TERROR TALES
OF THE
SCOTTISH HIGHLANDS

TERROR TALES
OF THE
SCOTTISH HIGHLANDS

Edited by Paul Finch

TERROR TALES OF THE SCOTTISH HIGHLANDS

First published in 2015 by Gray Friar Press.
9 Abbey Terrace, Whitby,
North Yorkshire, YO21 3HQ, England.
Email: gary.fry@virgin.net
www.grayfriarpress.com

With regard to the story The Fellow Travellers, all efforts have
been made to trace copyright holders, but these were
unsuccessful. If holders come forward, the publishers will be
pleased to make the necessary arrangement at the first
opportunity.

Typesetting and design by Paul Finch and Gary Fry

ISBN: 978-1-906331-99-3

TABLE OF CONTENTS

SKYE'S SKARY PLACES
Ian Hunter

We were back on the Isle of Skye staying in a caravan at the bottom of someone's garden in Portree. Not the holiday home we had expected; not even a home, I suppose. That's what happens when you book too late. The caravan door opened onto a lawn that was long and immaculate, where colourful flowers bloomed from every flowerbed, and, where there was no more earth, things grew in pots or hanging baskets or climbed up walls and wooden panels that separated this garden from the neighbour's.

Part of the deal was breakfast inside Mrs. Jessop's house, although after two mornings of a cooked Scottish breakfast, which was a generous helping of fried stuff served after a bowl of porridge ("No, sugar or honey in your porridge, mind, salt's best", she told us) and a kipper with toast; it was time to go continental style, or die – even if the closest to continental style was a variety of cooked eggs on toast wallowing in butter. Still, it did set you up for the day.

"What are your plans then?" she asked as she poured a little maple syrup onto a pancake man she had made for Molly. I glanced outside the kitchen door to see our dog, Jet, tied to a clothes pole by his lead. Otherwise he would have been pining at the back door. I half-smiled, half-grimaced at the ribbon of drool hanging from his mouth.

"A walk," Jenny told her.

"Hurrah!" said Molly, looking up and clapping her sticky hands together. She didn't mind Jenny's walks, which were usually conducted at forced march pace because she was either being carried or pushed.

"Mmmm," went Mrs. Jessop, lifting the lid of the teapot before stirring the contents with a spoon to make sure the tea was as dark and strong as possible. "There's something happening at the riding school on the Dunvegan road." She reached over to the island in the middle of the kitchen where a metal tree structure stood, branches catching letters, flyers and bills. She plucked down a flyer and looked at it, making a face." Why they can't call it Halloween anymore is beyond me."

"Call what?" I asked.

"This," she said, handing it over. The flyer was A5 sized and edged in white. In the centre, there was a large orange-brown leaf with writing inside it describing the autumn fayre the riding school was having.

"Face painting and dooking for apples, it says," Mrs. Jessop grumbled. "Now that's what I call Halloween if you ask me."

"It's not Halloween today, is it?" I said, pressing my phone to check the date. I was right; Halloween was a couple of days away.

"We could go, I suppose," Jenny said.

"What, and not climb a Munro before lunchtime?"

"Ha ha," she said, making a face. "More exercise would be good for you." At least she didn't reach over and pat my stomach, but I still pulled it in. Then she looked at Molly, who was licking syrup off her fingers. "Molly could ride her first horse."

*

The autumn fayre was in a field behind the riding school, a circle of tables standing in the tall grass like some modern-day equivalent of standing stones which car boot sale worshippers would come to visit. When I was a kid I used to go to jumble sales, usually in church halls, and bought books and old annuals that I thought would be worth money someday; but those are things of the past, maybe because churches aren't so popular anymore, or maybe thanks to all those TV programmes about antiques. People would rather try and sell something at a car boot sale or at an auction and get more money that way. Whatever the reason, I still like to get a 'bargain' as Jenny calls it, rolling her eyes as I produce yet another awful piece of colourful glass I have bought, or a Delft clog, or even a Delft clog with a windmill attached. Class.

But this fayre was disappointing. We were standing on the brow of a hill and if you looked over your shoulder the snow-streaked summits of some of the Cuillins peeked back at you as if they had sneaked up behind. The Cuillins were everywhere, both varieties, Red and Black. Skye was beautiful, stunning in places, but on the drive between the bridge to Portree, there were long winding roads going through bare hills and mountains that looked desolate enough to be on the Moon or Mars. The fayre itself matched this dreariness; it was small and tatty.

"Not much here," said Jenny.

I nodded. "Let's have a quick look round and we'll go."

An adult was kneeling on a mat, a fork in his mouth, while he moved his head, aiming to drop the fork onto one of the apples bobbing in a large tub. Call that dooking for apples, I thought, someone phone Trade Descriptions. Next to him was a little queue of children waiting to get their faces painted. A boy was getting his

2

face covered in a wonky-looking Spiderman mask. I wondered if Molly would want her face painted. She'd never had it done before. Hands in pockets, I ambled past the tables, eyes straying over jars of jams and chutneys of every flavour imaginable. Another table was covered in toys, mainly board games and jigsaws; below the table sat a plastic crate full of action figures. He-Man looked up at me, arm outstretched, plastic fingers curled to hold his sword, though now they were empty. Another crate contained figures that were given away with kids' meals. I crouched down and held Homer Simpson in one hand and Bart in another, and tried to bring them to life with my really bad attempts at their voices. The guy behind the table glowered down at me, possibly because he knew I was never going to buy any of them.

I stood up and Jenny jerked her head to the side. "What do you think, offski?"

I pointed to another table, this one selling books. "Last one, okay?"

The books were as expected. Chick-lit, thrillers written by guys who had been in the SAS, or wanted to be, as they saved the world from another terrorist threat. There were some ancient James Bond paperbacks that were too bent and battered to be worth anything. Still, I bent over and flicked through some hardbacks, hoping to find a first edition written by the crime-writing pseudonym of JK Rowling. That would be worth hundreds, if not, thousands and cover the cost of this holiday on Skye. Instead there were just some titles by Tom Clancy, some cookery books and ...

A little pamphlet held together with rusty staples, with a cover obviously drawn by a child in a mixture of felt pen and crayon, which showed two kids in a boat bobbing beside the coast, staring at a black cave in the rocks. From the darkness of the cave, red and green eyes seemed to be looking back at them. A lot of red and green eyes.

The thing was called *SKYE'S SKARY PLACES*, and the spelling seemed to be just as bad inside, but the drawings were good, if basic. Primitive, I thought, tapping into something. Childhood fears, probably.

I held it out. "How much?"

"Two pounds," the woman told me.

"You're kidding? I thought maybe fifty pence."

"A pound."

"Deal," I said, handing over a pound and gently rolled the pamphlet up and pushed it into my pocket, just as someone stepped into the middle of the tables and announced the highlight of the proceedings: a sheep-shearing competition.

"Sheep!" Molly cried. "Sheep! Baa! Baa!"

"Well, there's one vote," I said. "Shall we?"

Jenny smiled. "Ambassador."

We walked back towards the buildings of the riding school. A sort of sheep pen had been set up out of portable metal fences. The sheep waited inside and other bits of fencing allowed two run-offs where two guys were standing, hair hidden beneath beanie hats, clippers in their hands.

It started to rain, the wind picked up. We watched the sheep getting sheared until Molly could take no more. I knew how she felt. I sidled up to Jenny and held out my hand, catching raindrops on my palm, and sang, "That's en-ter-tain-ment!"

She laughed, and we left.

*

SKYE'S SKARY PLACES contained a paragraph or two about the 'skary place' on the cover and something that might have passed for a map, with directions – written by an adult, I suspected – and an accompanying illustration, much like the illustration that went with *The Battle of the Spoiling of the Dyke*, which told the story of yet another battle between the McLeods and the MacDonalds. There were so many dead that they weren't buried, just laid out beside the drystane dyke, which was toppled on top of them. The illustration showed rocks and tufts of grass and a skull and bones protruding from the ground.

"We should visit these places," I told Jenny.

She shook her head. "Scary places? Invented by some kid?"

"No, they're real enough. There's even directions how to get there." I flicked through the pamphlet. "There's lots of fairy places. Scary fairy places."

"Well, it is Skye and we've seen the flag," she said, referring to the shreds of the fabled fairy flag that were on display in Dunvegan Castle.

"There's a fairy bridge and a fairy glen, look." I opened the pages to show a pool of crayoned water and reeds and tall flowers that might have been foxgloves growing in front of it. Eyes peeked out between the vegetation and a long greenish hand stretched through some of them, reaching towards the reader.

The fingers were thin and sharp-looking. Some fairy.

"Don't let Molly see that," she warned.

"Okay, okay," I said, nodding, and turned the page. "The Kerrang," I said out loud, but it wasn't the famous heavy metal weekly magazine, it was something called 'the Quiraing'.

4

Really Spooky was written next to it, and eyes had been drawn in the two Os of 'spooky'.

"The Quiraing, you mean?" said Jenny. "It's up by Staffin. We've driven past it on the way to Uig." She sucked her bottom lip. "There's a walk there. We could do that with Molly and Jet."

"When?"

"Tomorrow."

I nodded, staring at the illustration, which showed various bits of rock and green grass.

The Needle, *The Table*, *The Prison* were written underneath them. I turned the page and saw a drawing of the bars of a cell with two hands wrapped around them and the word *No* written all over the page in different sizes, from whispers to shouts. Someone clearly didn't like being in the clink.

*

It was raining the next day, really chucking it down. So we scurried from tourist shop to tourist shop in Portree, managing to take Jet inside *The Isles Inn* and tie him to a table leg while a couple of people played the fiddle in the corner and someone else sang along with them, sometimes in Gaelic. I drank beer, Jenny drank wine, Molly drank juice and Jet's eyes never left us as we ate a packet of crisps. During a lull in the proceedings Jenny got her phone out and checked the weather tomorrow.

"Sunny with showers," she said, looking up.

"You know what Skye's like," I reminded her. "It could be a scorcher. It could be snow. Remember when we came up here at Easter and it was blowing a blizzard?"

She laughed. "Yes, and you still insisted on driving to Glen Brittle beach."

"Hey, it turned out to be a beautiful day, didn't it? The same could happen tomorrow."

She sighed and turned her head to look out of the pub window into the high street. She was in caged tiger mode. She had come to Skye to walk, but not bag any Munros; it had to be all low-level stuff for a while because we now had Molly, until she was old enough to join us on the hills. People scurried past in the rain, some with brollies up, some holding their newspapers above their heads, getting those soaked instead.

"I'm going to go for a walk down by the harbour," Jenny said, suddenly standing up. "You stay here with Molly, I'll take Jet. Get me another glass of wine in ..." She looked at her watch. "Half an hour?"

5

"Okay," I said, shrugging, not really surprised she wanted to go.

They left. We waited. I was the bad parent and ordered a side portion of chips and squirted them with tomato sauce. I checked my watch before I started sharing them with Molly, knowing I would have twenty-three minutes to use a baby wipe and get every trace of tomato sauce off her fingers and cheeks.

Twenty-three minutes later all trace of the chips were gone. Sadly, I didn't have a can of air freshener to spray above us. The half hour came and went. I wasn't bothered or concerned; Jenny would be late for her own funeral. Ten minutes later, with a large glass of Chenin Blanc waiting on the table, she burst into the pub and sat down beside us. I tied Jet to the table again. He looked like a drowned rat. I felt guilty at not keeping him a chip.

"Cheers," she said, raising her glass.

"Good walk?"

"We went down the hill to the harbour then took a left towards the hotel and into the woods by the sea." She beamed. "I think I saw a sea eagle."

*

It was Halloween the next day, and started off sunny, no showers, so we got our stuff packed together and headed for the Quiraing, where the land seemed to rise above us and a cathedral of rock formations stood on the left. There were a couple of cars in the car park. Jenny reached into the boot and grabbed Jet's lead as he jumped out.

We were taking the main path down to Floddigarry, but there were other tracks snaking out from the car park, one going into a little valley, another passing between two giant rocks like stone sentinels. I could imagine myself taking that path alone, not a soul in sight, but still there would be a niggle in my mind, making me look over my shoulder. I couldn't help remember the drawing from *SKYE'S SKARY PLACES* and all those *Nos*, like something that should have been put on a warning sign.

Then I heard something, a sound I rarely heard – our dog growling.

For some reason Jet was digging his paws in. His backside was up, but the rest of him was at an angle sloping downwards, front legs rigid. Jenny pulled and he pulled back, teeth bared, another low growl coming from his throat.

"What the?"

"He's going to slip his collar," Jenny warned, face contorted with effort. Jet was a fit dog, all muscle.

6

"Let him," I told her.

She shook her head. "No, we need to keep him under control. Suppose there're sheep over the next ridge, or cows, or something?"

"Cows? On Skye? You mean apart from the picture postcard shaggy ones with the long horns? No tourist attraction should be without one."

"Yeah, well, you saw the horns on them, didn't you? One of those would go right through Jet."

I held out my hand. "This is ridiculous, give me the lead."

She slapped the lead into my hand. I reached out towards Jet and he growled at me, but he wasn't looking at me.

He was actually looking out across the moorland. His mouth was open slightly, showing his teeth; the growl came out of him like distant thunder rumbling.

"Jet?" I said, and I could hear the incredulous tone in my voice.

"Jet's angry," Molly said.

No, scared, I thought.

"Pick him up and we'll leave him in the car," Jenny said.

I looked at her. "What?"

"Put him back in the boot and leave the windows open a little bit."

"Wait a minute, how long is this walk again?"

"It's only two or three miles."

"There and back?"

She looked away, voice almost lost on the breeze. "No, there, one way."

"So you really mean four or six miles? How long is that going to take with Molly? Unless you want me to leave her in the car too, with the window open wider?"

"Don't be smart, Joe."

"I know you can walk four to six miles in ..." I waved my hand vaguely in the air. "What? An hour and a half, the pace you go at."

"So?"

"We've got Molly with us. She stops at virtually every flower, bends over and tries to read the future in piles of whatever poo is lying there. We can't leave Jet that long. Someone would report us."

"You didn't want to come on this walk, did you?"

I felt myself frowning. "What?"

"You're so lazy, that's your problem, Joe. The thought of doing some exercise scares you to death before you even get round to actually doing it."

"Hey, this was my idea." I made a strumming gesture. "The Quiraing, right? Out of *SKYE'S SKARY PLACES*."

She sighed. "I'm fed up being stuck in that caravan. We should be in a cottage beside a loch, like we always are. I'm also fed up watching you stuff your face in Mrs. Jessop's kitchen every morning. We don't eat like that at home and we shouldn't eat like that here."

"I had porridge and toast this morning."

"Big deal, that's only because my nagging has begun to sink in."

"I'm glad you noticed."

"You can push Molly along the path."

"You're kidding?"

"The buggy is folded up in the back seat."

I gestured again. "Look at the state of the path."

"It looks fine to me."

"Really? It's uneven and full of jutting rocks, and wait until we see what it's like over the next hill. When we have to bounce Molly down parts of it, or take her out and carry her and the buggy down separately."

"Then forget the buggy, we'll carry Molly."

"Hey, health and safety in action. Pity I didn't bring the crash helmets with us."

"I want to go on this walk, Joe."

"Then go yourself. March down the hill and we'll get you at the other end."

"You're not coming?"

"No, it's not practical. We'd have to drag Jet all the way."

"Then put him in the car, like I said."

"We'd be gone a couple of hours."

"He doesn't want to come with us anyway," she said, telling me something I already knew. Why was that, I wondered. Jet's the friendliest dog in the world, a licking machine. He barks at postmen and tries to run through the door whenever he sees a cat on the path. Those are things that are in his DNA, but growling? At us?

I shook my head. "I'm not pushing Molly or carrying her either. You walk by yourself and we'll meet you at the other end. See if you can set a new record for your death camp walk."

"Fine," she muttered, turning away.

"I'll take you to the hotel for a coffee," I said after her.

She didn't turn round.

"And a cake!" I shouted.

Still she didn't turn round.

"Mummy's angry," Molly said.

"Yeah," I breathed, and looked down at Jet. "I'm where you live right now, pooch. Beside you in the dog house.

Of course, I stood there like an *edgit* and didn't know what to do. Should I put Jet in the car and open the windows a little bit? Should I put Jet and Molly in the car and open the windows a little bit more and run after Jenny? I'd have to run because she would have slipped into warp drive, chin down, mouth set, bending her arms slightly and swinging them as she walked. Fists moving forward as if she was punching an imaginary opponent in the gut; probably me. She was already out of sight, vanishing below the downward slope of the hill.

Still unsure, I walked back to the car and got a rubber grab toy out of the boot for Jet, and Molly and I threw it to him; not that he deserved it with all his carry-on earlier. Funny thing was, when I threw it towards the direction of the path, he wouldn't go after it. He would simply sit and look at us and look at the toy, yet would bound after the toy if it went in other directions. Who was the pet here, I wondered and put my back into massive throws that almost came down and clobbered him from the upper atmosphere, while Molly swung round and round and let go of the toy and usually fell over, flopping onto the grass.

My phone rang, I knew I was making a face when I saw Jenny's name come up on the screen.

"I'm sorry," we both said at the same time.

"Yeah, I know," I muttered. "So how about my idea?"

"What?" she shouted. "I can't hear you."

"Why not?"

"There's a bunch of folk coming my way. I can't see them because of the slope, but they are making some racket. Listen."

I did, thinking I could hear something like the sound of the wind blowing down the phone, and then some other noises. Cheers, and yelling, laughter. It sounded like a cross between a pub crawl and a hen night coming our way over the hills.

"Did you hear that!" she shouted again, and I could barely hear her.

"Yes!" I shouted back.

"What did you say?"

This was useless. I hung up and texted her: *I'll call u back when they've passed. Keep walking, coffee & scone @ other end xxx*

I looked at my watch and looked at the path, thinking I would wait until those noisy folk passed her and came into view, then I would head down to Floddigarry. Jenny would probably be waiting for us, unless she had gone down a gear and was walking at a normal person's pace. We played with Jet some more, and I watched the path. There was no sign of the other folk, the noisy ones. Somehow I imagined a group of excited foreign teenagers,

9

maybe Japanese, winding themselves up as they walked along the path. I remembered that some scenes in the fantasy movie *Stardust* had been filmed around here. The tourists probably recognised them and were getting a bit overexcited, if that's what rocked their boat.

Too excited to appear, I thought with a sigh, as I kept glancing down the path, before realising they didn't need to come this way after all. There were probably other paths snaking off in different directions. Jenny would be at the other end already and waiting for us, quietly fuming. Time to go. I dug into my pocket for a treat.

"Here, boy, here Jet."

Using the lure of the treat, I slipped the dog's lead on to his collar and walked him back to the car to jump back into the boot, before I clipped Molly into her car seat and we were off, driving down the single-track road towards the main one, which was where Jenny ought to have emerged by now.

Except she wasn't there. Not waiting beside the road, not walking along it. We passed some walkers, big rucksacks on their backs, some people on bikes, but no Jenny. I headed for the hotel at Floddigarry, and never passed her on the way. She wasn't there either, standing waiting in the car park with arms folded while she tapped her foot on the ground because there was nowhere else to go.

The hotel was closed, a FOR SALE sign practically hidden by some tree branches.

I dug my mobile out of my pocket. No messages, no reply to my text. I phoned her and it rang out until I got a message telling me to leave her a message.

"Hello, we're here. The hotel is up for sale, so looks like it's back to the pub in Portree."

I reached back and took a toy from the pouch on the back of the passenger seat and passed it to Molly. Her hands started moving immediately, making noises. She didn't even look up as I opened the car door.

I stood at the side of the road, hand above my eyes as if that would help me see Jenny as she trudged along the side of the road, or emerged through a gate at the foot of the hills, limping slightly, her jacket covered in mud from a fall. My phone rang.

Jenny.

I dragged an index finger across the screen to answer the call.

Static screamed in my ear. Static and other sounds: a cacophony. Screams, shouts, yells, shrieks, guffaws, everything.

"Hello!" I shouted. "Jenny is that you? Is Jenny there? Put her on, please."

The noises continued. I held the phone away from me and put it on loudspeaker and stared at my hand, as if I could see all those

10

different sounds swirling upwards into the air, Jenny's voice lost among them. I was worried something had happened to her and they were trying to phone and let me know. But I was more worried they had done something to her, whoever 'they' were, and that this was their idea of having some fun.

I hung up and waited, and waited. Went back to the car and waited until Molly fell asleep before I finally called the police.

*

They never found Jenny. They looked. I looked with them. Starting at the top next to the car park and taking the main path down, then all the other paths, going in every direction, places where she might have fallen and broke an ankle or leg, and was waiting for us to arrive, shivering. The local Mountain Rescue joined in the search, along with a police helicopter. All of them, all of us, turning up nothing.

They thought I had murdered her. Killed her and dumped her in a remote part of Skye or off a cliff into the sea, maybe even wrapped in plastic and weighed down at the bottom of the lochan.

Mrs. Jessop's testimony proved she had been alive that morning, so did the texts on my phone, I hoped, though one policeman said I could have used her phone to text myself.

I eventually got back to the mainland and almost lost Molly when Jenny's parents tried to take her away from me. I've lost friends too, everyone from Jenny's family. Almost lost my job, almost lost the house. It's a struggle now, down from two incomes to just one.

Eventually, Jenny will be declared dead and I can cash in the insurance policy that will pay off the mortgage, then things will get a little easier. I'm not trying to sound callous, honest, but I've developed a tough streak; comments made about you on social media will do that, especially the page set up by some of Jenny's friends. Calling me a murderer, packing it full of lies or every little thing they hated about me over the years.

Yes, I almost lost a lot of things, but I did lose the most important thing of all. My wife, my partner, my love.

*

At first, she used to phone me.

The noise started up as soon as I swiped my finger across the screen to answer. That cacophony of different sounds. I could just

11

about hear her trying to shout over the yells, the shouts, the jabbering, the shrieks and whoops.

Sometimes she managed to scream my name.

She texts, but like the calls it is always in the middle of the night, as if she is in a different time zone, a different zone altogether. The phone vibrates beside me, drilling against the top of the bedside table. It makes me think of a little matchbox with an insect inside, a scarab beetle, wanting to get out.

r u there?
It's me
Joe?
r u there.
Joe?
Joe?
Joe?
Where am I?
Do u know?
Joe?

The messages are pretty much always the same … like right now, as the phone chirps into life beside me. And I reach out for it, not even bothering with the bedside light. My thumb is poised to reply. I always try to reply, but words at the top of the screen tell me I have failed. That it will resend the message when I am connected to the internet. Except I know that I am always connected; it's where Jenny is now that's the problem.

PHANTOMS IN THE MIST

No land with as turbulent a history as Scotland would be complete without a whole clutch of native ghost stories. In fact, Scotland's annals are so crammed with battles and massacres, murders and executions that they could fuel the haunted imaginations of a dozen ancient kingdoms. Even in the Highlands, where so much land is uninhabited, and so much more of it impassable, there was clan feuding, guerrilla warfare, government brutality and incessant, widespread injustice. Never be fooled by the beauty and quiet of Scotland's far-off hills. Epoch-shattering events took place there, often involving profuse bloodshed and providing perfect fodder for ghost enthusiasts.

For example, the 'bookend battles' of the Jacobite era are famously commemorated by eerie visitations. At Killiecrankie on the River Garry in 1689, when the Jacobite forces of Viscount Dundee first charged the Orange Covenanter army of Hugh Mackay, they won a gruesome victory, leaving 2,000 of the enemy dead. The riverbank today, especially when bathed in a creepy crimson dusk, is reportedly still the scene of phantom troops marching. At Culloden near Inverness, where in 1746 the Stuart cause came to its tragic end and the Highland clans fell en masse to the muskets and gunnery of the Duke of Cumberland's Redcoats, spectral relics are said to linger on the moor, including a single blood-drenched Highlander, who appears at sunset, leaning on a broken pike and weeping as he mutters, "We are defeated."

In addition to these 'memorial' visitants, the Highlands can boast a wide range of ghosts who are celebrities in their own right. The mounted shade of freedom fighter William Wallace, hanged, drawn and quartered by the English in 1305, is still rumoured to gallop across Rannoch Moor, cloak billowing, broadsword at his hip. Claypotts Castle near Dundee reputedly houses the spirit of Marion Ogilvy, who was mistress to Cardinal Beaton and died in 1575. Lurking in the ruins of Ruthven Castle in Kingussie is the cinder-black wraith of Alexander Stewart, infamous to posterity as the 'Wolf of Badenoch' – he died in 1405, allegedly at the hands of a demon he himself had summoned.

Other Highland ghosts may be unknown in name, but often appear torn and mutilated, illustrative of their grisly ends. Glen Cainnir on the Isle of Mull is the abode of a long departed clansman named Ewen, who, as both he and his horse were butchered in battle, is often seen headless, mounted on a headless steed. Another headless figure is that of a Spanish mercenary said to appear at picturesque Eileann Donan Castle, which stands at the junction of three Highland lochs: Duich, Long and Alsh. According to folklore the Spaniard was killed there in 1719, amid a British bombardment in retaliation for the refuge the fort had offered to Jacobites during the rising of 'the Fifteen'.

In an almost unique local twist, several Highland ghosts are better known by their colour. Perhaps this comes in reflection of the Scottish tradition for colourising the names of the living; the Red Comyn for example, or the Black Douglas. In death, there are numerous Highland cases wherein green is the preferred shade. The ill-used Lillias Drummond died from a broken heart at Fyvie Castle near Aberdeen in 1601, but is now better known as the Green Lady of Fyvie, while the Green Lady of Mey Castle has been identified as the spirit of Elizabeth Sinclair, daughter of the 5th Earl of Caithness, who in the 16th century fell from the tower room in which she had been cruelly imprisoned. Green ladies have also been reported at Ballindalloch Castle near the Moray Firth, at Knock Castle on Skye and Ashintully Castle in Perthshire. By contrast, the Blue Boy of Loch Eck is said to rise nightly from the watery grave he accidentally found for himself while sleepwalking from the Coylett Inn on the other side of the nearby road to Dunoon.

Perhaps the most interesting of all the Highland ghosts is the White Horseman of Hestwall. In the 19th century on Mainland Orkney, two farm-hands fell in love with a local maid. In a fit of jealousy, one attacked the other while they were threshing together, and struck him dead with his flail. He concealed the body in the barn, and returned for it that night, transporting it on the back of a white horse to the top of the coastal cliffs, from where he threw it into the sea. On his way back, he became concerned that he was being followed. He turned and beheld a spectral horseman at his rear. At first, the murderer assumed it was the spirit of his slain friend, but on closer inspection, was horrified to see the shade of himself mounted on a white horse.

Terrified, he rode away, but in attempting to jump a farm wall, his steed fell, killing itself and fatally injuring its rider, who had just enough breath left to confess to those who came running before he too expired. For years afterwards it was said the wall in question could never be repaired, while the roads around Hestwall were the haunt of a despondent figure in white, mounted on a white horse. Well into the 20th century, a local woman was disturbed late at night by a knock at her front door. When she answered it, the ghostly horseman was waiting outside. He gazed at her sadly, before diminishing to nothing.

14

THE DOVE
Helen Grant

'Tradition has it that Mr. Denson, when led to the gallows, avowed his innocence of the crime, declaring that after his being thrown off, a white dove would fly down and land on the scaffold as proof of it. It is said that this really did happen.'

Who, thought Freya, *tries to prove their innocence like that? And how can it possibly have taken place?*

She took a sip of the red wine, taking care not to hold the glass over the book in case of spillages. The faintly mouldy aroma that clung to the browning pages might conceivably have been improved by a splash of Valpolicella, but she didn't fancy having to explain a purple stain to the librarian, or worse, having to replace the volume.

She'd meandered a long way from the original track of her research. Old local history books had a tendency to create diversions. They comprised anecdotes which had appealed to the writer, rather than anything structured. There were always huge holes in the information, so that it felt more like hopping from one stepping-stone to another than following a well-worn path.

Freya was miles off course now. Still, who could resist a story like this one, of murder and retribution and supernatural signs? Freya had come across it while researching a completely different parish, and become so engrossed in the grim tale that she had taken the shabby little book home with her from the library. Perhaps something might be done with it – an article or a blog post.

Two and a half glasses of red wine later and the story was filling her head like a grotesque dream; the more she pored over it, the more she thought she could see through the smooth prose to something far more brutal hidden within.

Imagine, she thought. James Denson, a young man not yet thirty, only recently licensed by his bishop, becomes the minister of a small Highland parish. For some years, things go well; there is not a murmur against him. He is, no doubt, a familiar figure in his sober clergyman's clothing, as he rides around the muddy roads or ducks under the lintel of a rough cottage.

But then the accusations begin. Drunkenness early in the day, language unsuited to a man of the cloth, lewdness, even brawling. The minister is said to have been so fuddled by drink that he dropped an infant into the font! Finally, even the word *witchcraft* is whispered; the Reverend is said to be adept in the dark arts, bargaining with the Evil One for his own personal advancement or the fulfilment of some atrocious aim. The congregation are loud in their protestations. The bishop, outraged, removes the Reverend Denson from his post.

Now the true horror begins. The disgraced minister having been flung out of the manse, workmen are sent into the house to repair the damage caused by violence and neglect. Even the hearthstone does not sit firmly in its place, but wobbles like a loose tooth in a gum when trodden on. They lever it up, meaning to reposition it. Underneath it, curled in the damp black earth like a pallid comma, they find the rotting remains of a tiny baby.

Appalling enough to kill an infant; worse to murder your own child, as the Reverend Denson has done. The mother is soon found: his servant girl, Margaret, a wretched, cowed thing, probably an unwilling partner in his unholy rutting. History does not record what happened to *her*, but James Denson is tried before the Earl, and soon after he is taken to the gallows and hanged, not before claiming that a white dove will land on the scaffold afterwards, to prove his innocence – not that he will live to see the truth or otherwise of this.

A nasty, brutish tale. In spite of the odd little codicil about the dove, Freya might have put it out of her mind; infanticide was a depressingly common crime in the seventeenth century. Still, she couldn't leave it alone, not yet. The more she looked into it, the more she could see that there could easily be another side to the story. The Reverend Denson's relationship with his parishioners, for example: *that* had started to go bad before the accusations were thrown around. He had inherited a parish church in a tumbledown state, and those who were responsible for contributing to the restoration of it were reluctant to pay up. The Reverend had pursued them energetically, seemingly unintimidated by considerations of local standing and influence. Had he made the parish too hot to hold him with his demands that people pay their dues?

Freya slid the glass of wine away from her. She felt faintly queasy; she was never much of a drinker and now she had had perhaps half a glass too much. She put her elbows on the table and her head in her hands, pushing back the strands of dark hair that fell over her face. Her eyes slid closed, the soft skin between her brows crumpling as though in pain.

Am I reading too much into this? she thought. Perhaps the story should be taken at face value. The corpse of a baby had been found under the man's hearthstone, after all – what could be more damning than that? A person must be a brute if he can sit of an evening warming his hands over the fire and know that under the stone upon which his buckled shoe rests is the mouldering body of his own child. How could he stand the evil scent that must have seeped from under it, rising on the warm air? Freya shuddered.

And yet – in cases of that kind, hadn't it usually been the mother who'd been prosecuted? Margaret, the servant girl, would have had much more to lose than the Reverend Denson did. He could have denied paternity, thrown her out into the muddy, frost-rimed street. There was no DNA testing in those days; it would have been the word of a servant against that of a minister. If she, Freya, had been the investigating officer in this crime, she would have made Margaret the lead suspect. James Denson – well, he might have been guilty of the sin of lust, but that didn't necessarily make him a murderer.

Freya opened her eyes. She stood up, a little unsteadily, and went into the kitchen to get a glass of water. Her mouth tasted sour with the wine, and her skin was hot, as though with fever or guilt. She let the tap run until the water was cold, standing with the glass in her left hand, staring at her reflection in the dark window. The glass was as good as a mirror, because there was not one single light out there.

If she'd been looking out of the window in the tiny dining room on the other side of the cottage, she'd have been able to see the lights of the town sparkling like fool's gold on the shoulder of the hill. On this side, though, there was nothing. In the pearlescent grey light of a damp Scots morning she would have seen a strip of overgrown lawn, an unkempt hedge, and beyond it fields stretching towards distant hills. All of this vanished in the darkness. It was an abyss out there now; it was the edge of the world.

Now, in the early twenty-first century, there were still great swathes of land here that were unlit at night. In the seventeenth century the nighttime landscape had lacked even those amber clusters of electric lights that marked out modern towns. The lanes, now smooth with tarmac, would have been deeply rutted, sticky with mud, impossible to negotiate after nightfall. Houses would be invisible; the feeble light of a candle behind window shutters would be lost in the darkness. Inside, there would be the dancing of long shadows and the stink of tallow.

James Denson had come here from the fine and bustling city of Edinburgh, where he had taken his degree. Edinburgh was not seventy miles from here; in the 1600s it might as well have been a thousand miles away.

Freya imagined him tackling the duties of a country minister, first with energy and then increasingly wearily. There would be many long evenings when he would pass the hours before sleep by reading or even writing something by candlelight, working until his head ached and the letters blurred before his eyes. In winter it would be dark by four or five in the afternoon, and bitterly cold when he stepped away from the warm radius of the hearth.

Chilled, comfortless and lonely, perhaps he had looked up one evening from some dry book and watched the servant girl, Margaret, moving quietly about, what blemishes she had smoothed away by the soft firelight. Perhaps she, sensing his gaze on her, had paused too and looked back at him, seeing not an employer nor a minister of the Church but a man.

You couldn't blame either of them for a natural impulse, Freya thought. If that was the extent of the Reverend Denson's sin, she could forgive it.

She drained the glass, set it down carefully on the draining-board, and went off to her bed, which was so cold that the sheets felt faintly damp.

*

Freya half-expected to wake up the next morning and realise that her imagination had run away with her. Mostly, what you saw was what you got; history said the Reverend Denson had killed a baby and been hanged for it, and that was probably what had happened. Even supposing that *wasn't* precisely what had happened, what could she do about it now? The man was dead three centuries. Even if she could *prove* he was innocent, who was going to care?

The story was still there at the back of her mind, though. Had justice been administered on the gallows, or had it, too, been murdered?

She went off to work, driving carefully along the country roads. There was a tightness around her forehead and the early light seemed very bright. Freya said to herself that she wouldn't drink red wine in the evenings any more; she wasn't hung over, exactly, but she didn't feel right. When she got to the distillery she'd start the day with an enormous cup of coffee.

The distillery was a small independent one, and Freya was the public relations manager. That was a smart name for a prosaic job; she was just as likely to find herself filing invoices or driving down to the village to buy the managing director's lunchtime 'piece' as writing a press release. She hoped that today would be quiet, that she could drink the coffee she was craving in peace and do the filing. It didn't work out, though. You'd have thought there couldn't be emergencies when a product took twelve long years to mature, but she'd hardly sat down before the phone was ringing. It seemed as though everything was urgent that morning; if her head hadn't been aching before, it was by lunchtime. Angus, the Managing Director, was short-tempered with her; Freya knew it was stress, it wasn't personal, but still it was difficult to listen to him ranting. As the last straw, the uneven autumn weather seemed to have caused the office heating to malfunction; she could see sunshine outdoors but she was shivering at her desk, fingers curled around a mug of coffee that cooled much too fast. When it got to five it was a relief to leave.

At home there was a single letter on the mat – nothing interesting, a circular from the bank, by the looks of it. Freya carried it into the kitchen, glancing at the answering machine as she went past. No messages.

What were you expecting? she said to herself. *You haven't called anyone either. You should call Sarah – or Karen. Karen's always telling you to get out more. 'You'll never meet anyone if you never go out.'*

The trouble was, Karen always wanted to go somewhere busy – a bar or a pub. Freya didn't like those places.

I'm an introvert, she said to herself defensively. *If we could go to the cinema, or just have a bottle of wine here ...*

Of course she really wouldn't meet 'anyone' if she and Karen sat at home sharing a bottle of wine. It was only in books that handsome strangers knocked on the door asking to borrow a cup of sugar or use the phone to call the breakdown services. Nobody was ever going to knock on *her* door, living out here; she didn't even get the ones trying to sell double glazing.

She told herself she would call Karen later, after dinner. Or perhaps tomorrow. She had a headache anyway.

Curiously, the wearisome pounding of blood through her temples was matched by repetitive strands of thought. Freya couldn't stop thinking about James Denson. His name throbbed through her aching head like a compulsion as she prepared and served her evening meal, the reproachful single portion as usual. Was he guilty or not? Somehow this seemed terribly important to her.

Supposing that happened to me, being condemned for something I didn't do?

Of course, that was ridiculous, because nobody was hanged any more in Scotland, whatever they'd done. But still – the idea of it –

Wouldn't it make a difference to me if just one person – just one – believed I was innocent?

She thought it would. To think of standing there on the scaffold, maybe shivering in just your shirt – because even in June, when he'd been executed, you could never be certain of warm weather – and smelling the stink of a seventeenth century market town, the animals, the rubbish on the street, the unwashed bodies pressing close as people strained to see the execution, and then looking up and seeing one person looking at you with pity. Perhaps even with love. That would be something to hold onto when they pushed you off, and the rope tightened around your neck, killing you instantly if you were lucky but more likely giving you ten minutes of agony as your legs kicked uselessly in the cold air and urine splattered onto the filthy ground.

Freya pushed her plate away, the meal unfinished.

Then there was the anecdote about the Reverend Denson foretelling the white dove. *He must have been desperate to prove his innocence to do that,* thought Freya. *He must have known the chances of it happening were practically nil. Perhaps he just wanted one last, faint try at proving he wasn't guilty.*

And it *had* happened, if you believed the eyewitnesses. A white dove really had flown down and landed on the scaffold.

Common sense asserted itself, suggesting explanations. Perhaps the condemned man had seen the bird perched on a nearby building and taken a gamble. Or perhaps he had said nothing about a white dove at all, but the bird had flown down to land on the scaffold anyway, and someone else had created an affecting story out of it.

Or maybe, she thought, *he really was innocent, and that proved it.*

The book was still lying on the table. Freya eyed it with a sense of suppressed eagerness, as though it were a letter from an ex-lover, a letter that should sensibly be burnt without reading.

She was aware that she was romanticising James Denson. There was nothing in the book to tell her what he had looked like, but she knew he wasn't *old,* he wasn't yet forty. She imagined a strong, intelligent face with sharp Scots features, grey eyes, and dark hair longer than the twenty-first century fashion, allowed to grow down over the collar, and curling slightly. The minister's dark garb would suit him, a counterpoint to the man's sturdy body underneath it. A country clergyman would hardly be rich; he would have walked or ridden about the parish rather than keeping a carriage, he might even have chopped his own firewood. Freya imagined muscle under the drab cloth.

The book was open under her fingers.

I want to know, she thought. *One way or another. Was he innocent?*

She couldn't imagine letting this go, not unless she settled it somehow, even just in her own mind. She wanted to be the sympathetic face in the crowd, the hand outstretched to the dying. The one to set something to rest.

Freya read the account again, unconsciously chewing her lip.

Now she saw that although those who had been so reluctant to pay for the rebuilding of the church had had their way for a while, eventually it had been done; if they had framed the unpopular minister, they had done it in vain.

It was then that she began to wonder whether the church still stood.

*

She parked the car at the side of the road, pressed close to the hedge in case anything else came along. After she had gone about twenty metres Freya glanced back. The car looked strangely insecure, as though it were huddling against the tightly-clustered hawthorn branches. *As though,* she thought, *nobody is ever coming back for it.*

It had taken some little time to locate the church. It seemed the seventeenth century parish no longer existed, and Google searches on her ageing laptop kept throwing up a similarly-named village in another part of Scotland altogether. Eventually she had found it on a local history site. *Ruined.* That was all it said. There was a snippet of a map but it wasn't zoomable so she'd spent more time finding the actual location.

She'd waited for the weekend, thinking she'd look over whatever was left of the church in daylight, but she'd forgotten how swiftly it got dark at this time of year. The sun was already low in the sky, so she had to shade her eyes when she faced west. Trees in the hedgerows threw broad stripes of shadow across the road.

She couldn't call this place a village, really. It was barely even a hamlet. There was a handful of houses strung out along the road. Freya didn't look closely at any of them; she already felt as though she were somehow trespassing, and didn't want any of the occupants to feel as though she were peering in at them.

The wind whispered urgently in her ears and plucked at her hair. Freya pulled her jacket closer around her body.

The only reason she found the church now was that she knew it was there to be found. The site was screened by trees and there was nothing to see from the road. She picked her way across rough grass that was wreathed with the subtle encroachment of brambles, and found a rusting gate between mossy stone pillars. Freya looked inside and her heart sank.

She'd known it was ruined, but she'd hoped for something more than this. The church that had stood here wasn't really James

21

Denson's church; it had been rebuilt, after all, years after his death. But it was on the same site, and she'd imagined herself standing in the nave – standing on the spot where *he* had stood, centuries before – the open sky above the naked stone walls simply bringing the destructive work of passing time more poignantly to mind.

I would have –

But she didn't even know what she would have done. This was a whim, coming here; she didn't understand her own need to do it.

The place didn't even *look* like a church. Whatever remained was buried under a profusion of overgrown foliage, the ends of it hanging down to meet the unkempt grass. It reminded her of nothing so much as the matted coat of some enormous shaggy creature. A triangular piece of stonework reared up at the east end, but that was overshadowed by a tree that had taken root and grown to a height in the heart of the ruins.

Freya went closer, threading her way between lichenous tombstones. There was a dark gap, a wound in the flank of the creature, that might have been a doorway, although it looked too low and narrow. It was choked with bare dead branches; she had to push at them before she could put her head through the gap.

Inside, the space was more cramped than she had expected, dim in the shadow of the clustering foliage overhead. Bushes thrust up through the rubble on the floor. Ivy snaked everywhere, binding the tumbled stones together.

This was only half of the interior, which Freya now saw had been divided by stone walls. She recognised what had been done here from visits to other churches; it had been converted into mausolea. She could see through a hole in the wall into the second chamber.

By turning sideways so that she could slide her shoulder through the space between the branches and the stone wall, Freya was able to get right into the church. She was wary of the ancient masonry, but there was no roof to fall in on her; she could see patches of sky through the leaves and branches overhead. She went over to the hole that led into the second room, debating on clambering through it. But when she put her head inside, there was nothing much to see, just more broken stones and branches. She felt the smooth sole of her boot sliding on something underfoot and looked down to see that she was standing on a shattered memorial. Feeling faintly disrespectful, Freya backed out of the hole.

What did you expect? she chided herself. *The ghost of James Denson?*

She wasn't even standing on the same floor he had; if there were original flagstones under here, they were buried under the rubble and encroaching vegetation. All the same, she was disappointed. She squeezed her way back out past the clutching limbs of the dead tree and straightened up amongst the tombstones.

What now? It should have been the end of the matter, but Freya was strangely reluctant to let it go. She felt a dragging melancholy, the feeling she might have had if she were saying a final goodbye to someone she was attracted to, without either of them ever having made a move towards the other. The obvious thing was to pick her way back to the gate and drive home; instead she lingered in the churchyard, gazing east over the gravestones as though over the shoulders of a silent congregation, at the distant river, turned to liquid fire by the sinking sun.

He knew this view too.

Freya imagined James Denson standing here, his clerical robes flapping in the autumn wind, his breath visible on the chill air, his grey eyes perhaps turned in the same direction hers now were. It was a short step from that to wondering where he had gone after visits to the church; where was the manse?

The logical thing was to go home and research it properly. She knew that. She hadn't thought of looking for the house until this moment, so there was absolutely nothing to guide her. All the same, she was moving before she was aware of it, making her way to the south side of the churchyard with the conviction of foreknowledge.

There was a crumbling wall here, and on the other side grass, then trees rooted in brambles and weeds. Freya scaled the wall easily. She was not generally a bold person, nor adventurous, yet now she found herself possessed with an eagerness foreign to her nature; she hurried over the rough ground as a woman might run to a lover long missed. The sun was very low now. She knew she'd never come back here. She was excited and terrified in equal measure; if she went home now she wouldn't bring herself to this point again.

I know – I know it's here –

And it was. Freya went to the spot as unerringly as if someone had taken her hand and led her there.

There would be nothing to see from the road or the churchyard; there was barely a thing to see even when you stood mere feet away. The house was as dilapidated, as overgrown as the church had been; the dank green of the moss that covered the stones blurred easily into the deep shadows of the overhanging trees. The door had gone; the lintel stone lay on the ground. Freya stepped over it, into the enclosure within.

The sense of desolation was absolute. Impossible to imagine this place as a home, even if you knew that was what it once was. Barely a feature remained besides the walls, and those were worn down so that not even the bottom of a frame had survived to show where the windows had been. As Freya moved about, small stones and splintered tiles crunched and clinked under her feet.

She saw at last that the stump of the chimney, though ruinous, still stood, like a grave marker over the hearth fire that had burnt out forever. Freya squatted in front of it, touching the stones with hands that were white and bloodless with cold.

What are you looking for? she asked herself. *You think the hearthstone's still going to be here, when half the chimney's fallen down?*

All the time she was thinking about it, her fingers were brushing stones aside, closing on the larger ones, tossing them away into the rubble at the side of the room.

What are you going to do if you find a flat stone under here? Pry it up?

Of course not.

But her palms were already smoothing dust and tiny chips of stone from a broad flat surface; her fingertips were questing for the edges.

She found the corners easily but she could tell the stone was heavy, it would take effort to lift it. Freya put one knee on the ground, wincing as the rough edges of stones pressed into her flesh. She grasped the edge of the hearthstone and pulled, the muscles in her back flexing ominously.

Somewhere deep down inside her, lost at the bottom of a dark well, a voice was screaming, *What are you doing? No! Don't –*

But she continued to pull, leaning back now to use all of her weight, and the edge of the stone was rising ponderously. The strain in her arms and shoulders was terrific; Freya bit her lip, grimacing. Her fingertips, now hooked firmly over the stone, could feel the cold slick underside of it; her nostrils were full of a thick damp smell of earth.

The setting sun was behind her; the stone threw its own black shadow, hiding what lay beneath it. It rose until it was balanced on its lower edge, and then Freya stumbled backwards as it completed the arc, like a heavy door moving on a hinge. She sat down hard on the stony floor and the pent-up breath sighed out of her.

I don't want to look.

But it was inevitable. She rose painfully, abrading her hands on rough things that bit into the flesh, and stared into the hole. She stared, and time seemed to stand still; the moment seemed to solidify around her like ice. There was no desire to see, she didn't *want* to see, but still she couldn't stop looking.

24

Curled in the rich black earth was something the size of a newborn infant. It was not a human child, Freya saw that. This was a thing begotten of far worse.

The bloating of the trunk and the sickly white colour of it suggested human flesh in a state of putrefaction, but the proportions were all wrong – the head was too small, the limbs etiolated, the digits rudimentary and too few. The face was a waxen horror: the eyes mere black pinpricks, the nose and mouth fused into something like a beak.

Freya saw this, and a long groan of distress oozed out of her, as though she had been wounded. At the sound, the homunculus stirred; the tiny limbs waved feebly, searching the air, and the pinprick eyes blinked white, then back to black again. The beak-like mouth opened and closed.

Shuddering, tears seeping from the corners of her eyes, Freya put out her hands. She looked down and saw them moving, her own hands, but she seemed to have no control over them. She lifted the homunculus from its dark bed of earth and where it had lain she saw the white bodies of maggots writhing away into the soil. She pressed the tiny creature to herself as a mother cradles a baby, and her lips were tight with disgust as she got to her feet and bore it away with her, over the rough stones and the grass, through the graveyard and out onto the road.

The drive home was a blur, a journey in a dream. Freya was not aware of parking in her own drive, opening the door, stepping inside with the bundle she still hugged to her.

Tired. So terribly tired. Have to sleep.

An alarm was ringing deep down in that place in her mind, but it was too faint, overwhelmed by the compulsion to lie down and give in to her exhaustion. Freya went into the bedroom and laid the thing she had been carrying carefully down on the cover of her single bed. She had tracked mud into the room on her boots, but the empty gaze that swept the room did not take it in. She took off the boots, her jacket, her woollen sweater.

The room was cool; it was natural to turn back the covers of the bed and lie down, the tiny bundle in her arms again, held close so that she could warm it with her body. Freya looked down and saw that it was not an ugly thing, as she had thought, but a real human baby, plump, bright-eyed and unblinking. The tiny hands, the fingers, the pearlescent nails, all were perfect; the soft mouth opened beseechingly, hungrily.

Freya unbuttoned the neck of her shirt and laid the child against her skin. She felt it nuzzle against her and smiled, relaxing against the pillows. Her eyes closed. The smile lingered on her lips until the tiny creature bit into her flesh, and she grimaced with pain, but did not open her eyes. Blood began to flow, but not for long. Then something flowed the other way, into Freya, and an essential part of her dropped into the dark.

*

Freya awoke to shouting, pain, a stink of something rotting. Her vision was blurred; she blinked hard, trying to clear it, and a sea of faces swam into view below her – lean, grubby faces with avid eyes, grimaces missing teeth here and there, straggling, greasy hair. She dropped her gaze and took in clothing in an unfamiliar style, the women aproned and in ankle-length skirts, the men in long coats, everything in drab colours. The attention of every single one of them was fixed on her; she saw a kind of hungry expectation in most eyes, a sorrowing sympathy in a few. They were waiting for something to happen.

Even before she looked down at herself she knew she didn't feel right. Freya was light-boned, slender; now she felt as though she were encased in a suit of armour. She could feel the bulk of this body, the way the great pads of fat on the chest and belly heaved with each tortuous breath, the tightness in the chest as the overburdened lungs laboured on.

It felt unstable up here; whatever was below her feet was rickety. Wood creaked as her weight shifted. She wanted to put out her hands, to hold onto something, but now she discovered that they were bound together, tightly. She tried to lift them, so that she could see, and instead of her own delicate arms and small hands she saw two limbs whose ham-hock thickness was not disguised by the dirty linen in which they were encased, and two large hands with bony knuckles and thick fingers terminating in spade-shaped nails.

A sound like a sob escaped her. She tried to turn her head, to look about her for some sign that she was dreaming, and felt the abrasion of coarse rope against the side of her neck. Now she knew.

It's a hanging. They're going to –

Still she struggled to take in what her senses were telling her.

Is this a dream? It doesn't feel like a dream. What's happened to me? I don't feel like myself – I feel like –

"Any last words, Mr. Denson?"

The words were uttered close by her, roughly-spoken but not unkind. A sharp whiff of stale sweat told Freya that the man was close at her shoulder. Was he preparing to push her off into space?

26

Terror exploded inside her. Freya wanted to speak, to protest that she was not who they thought she was, she was Freya Robertson, and not –

Mr. Denson?

A brief spurt of hope flared within her. *James Denson – they think I'm James Denson. I must be dreaming.*

That made sense of it all: the filth, the stink, the old-fashioned clothing, the thick rope around her neck, the waiting crowd with their eager eyes.

I've spent so long thinking about him – I'm having some kind of hallucination.

She wanted to believe that – she wanted it so very badly. But she couldn't keep up the illusion for more than a moment. If this were a dream, a delusion, wouldn't James Denson be the way she had imagined him – an athletic, dark-haired man? The body in which she found herself was gross and heavy; when she moved her head, the strands of hair that fell across her eyes were coarse and sandy. This was not imagination. The cool air on her skin, the murmuring voices, the creaking of the scaffold under her feet, none of that was imagination either.

Any last words?

So little time left to understand it. *Witchcraft – they accused him of witchcraft. Did he make this happen?*

Dimly she wondered whether in 2015, in the narrow bed in her own cottage, the body of Freya Robertson was stirring, sitting up, looking about with a watchful curiosity. She thought it was doing exactly that – and that gentle, bookish Freya was about to undergo a personality change.

James Denson had escaped. For *her*, there was no time left: no time to wonder how he had done it, why her? No time for anything but last words.

"I'm innocent!"

The voice that came out was deeper and harsher than she expected. The accent was a little strange, but then this was further away than a few hundred miles; this accent was from three hundred *years* away.

"I'm innocent!" she yelled again, and now the crowd reacted with jeers. The few faces that had shown sympathy looked down or away. Something flew through the air and exploded against the wooden scaffold with a wet splattering sound. Faced with disbelief and taunts, Freya fell silent, and seeing this the crowd stopped shouting too, waiting instead for whatever might come next in this morbid amusement.

Freya was very aware of the man at her shoulder, of time running out. At the very last, inspiration came.

"I've done nothing, and I shall prove it! When I am dead –" She faltered and then went on, "When I am dead, a white dove shall fly down and land upon this scaffold, as proof of my innocence."

A ripple went through the crowd again, but this time it was approval; this was a bold gesture on the part of the condemned. A greater part of the crowd looked up now with interest and rough sympathy; if these words were to come true, what a thing it would be to have seen it! Not one in twenty believed it *would* come true, of course.

Freya did. She had read it, after all.

PREY OF THE FIN-FOLK

It is difficult in the 21st century to attach fear to even the wildest corners of Scotland's Highlands and Islands. The rugged beauty of these far-away lands has never been in doubt; it is no surprise that in modern times even northern Scotland's most geographically hostile locales are visited with regularity by recreationalists. But in the ages preceding mechanisation it was somewhat different. In those distant days, terms like 'remote' and 'isolated' had entirely different meanings. The sheer emptiness of this scenic realm, its vastness and extreme inaccessibility, created a sense of mystery and awe, which, coupled with the Highlands' age-old melting pot of folklore and superstition, made it the perfect home for tales so eerie that not all of them are forgotten even today.

The Sound of Eynhallow is the ideal case in point. This stretch of storm-tossed water lies between Mainland Orkney and Rousay. Eynhallow itself is the small rocky island sitting in the middle of this turbulent passage. It is less than half a mile square, and aside from the ruin of a 12th century church, it bears few marks of man – the last crofters left the island in the 1850s. Now in the care of Historic Scotland, it is preserved as a bird sanctuary. However, even in modern times it is wreathed with spooky mythology which can dissuade all but the most intrepid visitors.

Most of those who make the journey these days are birdwatchers, eager to catch glimpses of fulmars, skuas, puffins, black guillemots and Arctic terns. By necessity, these visitors must be a hardy sort as the landscape of Eynhallow is bleak in the extreme. They must also be prepared to experience an awesome sense of loneliness. Few fishermen are ever seen off the shore here, for reasons that aren't all lost in the mists of time.

For example, in July 1990 a party of 90 bird-watching enthusiasts were brought to the island by a local boat firm, and quickly dispersed among the rocks and coves, hunting their feathered prey with cameras. Unbeknown to them, something else might have been hunting around the shores of Eynhallow at the same time. It was much later on, with darkness descending, when the party returned to their ferry, only to discover there were now only 86 of them. When the remainder scoured the island for the missing quartet, there was no trace. No-one was able to account for these individuals by name – no-one was even sure who was missing, which implied the absentees were all members of the same group and had likely been together when misfortune struck. Of course this made it all the stranger, because it meant that whatever had happened was of such seriousness that not one of four people had been able to raise the alarm. A report was made, and search-and-rescue operations were launched involving both the local police and the coastguard but no sign of the missing passengers was ever uncovered, either on land or in the sea. Eventually, the original passenger itinerary was checked and a suggestion made that perhaps there'd only been 86 passengers to begin with. Nobody could confirm or deny it, but on this basis the case was eventually closed.

However, some residents of the Orkney Isles had their own explanation. When pressed, they pointed to the fin-folk, a tribe of mermen who according to legend occupied the depths of the Sound and resented the presence of humans on Eynhallow to such an extent that they would seize any opportunity to snatch them away.

To modern ears it sounds ridiculous. But the notion of aquatic humanoids is common to almost all the cultures of the world, and theories have been voiced by paleoanthropologists that an alternate branch of mankind might have evolved in the ocean on a parallel course with its cousins on land (though it should also be mentioned that many scientists scoff at this hypothesis, and point to a complete absence of evidence in the fossil record).

Of course many parts of the British coast are home to merperson lore, but in general terms Scotland's seem to be the most frightening. The selkie, or seal-people, are indigenous to North Highland mythology, and though many of their stories possess charming elements, they rarely end well. Even less so those concerning the much feared Blue Men of the Minch, an ultra-aggressive species of merman believe to populate the wild straits between mainland Scotland and the Inner Hebrides. So fierce were the Blue Men's attacks reputed to be in olden times that modern scholars wonder if they might represent a folk memory of displaced corsairs, possibly former slaves from North Africa who were known to paint their faces blue as they ravaged the high seas. And if such origins explain the Blue Men, they might explain the fin-folk of Eynhallow, who were also said to possess non-traditional merman features. Not for Eynhallow a race of beautiful half-girls lolling on skerries and combing their lustrous, sea-green hair, with only clam shells to cover their modesty. The fin-folk are described as dark-skinned and thick with sinew, and often raiding coastal settlements in rowboats.

Does that sound familiar?

The Vikings, who claimed the Orkney Isles for their own in the 8th century, were notorious slavers. Could some of their captives *have escaped or even been released, to embark on similar missions of pillage and kidnap? It can't be discounted. In fact, the legendary reason the fin-folk were so defensive of Eynhallow dates back to the Viking era, when they stole the wife of a Norse jarl called Thorodale, who, in vengeance, drove them from their summer capital, Hildaland (modern day Eynhallow), by sewing it with salt and inscribing crosses in its turf.*

For all these tales, people still visit the tiny, wave-battered island each summer. The mystery and danger of the Orkneys only adds to their romance – until such time as the fin-folk rise again of course, and more innocent visitors unaccountably vanish.

STRONE HOUSE
Barbara Roden

"I'm glad to hear that your journey wasn't too arduous," said Campbell over dinner. "You're the first person to visit since we arrived."

Marsden waved a hand dismissively. "It was fine until Glasgow; there was a bit of confusion about the next train to Oban, but in the end I didn't have to wait long. I must say that I didn't realise quite how remote this place was. Thank you for sending a coach!"

"Yes," said Mrs. Campbell, sighing. "Remote is just the word. And here was everyone congratulating us on our stroke of luck, inheriting a Scottish estate, no doubt picturing something within easy striking distance of Edinburgh, or the Borders."

"You certainly kept your prospects quiet," Marsden said with a grin. "Despite your surname, you're one of the most thoroughly English people I know, Campbell; if that's not an insult to your heritage."

"Not at all," replied his host. "I've never lived anywhere except England. Of course I knew something of the family history, but . . . well, you know how these things are. My father came to England as quite a young man, and never spoke much about Scotland. There was some estrangement between him and his older brother; obviously a deep one, for he never discussed it with me. Perhaps he might have, but I was still quite young when he died, so never learned the details. Even my mother appears not to know much about it."

"The house looks quite handsome from the outside," said Marsden. "Puts me in mind of Vanbrugh."

"Well spotted!" replied Campbell. "From what I've been able to find out it was designed by William Adam, one of the great Scottish architects. He admired Vanbrugh, and was greatly influenced by him. It wasn't the first house on the site, however. There was a fortified tower house here from some time in the thirteenth century, although it was completely destroyed to make way for this house."

"It must have seen quite a lot in its day," said Marsden. "From what little I know of this area, stability does not seem to have been a watchword."

"Oh yes, the original house saw a fair bit of violence over the centuries, and changed hands several times as family strength waxed and waned, and political favour was bestowed and then snatched away. It finally came into the possession of the Campbells through marriage, sometime in the seventeenth century."

"You've put your time to good use," said Marsden, "to have learned so much so quickly."

"There's quite an extensive library," said Mrs. Campbell, "and any number of old papers, although everything is in such terrible order that we've only just begun to be able to make sense of it."

"We had no idea how badly run down the house was," added Campbell. "Uncle Donald appears to have lived in only two rooms, and had closed everything else up. There was no staff to speak of, and the place was left to rack and ruin. Some of the rooms have been so badly affected by damp that we'll be fortunate to salvage anything in them. This"—he waved a hand around the dining-room—"is one of the few rooms we've been able to make habitable."

"Seems a prime location for a haunting or three."

"We've not come across any ghosts; at least, not yet," said Campbell. "Although I'm sure that as I do more research I'll come across some rather colourful stories."

"What are you going to do with the house?" asked Marsden. His host shrugged.

"Heaven knows. Uncle Donald leaving me the estate was a huge surprise, given the relations between him and my father. I'm beginning to wonder if the old boy didn't purposely hand me a poisoned chalice, out of spite."

"The grounds, too, are in a terrible state," said Mrs. Campbell. "We've been so busy in the house that we've barely set foot in them—everything is so massively overgrown. And the weather has hardly been conducive to venturing outside."

"The grounds at Strone House used to be famous, didn't they?" asked Marsden.

"Yes indeed," said Campbell. "The ancestor who had the current house built was determined to turn the grounds into a showpiece; I found a reference to Capability Brown in an old letter, although I think it more likely that one of his pupils oversaw the work. All manner of statues and ornaments and whatnots were brought in to decorate the place; money was apparently no object! Dr. Johnson visited the estate more than a century ago, during his journey through Scotland with Boswell, and spoke of—how did he put it— 'the extent of its prospects, the awfulness of its shades, the horrors of its precipices'. It would be lovely to restore the grounds to their former glory." He caught his wife's eye and added hastily, "But that is hardly a priority at the moment. The grounds can wait until we decide what to do with the estate."

"It's an extensive one, is it not?"

"Yes, several hundred acres. My ancestor used the natural cliffs to create a network of paths; then, not content with that, carved out a Grotto, sprinkled follies about at random, and cut an archway through one of the cliffs. There's a tower as well, built on the site of an earlier structure; some say a watchtower, others a cell of some kind. There was even a Lion's Den, complete with a stone lion."

"And the Hermitage!" laughed Mrs. Campbell. "You forgot the Hermitage."

"Complete with an authentic eighteenth century hermit, I hope," said Marsden.

"Not a real one," admitted Campbell. "It was an automaton of some sort, apparently. Moved, and spoke a few words, and was infamous for his terrible cough. He apparently fooled a good many people."

"Is there any sort of map of the grounds?"

"Yes," said Campbell. "I came across one the other day. I'll find it out for you."

"We've no real idea what the park is like now," said Mrs. Campbell. "We did ask, when we arrived, but it's been so long since the grounds have been open to anyone that the locals seem to know no more than we do."

"There's an old chap named James McLeod whose father was the last guide here, and whose grandfather was a guide before that," added Campbell. "He was being trained in the family business as a lad, and then the house was closed to visitors. He's been ill, and I haven't been able to speak with him, but he undoubtedly has a better knowledge of the grounds than anyone else alive."

"I shall take a look tomorrow, and give a report," promised Marsden. "Perhaps I shall find the hermit, or what's left of him, and send him your apologies for not having paid him a visit yet."

*

Next morning Marsden surveyed the view from his window. The lawns and gardens closest to the house were overgrown, but he could still trace their shape and pattern; a task which grew impossible as the land sloped away towards the area which had, more than a century earlier, been turned into a fantastic playground.

"Much of it is almost certainly well-nigh impassable," said Campbell later, as the two men stood outside the house. "I made it as far as the entrance to the Grotto, and that took me the better part of a morning. The path is choked with plants and dead leaves, and is quite treacherous underfoot, positively covered in rotten vegetation.

It will take a large team of men some time to clear it all out. And it's done little but rain since we arrived, which hasn't helped matters." He glanced at the sky. "By the look of those clouds, we're in for more rain soon. Are you sure you wouldn't rather stay at the house?"

"No, I'm keen to see some of these famous grounds," replied Marsden. He held up the map. "Armed with this, I should manage to find my way about. And I have a candle and some matches, for investigating the Grotto."

"You'd best take this, too." Campbell handed his friend a stout billhook, its curved blade glinting in the light. "You'll almost certainly need it. You should make it to the Grotto without much trouble, but I don't know what you'll find beyond that."

Marsden consulted the map. "I shall try to make it through the Grotto, and as far as the Hermitage and the Tower. I'll let you know the extent of the damage when I return."

*

At ground level the gardens lost any semblance of the order Marsden had discerned from his window. Hedges were overgrown into a riot of foliage; bushes overhung the grass- and weed-choked paths; and what had once been called the Topiary Garden had become a field of grotesque shapes of monstrous size. Every statue he passed was covered with dirt and moss, and few were intact. Atop a derelict fountain was a pair of legs ending just above the knees, and when he peered over the rim of the basin Marsden recoiled at the sight of a head raising its faceless countenance towards him. A breeze rippled the surface of the scummy green water surrounding the head, and he shivered and glanced skyward. Clouds were building up, and for a moment Marsden considered returning to the house, but the lure of Strone's grounds proved too strong. He turned and continued in the direction of the park, and was soon descending the narrow, twisting path from the lower gardens.

A rough trail of hacked branches showed where Campbell had cut through. Even so, Marsden found he had to use the billhook more than once and proceed with extreme caution, down steps that were slick with moss and leaves. The deeper he went the worse it became. With each step he took, the grey cliffs rising stark on either side of him reduced the light even more. Eventually he was proceeding almost blindly, and was beginning to think of admitting defeat and turning back when he realised that the path had levelled out.

35

Marsden pulled the map out of his pocket. There were three possible routes through to the other side of the grounds. He could go left, and continue along a series of pathways cut through the cliffs; straight, down a narrow defile called the Cleft; or right, through the Grotto. A quick glance at the first two routes was not reassuring: both were choked with more of the dense foliage he had just come through, and it was clear that no one had passed down either way for some decades. The prospect of venturing along either route, without anyone having acted as trailblazer, was not appealing. The Grotto, then, was the only practical option.

He had just reached this conclusion, and was tucking the map into his pocket, when Marsden was startled by a noise behind him, somewhere further up the path he had just come down. He turned sharply, and listened. For a moment there was silence, then a rough, rasping sound, followed by a sharp clattering as of stones falling.

"Who's there?" he called out. "Campbell, is that you?"

There was no reply and, even though he listened intently for several seconds, no further sounds came to his ears. He turned to the entrance to the Grotto, barely discernible through a screen of bushes. Then, once more wielding the billhook, he fought his way through to the Grotto itself.

A certain amount of wan daylight penetrated the entrance, but there was no corresponding exit visible. Marsden fumbled in his pocket for the candle. It did not provide much illumination, but was sufficient for him to be able to pick his way along the rough ground, which was obscured by drifts of rotting leaves. It was not long before he had left the daylight behind, and the darkness outside the small circle of light thrown by the candle seemed oppressive. The passage narrowed as he continued along it, and Marsden was conscious of the weight of stone pressing down upon him from above. He was beginning to wonder whether or not there was more than one path through the Grotto, and if he should stop and consult the map in case he had taken a wrong turning, when he rounded a corner and came to an abrupt halt.

The darkness seemed to open out around him as the walls of the passage fell away, and he realised he was at the centre of the Grotto, a huge arched cavern cut into the heart of the cliff. He held the candle high above, and saw that the wall closest to him was adorned with niches, some of which still held barely visible carvings and ornaments. The niches, so far as he could tell, stretched round the interior, and shells and stones had been set into the walls, although many had come loose and fallen to the ground. There was, he knew, stained glass set near the top of the Grotto, which had originally let in some illumination, but he could see no sign of it; it was far too high for the light from his candle to reach, and he suspected that it was covered over with vegetation on the outside, shutting out any of the light that might once have come through.

He was gazing upwards, trying to see the extent of the place, twisting round as he did so. He had, without looking down, moved into the centre of the Grotto, and his foot came into contact with something hard. He stumbled and almost fell, regaining his balance just in time but dropping the candle in the process.

"Damn," he muttered, bending down and fumbling with his free hand, still clutching the billhook with the other. He touched something large and round and rough—probably what he had stumbled over in the first place—and continued groping for the candle; then froze as he heard a sound—raspy and hoarse, definitely not rocks falling—emanate from the direction from which he had come.

For a moment he remained immobile. Then his hand moved once more and his fingers felt the smooth wax of the candle. With a sigh of relief he picked it up and managed to fumble the matches out of his pocket. Still crouching, he lit the candle—and almost dropped it again when his eyes encountered a face staring up at him.

Marsden jerked upright and, when his heart had slowed, looked down again. His gaze fell on a carved stone head, which could have been the twin of the one he had seen in the fountain. It was grey against the white stone of the ground, and seemed to glimmer dully in the dim light of the candle.

Shaking only slightly, he stood up. It was clear that the head had once adorned one of the niches high up in the Grotto, but time and neglect had brought it to the ground. He stared at it for a further moment, and it gazed up at him, its unblinking stare unnerving in the dimness.

There had been no repetition of the noise behind him, and Marsden began to think that he had imagined it, or that it had merely been the wind blowing through the dead leaves. He had no wish to linger, however, and without glancing behind him he hurried on. There was only one passage leading out of the Grotto on the far side, and as he made his way along it he took care to keep his gaze directed downwards lest he stumble again.

It was with considerable relief that he saw a glimmer of daylight ahead, and it did not take him long to hack his way through the screen of bushes obscuring the far end of the Grotto. He took several deep breaths when he was once more outside, surprised at the relief he felt being back in something like the open. Indeed, he was pleased to see, now he had reached the far side of the cliffs, that the land opened out somewhat, and the bushes, with more room to

37

spread, were not as formidable an obstacle as they had been. The top of the Tower was visible before him, two hundred or so yards distant, and Marsden cast an appraising look over the foliage that stood between. It would not, he thought, take more than a few minutes to cut his way through. Hefting the billhook purposefully, he set off.

In the end, it took almost a half-hour to carve a passable trail through the undergrowth, and when Marsden emerged near the base of the Tower he was sticky with perspiration, despite the chill and damp of the day. It had become cooler since he had set out from the house and, glancing upward, he noted that the clouds were thickening. Rain was not far off but he had, he decided, a bit more time before he had to turn back.

The Tower was a slender column of white stone, with narrow slits at intervals down its sides. There was no sign of the original structure, and Marsden wondered idly what had once stood on the spot. He craned his head back to see the top, some hundred or so feet above him. The stonework looked solid enough, and he approached the stout wooden door which faced him. He gave it a firm push, fully expecting that it would be locked, or otherwise impassable. To his amazement, after an initial moment of resistance it swung open, albeit grudgingly, and with a harsh squealing grate which spoke of unoiled hinges and wood dragging across stone. A gentle sigh of damp, musty air, long unbreathed, wafted over him.

He stepped through the open doorway. A pale stone staircase twisted up out of sight away from him, the centre of each step worn to a slight concavity. A thin metal rail was set into the wall, and Marsden reached out a hand to test it. It seemed stable, and there was enough light penetrating the stairwell to enable him to see his way, so with only the faintest hesitation he began making his way up.

The steps were slightly damp underfoot, and slippery, and before he had gone very far Marsden began to wonder how wise an idea it had been to climb the Tower. Still, he told himself, as long as he took care he would be safe, and it seemed a shame to have come this far and not get to the top. The view would, he imagined, be spectacular; Campbell had told him the night before that from its top one could, on a clear day, see for several miles in any direction.

So he continued upwards, pausing occasionally to catch his breath. He tried squinting through one or two of the window slits he passed on his way, but could see little beyond a jumble of trees. Once, when he stopped, he thought he heard a scuttling noise echoing up the stairwell, but although he listened for some moments it was not repeated.

He was beginning to wonder how much longer he would have to climb, when an increase in light told him he was nearing the top of the Tower. He made a final turn of the stairs and was startled to find himself in a narrow aperture leading out to an even narrower walkway which, so far as Marsden could tell, went all the way round the outside of the Tower. He did not dare proceed out on to the walkway and investigate its full extent, for while there had clearly once been a rail or fence of some sort, the barrier itself had long since crumbled away, and the stone ledge looked to be in a precarious state at best.

Having come so far, Marsden tried to admire the view, which might well have been impressive on a good day, but he was somewhat hampered by the necessity of staying within the doorway. The weather was also a factor. In the relatively short time it had taken him to climb the tower, the clouds had built up even further, and it seemed likely that a downpour was imminent. Marsden turned back to the stairway, but had not taken more than three steps down it when a sound came to his ears: a harsh squealing grate, as of unoiled hinges, and wood scraping across stone.

Marsden froze. The sound was unmistakably that of the door to the Tower being opened—or closed—by someone below. It echoed up the stairwell, bouncing off the steps and walls. He waited a moment, then called down the stairs "Hello? Is someone there?"

Silence. He tried again. "Who's there? Campbell, is that you?"

He did not really think it was his friend, but that seemed the best possible option. He recalled the noises he had heard earlier, on the path down to the Grotto and in the Grotto itself. Could someone be living rough in the grounds; a tramp, perhaps? Or perhaps some of the locals, knowing they had the run of the place, came in and did a little poaching on the sly. He had seen no evidence of anyone else having been in the gardens, once he had passed through the Grotto, but if someone was following him, was even now waiting inside, or at, the base of the Tower …

Marsden shivered at the thought. Perhaps it had been the wind, blowing the door, although it was a very heavy door, and there wasn't much wind …

He hesitated, wondering what he should do. The thought of making his way down the stairs, rounding the final turn, and coming face to face with—someone—unsettled him, but it did not take him long to realise he had no option. There was no other way down, and he could not stay at the top of the Tower indefinitely. It would be some time before anyone at the house realised he was overdue, and longer still before there was a possibility of anyone coming within hailing distance of the Tower. He had no choice but to proceed down the stairs, whether there was anyone there or not. Which there couldn't be, of course. However ...

"I'm coming down now," he called, trying to make his voice sound jaunty. "Best clear out of the way, whoever you are, as there isn't enough room for two on these steps."

Was it his imagination, or was there the faintest whisper, the tiniest hint of movement, from the base of the stairs? He could not be sure, and a moment later, after taking a deep breath, he started down the steps.

He had thought it would be easier descending than ascending, but the steps seemed even more slippery than when he had made his way up them, and his tread seemed ever so slightly off, so that he was forever catching his feet and stumbling, clutching at the railing that circled the wall. Every few steps he would pause, listening intently, and once or twice he thought he heard a sound from below: a rasping noise, rattling and sharp, similar to the one he had heard in the Grotto. Still he made his way downward, until he knew that there were only a further two or three turns in the stairwell until he was at the bottom. Then he stopped once more to listen.

All was silence, yet Marsden had a sense that someone was there below him, that indefinable sense which alerts one to the presence of another close by. He was sure of it, so sure that he hefted the billhook and called out loudly "I'm almost at the bottom, and I have to warn you that I have a weapon, so don't try anything foolish. It might be better if you cleared off now, whoever you are. I won't tell the owner, as long as you don't do anything silly."

Was it his imagination, or was there a faint shuffling noise, as of footsteps over rough stone? Marsden hoped it indicated that whoever was waiting below was leaving, rather than advancing further up the stairwell. Without giving himself the opportunity to think any further about this second option, he gathered himself up and rushed down the final two dozen or so steps, almost losing his footing more than once, and arrived at the bottom breathless, and with the billhook extended before him.

There was no one there.

Marsden paused, and glanced round the small base of the Tower. There was nowhere for anyone to hide; he was completely alone. But the door, which he had left open, was now closed.

He gave it a tug, and it opened grudgingly, as before, with the same squealing grate. Impossible to think that the wind had blown it shut, but that was the only explanation. Either that, or someone was waiting outside ...

But when he exited the Tower, there was no one in sight, and no indication that anyone other than himself had passed that way recently. He could see his own tracks, coming from the direction of the Grotto, and no sign of anyone else. He shook his head. "You're imagining things, old boy," he muttered to himself; then flinched as a fat drop of rain spattered against his arm.

He looked up. The clouds were angry and grey, and the first drop of rain was soon followed by others. Within seconds the rain was falling heavily, and Marsden realised that the predicted downpour was upon him. He could make a dash back the way he had come, and trust that the foliage would protect him to some extent; or he could seek refuge inside the Tower until the rain let up. He was, for some reason he did not want to consider, unwilling to adopt the latter course, and while he did not fancy making his way back to the Grotto in the rain, it seemed the only choice.

He was weighing this option, glancing about him as if hoping for inspiration, when he saw to his right the corner of a small building, tucked into a grove of trees. At this moment the rain grew even heavier, and without another thought he turned and ran towards the building, ducking under branches and following a barely discernible path to what he realised, as he drew closer, must be the Hermitage.

It was a small, roughly built structure surrounded by a stone wall and surmounted by a steeply pitched roof that was thick with moss. Marsden ascended the uneven steps and pushed at the door, which yielded after a moment, as if something had given way on the other side. With a sigh of relief he entered the hut, blinking against the sudden dimness. The only light came from a small window beside the door, and it took some seconds for his eyes to adjust to the gloom. When they did, he started for the third time that day, as he realised someone was sitting in front of the window.

It was a man: old and dirty, and clothed in curious garments that Marsden took some seconds to identify. When he did, he almost laughed aloud, so great was his relief. It was the eighteenth century Hermit of which his friends had spoken, still keeping watch after well over a century.

Marsden approached the figure. As he drew closer, he could see that decades of neglect had taken their toll. The Hermit was begrimed and dingy, his clothing even more tattered and worn than his creator could have envisaged. He was wearing a kilt, which had been of muted colours to start with and faded considerably over the years, although Marsden could trace out heavy dark lines over squares of green and blue threaded with red.

Despite everything, however, the Hermit still looked amazingly lifelike, and Marsden, when he was close enough, reached out a hand to touch it, as if to reassure himself that it was indeed an

41

automaton, and not a real person. The figure did not move, and Marsden drew a deep breath.

"Well, Mr. Hermit, I'm pleased to make your acquaintance," he said. He gave a slight bow. "The owners promise that they will soon be here to pay their respects."

A quick glance round the rest of the interior showed that there was little of interest remaining in the Hermitage. A dusty table had probably once held a few relics, and a low bookcase, its one shelf sagging, had almost certainly contained a few impressive tomes suggestive of a man of deep learning and much wisdom, but the books had long since vanished. Presumably the Hermit had been the main attraction, and little attention had been paid to anything else.

Marsden returned to the door, to see if there was any sign that the rain was ceasing. He had just begun to allow himself to think that it was tapering off slightly, when he heard a now-familiar rasping noise behind him.

A cough.

He jumped; then turned, somewhat unwillingly, towards the Hermit. His breath caught in his throat when he realised that it was moving, slowly and jerkily, the head turning towards him.

That cough again—*He was infamous for his terrible cough*, Marsden recalled his friend saying—and one arm moved slightly, until it was pointing directly at him. Another cough, and then he heard, faintly but unmistakably, words.

"*Say kind.*" Cough. "*And.*" Cough. Then silence for several almost unendurable seconds, before the figure rasped "*Tour.*" The head turned a fraction more in his direction, the eyes of the figure locked on Marsden's face, and the words were repeated, slowly and harshly: "*Say kind and tour.*"

Marsden gave a faint cry and scrabbled at the door for the handle. Then, oblivious to the rain that was still pelting down, he ran down the track he had made towards the Grotto. Branches clutched at his clothing, and he stumbled more than once, but he kept up his blundering flight, not resting until he stopped, panting, at the entrance to the Grotto. He paused only long enough to light his candle, then entered the passageway, which was even dimmer now than it had been before. The uneven ground forced him to slow his pace, and when the passage at last opened up into the main chamber he made sure to keep his eyes down lest he stumble over the head—or anything else—on his way across.

It was not until he was entering the passage on the far side of the central chamber that his brain registered what he had not seen on his way through the centre of the Grotto. Almost unwillingly—but he had to be sure, he *had* to—he turned and retraced his steps to the middle of the chamber. Bending, he shone the candle close to the ground, sweeping it back and forth so that it illuminated the entire floor. He was right. The head which he had stumbled over on his initial journey was nowhere to be seen.

A sound—*Was it a cough? Please, God, not that*—from behind him echoed around the chamber, and with it a noise as of footsteps dragging along the passage which led in the direction of the Hermitage. With a whimper Marsden fled, heedless now of caution, intent only on getting out of the Grotto and into something like open air once more. It took some time to claw his way back up the path he had descended in such good spirits only a few hours earlier, but he did not pause until he was at the top of the pathway, the reassuring bulk of Strone House in front of him. He shuddered as he passed the ruined fountain, and did not look into the basin as he made his way past it.

*

They all agreed, when Marsden had told his tale, that the automaton must still have been in working order, and that Marsden had activated some mechanism within it when he touched it, which had set it off again; remarkable, after so many years, but not out of the question. It was a fine theory, and seemed to answer some—if not all—of the questions racing though Marsden's mind, although he remained silent about those, at least while Mrs. Campbell was present. When discussing the matter afterwards, over more than one stiff brandy, the men decided that while there could, perhaps, have been an intruder in the grounds, it was more likely that wind, rain, solitude, and Marsden's imagination had been at work.

The next morning a wan sunlight made the grounds look somewhat less foreboding, and Marsden was able to view the previous day's events with equanimity. He was given a tour of the house, which ended in the library, where piles of paper and a stack of books lay on a huge desk. Campbell pointed to them and smiled ruefully.

"And that is only a part of it," he said. "I've barely been able to make a dent. But while you were out exploring yesterday, I did come across one of those colourful tales I told you were sure to be found." The smile faded from his face. "More gruesome than colourful, if truth be told." He pulled a small volume, bound in faded calf, from the top of the stack of books. "I had thought that once the property came into the hands of the Campbells by marriage all would have been peaceful here; but I underestimated just how bitter the enmity between certain families was."

43

He opened the book and leafed through the pages until he came to a certain spot. "It seems that the MacDonald family had long had their eye on the house and lands here, and resolved to take it from the Campbells. As the then-chief had little idea how strongly defended the house would be, he sent a spy in; his piper. The man came in undercover, as it were, and soon found that the house was well-fortified and almost unassailable. Unfortunately for him, he was discovered before he could return with this news, and imprisoned; quite possibly in whatever building stood where the Tower is now, although that isn't clear from this account. His chief decided to march on the house, but the piper was able to warn him by playing a song which told him to 'shun the tower, I am imprisoned'."

"And what happened to the piper?"

Campbell shook his head. "The man paid for his loyalty with his life, apparently, as a warning to anyone else who might try the same trick. It must have worked, for I can't see that any other attempts were made on the house."

*

The next day dawned brighter still, and brought a message that James McLeod was well enough to meet with them. Campbell and Marsden promptly paid a visit to the man, who received them in great state. He could not recall how old he was, precisely, but his grandson, who sat beside him and was at least of middle age, assured them that the old man was well into his nineties. He could recall, with remarkable clarity, his time spent assisting his father as a guide at Strone in the very last days of the previous century. Mention was made, eventually, of the Hermit, and McLeod laughed.

"Aye, it frichtened me when I was a bairn, gaun wi' my father. He'd tak fowk tae the windie an' there the auld deil was hunkerin' intil, keekin' oot as they keekit' in tae the mirk. Then the auld deil begood crackin', an' some o' the leddies cam near skirlin', he was so rale. His hoasts were braw."

It took a few moments, and some translation on the grandson's part, before the old man's listeners understood him to have said that his father had taken visitors to the window of the hut to see the Hermit within, sitting in the gloom; that once the figure began speaking, some of the ladies in attendance had almost fainted; and that his coughing had been particularly impressive, undoubtedly lending to the effect.

"Well, you'll be pleased to know that he's still there, although somewhat the worse for wear," said Marsden, with a laugh that was slightly forced. "Amazing what they could do with automata then. The machinery still works, in a small way." When the old man looked puzzled, Marsden continued, "Automata—mechanical figures with some sort of machinery inside that could make them move, and even seem to talk. Very convincing he was, too."

"Nay, he wasna"—the old man hesitated over the word—"mechanical, sir. He whaur nocht but a *gille-mirein* happit in auld claes."

Seeing their look of confusion, the grandson spoke up. "Puppet, sir. He says it was nocht but a puppet in old clothes."

"Puppet?" said Campbell. He glanced at his friend, then looked at the old man. "Are you sure?"

"Aye, sir. My father wad gang ahin it in the mirk an' hunker doun an' mak it gee an' blether an' lauch an' hoast. T'was unco rale."

Marsden had gone quite pale. To prevent an awkward silence his friend said, in a voice of forced cheeriness, "As Mr. Marsden said, he's still there, and still wearing his Campbell tartan."

McLeod shook his head. "Nay, sir. The puir cratur's caes were the auld Clan MacDonald tartan, frae wanchancy piper kilt gin there lang syne, wha sang *pibroch* tae warn his maister." He cleared his throat and began to sing in a thin voice.

"A cholla mo run seachain an tur, seachain an tur
A cholla ghaoil seachan an caol, seachan an caol
Tha mise an laimh, tha mise an laimh."

Marsden looked up sharply. "That first line, the end of it—'say kind and tour'," he said, his voice tight. "What does it mean?"

The grandson looked at them. "*Seachain an tur?*" he asked. "It means 'shun' or 'stay away from' the tower. And the last line means 'I am a prisoner'. Mr. Campbell, is your friend not well? He's gone quite pale. Let me get you a glass of the *uisge beatha* ..."

THE WELL OF HEADS

Loch Oich, which lies between Loch Ness and Loch Lochy, is one of the most famous Highland lochs, but in this case that isn't simply because of its pristine beauty. Indeed, the story behind Loch Oich's notoriety is a gruesome one. Visitors will gain their first intimation of it if they use the A82 trunk road from Inverness to Fort William, which follows the loch's pretty west shore. Along that route they will pass a very curious object: a single stone column, on top of which are mounted the stone images of seven severed heads.

Its origins, perhaps not unexpectedly, can be found among the clan wars of ancient antiquity. On September 25th 1663, two brothers, Alexander and Ranald MacDonald, were knifed to death by rivals for their chieftainship of the Clan of Keppoch. The prime suspect was another MacDonald, Alistair, who had allegedly attacked the two young captains with six accomplices, most likely his own sons. Alistair MacDonald was an influential man, and initially no action was taken against him. However, a local bard and friend of the two victims, Iain Lorn, agitated for justice for two whole years, and eventually two clan high-chiefs, MacDonald of Glengarry and MacDonald of Sleat, chose to act, now armed with a 'letter of fire and sword' issued by the Privy Council in Edinburgh. Fire and Sword was an old Scottish legal mechanism by which the local sheriff was entitled to use all powers necessary to bring justice on malefactors who persistently resisted the law.

The murderers attempted to flee, but were overhauled by a posse from Inverness, which contained many members and supporters of the bereaved Keppoch family, including the fearsome Ian Lom, better known as 'Bald John'. All seven were tried by their captors at the scene, and then dragged to a fallen tree, where their heads were lopped off.

At this point in the tale, history makes way for spooky mythology.

En route to Invergarry Castle to present the severed heads to the chief of the Glengarry MacDonalds, Bald John, who was carrying his gory trophies in a single Hessian sack, heard them snarling and groaning about the injustice of the vengeance wrought upon them – hissing that none of them had been awarded a fair trial. Thus, Bald John stopped at a spring on the loch-side and dunked the heads repeatedly in order to drown them and silence them for good. This appears to have done the trick, as the heads *were accordingly transported to Invergarry without further incident, and from there to Edinburgh, where they were "affixit to the gallowes standing on the Gallowlie". This latter part of the tale is definitely true, as indicated by the official record quoted above, and by the seven headless corpses which were later disinterred from an unmarked grave near the site of the summary execution. The monument currently marking this spot on the loch side – 'Tobar nan Ceann' (in English, 'Well of Heads') – was erected in 1812 as a permanent memorial to the crime committed and the harsh justice that rectified it.*

But most likely, Bald John actually stopped here to wash these bloody fragments of his enemies and make them less repulsive a trophy for his chief, rather than to still their undead tongues.

FACE DOWN IN THE EARTH
Tom Johnstone

Sunlight bouncing off wet tarmac dazzles him as he drives along the hair-raising, hair-pinned single-track road. It is a blazing gold-white ribbon stretching into the distance amidst mountains garlanded with foaming burns, flanked by banks of dripping, green ferns and tough, violet heather arching above rocky out-crops on one side, and a drop down to a silver loch on the other.

All very picturesque, reflects Ramsay sourly, wishing he was back in Edinburgh with Fiona. Ah, Auld Reekie, where two vehicles can get past each other on the road, without having to rely on passing places.

Lucky for him that one of these turns up when the sudden, intense burst of sunlight plays the trick on his vision.

For that's what it was, his mind insists as he sits in the passing place, trying to calm down after skidding to a halt there, nearly aquaplaning the car through splashing rainwater, to avoid the shape he thought he saw in the way.

One of the sheep perhaps? They're always wandering out and playing with the traffic. The stupid creatures think they own the roads as well as the hillsides they inhabit.

Still, he shouldn't be too hard on them. After all, he wouldn't be where he is today without them! Not that he's a sheep farmer or shepherd, though one of his illustrious forefathers was a major factor in their introduction to these rugged hills and glens, admittedly at the expense of the rural human population.

A major Factor.

He smiles at this play on words, breathing a little easier. He doesn't like to dwell too much on the past though. It's here and now that matters.

It can't have been an errant sheep. Too dark. And too tall, though squat compared to him.

And sheep don't stand on two legs.

Spots, motes of light, dance before his eyes, as he squints through the windscreen. There's no sign of the figure he almost collided with. He rubs his eyes until the backs of his eyelids turn into a congeries of fuzzy, grey polygons and splotches of light. Then he looks out towards the loch. In the distance, white blobs of sheep graze near the ruins of an ancient crofter's hut: just four squat, dry stone walls without a roof. The blinding evening sun chases away the tatters of cloud that loomed dark and wet over the glen only moments before.

He should have known it was a mistake to drive west at this time of day. But Dougie was insistent that Mr. Ramsay should come and look at the shower block in person. Why can't the man deal with a simple problem like this himself? That's what Ramsay pays him for, after all.

He needs to make up some time if he's going to catch the last ferry across the Sound. The light dies very late in these parts at this time of year, yet he knows that it'll be fading fast by the time he makes the crossing. Of course, he'll be permitted to take his car across. A far cry from the days when the islanders used to have to swim their horses across the Sound, tethered to their fishing boats. He's not an islander, not really, as far as anyone who lives there is concerned, and only islanders are permitted to take their cars across, just a few at a time, on the wee rust-bucket Caledonian MacBrayne ferry.

But they let him on just the same, though as usual he senses the granite disdain in the cobalt eyes of Shona, the hard-hatted, high-viz-jacketed ferrywoman, full of that mixture of hostility and deference he's come to know from his previous visits. He doesn't actually live there; he owns a small croft with a campsite on his land, which makes him an islander on paper.

He's trying to avoid that cobalt stare by gazing out over the choppy waters, when the thing appears bobbing between the waves. He sees a luminous, silver shape keeping pace with the lumbering Cal Mac hulk, hears snatches of a crooning chant in an unfamiliar tongue. Or not so unfamiliar: Gaelic. He doesn't know any of course, but he recognises its sounds, its lilts and cadences. He remembers the legends of the water-horses he read about at a more impressionable age. But the creature's too small for that. A woman? He can't quite make out the face, which seems to be immersed in the black turbulence of the sea. The spray must be blinding his eyes to give him such a daft idea. His heart quickens pleasantly at the undulating feminine shape with its silver sheen, less pleasantly when the face rises up. The blank, black eyes. The head grey and shiny, tapering to a white-whiskered snout.

He laughs at himself for getting spooked by a seal. And the Gaelic incantation? Just the pre-recorded piped safety announcement, read first in Gaelic, then in English. *For the Sassenachs like him*, he can imagine some of the islanders thinking, the ones like Shona at any rate. Not that they mind taking the money spent by the Sassenachs his campsite attracts, he reminds himself. And anyway he's no Sassenach, any more than the countless other

49

Scots that no longer speak a language which is all but dead, despite official attempts to revive it.

Though the crossing only takes about ten minutes, it seems like an age before the ferry lowers its creaking metal tongue to disgorge its passengers. His car's facing the wrong way now. He suspects Shona of arranging this deliberately with the pilot, to force him to reverse onto the narrow, concrete jetty, and to carry out an agonising five-point turn that threatens to plunge him and his Range Rover into the dark, lapping waters.

When he's completed this under her amused gaze, he edges the car slowly up the concrete ramp, past a huddle of huge men muttering and smirking over their lobster creels. The blood rushing through his skull seems to whisper at him in the dead tongue: *Mortair*[1]. The wind's dropped now. The weather turns on a sixpence out here. While flecks of mackerel cloud charcoal the darkening sky, he drives past the shop selling everything from wellies and waterproofs to midge repellent and the kinds of books on Scottish folklore he remembers from his youth. He follows the narrow road along the shoreline, which bends round to the West, taking him to a crossroads. His property is just beyond.

As he climbs out of the Range Rover, his feet crunching on the gravel, the sheep on the nearby hills bleat their greeting to him. Dougie's there too, standing there expectantly. So are the midges, out in force in the suddenly oppressive stillness of the air. Not even a breeze stirs the sea, which lies as flat as a mill-pond. He can feel a faint but insistent tattoo on his scalp. He claps his hand onto the clammy skin of his forehead. His palm comes away dotted with swatted insects too hungry for his flesh to get away in time.

"Damn things," he mutters.

"Have ye no tried that Avon Skin So Soft, Mr. Ramsay? It's just the thing for –"

"You've not dragged me all the way up here to discuss beauty products, Dougie …"

"No, Mr. Ramsay. Right enough."

Crestfallen, Dougie ushers his boss-cum-landlord inside the croft's modest, pebble-dashed bungalow, away from the insects' relentless gnawing. Dougie's ma stands in the kitchen, her arthritic hands clasped together. It's hard to imagine her frail, miniscule frame giving birth to her stocky, broad-shouldered son.

"Ah, there ye are, Mr. Ramsay," she smiles. "Ye'll be tired after all that travelling, eh?"

---

[1] Murderer.

"Oh, it wasn't too bad. Mind you, that Shona gave me the evil eye, as usual …"

"Och, ye shouldna pay her no mind," she says. "You sit yersel' down, Mr. Ramsay. I'll put the kettle on."

"Have you been on Facebook, Mrs. MacPherson?" Ramsay asks in a teasing tone he knows amuses her, glancing at the laptop on the spotless kitchen work-top. Despite himself, he likes being mothered by the tiny, neat, old woman. She laughs.

"Oh-ho, no, Mr. Ramsay! Ancestry Dot Com … It's awfie interestin'! Eh, Dougie?"

Dougie, who has remained silent in the corner up to now, mutters his agreement.

"Well, son," she says, eyeing the gloaming outside the window pointedly. "Go ben and get yer bits."

Dougie frowns uncertainly.

"Mr. Ramsay'll have to stop here the night, and we canna expect him to go in the caravan. So you'll have to do that."

"Aw … aye, right enough."

"Sorry about this, Dougie," puts in Ramsay. "It won't be for long, probably just one night. Then, you can show me what the … er, problem is in the morning."

There's a slight edge to Ramsay's voice. Dougie lowers his eyes: in embarrassment?

"Wi' the dunny? … Aw, aye, right enough, Mr. Ramsay. I'll go ben then."

He goes through the door to the back bedrooms.

"He's a good lad, Mr. Ramsay," Mrs. MacPherson says.

"That he is, Mrs. MacPherson."

He wouldn't like to say that Dougie's 'slow'; certainly wouldn't dream of saying it aloud in the old woman's presence. The way he'd put it is that Dougie is phlegmatic where his mother is quick-silver spry.

"I just canna understand why he needs ye to come all the way out here for a wee plumbin' problem!"

"I dare say he has his reasons. And it's nice to feel wanted, I suppose."

He's being diplomatic, for her sake. Changing the subject, somewhat to his relief, she moves onto the ritual of showing him to Dougie's small, spartan room, checking he's comfortable there, asking if there's anything else he needs, etc.

She must have slipped a wee nip of something in his tea, because before too long he's lying exhausted on the bed, fully-clothed, staring at the corrugated metal of the ceiling, where the heads of two rusted nails might be eyes. Closer scrutiny shows him

51

their pupils' odd shape, with the dip in the middle of each suggesting a rounded hour-glass. Curled horns crown the woolly face from which they stare at him, though the head sits on the hempen-smocked shoulders of a man.

"Thought ye might like the new heid, Mr. Sellar," the head's voice bleats. *"I've heard ye prefer sheep tae folk ..."*

He rolls over in bed, away from the creature's face. But in the small, grave-like gap between bed and wall, a naked, wrinkled body lies on its stomach. 'Face down' would be the right expression, except that the hag's face grins up at him as if her head were twisted right round one hundred and eighty degrees, crooning softly and horribly in a dead tongue. With a dead tongue.

Mortair.

Her spindly arms reach out to wind themselves around him.

Gasping awake, he struggles free from the tangled, sweat-soaked sheet.

He lies there for a while, breathing hard.

Why did the sheep-thing call him Sellar?

His great grandmother's maiden name.

*

"Sorry for turfing you out last night, Dougie."

"Aw, it's nae bother, Mr. Ramsay."

They're crossing the field, their galoshes squelching through the flat expanse of water-logged grass, which was broken up by a handful of bedraggled-looking tents, and hillocks bristling with grey rocks and coarse grass, as if the cropped sward of the campsite were breaking out in defiant warts or boils of the surrounding wilderness.

As the sodden ground sucks at his boots, Ramsay feels the full Scottish breakfast of square sausages, potato pancakes, pikelets, coddled eggs, beans and white pudding, lovingly cooked for him by Mrs. MacPherson, sloshing around in his stomach.

"Of course," adds Ramsay, "I wouldn't have had to do it if you'd been able to ... Did you not try digging some kind of drainage ditch around the block?"

"Aye, I did that. It's just ... Well, as I was digging, I found something."

Ramsay sees the narrow trench like a miniature moat around the breeze-block shower and toilet block, to help drain off the excess waste water that Dougie's told him has been building up in there. It branches off into a wider trench that extends into the neighbouring field, a boggy no man's land where heather bristles from soft, spongy, yellowish clumps of marshy ground. Ramsay notices the

52

rusty darkness of the ditch water, and reminds himself that the black, peat-rich soil stains the water that colour.

The trench comes to an abrupt halt. Four iron posts have been driven into the surrounding area, festooned with red and white hazard tape. As they approach it, Dougie begins to speak with a manic fluency Ramsay has never heard in him before.

"Ma doesna ken aboot it, Mr. Ramsay. If she got wind of this … With all her Ancestry Dot Com blether, she'd have a field day! Didna want the happy campers gettin' wind of this either, by the way. There's enough of them clearin' oot as it is, what wi' the dunny floodin'…"

Ramsay peers back at the campsite. The tents do indeed look a little thin on the ground over there. In fact, the campsite's almost deserted.

"You said you dug something up," he prompts Dougie.

"Dug? What d'ye call a man wi' a spade in his heid? Doug. What d'ye call a man wi' no spade in his heid? Douglas …!"

Dougie grins in the expectation of mirth from Ramsay, which never comes.

"You dug something up?"

"What? ... Oh, aye."

Dougie lifts the hazard tape, ushers him into the red-and-white striped enclosure. Ramsay stares down at the long, yellow-brown, tapering shapes just visible in the dark water. He can just make out the triangle of a scapula, the featureless dome of the back of a cranium …

The back of a head.

"Did you not call the police?"

"Well, even if I had, it'd take them half a day to get here fae the mainland, Mr. Ramsay …"

Why is Dougie grinning at this? And why are the midges out already at this time of day?

Ramsay slaps his hand against the back of his head as their relentless gnawing begins.

"Aye, the wee beasties come oot earlier and earlier," says Dougie, though he seems unaffected by them, and his eyes have a disconcerting glint in them. "They just love these marshy conditions. But you shouldna worry aboot the polis. She's no a victim o' crime. Well, no in the normal way … See the way she's lying? Face doon. That's the way I found her, by the way …"

Her? How does he know the sex of the skeleton? And what's the significance of her being laid to rest face down?

"Face doon in the earth," another voice calls, a female one from the direction the two men have come from. "The way they buried

53

the Gaelic Bards during the Clearances, to make 'em haud their wheesht when they were deid. Mary MacPherson was one of them, Mary Mhor nan Oran. Oh, aye, ye can learn a lot fae Ancestry Dot Com ..."

Ramsay spins round, sees Mrs. MacPherson's tiny frame through a blur of frantic midges, which seems to take on a vaguely female shape in front of her. Somewhere in their humming drone, he can hear the skirl of a mournful Gaelic lament, a dead tongue singing the song of the dead. She seems such a fragile figure in that vast, ancient landscape. Yet her voice rings out, and her laughter too. When he sees the ancient blades she and her son are holding, he suddenly wishes he'd rung Fiona last night before he dropped off to sleep. Will he never hear her smoky voice again? He looks desperately over to the campsite, thinking to call for help.

Empty.

Have Dougie and his ma used the flooded shower block as a pretext to evacuate the campsite, to isolate him in this lonely place, this deserted, depopulated place? And he's come here willingly, like a lamb to the slaughter. He could fight off the doll-like old woman, but her huge, granite-muscled son ...? Not likely. He could run, but the weight of history is dragging him down, along with his condemned man's hearty breakfast.

The female-shaped cloud of midges dances towards him, buzzing arms locking him in a toxic embrace, lips composed of hovering black dots locking with his in a kiss that itches and burns, driving all thoughts of fight, flight or for that matter anything else from his maddened brain.

He retreats into the ditch, as much to escape the midges as the MacPhersons' blades. All this does is enable the diminutive old woman and her squat son to tower over him.

"Ancestry Dot Com," continues the old woman, almost dwarfed by the huge blade. "That's where I found out about Mary. It's where I found out about yer great granny's maiden name too, Sellar. Descended fae Patrick Sellar, the Duke of Sutherland's Factor, who burnt folk fae their homes, so he could graze the Cheviot sheep on their land. That song ye can hear. It's about the Factor... Ye can see why he wanted to shut her up! Didna work though, eh? Look: all this haverin' on about the Factor is makin' her turn in her grave ..."

Well, part of her anyway. The skull is no longer facing down. Ramsay's jumping in there must have stirred the peaty water, so that it grins up at him like the face of the hag in his dream. Is it this turbulence that's making its jaw wag as though miming the singing?

Sellar. The dream hag called him that.

54

But he remembers his history, family history too, on his mother's side:

"Factor Sellar was arrested," he blurts out, dodging the blade, "charged with murder..."

Mortair, the breeze seems to echo.

"Aye, and he got off wi' a skelpt wrist," Mrs. MacPherson mutters.

A flick of the blade in the old woman's bird-like wrist slashes his cheek, but the midges' onslaught is such that he barely feels it. They even get in his eyes, nibbling at his eyelids when he tries to blink them away.

He tries to speak, to plead, but his mouth feels as if it's crammed with wool, and the words come out as a bleat.

"But I'm ... I'm not the Duke of Sutherland," he splutters, with midges invading his mouth, peppering his tongue with tiny bites. "I'm not even Patrick Sellar ..."

"Aye, but ye'll have to do," she says. "Ye're the closest thing we've got."

"It was nearly two hundred years ago!" he chokes out.

"Not to her," she hisses, pointing her blade towards the singing skull at his feet. "To her, it's like yesterday ..."

THE VANISHING

If there is one occupation that has caught the imagination of horror and mystery writers the world over it is that of lighthouse keeper. The iconic image of the lone signal tower in the midst of roaring spume is nightmarish. Countless spines have shivered at the mere thought of occupying such an outpost. It helps of course that lighthouses, those marvellous innovations of the Ancient World, have traditionally occupied some of the scariest places on Earth. Their sheer remoteness and the wildness of the elements besetting them have created a perfect breeding ground for thrilling tales and creepy legends.

Like most landmasses, the United Kingdom is surrounded by lighthouses. They play as vital a role now as they ever did, though in modern times they are automated. No longer are hardy crewmen despatched to these isolated structures, where the screaming wind, the bitter salt spray and the roiling dark of the ocean fog may engulf them at a moment's notice. Even so, Britain's far north, the Highlands and Islands of Scotland, still boast some of the most extreme lighthouse locations, and lay claim to what is possibly the eeriest lighthouse story on the planet.

It is almost impossible to imagine a more desolate spot than the Flannan Isles, or the 'Seven Hunters' as they were known in medieval times. These bleak, wind-blasted rocks sit 20 miles northwest of the Isle of Lewis in the Outer Hebrides. They are literally the farthest flung fringe of Britain, and are exposed to the most brutal Atlantic gales. A posting here would pose a challenge for even the toughest seadogs employed by the Northern Lighthouse Board.

Construction of the Flannan Isles Lighthouse commenced in 1895 and was completed in 1899, but long before it commenced operations there were odd stories about this Godforsaken place. The so-called 'Phantom of the Seven Hunters' was a disembodied entity whose shrieking voice numerous passing boatmen insisted they had heard. This myth was well-known across the Hebrides, and may predate St. Flannan himself, a 7th century hermit whose ruined chapel can still be seen on Eilean Mor, the main island. Certainly by the 9th century, when the last Christian occupants were driven from the Flannans by Viking raiders, stories were rife that curious daily rituals had been required to keep the islands' unquiet spirit at bay.

In respect of all this, it is perhaps no surprise that the Flannan Isles Lighthouse had only been in operation one year before it was stricken by a bizarre tragedy. In December 1900, the lighthouse's three-man team of Donald Macarthur, Thomas Marshall and James Ducat – all regarded as a reliable, disciplined men – vanished from their posts.

Simply that.

Vanished.

Concern was first felt on the mainland on December 15th, when the crew of the steamer Archtor came ashore at Oban and complained that no light had shown from the Flannan Isles signal tower. Other seamen confirmed this. The Isle of Lewis relief boat, the Hesperus, was not immediately despatched – difficult weather delayed it a week, but on arrival on December 20th, there were immediate ominous signs. No supply crates were waiting on the Flannan Isles dock to be restocked. Likewise the men themselves were absent, whereas normally they'd be waiting to welcome any visitors. The lighthouse itself stood closed and locked.

When the relief crew gained entry and searched the buildings, no-one was on the post.

They searched the islands too. But there was no-one there either.

There was no note, and no indication of where the men might be.

No-one would ever see Donald Macarthur, Thomas Marshall or James Ducat again.

Inside the lighthouse, evidence of major disruption was thin on the ground. A single chair lay on its side, and two sets of the lighthouse's three oilskins were missing, indicating that at least two of the men had gone outside voluntarily when disaster struck. Reports circulating at the time that uneaten meals sat on the crew-room table were found to be untrue, an embellishment added by tall tale-tellers to create a Mary Celeste type atmosphere of weirdness.

In fact, imaginative embellishments have been the bane of modern investigations into the case. For example, much distraction was caused by the supposed curious entries made in the lighthouse logbook just before the disappearances. On December 12th, Thomas Marshall was reported as having written: "Gale north by northwest. Sea lashed to fury. Never seen such a storm. Waves very high. Tearing at lighthouse. James Ducat irritable." His second entry that day read: "Stormbound. Cannot go out. Donald Macarthur crying." On December 13th, he added: "Me, Ducat and Mcarthur prayed." In his final entry on December 15th, he wrote: "Storm ended, sea calm. God is over all." All of this concerned the three men's colleagues because it sounded out of character. Donald Macarthur was known as a tough old veteran who was unlikely to cry for any reason, while none of the trio were regarded as the sort of God-fearing men who would resort to prayer just because it was stormy. These log entries fuelled the mystery for ages, until it transpired much later on that they had never been made, and were in fact the invention of a journalist seeking a more sensational story.

But even without such exaggerations, there are some extremely odd facts in this case.

On arrival, the relief crew found that all the clocks in the lighthouse had mysteriously stopped. In addition, the West Landing had been destroyed, its steel handrails broken, bent or uprooted, a huge piece of stonework weighing close to a ton displaced. Other men in the service had seen storm damage of this magnitude before – the problem was that the West Landing was over 100 feet above sea level. A truly cataclysmic tempest must have struck the Isles to cause such havoc, and yet meteorological reports showed that on the nights in question the Western Isles had enjoyed a calm sea and an easy wind.

Subsequent outlandish rumours ran riot: that mer-folk were responsible; that some indescribable sea monster had come ashore; that witches or ghosts were the culprits.

For a brief time the ghostly explanation was taken partially seriously. When a fisherman claimed he'd seen a rowing boat filled with the spirits of downed mariners glowing in the dark as it rowed away from the Flannan Isles, investigators wondered if what he'd actually seen was the three men deserting their posts. Had despair at the bleakness of their location overcome them? Had something frightened them? Others wondered if the fisherman had witnessed an abduction – could the crew have been seized by pirates, smugglers or enemy agents (though none of these unlikely explanations would have accounted for the damage on the West Landing).

Modern analysts now point to the possibility of a freak wave, the sort of monstrous surge that has occasionally risen without warning in the North Atlantic. Could two of the men have been working on the West Landing, and had the third member of the crew, seeing the approaching wave from the lantern gallery, rushed down to warn them, only to fall victim to it as well? That would certainly explain the damage and why only two sets of oilskins were missing.

Of course, even that theory doesn't account for the lighthouse being closed and locked when help finally arrived. Not even nature's most destructive elements could have managed that.

THE DREAMING GOD
IS SINGING WHERE SHE LIES
William Meikle

For the thought of her is one that never dies,
She's sleeping in the depths, the depths, the depths,
She's sleeping in the depths,
And the dreaming god is singing where she lies.

John Brookes knew he was in the right place when the man with the yellow front tooth smiled at him.

"Tam McLean, you say? Nope. Never heard of him."

The man went back to his beer, and Brookes took a glass of his own to a quiet corner of the bar and settled in for a watching brief. He was waiting for someone, the aforementioned McLean, a man who had sent a letter that got every one of Brookes' reporter senses tingling.

There's a story in this. A good one too.

The letter had come in to the newsroom in Glasgow three days before, and it had taken him two more days to convince his editor it was worth following up.

"Sweetie wives tales," Dave had said. "They're ten a penny up that way. What was it the man said about the Teuchters ... *antediluvian*? That just about sums them up. Inbred, unbred and willing to believe any old shite."

It was only when Brookes had dug up the details of a missing reporter from their biggest rival in Edinburgh that the editor relented.

"You've got forty-eight hours, John," he said. "No more. And a hundred quid on expenses ... that should keep you off the beer long enough to get the story ... if there is one."

And now here he was, sitting in a quayside bar in the West Highlands, waiting for the man who had started it all, the man who sent the letter. The bar was quiet, but it was early yet. He had given himself plenty of time to get here, and the car journey had proved easier than he'd thought, mainly due to the lack of traffic north and west of Inverness. He took a long chug at his beer, and felt the pull of a second starting to call.

Brookes let his mind wander, to tales of haunted houses, and missing reporters. He knew from experience that the paper's readers lapped this kind of shite up. Anything about haunts or spooks meant more copies sold. Dave, the editor knew it as well ... he'd never have let Brookes out here otherwise.

He had already composed most of the article in his head.

Hell, I hardly even needed to come here to get the job done – this shite writes itself.

But he had just enough respect left for the job to do it right. So he waited, and he sipped slowly at the beer, despite the increasing clamour for a second one.

The bar door slammed open. A tall, thin, black haired man entered. If Brookes hadn't looked up at just the right time he'd have missed it – one of the locals made a gesture with his right hand, slashing it across his neck. The black-haired man – Brookes guessed it must be Tam McLean – ducked back out of sight. Brookes drained the dregs of his beer and hurried out into the parking lot. A battered Volvo was just pulling out, and he caught a glimpse of a mop of black hair and a pair of wide, startled eyes.

He got into his rental car and followed.

It wasn't a long journey. The Volvo drew up outside a run-down timber house just beyond the quay, which looked like it had started falling down a hundred years ago and was near to finishing the job.

McLean was out and into the house, door slammed behind him, before Brookes pulled up and parked.

Got you!

Brookes smiled as he walked up the weed-covered driveway. He rapped hard on the door.

"Come on, Tam. I got your letter. You obviously want to talk. I'm here to listen."

There was no sound from behind the door.

"Don't you remember, Tam? You sent me that tape yourself. You sent it ... and I listened to it. That's why I'm here."

The door opened slightly and Tam McLean peered out.

"You listened to it?"

Brookes nodded.

"And you're no' feart?"

Brookes tried not to laugh.

"I'm here to help ... I need to know the rest."

The door opened wider.

Now I've really got him.

"You'll write it down, right?" McLean asked. "About how I went an' looked for him in yon house? How I didnae leave him there? I'm nae coward – I'm no' like the wankers are sayin' aroon here."

Brookes stepped forward, making sure the door couldn't be shut again.

60

"I'll do right by you, Tam," he said. "I just need the whole story."

The door opened fully and Brookes was shown into a dingy main room that smelled of smoke and damp dog. He cleared a swathe of magazines to one side and sat down. McLean went to the kitchen and came back with a beer for each of them. Brookes let him get settled in the armchair opposite before starting to question him.

"You're no' gonnae record me?" McLean said.

Brookes shook his head.

"Just tell me about the tape you found at the house," he said. "Then we can fill in the rest of the story and decide what's what."

McLean sat and sucked at the beer for a while, not speaking. Brookes knew what was required ... this wasn't his first time at the dance.

Time to reel him in.

"There's three hundred in it for you if you give me the real gen."

McLean's eyes lit up. He started talking without any further prompting, staring into the distance.

*

"I found it on the porch of the hoose two days after I'd left the reporter there. There was nae sign of the mannie and I thought there might be a clue on the tape, so I played it on the machine in the motor. The start of the tape was all just the reporter yakking ... local legends this, haunted hooses that ... nowt I hadnae heard afore. The good stuff was further on. The tape made a faint hissing sound as I ran it forward a wee bit. Then I pressed play.

"There was some chat fae the reporter about the history o' the place – I cannae hae mind o' the details now – but his voice was cut off by a loud bang. I heard heavy steps on the floor ... then it went quiet. Then a piano played. It was an auld song, but abody aroon here kens it weel. It was *She Sleeps in the Depths*.

"And worse than that – folk started singing along – hunners o' folk it sounded like.

"The dreaming god is singing where she lies."

*

Brookes took a cassette tape from his pocket.

"This was the one?"

McLean eyed it warily.

"Aye. That's the wan. You've played it? You've heard it for

61

yersel'?"

Brookes smiled sadly.

"There's nothing on it but static and hiss. *White noise* the lab boys called it – but whatever it is, there surely is no piano playing or singing on this tape."

McLean sat back wearily in his chair.

"Aye. There is," he said softly. "I heard it."

Brookes nodded.

"I'm sure you did," he said. "But if you want me to write this up properly, I'm going to need more – I'm going to need you to take me to the house."

McLean's beer fell from his hand and rolled across the carpet, but the man paid it no notice. His eyes had gone wide, staring. He shook his head from side to side.

"No way, mister. No fucking way. I'm no' setting another foot on that hill."

Brookes smiled thinly.

"Well in that case, I'll be on my way. There's no story here. Just a coward."

For a second he thought he'd miscalculated, and McLean was just going to sit and take it. But to his surprise the man pushed himself up out of his chair.

"I'm nae coward," he said softly. "I telt ye that afore."

He walked to the door.

"Well?" he said. "Are ye coming? It'll be daurk soon. It'd be best to get this done afore then."

Brookes chugged the last of his beer and followed McLean out.

*

They took the old Volvo and there was no chat

Brookes broke the silence five minutes after they left the town behind and followed a rutted track out into open countryside.

"Tell me the story," he said to McLean. "How did this whole legend get started in the first place?"

McLean bit the filter off a cigarette and spat it out the open window. He took a long deep draw from what was left before replying.

"There's no' much tae tell," he said. "A mannie buys a house in the middle of naywhere. The wifie wants a piano, mannie buys piano, wifie thinks *something* in the sea is singing to her, and she plays the same song tae it, day efter fucking day until mannie goes doolally and takes an axe to her. You can hardly blame him, being out here with naywhere to go to get awa' fae it."

It was Brookes' turn to laugh.

"Well, when you put it like that ... but what about the husband? What happened next?"

McLean fell quiet.

"They never found him," he said. "John Doyle fae the insurance company called in the spring, but found nowt but bits of the dead missus and that old piano, chopped up into kindling with the same axe. John only ever talks about it when he's pished ... but even then, you'll never get him anywhere near a bar wi' a piano player."

Brookes looked out the windscreen. They had just rounded a headland. The shore along here was a series of tall sea cliffs. Up there on the tops in the next bay along, distant but getting close quickly, stood a squat white wooden house, jutting up out of what looked like a small hill of bare rock.

McLean was whispering now.

"There's naebody fae aroon' here goes close now ... no' if it can be helped. That reporter was the first for a while ... and him not coming back put paid to any other visits. I doubt there's been any foot set in the house since I left two year ago."

"Good," Brookes said. "There might still be some evidence."

McLean spat out some soggy tobacco strands.

"I dinna ken what kind of evidence you're after," he said. "But I can tell you now, you're no' going tae find nothing. Nothing solid at any rate."

McLean had gone pale again. He reached down into his glove compartment and took out a half bottle of whisky. He drank straight from the mouth, taking a long chug, and had some color back in his cheeks as he passed it to Brookes.

The reporter was about to refuse, but his glance had fallen on the house, and a deep cold took hold at the base of his spine, alongside a sudden urge to retreat to the bar and let the booze give him oblivion for a while.

He took the bottle and slugged a mouthful down, resisting the urge to suck hard at it.

"Just get me there," he said to McLean. "And we'll see what we can see."

*

McLean brought the Volvo to the end of the track some five minutes later. He turned the engine off but showed no signs of climbing out.

"I'll wait here," he said. "Dinna be long. I want to be away by daurk."

63

Brookes looked back the way they had come. The sun was already well on its way down, hovering above the town in the far distance.

"It might go faster if you showed me around," he said, but McLean wasn't going to be budged.

"There's the hoose," he said, pointing up a steep slope ahead of them. "There's nowt else here but rock and bird-shite."

Brookes would have pushed harder, but he saw that the fear was big in the man's eyes. He climbed down out of the car. He only looked back once – McLean had the whisky bottle raised at his lips.

I hope he's sober enough to get me back.

He turned away, and made for the house. It was a bit of a scramble up to the building, and Brookes came to regret not dressing appropriately, even more so when he got up to the level on which the house had been built. A cold wind whistled around him and through the thin material of his jacket and trousers. He made quickly for the door, hoping for some shelter.

A call came from the road below.

"Can you hear her?"

He turned. McLean stood in the road, hands raised to his mouth. Brookes gave him a wave, turned the door handle, and headed inside.

It was as if someone had turned the volume down. He was immediately enveloped in a silence that felt somehow heavy. Dust motes soared and swooped in the thin sunlight that came in through the windows, but there was no other movement. It was obvious that no one had been here for quite some time.

A small hallway led into an open living area. As Brookes strode across a hardwood floor he realised it was growing darker quickly. The room was bathed in a yellow glow that was even now turning red. He walked over and peered out the window. The sun was almost down, sinking beyond the horizon. But that wasn't what got his attention – the Volvo was pulling away back down the track, the sound of the engine only just audible through the thick glass.

"Hey!" Brookes called. He banged on the window for several seconds before realising the futility of that approach. He ran outside, yelling now, but the car was already a hundred yards away.

Brookes yelled until he was hoarse.

McLean never turned and soon the truck was gone from sight round the headland. At almost the same moment the last of the sunshine went from the sky and Brookes was left alone in the gathering dark.

*

His cell phone was no help, showing no bars, no signal. All it was good for was as a light to show him the way back into the building. He surveyed the whole ground floor and found a supply of firewood and a pile of old newspapers in a deep cupboard – sufficient for him to start a fire in the main living area. Once he'd got that going he felt slightly better about his situation – but he was far from happy.

For the first hour he jumped at every noise and every shadow, but he settled once he took his notebook and pen from his pocket and started to flesh out the story he would tell on his return.

McLean is a wee coward ... and I'll make sure everybody knows it.

He even got so warm that he had to move away from the fire. But that broke his feeling of wellbeing. At the same time something *shifted* in one of the other rooms. His enforced incarceration suddenly ceased to feel like an adventure.

"McLean? If that's you, I'll break your fucking neck."

He listened, but heard no reply. He stood and moved to the window, but there was only darkness beyond, and his own wide-eyed reflection looking back at him. He turned towards the welcome roar of the fire ... just as someone whispered in his ear.

"Can you hear her?"

He did a three-hundred and sixty degree turn, but he was completely alone in the room.

"Oh shit," he whispered softly. He moved closer to the fire, to the relative safety of the light and warmth. Once again something *shifted* in one of the other rooms. There was a soft thud, and a vibration ran through the floor, a throb that reached through the soles of his shoes.

"McLean? I get it ... the Teuchters are getting their fun at the expense of the reporter. Just stop now, and you can have your three hundred. I'll even stand for a round of drinks in the bar."

There was no reply.

It became hard to breathe, panic tightening at his chest, heart thudding in his ears. He lit a cigarette and tried for calm, but it wouldn't come.

The *shifting* noise came again.

"That's it," Brookes shouted. "That's fucking it."

He strode towards the noise and threw open a door to a dark room beyond. The fire threw flickering shadows ahead of him, but the room was too dark to make out any detail.

"This is not funny," Brookes said, his voice suddenly too loud.

"Can you hear her?" the voice said in his ear.

Without being aware of moving, Brookes found himself outside the building, sucking in deep gulps of cold night air, his hands on his knees as he bent over and threw up what was left of the earlier booze.

He headed for the road, but after just three steps he realised that would be folly. In the darkness the clamber down to the track would be more than dangerous ... it would be suicide. He made his way back to the door, but couldn't bring himself to go back inside.

He stood outside for the space of three cigarettes, staring longingly at the lights of the town in the far distance before the cold of the night bit at him inside the thin suit. He could see through the window that the fire he had lit earlier was beginning to burn down, and the thought of spending the whole night without any warmth whatsoever gave him impetus to go back inside.

The next ten minutes were spent stoking the flames with anything he could find. The fire roared in the grate and the skin of his face tightened slightly, but he did not move away. He took out his notebook again and added some notes to the pages. For a time he was once more able to find a certain distance from reality in his writing, but that was again shattered by a heavy *thud* from the next room.

Ignore it.

But that was impossible. He strained to hear ... then wished he hadn't as the faint strains of a piano playing wafted through the house. A woman's voice rose in accompaniment.

For the thought of her is one that never dies,
She's sleeping in the depths, the depths, the depths,
She's sleeping in the depths,
And the dreaming god is singing where she lies.

He walked towards the music, then thought better of it and retreated back to the fireside. After one round of verse-chorus the house once again fell silent, but Brookes could still hear the mocking voice in his ear.

"Can you hear her?"

He tried to go back to his writing, but his mind raced and he couldn't find focus. He was dismayed to look down at one point to find he had been writing more of the song's lyrics.

Listen to the depths, listen to the depths,
The dreaming god is singing where she lies.

He tore the page from the notebook and threw it into the fire. It went up with a *whoosh* that made him step back.

66

The piano started up again.

"Fuck this for a lark," Brookes said. He walked, almost ran, across the floor and threw open the door to the room beyond.

The first thing he noticed was that the room seemed to be lit in faint blue phosphorescence. Then he saw the piano, and the woman who sat playing. She wore a long dark dress that hung in swathes to the floor, a hood hanging over her face. Thin white hands danced over the keyboard.

"What the hell is this!" Brookes shouted.

The piano player turned to him. The hood fell back, and suddenly all breath left Brookes' chest in one gasp. The face was too pale, skin thin enough to be translucent, huge, unblinking eyes staring back at him, too-wide lips smiling from a mouth that belonged more on a cod than a person.

Brookes stepped back, into the doorway.

"Can you hear her?" the voice said in his ear.

The piano player got up from her seat.

Brookes turned and fled, heading for the fire as the piano rose to a crescendo and the lyric ran in a loop in his head.

The dreaming god is singing where she lies.
The dreaming god is singing where she lies.
The dreaming god is singing where she lies.

*

Tam McLean was feeling ashamed of himself as he walked up the hill in the early dawn. A thin plume of smoke rising from a chimney gave him hope that leaving the reporter here overnight on his own hadn't proved fatal.

He almost ran up the slope to the house.

"I'm sorry, Mr. Brookes," he shouted as he pushed open the door. "I'm really sorry."

The room was empty, with no sign of the man. The only trace was a pencil on the floor lying on top of a notebook. There was one word written on the top page.

No.

67

THE CURSE OF SCOTLAND

There are many reasons why certain Scots feel distanced from the British government in Westminster – and they aren't all concerned with modern-day politics. Numerous events have occurred in history which have deeply disenchanted the Scottish nation with its role in Britain. One such was the bloody massacre at Glencoe, which though it took place before the Kingdom of Great Britain existed, was the work of the British government and left an indelible mark on British/Scottish relations for generations to follow.

There had been trouble between Scotland and England since long before the Glorious Revolution of 1688. Up until 1603 they had been separate and rival kingdoms who fought frequently, while for much of the mid and early 17th century both countries, along with Ireland, were embroiled in a series of complex and debilitating civil wars known collectively as the War of the Three Kingdoms. After 1689, when William III (of Orange) came to the throne, it was hoped a more peaceful era would ensue based on a general acceptance of constitutional monarchy. But sectarian issues remained. James II and the House of Stuart had been deposed, and Catholics were prohibited from ever sitting on the joint-throne.

This alienated many groups in the British Isles, especially in the fiercely Catholic Highlands of Scotland. The direct result was the Jacobite Rising of 1689, which only ended with the defeat of James II at the Battle of the Boyne in 1690. King William subsequently offered the Highland clans an amnesty if they would declare their allegiance to the Crown, the deadline for which was January 1st 1692. The Highland chief most reluctant to comply was Alasdair Maclain of Clan MacDonald in the ruggedly beautiful Glencoe region. However, Maclain only delayed in accepting the deal; he didn't refuse it outright. Heavy snow that Christmas and New Year further delayed him, as he would need to travel to Fort William to make his pledge in front of a magistrate – and as such, when he finally signed on the dotted line, it was six days late.

It is a matter of debate whether King William would have accepted this. Highly possibly he would as it would have meant there was peace at last in the British Isles – had it not been for the intrigues of one John Dalrymple, Master of Stair and Secretary of State over Scotland. Dalrymple, a modernising lowlander who was embarrassed by what he saw as the feudal clan system, advised his royal master that Maclain had treacherously declined to pledge, and named the MacDonalds of Glencoe as a gang of thieves and rebels. An order was thus passed to make an example of them, which task was taken up by Clan Campbell, firm Protestants and old enemies of Maclain and his people.

On February 1ˢᵗ, Captain Robert Campbell led two companies of Campbell militia from the Earl of Argyle's Regiment to Glencoe, where in the traditional fashion of the Highlands, he and his men were offered unconditional hospitality, which, rather surprisingly given the bad blood between these two groups, continued for the next two weeks. There is some evidence the troops themselves did not know why they'd been sent there – theoretically it was to collect outstanding tax – but on February 11ᵗʰ they received orders to eliminate the village where they were staying, and kill all MacDonald men under the age of 70.

The systematic massacre began that night at midnight.

Maclain himself was slain in his bed by Lieutenant John Lindsay, while others in the troop rampaged through the village, burning cottages and shooting those villagers caught fleeing. Despite overwhelmingly superior weaponry – muskets, bayonets, cutlasses and pistols – the government force was not entirely successful. They managed to murder 38 men in the village, while some 40 women and children froze to death after fleeing up onto the icy moors. But others survived, and there were many witnesses to the atrocity. Witnesses were also found among the troops themselves, several of whom refused to participate. Lieutenants Farquhar and Kennedy broke their own swords rather than join the slaughter, for which they were later arrested and tried for mutiny (though both were acquitted).

The bloodbath at Glencoe caused widespread outrage, in England as well as Scotland, though under Scottish law it was classified as 'murder under trust', a particularly despicable crime. Despite this, and despite King William's expressions of regret, the subsequent enquiry spared almost all those involved from any meaningful punishment. The king himself protected Dalrymple from censure, and in 1703 Queen Anne promoted him to the rank of Earl of Stair (though the Dalrymple family emblem, which resembles nine diamonds arrayed on a blue saltire, was reviled ever after and is often given as the reason why even today the Nine of Diamonds playing card is referred to as the 'Curse of Scotland').

Despite this attempted whitewash, the shameful episode at Glencoe would go on to claim many more victims, fuelling the Jacobite rage that would manifest itself in further battles and slaughters over the following decades. As so often happened in the

Highlands, one grave injustice proved the touch-paper for numerous others.

Glencoe today is still one of the most scenic regions in Scotland, and yet it has a strangely oppressive atmosphere. Whether this owes to the brooding presence of Etive Mor, Bidean nam Bian or the Three Sisters of Glencoe, all of which stand guard over it, or to our knowledge of the terrible deed that was done there, is uncertain. But there are repeated reports that ghosts linger in this place. Even now, especially in winter, shadowy forms have been seen crouched in the heather or hiding behind boulders or tree-stumps, still taking shelter from the executioner's blow that would fall on them so many centuries ago.

THE HOUSEKEEPER
Rosie Seymour

Whether Stanley loved Gwen more than Gwen loved Stanley was a debate that had raged throughout the course of their fifty years of married life. As a sixteen-year-old apprentice at the fish smokery, Stanley had admired from afar the young Housekeeper who had taken weekly delivery of Laird and Lady Hamilton's supply of the finest smoked salmon.

To the worldlier wise and seemingly sophisticated two years older Gwen, a match with an apprentice smoker did not represent the most effective means of rescue from a life of servitude to Scotland's aristocracy. His advances were politely but firmly rebuked and thus was Stanley was obliged into weekly contact with a woman who failed to see their imminent compatibility. He was, nevertheless, relentless in his pursuit of her and channelled his unrequited love into his work, moving quickly through the ranks.

One Tuesday, some three years after his initial rejection, Stanley was able to knock on the door of the big house and respectfully request of the Butler that "the Master Smoker" wished to see the housekeeper. Gwen's earlier rejection of Stanley had been at the root of a great many debates that had quietly smouldered in the fifty years that followed.

Now, since retiring from the position of bookkeeper to her husband's fish and meat smoking business, Gwen had begun to slow down. She'd remained active as long as she could, careful to hide her increasing breathlessness from the watchful eyes of her husband, but retirement beckoned and then it called and when it began to shout from the rooftops Gwen had finally conceded. She no longer had the great grandchildren over for tea whilst their mother ran errands; the laundry was sorted by another's hand and Stanley's favourite venison pie was a distant memory. Not that Stanley would have said a word about the pie; Stanley cared for nothing less than the very best for his wife.

That day, the Master Smoker set about preparing the ovens for the oak-smoked salmon that would grace the finest of tables. Since making the business his own in his twenty-first year, Stanley had pushed its boundaries from the humble kipper and the more upmarket salmon and was now renowned for smoking anything that was presented. Locally shot venison, wild boar, rabbit, Stanley's skill and attention to detail had more than earned him the right to call himself the Master Smoker. It was generally acknowledged amongst the many Scottish smokeries that Stanley was the best in the business and Stanley's opinion was frequently sought. His competitors were not, however, without a sense of devilment and when word got out that Stanley believed that there was "Nothing on God's green earth that couldn't be smoked", he was taken quite literally. Over a period of several months, a variety of creatures began arriving at the smokery gates. It was only when Stanley opened a package addressed to 'The Master Smoker' containing a recently deceased cobra that he amended his statement. He now told his apprentices that "Everything on God's green earth can be smoked, but not everything deserves to be smoked."

Venison pie, Gwen decided, would be an unexpected end of the working week treat for Stanley. He was such a hard worker, had provided for the family, consistently putting himself last for five decades. Gwen sifted the flour whilst the butter chilled. Her pastry was something to be proud of. She'd learned her art as a young housekeeper at the big house, when the cook had to leave unexpectedly due to an indiscretion and Gwen had stepped into the breech until a suitable replacement could be found. Her pastry had earned her the enthusiastic praise of Laird and Lady Hamilton and a great many of their distinguished guests. She was, it was generally acknowledged, destined for a prestigious future in servitude until the independent Master Smoker knocked.

The trick, she learned, was to keep the hands as cool as the butter and to work briskly. Gwen lined the dish with the freshly rolled pastry as the venison bubbled in its dark, rich bath. Another hour and he'd be home. There'd be ructions if he caught her at her work; she was supposed to be resting he'd tell her. He was perfectly happy with a simple sandwich. Gwen knew that there was no love in a sandwich, no joy in between the slices of shop turned-out, thin white batches.

Two capfuls of ruby port, a 'thank you' gift from a well-heeled customer, were stirred into the stewing meat. They'd grown old together, like they'd always hoped. He was a good father, firm but fair, and their girls had turned out well. People often asked how they'd stayed happy together for so many years. As if they had a secret formula; Gwen didn't understand the question. She was happy with Stanley because to not be happy with him would be like being unhappy with her foot or her arm.

Stanley locked the door to the smokery. He'd be home soon, he'd put his key in the lock and call out to his wife that he was back. Fifty years and he still felt a surge of excitement at the thought of once again being in her company. Things had changed; of course they had. Her trim figure had blossomed once she was no longer running around after rich folks and his hairline had crept away from his forehead until it had disappeared altogether somewhere around his forty-fifth year. She was, he never tired of telling her, more beautiful than ever before. The creases on her face were the tracks of love. This one, he'd say was made the night she'd stayed up nursing him through a fever. This one was from the smiles she'd given him every morning as she opened her eyes and looked upon the man that she loved and who loved her more than life itself.

He'd make her a pot of the perfumed tea she liked so much when he arrived home. He'd pat her on the hand and she would know.

Gwen opened the door to the oven. He'd smell it as soon as he walked in. He'd be cross at first but the moment his fork broke the buttery crust of the pie, all would be forgiven. The heat of the oven and the effort of bending down had made Gwen faint and lightheaded. She sat down at the kitchen table that had been the heart of the home for so many years, and she waited.

When Stanley returned home the smell of burnt pastry filled his nostrils and his eyes stung.

Whether from the tears that had sprung up upon seeing his wife of fifty years slumped lifelessly at the table or from the acrid smoke that hung in the air didn't really matter.

*

It was Sunday evening and Stanley was alone. Should anyone pass the smokery windows and see him at his work they would not have recognised the hunched, broken old man.

There was a tribe he'd once heard about, deep in Papua New Guinea. When their loved ones died they'd stitch up their eyes and their mouths. They'd make small incisions across their bodies, the knees, feet, elbows. Skewers would be inserted into their soft organs to allow their body fat to drain out. Men, women and children would be smoke-cured and kept for posterity. They would become guardians of the village, an honour bestowed upon those whose relatives could not bear to be parted from them.

The oven was hot. The smoke was ready.

FROM OUT THE HOLLOW HILLS

During the later Dark Ages, the whole of Britain and Ireland was subjected to regular, brutal raids by the Vikings. The Scottish Highlands and Islands were no exception and recorded several spectacular acts of viciousness, as well as inheriting an extra layer of mystery and superstition.

In 806, on the Isle of Iona in the Inner Hebrides, the famous monastery's library and scriptorium was despoiled by pillaging Northmen, and 68 of the monks were taken down to the sea's edge, where they were drowned in the waves. Many local ghost stories are now connected to this atrocity. Meanwhile, on the mainland, Viking armies are said to have marauded so relentlessly that legend holds it was they who burned the great Wood of Caledon while searching for any native Scots who had evaded them. But in truth, the Norse influence in northern Scotland wasn't always negative. History indicates that many of the Vikings who entered Britain through the Highlands were looking for land rather than booty, in exchange for which they sewed this wild realm with their own lore and tradition. For example, the Clan McLeod of Skye were convinced their famous Faerie Flag – Bratach Sith, an emblem beneath which they could never be defeated – had been handed down to them from their ancestor, the Norse warrior-king Harald Hardraada, who had known it as Land-Waster, Odin's Raven. And of course, Scotland's northernmost isles, the Shetlands, celebrate their Viking heritage in amazing fashion with the annual Up Helly Aa, or midwinter fire festivals, which have become massive money-spinners for the local community.

But one other aspect of Norse culture with which Shetland was imbued is the myth of the so-called 'trows', and this harks back to that much darker, more violent side of Viking nature.

In ancient Scandinavia, by far the most feared denizens of the night were the trolls. It is very important not to confuse these mysterious beings with those gnarly faced toys available at tourist shops, or those anonymous weirdoes who pervade the internet. Trolls in Norse myth were terrifying entities; ogre-like cannibals, all but invisible during the day as sunlight would turn them to rock or soil, but at night real beings who would emerge from the hollow hills to prowl the woods and pastures, preying on men and their animals. It was also said that some trolls had magical powers and despite their brutish, barbarous appearance, an arcane knowledge. In Shetland, these more intelligent beings were called 'trows', and *they were part of the island chain's folklore for a very long time. On Foula, the most westerly isle in the archipelago and possibly the most remote constantly inhabited island in the whole of Britain, there was a very real fear of trows until well into the 19th century.*

Not as large or as openly fierce as their Scandinavian cousins (in Old Norse, this special breed of troll were called 'underjordiske'), the trows were believed to inhabit barrows, grave-mounds and other underground chambers, and were considered exceptionally dangerous, carrying the blame for all kinds of mishaps in the local farming community – from thefts to animal deaths, from fatal accidents to the abduction of children, who they would replace with idiot changelings or sometimes wooden dolls. On Foula, the trows were most active during the long, dark winters, especially around Yuletide, which was as sacred to them as Christmas was to the islanders. At this time of year, the locals would take extensive precautions against the trows, fixing crucifixes woven from straw over the entrances to yards and outbuildings, and carrying a clod of burning peat around the homestead to the accompaniment of protection prayers. They would even invoke a pagan spirit of their own, the 'haugbonde', whose sole duty was to defend the farm against these evil forces.

So far this sounds like a typical old wife's tale, yet there is one story concerning the Foula trows which was attested to by many witnesses, and it doesn't date from the Dark Ages. A craggy area of cliffs called Hamnafjeld was known to have a fault that descended in a straight 1000-foot shaft to a flooded cave, from where a man, if he could climb all the way down, could reach the sea. This was believed the main hiding place of the island's trows. Sometime in the 1670s, a Dutch naval crew resting on Foula laughed at the stories and promised to investigate the Hamnafjeld shaft. But of the two men lowered down with ropes, one was brought back to the surface dead and the second had gone insane, though he too died as he was taken back to his ship, raving about the things that had attacked them. Though the entrance to the shaft was well known about before, it has never been located since – and most researchers will agree that a 'spell of permanent concealment' is one of the oldest faerie tricks in the British folklore manual.

THE EXECUTIONER
Peter Bell

'For from the mountain hoar,
Hurl'd headlong in some night of fear,
When yell'd the wolf and fled the deer,
Loose crags had toppled o'er.'
Walter Scott, Lord of the Isles

1

As the motorboat bounced back over the stirring waters of Loch Scavaig, Hans gazed at the receding magnificence of the Black Cuillin. A few days into April, the equinoctial winds had not lessened, nor had winter yet been banished from the Hebrides; the chill of *Ultima Thule* still besieged the land.

The lowering sun silhouetted the grim blackness of the jagged peaks, a slanting, golden light shining through the crags and corries and over the turbulent sea, lending to the scene an ethereal, sinister glamour. Passing seal-inhabited islets, sunbeams touched the pelts of the inquisitive creatures, tinting them a burnished gold. High above on a rising north-westerly an eagle soared, and gannets sleekly dived beneath the white-flecked waves. The scene was changing all the time, mists drifting off the chilly sea, curling in tattered banners round the peaks, emerging as if from nowhere. The low-beaming light, through a squall of biting hail, illumined the hazy vista, rendering the narrow gorge of Coruisk—'dark, brooding, wild, weird and stern' – a cauldron of fiery glory, as if it were the portals of Valhalla.

"Gars-bheinn, Casteal a' Gharbh Choire, Sgurr na Banachdich, Sgurr a' Ghreadaidh, Sgurr a' Mhadaidh, Bidein Druim nan Ramh, Sgurr nan Gillean, Sgurr na Stri ..." Sara reeled off the forbidding litany, naming each peak in turn, imbuing her recitation, as only a child of Skye knew how, with cadences of mystic beauty.

It was Hans's first visit to Skye. He was taking the opportunity to visit lands which, before the falling of the Wall, had been out of bounds for citizens of the Democratic Republic. The Cuillin of Skye were, for climbers, the Holy Grail. The previous summer, when he and Sara had met, he had climbed the Cumbrian peaks – Great Gable, Skiddaw, Hellvellyn, Scafell Pike – and now felt ready for the greater challenge. It was upon that trip – designed for people who, still reluctant to admit to middle age, were decisively no longer in the full bloom of youth – that he and Sara had met. In a foolish moment over a beer too many she had invited him to the island, where she would "show him the sights". She had not realised how literal-minded Germans were, nor with what alacrity he would seize her offer. And now she was, with difficulty, explaining to a man with an excessive estimation of his own capability – a few hikes through the Harz Mountains the limit of his experience – what many a foolhardy pilgrim to the Misty Isle learnt the hard way.

Few of the Cuillin summits were attainable without climbing. The heights were exposed. The terrain, rough, arduous and complex, traversed bare rock and scree without obvious tracks. Mist and cloud formed rapidly even on fine days, and there were no easy exits. In poor weather, mountains, corries and passes were universally treacherous. A quirk of the magnetic rock rendered a compass useless, even dangerous. There were on average a dozen fatalities a year, from hypothermia and falls, numerous grave injuries, and many a terrifying benighting.

"So," she concluded, "if you get lost up there in mist a strong religious faith is an asset."

"They sound ferocious!" laughed Hans. Was there a hint of mocking irony in his tone? Or was it just the German idiom?

"They *are* ferocious! Consider the names! 'Sgurr a' Ghreadaidh – the Peak of Torment. Casteal a' Gharbh Choire – Fortress of the Rough Corrie. Sgurr na Stri – Peak of Strife …"

Hans pointed at a serrated peak, black against the sun's diffused beams. "What is that?"

"Sgurr na Banachdich – the Smallpox Peak. It's the surface, all pitted and bumped like a pockmarked face. It's the rock – gabbro. It's everywhere here. Oh, it's a blessing to climbers because it gives good grip; they run up slopes like spiders, and it's good for the holds. On the other hand, it causes terrible injuries. Rips the flesh right off the bone – if it doesn't bash your brains out! And there are slippery intrusions that fool people."

They were now ashore. The launch bounced away over the white horses, splashing furiously on the stony strand.

"So, you have climbed the Cuillin?" he asked.

"Only into the corries – they're intimidating enough. The only mountain walkable without putting hand to rock is Bruach na Frithe – Brae of the Deer Forest."

"That has the 'tourist route'?"

"No, that's Sgurr nan Gillean. Peak of the Young Lads. Don't be fooled by the word 'tourist'. The last hundred feet you crawl up a narrow ridge – you need a good head for heights! A woman died there, this time last year. Went up in icy conditions with her husband. Ignored local advice. They weren't even halfway and she slipped down a slab. Only twenty feet – dead by the time rescue arrived. Came from London. Left a two-year old daughter with grandparents."

"So," persisted her indefatigable companion. "Shall we perhaps go up the easy one? The one which is a walk?"

"I never said it was easy. Well – we'll see! Much depends on the weather. It's not looking promising."

Persistence, inexperience, arrogance – a lethal combination, she reflected. Hopefully, the weather would remain its usual miserable self.

2

For the next few days a grey shroud lingered over the Cuillin, laced with icy squalls that blustered viciously from the far north. Occasionally, the upper slopes appeared through a misty veil, the crags wreathed in a mantle of snow. At ground level the wind was chilling; it would be lethal on the tops. Instead, amidst hailstones, they explored the Quiraing, that weird chasm with its monolithic bastions in the northern hills, where farmers once corralled their sheep. In pouring rain, they clambered up to the Old Man of Storr, the immense, detached buttress which, on close approach, looked from its undercut base about to topple down on them. They ascended MacLeod's Tables, flat-topped summits beside the western seas, where they gazed, across a desolate landscape, to the Cuillin twenty miles away.

"Look!" cried Hans, as they ate their lunch, huddling from the gusts. "It is clearing!"

The familiar jagged outline was emerging, and for those so minded, Sara supposed, looked beguiling. Snow still cloaked the tops. From their vantage, with the summits extending either side of a lower central peak, the ridge resembled a huge, black eagle with its wings unfurled. At Hans's request, once again she ran through the names of the visible summits.

"And what is that?" he asked. "Like a tower. I do not think you named that one?"

"The Basteir Tooth. Part of Am Basteir. See, the sharp peak beside it? Before Sgurr nan Gillean? The Tooth's the most difficult pitch on the ridge for climbers, after the Inaccessible Pinnacle."

"The Inaccessible Pinnacle!" repeated Hans, bemused.

"That's on the far side. I'm not sure you can see it from here."

"And what is Basteir, please?"

"It means 'the Executioner', or more exactly 'Death-Dealer'."

"It sounds ominous."

"They say the Tooth looks like a raised executioner's axe … Actually, the name's disputed by purists. They say it's a corruption of 'Bhasteir' – with an aitch – meaning 'cleft'. The corrie below is reached by a narrow gorge, spelt on old maps Coire a' Bhasteir. Probably the other form – 'Basteir' – has become accustomed because it's a more fearsome name. Fatalities are frequent."

"I would like to see this Tooth," said Hans. "It is near this Mountain of the Deer?"

"Bruach na Frithe."

"Maybe we shall go tomorrow if it is becoming clear?"

"Not while it's still winter!"

"But it is spring."

"Not here! I told you, we have our own weather."

A sable shadow fell across the snowy summits. Across the broad expanse of the brown, featureless hinterland, and over wild Loch Bracadale, a shower of horizontal sleet was racing in from over the sea, lashing their faces with icy ferocity.

"Come on!" Sara shouted. "Time we were away!"

3

It was Hans's penultimate evening. They sat in comfortable wicker chairs in a windowed alcove in the luxurious lounge of the Sligachan Hotel, awaiting a call to dinner, sipping aperitifs. Stags' heads surveyed them with morose indifference, each doubtless associated with some long-forgotten feat of hunting prowess, now merely dusty, yet nostalgic for a fading Scottish elegance which the hotel – beyond the rumbustious Climbers' Bar – worked assiduously to maintain.

Sara felt a twinge of guilt for not being sorry her companion would soon be going home, but his presence she had begun to find irksome. Though outwardly he deferred, with exaggerated politeness, to her hospitality, she felt constantly pressurised by his agenda, notably his pestering about the Cuillin; his refusal, moreover, to concede her local wisdom, she suspected, was because she was a woman, her reticence a weakness to be overcome, rather than a caution to be respected.

After fierce gales, calm had descended overnight; and conditions through that day had continued to improve. In the perpetual battle of the Hebridean seasons, spring had advanced, though a pall of snow remained upon the tops; indeed, quite low down in the corries. The forecast for the Hebrides the next day, however, was not too bad.

"So!" Hans declared, sipping his cognac. "Tomorrow, my last day, shall we walk up this Mountain of the Deer?"

"Bruach na Frithe. We'll see," replied Sara diffidently. "You never know what the next day brings. No use listening to the weather forecast. The sun can be blazing one end of the island, and a blizzard at the other. And the Cuillin are a law unto themselves. Like I said, mist forms from nowhere. There's still snow and ice up there, look!"

"It will thaw."

"Not up there. They're north-facing corries. The snow lasts well into June sometimes ... Look, maybe we can walk into Fionn Choire – the Fair Corrie. It leads up to the ridge beneath the Basteir Tooth, so at least you can get a taste of what it's like ... and, well, if the weather turns out fantastic, then we can have a think about going further."

Even as she spoke, she regretted her qualified words – a hostage to fortune.

"I wouldn't mind betting," she said, changing the subject, "we're sitting in the same corner where Norman Collie used to sit in his old age, sipping his wine and looking up to the summits he used to climb in his younger days. A sad figure, they say."

Through the window Sgurr nan Gillean loomed pale in the moonlight. Twinkling stars glittered in the frozen night.

"Norman Collie?" queried Hans, with that puzzled, sceptical look which had so come to annoy her.

"Yes!" she snapped. How could anyone serious about mountains not have heard of Collie? "One of the great Cuillin pioneers. Professor of Organic Chemistry at London University. Fellow of the Royal Society. An Aberdeen man, he knew the Cairngorms inside out, but spent most of his time here in Skye. One of the peaks is named after him – Sgurr Thormaid."

"Thormaid?"

Hans sipped his drink, fixing her with inquisitorial blue eyes, brows furrowed – like a schoolteacher querying an inaccuracy!

"Thormaid. Gaelic for Norman. There's Sgurr Alasdair – the highest peak – for Alexander Nicolson. Sgurr Thearlaich, for Charles Pilkington. And Sgurr MhicCoinnich, for John Mackenzie. Pioneers all. Mackenzie was a local Cuillin guide – knew them like the back of his hand.

Sara swept her hand round the room.

"Look! There are photographs of them on the walls. Famous climbing expeditions."

They arose and circulated, examining the old sepia prints in their plain wood frames, showing various groups in improbably precipitous situations beside menacing crags, stark summits or vertiginous chasms, attired in still more improbable gear. The men wore tweed jackets, deerstalker hats, plus-fours, and hobnailed boots that looked scarcely capable of getting a grip on anything.

The boots amused Hans, contrasting so markedly with the lightweight, brand-named, smart walking boots he had bought specially. So too did the number of women who appeared in the climbing parties, even more quaintly dressed. His disposition to find amusement from the female of the species stung Sara.

"Actually," she declared, "women have been active mountaineers in the Cuillin – not that they get the credit!"

"So, these were the first to conquer the Cuillin?"

"Supposedly. But I'm sceptical. Established history. This was the late nineteenth century. Here come the enterprising Victorians! Don't tell me no-one ever climbed the Cuillin before. It just wasn't recorded. Victorian myth-making! … That's why women don't get their due!"

"But there was a woman on the throne," insisted the accurate German, smiling.

"There!" she declared. "We're being called to dinner."

*

The dining room was no less elegantly Scottish than the lounge. Antique silverware, fine crockery and cut glass equipped the white-clothed mahogany tables; discreet standard lamps gave a cosy glow; there were richly patterned carpets, and the walls, clad in lavish paper, were divided into sections by ornate, wooden dado rails. Gilt-framed oil paintings of wild landscapes and scenes from the stag-hunt crowded round, and logs blazed in a huge oaken fireplace. A delicious meal was served by a deferential, silver-haired waiter, ever ready to replenish the crystal wine-glasses. The highland broth, roast pheasant and cranachan met the highest standards of Caledonian cuisine. The good food and wine, the sybaritic atmosphere, smoothed away their tensions, and the evening proceeded more easily than it had done so far. Over a sharp Talisker whiskey, selected from the multitude of single malts that glimmered in the firelight, they fell into a discussion of old Skye lore, of Flora MacDonald, Bonnie Prince Charlie, and the many eldritch beings said to inhabit the wilder quarters of the Misty Isle.

Sara told Hans of the numerous *sithean*, fairy mounds, associated with mysterious vanishings; of the Bean-nigh, crooning and washing her shrouds in the burn, prophesying imminent demise; of the Gruagach, after which certain standing stones were named, recalling bloody sacrifice; of the Baobahn Sith, demon-women who sucked the blood of victims, male and female alike; and of various black dogs, bewitched cats and primeval creatures lurking in the deepest lochans, occasionally arising to inflict a shocking fate upon lost and benighted travellers.

"So, you have vampires here?" remarked Hans.

"Well, I'm not really sure the Baobahn Sith *is* a vampire, it's more to do with witchcraft."

"If it sucks the blood, it is a vampire," announced Hans with finality, as the waiter materialised to refill his glass from a gleaming decanter.

"What about the Cuillin?" he continued. "Are there any horrid creatures living there?"

"Strangely, very few," replied Sara. "No fairy mounds there – even the wee folk keep away! Oh, there are all sorts of vague tales about weird voices, climbers' ghosts, and so on – the winds make peculiar sounds howling round the crags. But the only creature linked specifically with the Cuillin is the Uraisg. There's a corrie and a pass named after it. It's supposed to look like a goat in a man's shape, all shaggy, with sharp teeth and claws. Very frightening to behold."

"Like the Yeti!" observed Hans.

"Sort of ... but, really, more a version of Pan. Spirit of the wilderness, and all that. But very nasty."

"Like the Big Grey Man of Ben MacDhui? I read of him in the *Fortean Times*.

"The Fear Liath Mor," translated Sara, ever keen for the Gaelic. "No, not really."

"Then, who is this Grey Man?"

"Some say the Brocken Spectre – the sun casting your shadow on mist, circled by a rainbow we call the 'Glory' or Ulloa's Ring."

"Ah!" interrupted Hans. "The Brocken Spectre, I know him! That is in the Harz. Where witches dance on Walpurgisnacht."

"Yes, I know," she replied testily. "But there's a better explanation. The Grey Man is heard not seen. In certain snow conditions the hollows made by walkers collapse in on themselves after a time lag. So it sounds like footsteps following. That's why huge footprints are sometimes seen, the dent in the snow is enlarged. Add to that the terror of a white-out, mist all around, especially if you're on your own – no wonder people get scared and imagine things. Sounds get magnified. Witnesses report a feeling of terror at a presence they can't see. Shackleton's party experienced similar in the Antarctic, like they were being accompanied by an extra man.

"As a matter of fact, one of the earliest recorded accounts of the Big Grey Man came from Collie. It happened when he was young on Ben MacDhui. It was so traumatic he never spoke of it for decades. He'd climbed all over the world, the Alps, the Himalayas, but he said he'd never felt so frightened as on that occasion. He fled down the mountain in a blind terror. For all his scientific training he continued to believe that there was something up there beyond human understanding."

"And so, perhaps the Uraisg?"

"Well, no, this was in the Cairngorms. Collie never saw anything like that in the Cuillin."

"Then what does the Uraisg do? What is the legend?"

"The Uraisg is said to tear its victim limb from limb."

"And you believe these legends?"

"Like I say, all these names – the Uraisg, the Big Grey Man, the Executioner – they embody the terror of the wilderness. There's lots of bodies torn to bits in climbing accidents in the Cuillin. It's symbolic, a metaphor. The only death-dealers here are the scenery and the weather … I'm a bad Celt – I'm not superstitious!"

4

In Sara's opinion, conditions the next day were still insufficiently clement to warrant an expedition into the Cuillin. The mountains, certainly, were visible, but with no guarantee of permanence; snow still lay extensively in the upper corries and on the ridge.

Hans, however, remained adamant.

"It is my last day. I have spent all my life in a political prison-house. I have come all this way for a dream. Look! It is clear!"

The relatively pleasant weather, in contrast to previous days, made it difficult for Sara to gainsay his case. A compromise was reached: they would ascend the Fair Corrie as far as the Tooth, so long as conditions underfoot allowed, then review the position.

On the wearisome trudge up from the Sligachan Hotel, Sara's qualms failed to diminish. Wisps of cloud kept forming on the ridge, obscuring the summits. The Fair Corrie, judging from the scree-shattered desolation, was a relative concept, being the only one, rumour told, where green shoots grew; yet the sole evidence of Nature's bounty was a disconsolate clump of primroses beside the burn, which, nevertheless, lent a welcome vernal touch to the inhospitable scene. The Tooth, so precipitous as to bear no snow, loomed black against the skyline, a grim sentinel counselling retreat.

Sara, ever a careful planner, had made sure they had prepared for the worst. Hans, for one so intent upon the mountains, had arrived, she thought, singularly unprepared, with footwear more suited to a moorland tramp than tackling challenging terrain. In their rucksacks she packed extra food and drink, woollies, waterproofs, map and guidebook, survival sheet, torch and – useless as it was reputed – a compass; but, as she clambered up the punishing gradient, she cursed herself for not remembering – essential for the mist-girt wanderer – a whistle.

The Fair Corrie, according to her *Scrambler's Guide to the Cuillin*, was 'a walk only in name' – and so it proved, as they struggled laboriously up loose scree. Claustrophobic, ominous, the summits crowded round – puny humans faltering in giant-land. Stern warnings applied for the mist-bound in the area around Am Basteir, where the unwary might 'encounter difficulties', the exit from the ridge being 'by no means obvious'. It was vital to ensure that, of the various routes and bogus routes, the correct one was identified, as the compass was 'not to be relied on'. Erring west led to 'a rough scramble' but eastward a 'promising but challenging descent terminated in cliffs'. Except in clear weather walkers were advised 'to avoid the area altogether'. Hans remained obdurate, his literal-minded idiom failing to detect the subtle menace of the laconic, understated prose.

"Look!" cried Hans, grinning. "It is like a face! A monster's face!"

They had almost attained the ridge, peppered with fresh snow drifting to several feet, a cornice forming at the corrie's head. The black battlements of Sgurr a' Fionn Choire, Peak of the Fair Corrie, shut out the sun, but it was the Basteir Tooth to which Hans referred, looming to their left above them, stark and monumental.

By screwing up her eyes, and a generous dose of imagination, Sara could see what he meant. Indeed, the more she looked, the more distinct became the impression, such that, eventually, it was hard to banish it from the mind. It was of a magnitude that awed, and again she reflected on their fragility before the mighty Cuillin. The pyramidal summit of Am Basteir towered beside the Tooth, and, beyond, the pinnacle of Sgurr nan Gillean. In the heavens an eagle soared, then another, the vast spread of their golden wings illumined by the sunshine excluded from the Fair Corrie.

"This is the Bealach nan Lice," announced Sara. "I'm not sure it's wise to go on – look at those clouds." The vapours, like spectral, wreathing fingers were creeping round the summits; yet, above, blue skies peeked through. Whether the wind had dropped, she was unsure, as they were somewhat shielded from the west. If it had dropped entirely, it did not bode well, as the stealthy, sinuous creep of the mists, unswept by gusts, warned only too clearly of the perils in such temperatures of total calm, especially as the sun hastened after noon on its rapid descent.

"It is nothing," responded Hans impatiently. "It will clear. We have come so far. It is just a little way now."

They looked towards the whitened top of Bruach na Frithe, deceptively near.

"That's at least half an hour away," warned Sara. "With a stop, we won't be back here for another hour-and-a-half at least. It's very treacherous around this bealach if the mist comes down."

"What is 'bealach', please?"

"It means 'way through' or 'pass' but not as you or I know it. See – to the south it drops down a thousand feet."

They waded through the drifts and looked down a vertiginous wasteland of scree-strewn crags.

"That is a pass?" remarked Hans, incredulous.

"It's one of the better ones. The book describes it as 'easy'. If you take a wrong turning here, past the Tooth on the north side, you get to the Bealach a' Bhasteir. The book says that one's 'very unpleasant'. Then, beyond that is the west ridge of Sgurr nan Gillean. Climbers only. The last lap on the circuit of the ridge."

Hans insisted on proceeding; if she did not wish to accompany him, he would go on alone to Bruach na Frithe. Dismissing a temptation to leave him to his fate, Sara yielded. Cagily, they picked their way over the snow-clad, ankle-twisting rocks beneath the cliffs.

The journey took longer than distance appeared to merit. The last few hundred yards to the summit were arduous, a wilderness of obstacles rather than a route, a confusing three-dimensional labyrinth. Gargantuan boulders, as after a battle between angry gods, lay tumbled in mayhem, such that a recognisable reverse route could scarcely be memorised, while a checking of the compass confirmed the deceitfulness of that device – vain foible in the presence of Nature's omnipotence.

At the top, however, there was rich reward; for a time Sara's uneasiness faded before the splendid panorama. It was said that Skye took its name from the island's shape as a bird with outstretched wings, as the scene below strikingly supported. They could see, beyond Loch Bracadale, Macleod's Tables, their vantage of the other day; while, west, the hundred mile chain of the Outer Hebrides glistened in the sun, and far distant, the isles of St. Kilda, as numinous as a vision of Tir nan Og. Eastward, rolled the sweeping panorama of the Scottish Highlands, interrupted only by the nearer perspective, where the jagged procession of peaks to Sgurr nan Gillean marched in terrifying array, uncomfortably reminding her of their perilous elevation.

They settled down for lunch on the rocky summit, gazing south over the entire Cuillin ridge, a vast S-shaped curve, over thirty fearsome peaks packed densely and bewilderingly into a mere eight miles. The dizzying effect was enhanced by the deep chasm separating them from the ridge's continuation. It was grand, awesome, yet in some indefinable way, dismaying; and all the time they sat, Sara felt increasingly ill at ease, anxious to depart this stronghold of the fickle gods, where they trespassed at their peril. All the time she kept monitoring the weather, every nuance of the cloud configuration. The wind, indeed, had dropped, except for a light breeze that only served to hone the bitter chill. The sun had disappeared behind a dark bank of snow-heavy cumulus. Deprived of its rays, the mountain top suddenly felt menacing. Mist was rising from the chasm like drifting smoke.

An abrupt depression of the spirits intruded, her wellbeing waning with the sun. Mist was approaching, unmistakably: over Sgurr Alasdair, Sgurr Dearg, Sgurr na Banachdich, trailing the several summits of Sgurr a' Greadaidh, and around Sgurr a' Mhadaidh, drifting across the long shoulder of Bidein Druim nan Ramh, obscuring Am Casteal ... creeping ever closer to their lonely eyrie. Sara began to worry about getting off the top; the way through the colossal rocks was not apparent. An inkling of oppression behind her made her turn. Her stomach churned. Swirling like a swollen river over Am Basteir and Sgurr nan Gillean, billowing in the corries and along the ridge, was a thick, grey mist that, in its eerie shifting, appeared imbued with a malevolent intelligence. It was happening at a swift, unreal pace, like a speeded-up film of weather movements. For an instant, the Tooth stood out sharp and alone, separated by the swathes from its parent summit, before vanishing. A dull silence gripped the land, and the cold grew venomous. It was time to leave.

Hans strode ahead. His outward aplomb, his arrogant disrespect for hazard, were a naïve façade, crumbling before true danger. An unreliable companion, she felt, liable to plunge them both into disaster, while offering her scant protection or moral support. Already, he was veering out of line for a sensible escape, too far left, where the mountain was bounded by long, steep screes shunned by the guidebook.

"That's not the way!" she cried after his retreating figure. "We must go back the way we came."

"It is going down, look. It is a short-cut. We can bypass the top. See, there is a cairn."

There was indeed, a tiny one.

"Don't be stupid," she cried. "There are no short-cuts here! That might only mark a climbers' pitch!"

Fear was mounting inside her, spreading like wildfire from her hurrying companion. All she could do was follow, vexed at his irresponsibility. She felt her ankle give, then saw a bootlace had come untied, but by the time she had refastened it Hans was nowhere to be seen. Nor did her calls, increasingly impassioned, elicit any response. Panic welled over her, fired by anger, most perfidious of counsellors.

As far as Sara could guess, she was several hundred feet down on the east side, beneath the summit cliffs. God willing, a straight course should set her on the right way, providing no obstacle intruded. The vista kept opening and shutting, the mist receding and reforming with baffling effect; but the brief windows, far from establishing her whereabouts, tended rather to befuddle. An opening left looked promising, but a few yards on a downward ledge ended in a loose scree slope of indefinable depth and gradient. Instead, she pressed on with her original course, soon catching sight of another cairn. She found she had reached a hollow beneath impassable crags, a cul-de-sac.

Then, as the veil thinned, she noticed a narrow chimney ahead. Above was a ledge, and upon it another cairn. Did it lead on to the ridge? The direction was right. She called out to Hans, many times, but with mute response. On close inspection, the cleft looked daunting: a bad step with a long reach up a slab. She put hand to rock, trying to haul herself up, but her reach fell too short; nor could her legs stretch far enough, nor provide the necessary leverage. Conceivably, by awkward contortions, the move could be achieved, but it was too risky alone. Had Hans come this way? Maybe he had gone down the scree? The more she pondered, the more she suspected that what she faced was a climber's traverse that might well lead to insuperable difficulties. All the time, the light was fading and she was getting colder. On balance, the lesser risk was to relocate the gap and descend by the screes.

Hans, plunging ahead into the mist, was stepping too fast, stumbling over intolerant terrain. His lightweight boots, with limited ankle support, kept sliding on the loose surface. The cold was astonishing, penetrating his expensive outfit. The image of the old climbers with their high hobnailed boots, their gloves, their balaclavas, their tweeds and woolly pullovers returned to him, rough and ready, eminently practical.

And where was Sara? He had assumed she was following. He had no idea how long it was since leaving the top. A minute passed, then another, then five. Irritation became guilt – he had abandoned his companion in a panic, a cardinal sin of the mountain code – though there was too, in his remorse, an element of self-preservation: for Sara had a better idea of the layout of the land than he did, bereft even of a map. She was also carrying the extra clothes, and water. How would he get down without her? Had she taken another way? Gone back to the summit to the route they came by? Had she fallen? Numerous times he called her name, yet always in the muffling mist his voice faded. The best thing was to get off the mountain as quickly as possible. There were more wholesome places than here to be wise after the event.

But what to do about Sara? He stood in a hollow beneath soaring crags with no clear way forward. Several times, again, he called, but met only the silence of the mountains. Then, as he considered going back to look for her, he heard a faint cry: a woman's voice. It was difficult to locate it, though it came, he fancied, from ahead, where he presumed the ridge to be. Somehow, she must have found another way, bypassing him; it was he who was lost. Again he heard her voice, curiously ethereal, infused, it struck him, with a timbre of anxiety. No words could he discern, not even a suspicion of his name. A third time he heard it – echoing off the crags like several voices. Yet, as he yelled, his own voice fell flat and dead.

Considering his options, he saw beyond a small cairn a cleft in the crags, with a promising suggestion of an ascending ledge above. Maybe this would take him to the ridge; it was in the right direction. As far as he could judge, it was the direction, too, of Sara's voice. The prospect of returning back over the summit to search for his companion, missing one another in the mist, had not been inviting; the matter was decided.

The chimney proved more difficult than expected, with a bad step; but by stretching his long arms up to a hand-hold, and propelling his body upwards by a contorted movement, his right heel jammed into a hairline crack, using the full length of his legs, he managed to attain the ledge. Then followed a discernible track across a scree slope, but it ended in more crags which he only negotiated by a hair-raising scramble.

At last, he stood on the snow-clad ridge. But the mist was thickening. If only he could see the Tooth, he could orient himself. Whether it was the bad visibility or his anxious mind, as he made his way the landscape seemed utterly unlike he recalled, with no feature, as he stumbled over endless boulders, remotely recognisable, only an unceasing monotony of scree, stone and snow …

Eventually, after an interminable struggle, his stamina depleted, losing all sense of time, Hans found himself going down. The relentless mist had afforded no glimpse of the Tooth: presumably he was dropping down into the corrie, but it felt much steeper than on the way up, jarring his knees.

He descended a considerable distance; then found to his consternation that the track was beginning to climb up again, unceasingly. He had not the faintest idea where he could be. The dreadful vertigo of lost direction besieged him.

Panicking, he fumbled in his bag for the compass. The needle whirled futilely whichever way he located magnetic north. Had he gone too far? Or far enough? Had he even reached the Tooth? Or, horrid to contemplate, had he descended on the wrong side of the pass? Those lost in mist, he recalled, walked in circles. He hesitated, torn between retracing steps and going on. Suppose, not far ahead the confused contour became clear and he was on the right route after all? All the time he was getting colder …

The track terminated suddenly at boulders. He was standing on a narrow ridge of shattered rock, and on each side sensed rather than saw a yawning void seeming to draw him down from his precarious position. Slowly, the vapours parted, an immense V-shaped rift, at the top of which the tip of a ferocious peak, horribly near, soared through the tattered tendrils like a scudding moon through racing clouds. Immediately before him, emerging from the swirling cauldron, towered a forbidding pillar of rock, blocking the way. Here, surely, at last, was the Basteir Tooth …

Or was it? … Immense and portentous though it was, it lacked both the height and bulk of the Tooth … Nor did it really resemble it – except, maybe, in its malevolence, like a grim sentinel at the gates of Hades.

Hans sank shuddering to his knees, bereft of all energy, all resolve, all hope. His mind was reeling in strange daydreams. Again he heard Sara's voice, indisputably proximate, echoing around the wasteland as if there were many voices, suffused with urgency, apprehension and bone-chilling fear. And then there came a screaming, awful to hear, and a wailing as in an extremity of terror, accompanied by a rumbling crash and a harrowing final ululation. It echoed round the corries, followed by a dead, chill silence. And it drifted through his rambling mind that, all along, he had been hastening not towards salvation, but hurrying to calamity ...

6

Bruised and exhausted, Sara trudged the long, hard miles back to Sligachan. The scree had proved so loose, so precipitous, she had effected the thousand foot descent on her backside, at terrifying speed and considerable discomfort. She felt very shaken. But where was Hans? Her emotions flitted from remorse, to anger, to trepidation.

The car awaited, forlorn in the hotel's car park; there was not a sign of her companion. She stared back towards the invisible mountains, fearing the worst. A pall of dank grey hid the fearsome peaks, such that one might have imagined they were never there, phantoms of nightmare. A gathering gloom signalled the imminent demise of the short day.

An investigation of the Climbers' Bar and queries at the hotel proved fruitless; after a decent interval, as twilight gathered, she rang Mountain Rescue from Reception, feeing a sense of disbelief to be involved in this grim drama – so common here that one hardly gave it a passing thought – something that only happened to 'other people'

Assistance arrived with commendable speed, two men, one in his forties, the other somewhat younger. The older of the two, Alan, she knew slightly, but the younger, David, was a newcomer recently arrived from North Wales, where he had worked with Snowdonia Mountain Rescue. They would lead a team right away to search the region, Alan explained; and a helicopter would join the search if necessary later, weather permitting.

They questioned Sara so precisely about their movements and knowledge of the landscape that she felt like a foolish pupil babbling before a sceptical headmaster. Was it guilt, a sense of failed responsibility that caused her to detect a hint of rebuke in their questions?

"Did you not see the warning signs were out this morning?" asked the Welshman.

"The forecast for the Cuillin was bad, you should have checked with the Tourist Board," added his colleague.

They raised their eyebrows in disbelief when she described the way she had descended.

"You're lucky you didn't hit crags on the way down," said Alan. "There are very few gaps."

They asked her how well-prepared Hans was likely to be, appearing less than reassured at her description.

"Has he a torch and a whistle?" asked David.

"A torch, yes. A whistle, I, er … I don't think so."

"Always carry a whistle," he reprimanded.

"Do you think he'll be alright?" Sara asked.

The men looked at each other, as if hoping the other would answer.

"It's early days, yet," said Alan. "He might just turn up. Or we'll find him walking down the corrie. Don't underestimate the capacity for delay if he got lost."

"What are the odds if … he's stranded up there?" asked Sara.

"Depends," Alan replied. "If he keeps his head and battens down till it gets light, he may be okay. But if he's fallen, or in shock, or if hypothermia sets in … who knows?"

"It depends how quickly we find him," added David. "We've known people hold out for surprisingly long periods. And he's got a survival sheet. Don't despair, we've had many successes."

And many failures, Alan reflected, though he dared not voice his thought, nor give an honest view.

Sara was advised to stay in the hotel, overnight if necessary, and await further news.

It was gone eleven before a message reached her, via Reception, that the search 'would be continuing through the night'.

*

Sara was awoken at seven-thirty, after a largely sleepless night fully dressed beneath the counterpane. Mountain Rescue were waiting in the lounge, said the maid.

The cold, grey dawn shed an unprepossessing light on the room, as if the bright, gay elegance of their last evening together here had faded to the sepia tones of the old prints. She sipped a hideous black coffee in a plastic cup from a machine in the Climber's Bar. Alan was alone, sitting in the very same window where she and Hans had sat. The morn was clear and bitter, as she looked up to the ferocious bastions that ripped the skyline.

"You've found him?" she asked as she took a seat, spilling her scalding coffee with a shaking hand.

"Not exactly."

Alan's response nonplussed her.

"Not exactly?"

Alan gave a terse explanation. They had surveyed the area last night in shocking conditions, finding no sign of Hans on the route she had described, but there was a clue.

"We've found a fell-boot, and his haversack."

He described the boot, which, horrified, she confirmed.

"So what does this mean? How …?"

"How did it come off?"

Alan, she thought, looked reticent, shifty even, as if pondering whether to tell all.

"Obviously," he continued, "we don't really know yet. A helicopter's searching the area now ... but I'm afraid the likeliest explanation is a fall of some kind. The rucksack was upturned, the stuff scattered. The boot may have come off in the fall."

"Where?"

"Way off course. We found his effects just this side of the west ridge of Sgurr nan Gillean at the top of the Bhasteir Corrie … He probably missed the turning down – easily done – carried on past the Tooth, and then got into difficulties … but at the moment it's still speculation."

Effects! It certainly sounded bad.

"Could he still be alive?"

Alan's walkie-talkie crackled. She could not make out what was said. He left the room.

He returned after a few minutes. Sara did not need to repeat the question. She read the answer in his eyes.

"That was Dave, Sara," he said. "It's bad news, I'm afraid. They've found your … friend's remains."

"But are they sure?" she persisted. "It *is* Hans, isn't it?"

"Yes, they're sure – he had his passport on him."

"Don't you want me to identify …?"

"It's not advisable after these kinds of accident; the authorities will do what's necessary."

7

Alan and David sat in the Land Rover, the engine running to offset the bitter cold. The summits, draped in frosty majesty, starkly beautiful, glittered up on high.

"I can't decide whether I love or hate these hills," Alan sighed. "Twenty years in the trade and it never gets easier."

"Did you tell her about the boot?" asked David.

Alan gave a mirthless laugh.

"I didn't tell her the foot was still in it, if that's what you mean! ... And I didn't repeat what you told me the helicopter found – except that he was dead. Remind me of the detail."

"You know they found the rest of the leg not far away? It was severed, in an odd way. You'd expect the knee or the hip, but this was torn halfway through the thigh. The other leg's still attached. The right arm's missing the hand. But the left arm, up to the elbow, was discovered on the other side of the west ridge, just down into Lota Corrie, not far from where they found the boot and the bag. Maybe he fell from further up the west ridge and the body parts dispersed either side?"

"Maybe. More likely dispersed by eagles, or possibly a fox – that would explain the thigh, it's been gnawed."

"Well, they must have been at work early; the chopper was there at first light."

"It happens ... What do the head injuries tell us?"

"They're still looking for his head."

"Jesus Christ!"

They were interrupted by the roar of an engine. Another Land Rover pulled alongside them and the window dropped. Alan recognised the grizzled visage of James MacDougall – Jimmy Mac – one of the oldest hands on the Mountain Rescue team, now retired; bad tidings travelled fast.

"What happened?" Jimmy demanded.

Alan introduced David, and gave a brief account.

Jimmy shook his head. "That whole area round the Tooth is treacherous. Over thirty fatalities in the last ten years. If he strayed onto the west ridge of Gillean in mist, that's practically a death sentence. It was better when it was totally impassable. Ever since the Gendarme collapsed, people think they can walk it, but they can't."

"The Gendarme?" David looked askance.

"The Welshman doesn't know his Cuillin!" quipped Jimmy.

"The Gendarme," Alan explained, "was a huge pinnacle at the foot of the west ridge. Completely blocked the way. It was undercut on both sides, no way past without abseiling below or a rope job over the top. It collapsed in 1987 in a terrific thunderstorm. Struck by lightning."

"That's where the Donaldson party came to grief," said Jimmy. "First recorded attempt on the Gendarme. 1885. Two women, one man. They were trying to complete the Cuillin circuit, but the mist clagged in as they came over Am Basteir. They never got past the Gendarme. Fell down into the corrie – they think. Never found the bodies. But they found their ropes in position on the Gendarme. Spooky! Like the *Marie Celeste* or the Flannan Lighthouse! Some say you can still hear their voices screaming when the mists are down … Aye, it's a bad place!"

He revved his engine and drove off.

"Doesn't bear thinking about, does it?" David remarked. "I mean getting lost up there, stumbling round in mist, all those crags, not knowing where the hell you are …"

"Yes, well, it's best we don't. We'd never do our job. Come on, the bar's open, I'll buy you a pint."

SAURIANS OF THE DEEP

Purely in folklore terms, northern Scotland's plethora of monster mythology is the envy of the rest of the British Isles. This is mainly thanks to its multiple deep, dark lochs wherein the bulk of these mythical horrors are said to be found. Of course, this is a tradition everyone in the world is familiar with, and as such it adds millions of pounds per annum to the Highlands tourist industry. Yet its origins go way back virtually to the dawn of human occupation in this region, and as such it has caught the interest not just of holidaymakers but of historians, journalists and even scientists, despite whose best efforts the institution of the Scottish loch monster, in particular Nessie, the much lauded and feared 'Great Orm of Loch Ness', continues to defy analysis.

The earliest report we have of Nessie come to us from the 6th century, when the missionary Saint Columba performed a religious service on the banks of the loch to lay a monstrous serpent that had been devouring villagers. This curious tale should not surprise us. During the Dark Ages, the Celtic quarters of Britain traded mightily on their legends of fearless heroes battling with serpents, many of which would arise from bottomless lakes or flooded caves. As such, it would have been completely wrong if one of the new breed of Christian heroes had not adopted the same policy, but using prayer rather than the sword.

The odd thing about the Loch Ness myth was that it persisted even after the saint had departed. Later stories refer to a monster that dwelled both in the loch and the River Ness, describing it as a 'water-horse' or 'kelpie', a much-feared Highland spirit. Very detailed written reports of these sightings can be dated to 1771 and 1889. Of course, Loch Ness lies in the Great Glen, a fault line that bisects northern Scotland between Inverness and Fort William, and which back in those early days made it a very isolated spot – so the rumours didn't spread far at the time. But when in the 1930s a new road was built around the loch, the whole thing seemed to explode. A rash of sightings followed, and not only that; much photographic and cine-film evidence was supplied. Cinema audiences from John o' Groats to Land's End watched goggle-eyed as flickering black and white images appeared to portray an enormous, long-necked something swimming in the dark waters off Urquhart Castle. Thanks to the publication in 1912 of Arthur Conan Doyle's 'The Lost World', and the first screening of 'King Kong' in 1933, dinosaurs were firmly in the public consciousness, and it didn't take long for *people to start commenting that the strange creature in Loch Ness looked remarkably like a plesiosaurus.*

Reasonable arguments were put forward to this effect. Could a brood of these ancient sea reptiles have somehow been cut off in the loch during their heyday, which was the Jurassic period? When marine biologists replied that Loch Ness didn't even exist in the Jurassic age, and that plesiosaurs, like many other sea-going reptiles, could probably not tolerate fresh water, another proposition was aired. Was there a hidden channel connecting Loch Ness to the sea? Was it perhaps an ancient breeding ground, and were these magnificent dinosaurs coming and going by that route? When the scientific community responded that Loch Ness was only connected to the sea by the River Ness and the Caledonian Canal (constructed in 1847), and that nothing so large, especially a breeding population of such nothings, could traverse these routes without being detected, it only deepened the mystery.

Since then, the exposure of numerous hoaxes has failed to dim the monster hunting community's fascination with Loch Ness. When the notorious Surgeon's Photograph, which had stunned the world in 1934, was revealed in 1975 to have been an elaborate prank, there was disappointment but no let-up in the community's enthusiasm. Many viable explanations for sightings have been forwarded: underwater currents, the eruption of sub-aqua gasses from the loch's bed, the emergence of rotted logs, the presence of other forms of rare wildlife (from time to time, seals, and even a walrus are reported to have strayed into the loch). This has diminished the body of evidence hugely, but belief in the monster lingers. It even survived a BBC-funded survey of the loch in 2003, which utilised satellite tracking and 600 separate sonar beams, and still turned up negative results.

Partly this is because, despite all, there are few scientists who will unreservedly assert that nothing strange or unknown exists in Loch Ness. It is the largest lake in Britain in terms of sheer volume – 23 miles long and nearly 800 feet deep – and is permanently fogged with tea-coloured peat; so there is no easy way to thoroughly and reliably investigate it. In fact, some scientists, rather than erring on the side of caution and simply dismissing the myth, have suggested plausible biological theses. For example, the Atlantic sturgeon has been proposed as a possible candidate. The sturgeon could swim up the Caledonian Canal to the loch far more easily than a family of plesiosaurs could, and has been known to reach an amazing 27 feet in length. Others have spoken about as yet undiscovered species of giant eel.

Of course, until an outsize version of some such creature is proved to be the occupant of Loch Ness, Loch Morar, Loch Maree, Loch Arkaig, Loch Shiel (yes, there are many such aquatic mysteries in the Highlands), the world's monster-seekers will keep on coming, and cameras will continue clicking along northern Scotland's beautiful inland shores.

YOU MUST BE COLD
John Whitbourn

"**Y**ou must be cold!"

The Director spoke not to me but the brave soul atop Dunadd. There was no chance the distant figure would hear: he was a mini-mountain and good quarter-mile away. Even so, we could plainly see he was in his shirtsleeves, so he got co-opted into my briefing.

"I'm not your mummy," the Director continued, back to me and only me again, "but I'd advise you wrap up warmer than that twit when you're atop. It blows a breeze there twenty-four/seven. You'll sweat during the heavy work, then chill. That way you get colds. I don't hold with colds or days off sick – save maybe for pickaxe wounds. *Maybe*. And even then I expect you to wait till lunchtime to get an ambulance."

I'd heard tell this dig was hard-line, though I think the last bit was an attempt at humour. I reviewed it by failing to smile and keeping strictly to business.

"Where will I be?" I asked.

I saw three separate trenches started on Dunadd, plus a fair start on sectioning the ramparts. All looked equally promising and my settled stance was not to care. From finds-washing and finicky whisk-work, right through to brute-force-and-ignorance pickaxe stuff: it was all the same to me nowadays: all archaeology – the only thing I had left to love.

"You've been around," the Director conceded. "Your references are good. So, the summit I reckon, plus your fair share of the ramparts, naturally. Every hefty bloke takes their turn there. But up top is where I mostly see you: that's where I've greatest hope."

I think he wanted me to ask *"of what?"* but I passed on that, boss or no. I knew his reputation as he knew mine. Like he said, I'd been around: a *'nomad'* as we're termed, a pittance-paid professional digger, at home on any site from Palaeolithic to post-Medieval, from Afghanistan to Argyll, as now. My 1990s-spanning CV spoke for itself. I'd earn my money, such as it was.

The Director accepted I wasn't another of his archaeology undergraduate conscripts doing their compulsory fieldwork, nor yet some volunteer from the local leisured bourgeoisie. Not only did I have a decade or two on the former, but my skills could command payment, unlike the latter. There were plenty of other places who'd have me and be glad of it. So, he'd have no fun from psychological games with (or from) me – only competent graft. Of course, he wasn't privy to my cheap scotch habit: that was an in-my-tent-only secret. In public I was staunch teetotal.

I don't think he was disappointed as such. Every excavation needs a leaven of *'leave 'em alone and let 'em get on with it'* types. All the enthusiasm and *joie d vivre* can be delegated to the far greater number of youngsters (of all ages).

"Okay," he said, still surveying his site, seeking out imperfections after having failed with me. "Start this afternoon. Pitch your tent: settle in: help yourself to some lunch. We kick off again at 14:00 – sharp. Report to Duncan on the summit. Tell him I said you can jump straight in."

Viewing where I'd soon be made us both notice the lone figure again. He was still at the very top of Dunadd, indifferent to the elements. I presume the view was distracting him: the dig prospectus said it was spectacular – over to Mull and Jura, even across to Ireland on a clear day (i.e. rarely).

"Twit!" the Director repeated. "He'll catch his death – though maybe that's what he wants …"

There was a definite hook in his words that he really hoped would be bitten. Gruff might be my chosen default, but rarely rudeness – so I bit.

"What do you mean?"

The Director did his 'sort-of' smile that *hinted* at a human side yet didn't commit him further.

"Well," he said, still wearing that annoying 'man of the world' smirk. "Dunadd sometimes gets used for flying lessons, y'ken ..."

I could guess, but wanted him to spell it out – just so all the crassness should be on his shoulders alone. It also didn't help that his overdone, *'have I mentioned I'm Scottish?'* accent had started to grate. I'm born and bred myself but never felt the need to provocatively roll my *rrrrs* all over the place like that. The next station along was saying *"hoots mon!"* and wearing a kilt other than under duress at weddings. Include me *out*.

"What?" I pretended to be slow, even trying to sound English. "Hang-gliding do you mean?"

A snort of pseudo-amusement. "*Och* no; I mean the free, solo, amateur sort. *Failed* and once-only flying lessons. Fine take-offs but crap landings …"

My, *how* I laughed. *Not*.

That accent didn't only soar, from time to time it also slipped. I suspected this born-again was actually born in Birmingham. Another bandwagon-boarding *'bonnie-prince-shortbread-tin'* Scot slapping down the ethnic trump card.

"Don't worry," I told him – *told* him, and with his own words too. "I'm here to *'jump in'*, not jump off. Anyhow, whereabouts in Wales do you come from?"

*

"Dunadd," said the Director, "as a hilltop stronghold has its origins in the Iron Age, but only really achieves prominence from the seventh century CE – that is to say, *Current Era* – onwards. Its name derives from the Goidelic Gaelic – *not 'Celtic'* if you please…"

Polite titters met this scornful reference to common if misplaced parlance. He and his informed audience were at self-congratulatory one regarding discredited and racially tinged terminology.

The Director's *Braveheart* meets am-dram *Macbeth* accent had gone down a notch or four for this spiel to distinguished guests. They were, after all, *distinguished.* Who knows? Maybe some of them carried keys to *funding* in their pockets or purses (not sporrans). Or even *recommendations*, and thus the Holy Grail of *tenure*. It was important he be inclusive and *sensible*.

"… meaning fort on the – river – Add, hence *Dún Add.* The site is notable for its – count 'em: one, two, three, four – successive circuits of cyclopean dry-stone ramparts, and for featuring in so-called 'Dark Age' chronicles as the capital, for want of a better word, of the Kingdom of Dál Riata. Popular attention is also caught by the famed 'coronation stone', complete with footprint-shaped indentation, which we shall see on the summit. I shall also point out the highly significant Pictish incised boar symbol and the Ogham inscription."

Us foot-soldiers knew this stuff from the dig prospectus or else had heard it all before. So we just carried on scraping away on our hands and knees, pretending we weren't being observed like zoo animals and the more shapely raised arses covertly admired.

I was pretty safe in that last respect, but still felt the creepy caress of *'wonder what's he doing?'* looks along the spine. It is the one thing even veteran diggers never get used to: being conscript mime-artists performing for free. It might help if the audience sometimes brought bags of buns along to throw. Especially since tea break times were strictly enforced on this excavation and dinner often seemed stomach-rumblingly distant.

But no buns flew, only guilty glances at bums, so there was nothing for it but pretend we occupied separate realities. I turned my back on the invaders from Planet Academia.

And thus towards my companion in this section of *'Trench Two'*. Flora was a sweet old soul, not, I soon discerned, exactly overtaxed by playing housewife to the retired mathematics professor who'd heard about Dunadd on the departmental grapevine and suggested she volunteer. I could almost hear the conversation over the tea-things that brought her here and into my less-than-convivial company: *"Might get you out of the house, old girl: give you an interest. Leave it to me, my dear; I'll have a word with the Head of Archaeology ..."*

So he had and here she was. But no one had told her that buying a *riveted* trowel was no good – they don't last five minutes. And though someone had loaned her a proper one and devoted all of five seconds to demonstrating its use, she was left in the dark about why and what for. Why scrape so slowly down through the mantle of Mother Earth? What might be revealed that a spade couldn't tell you ten times quicker?

I'll admit the milk of human kindness has pretty much curdled in me, but I felt sorry for Flora, who meant well yet hadn't turned out as she'd once upon a time hoped. The ghost of her girlish smile now had a gravitational pull towards *'20 past 8'*. That much I could readily empathise with.

"Here," I chose then to say – even though the Director was still in full flow and conversation was *'discouraged'* during working hours, "try it this way: sweep *towards* you – and with the fingers, not the wrist. That way you get more control in it and don't go home sore. *That's* the stuff: good. See that chocolate colour layer coming up through the lighter stuff? Gently: scrape at the edges of it and get some more. Reveal the shape like it's a puzzle. Right? Now, that's *fill* you're revealing: a back-filled pit no one but you has seen since it stopped being useful a millennium ago..."

Us nomad-diggers no longer leap like salmon at the *'chasms of time'* aspect of the job, but I could see Flora was – why mince words? – *thrilled.* She'd have something to tell hubby about what *she'd* done today over this evening's *aperitifs.*

I sensed bad vibes bathing the back of my neck and guessed the Director wasn't digging (if you'll excuse the pun) my little seminar. Not only was I breaching the no chitchat rule and distracting from his spiel, but he hadn't forgiven me for the *Welsh* crack last week either.

"As I was *trying* to say, ladies and gentlemen," he said, voice raised, "Dunadd has been excavated on a number of occasions: in 1904-5 and 1929 and, most professionally, in 1980 by the then University of *Wales* ..."

101

Was it my neck hairs' imagination, or was someone dancing on my grave, inspired by that last word?

"Accordingly," he pressed on, "the primary purpose of our 2001 digging season is to ascertain if there remain any significant areas undisturbed by those previous investigations, and to seek evidence, such as firing or deliberate demolition, of the two attested sieges of the site, in 683 and 736 *CE*, as per the annals of Ulster. This will primarily be tested, as you can see, by a thorough sectioning of each of the ramparts ..."

And somehow I knew, with all the faith of a saint in Christ, that I would be working on the ramparts that afternoon, even though it wasn't my turn – and doubly sure if it came on to rain as the clouds threatened. Meaning moving monstrous rocks in inadequate wheelbarrows until, by knocking off time, I resembled Argyll's answer to *The Beast from Fifty Fathoms*.

So be it. I no longer expected any day to be my day. In the immortal words of my hero, Ho Chi Minh, *"so much of misfortunate have I seen that I have set my face like stone"*. No one would ever know what I thought of extra ramparts work – or anything else.

"What should I do about this?" Flora had leant across and whispered in my ear, so keen was she to avoid Directorial reproof. "There's a stone in my – the – pit ..."

And then I saw that today could never have been my day – or anyone else's bar Flora's. There, revealed by her timid scrapes, was a slab of slate: non-native to Dunadd geology but precisely what the Picts favoured for their enigmatic messages to futurity.

I went over and reverently puffed the remaining crumbs of earth away, never really doubting what I would see. Sure enough, though still begrimed, there were the etched lines, white on grey: swirls of surprising calligraphic skill.

Before the invader Scots (probably) wiped them out, the Picts had sealed Flora's pit with this last token of ... something or other. It was one of the rarest kind: the mysterious *'swimming elephant'* symbol: the headlines-worthy find of a lifetime.

I indicated Flora should look closer. So she did and she saw – but yet didn't.

"Oh, God!" she said, actually *scared*. "Those marks – have I scratched it? I'm *so* sorr –"

"*'Sorry'* is it?" I echoed – but for her ears only. *"Au Cointreau*, hen: in the immortal words of that witch Thatcher*: 'Rejoice! Just rejoice!'* Now, prepare to bask in glory ..."

I backed off and whistled, high-pitched like a shepherd, suggesting the Director should shut up and come over. It was another total certainty that his frown would be turned upside down (and stay pinned that way for days) the second he got here.

"Look what Flora's found!" I told all promiscuously, from Director to lowest pickaxe-pleb (just so that it couldn't be ... *nuanced* later). "And cleaned off perfectly too! She's gonna be *famous!*"

Then, without asking for permission, I knocked off for a smoke, knowing there'd be no more work on Trench Two that glorious Flora-made morning.

*

I suppose I could have stayed to share the joy, and hear the honeyed words poured over a stunned Flora, but bright scenes like that were no longer my scene. I took myself away from humanity and left them to their happiness. At least then I wouldn't spoil things with my brooding presence.

On Dunadd's summit I stood beside (not *on* – I was still an archaeologist) the foot-imprinted stone used in the coronation of umpteen Dark Age kings, drawing on a menthol-tipped fifty-fifty baccy/weed roll-up. The view over the Add and its *'Great Moss'* bog, the little farms and hamlets all the way to Lochgilphead and the Crinnan canal, and then the horizon-forming pine-twilight of Kilmichael forest – it was *splendid*. Even the storm clouds did the decent thing and made way for a rare bit of sunshine. Aside from the omnipresent biting midges (probably proof against *ack-ack* guns, never mind mere smoke) things looked and were as good as they were ever going to get.

But not for me. How could I feel joy when Joy had said definitively *"No"?* And how to get into the party spirit when the Party was no more?

High up – washed up – atop Dunadd at the tender age of forty, I realised I was high and dry.

*

Communists are often at a loose end on Sundays. Especially since their Party dissolved itself (or committed suicide) in 1991. And you'll not be surprised to hear that church-going isn't high on the alternative to-do list – though it *may* amuse to learn that many have taken up bird-watching since. And, no – I don't care to analyse that for fear of what it might say about *me*. For the record, I've no intention of emulating them. Where's the pleasure in living under a cloud of suspicion of being a peeping tom?

103

And, as with my life-long cause, likewise with the love of my life. Joy was (as best I knew since we no longer spoke) hundreds of miles and a routine I knew nothing of away. Our last still-searing conversation has cauterised any lingering hopes I had on the *'us'* front. That's what happens when you only get to meet the one – THE ONE! – sister via being already engaged to the other.

This excavation started late on the Sabbath. Some reactionary diggers went to Mass, others had a lay-in and nursed their hangovers. Me? Oblivion in a bottle being out of the question, my round-and-round-about thoughts drove me out of my sleeping bag bright and early.

The nearest farm to Dunadd had a Sabbatarian *'Wee-Free'* tenant, but a workaholic sheepdog. The latter couldn't abide idleness and so, whilst his master attended chapel, read the Bible or did whatever it is Calvinists do when they feel God's call, he went out *looking* for work. This took the form of shepherding flocks of walkers, whom he'd guide, darting and barking and nipping as he did with four-legged sheep, up to the top of Dunadd, and then back down again. I'd seen him do it from Sunday dawn to dusk, amusing or annoying folk according to type.

That morning all he could find was me, but a flock of one is better than nothing. Being ever fonder of animals the more I learned of humans, I swallowed my pride and allowed myself to be herded aloft. It was where I was going to spend the day in any case. This way at least someone would get a little pleasure out of it.

Then, near the top, workaholic-dog suddenly changed his mind. Instead of urging me on he counselled retreat. In fact, he tried to enforce it, placing jaws round my jeans, trying to draw me back. That was the stick: his carrot was whimpering, tugging at the heartstrings as he did my trousers. *"Humour me, oh two-legs,"* he was saying. *"Don't make a hard-working hound unhappy just because you can..."*

I fully approve of overturning *human* hierarchies but that's as far as it goes. Giving in to him would be taking animal rights consciousness (a *petit-bourgeois* deviation in any case) a step too far. So I took *contrary* steps and said something not for delicate ears and shook the moody beast off and away. Its advice slighted, it soon showed me a clean set of pads.

Whereupon I reached the top and saw that 'fresh air freak' was back, still only shirt-sleeved. Yet somehow the man was managing to keep his old-style trilby on without having to clamp it down. The wind blew and buffeted him and me but kindly relented re his headgear. Odd.

Thoughts of how that might be reminded me of the weather. I was in my parka and glad of it too, unfashionable fur trim and all. Whereas my surprise (and unwanted) companion was high-summer clad.

There was no escaping conversation: we'd happened on each other at point blank range. To say nothing at all would be tantamount to rudery. So:

"You must be cold ..."

I didn't mean to take him by surprise. I assumed my arrival, complete with towed cur, had been heard but politely ignored. Yet when he turned the middle-aged man was a picture of horror. He didn't expect to see me. He didn't see *how* he could see me.

And then I couldn't see him because he vanished.

*

Back at the tent lines the Director caught me and started to say what I could do today. Still in shock, I told him precisely what *he* could do.

And then I arbitrarily took the day off, heading for habitations and people and noise and anywhere *not*-Dunadd, meanwhile telling myself repeatedly:

"That did *not* happen. That did *not* happen ..."

*

But it *did* and nothing I could say, however often, could shake that. So when I got off the bus in Tarbert I headed for the nearest pub.

Soaking in four pints of *heavy* made me feel a little better, maybe even made me look better, because the landlord then engaged me in conversation, which I'd seen him decide against before.

"What brings you to Tarbert, pal?" he asked, skipping the pointless *"you're not from round here, are you?"* foreplay. He meant well – but thereagain so did Stalin.

'Archaeology' was just too complicated, and sometimes even controversial ('grave-robbing' and all that), so I said I was a dry-stone waller. I saw him check out my hands but they fitted the bill, meaning the bogus conversation could stumble on a few more clauses. I don't even remember what other lies, if any, I told.

Afterwards I went and explored the town – which occupied all of ten minutes, including a fair while staring entranced into a record shop window display of antique Andy Stewart and Moira Anderson *'White Heather Club'* LPs. *'Warning!'* said the cheeky placard placed above, *'These records may include phrases such as "Och aye the noo" and "D'ye no ken?" May also contain traces of tartan-tomfoolery.'*

Then I bought a *bridie* and chips and went and sat by the harbour, watching the fishing boats. Having been bitten before I should have known better. Blame the beer. The mutton (maybe) and greasy pastry *atrocity* was rejected by every taste-bud even before I chewed. That first and last mouthful went into a handy bin and the balance got chucked onto the beach. A vigilant seagull swooped, sniffed – and then flew away empty-beaked! Which is something I have never seen before in my entire life, anywhere in the world ...

Whereas my new companion I'd met before. He wasn't there when I arrived; now he suddenly was, though how I couldn't tell. The half-gallon of *heavy* evaporated instantly.

Shirtsleeves from Dunadd recognised me.

"Oh, you again," he said. "How d'you do?"

There was surprise at seeing me – or at me seeing him – but not the dismay of before. He now seemed reconciled to the encounter.

I couldn't say the same – I couldn't say anything at all – but hardwired behavioural traits made me match the friendly hand he extended.

Mistake – worse than the *bridie*. His hand was so frigid that when I shook it my skin stuck.

I was able to tear myself away from that grip, but not, alas, from the bench and *off*. That was asking too much of my trembling legs.

He studied the little patches of me I'd left adhering to his palm.

"We seem to be connected in more ways than one," he said. "Sorry about that, my friend."

Again, ancient engines cut in to say the *'polite thing'* instead of what I felt.

"That's okay ..."

"I'm John, by the way. John Maclean. Nice to meet you."

And in a funny, totally implausible, way, it actually *was. Now* I knew why that open, friendly face seemed familiar. He was someone I'd long admired but never thought to meet. What with him dying in, what was it – 1923? I'd sort of ruled it out.

The warm flood of data was now the sole thing that kept me there in that frost-generating presence. Otherwise, I'd have been away down Tarbert High Street wailing like a banshee. As it was, I *had* to know ...

"What?" I asked, through chattering teeth. "*The* John Maclean? Hugh MacDiarmid *poem* John Maclean? *'Red Clydeside'* and all that? *'Scotland's Lenin'*?"

He smiled. "I'd not go that far, though I'm flattered to be compared to the great man. But MacLenin? No: though the Bolsheviks were kind enough to make me their Scottish consul ..."

And ... and I believed it. Believed *him*. The modesty, the charm, accorded with all I'd read. He fitted every grainy photograph I'd seen. Even the shirtsleeves detail was spot on. I remembered now: he died young, before his time and way before he ought – of pneumonia. It was part of the Maclean legend and typical of the (living) man. Though weakened by prison hunger-strikes and forced feeding, he'd loaned his only overcoat to a Jamaican comrade suffering in a Scottish winter. Whereof he died ...

Died. John Maclean was *dead*. Did that mean ...?

"No," he told me, still looking straight ahead at the same scene as me – or so I then thought. "You're alright, my friend. Or so-so anyway. Although obviously in some sort of trouble if you can see me. Mebbe that's what drew me here. I always had a habit of heading towards trouble ..." He suddenly turned to me and, faced with that sincere countenance, I felt ashamed for feeling fear. "But only ever to help, mind," he added to reassure me. "Only ever for the Cause ..."

Wasn't that the truth! He was *our* hero; of Highlands stock, in and out of prison till it was a second home; fearless before raw power in the second *'Killing Time'* of WWI. A proletarian internationalist to his fingertips, but a better Scottish patriot than Wallace or Bruce ever were!

So I stayed. My coat was crisped on one side by the chill he radiated, but I stayed because here was a *man* ...

Was ... Second-thoughts time. I didn't believe in ghosties or *any* mumbo-jumbo. To do so would require a revolution in everything that made up the nation state of *Me*. A dilemma.

John Maclean sensed and solved it.

"Don't fret," he said. "Just accept there's a Court of Appeal – justice arriving eventually. I don't even try to think it through any more. I'm just grateful ..."

It was no longer possible to resist hugging myself. His cold had entered my bones.

"How do y'mean, Mr. Maclean? What court –"

"It's *John*, please," he cut in. "And have you no heard a picture's worth a thousand words? Look about. Tell me what you see."

For a teacher by trade he had brawn in his arms. He waved one to encompass Tarbert.

107

I looked and duly reported. An alleged town little bigger than a village. Water to two sides. A withered fishing fleet. The chippie where my *bridie* was born, that jokey record shop …

And yet, truth to tell, all that seemed less … clear than before. Squinted at just right, some other scene slipped in and out of sight behind *my* panorama. Something busier: and better?

Maclean nodded.

"You can almost glimpse it, can't you, son? Which means you're sharing my vision. And shall I tell you what that is? It's *Socialist* Tarbert, in collectivised Argyll, part of the *'Red Highlands'* and SSSR: the good old Scottish Socialist Soviet Republic! Which is in turn not the least part, if I may say so, of the USSE …"

Because he wanted me to I played 'guess the acronym'.

"The U.S.S … Europe …?" I ventured.

Maclean grinned. He had better news than that even.

"*Earth*," he told me.

I looked again and now saw more. When the vision chose to firm up, I viewed superior, safer, trawlers. Red flags flew from church and kirk spires; and all the workers' towerblocks too. Passers-by looked healthier, *happier*; less abraded by Capitalism's relentless war of all versus all.

A part of me is incurably frivolous: it's why I never aspired to Party office when it was still around. At that sublime moment I saw fit to wonder if there were *bridies* in that ideal world. If so, likely they were *delicious* ones …

"Remember?" said my companion – *'friend'* even. "A Court of Appeal, like I told you."

And now it was staying with me for whole seconds at a time. I saw the world the great John Maclean had fought and, aye, *died* for. And now had to hand. For those snippets of time I stopped wanting to scream or flee.

Yet, still a residual rationalist, I tried to rationalise things.

'It could be the *'Many Worlds Theorem'*," I suggested. "Modern Physics, you know. That every *possible* world actually does ex –"

Maclean shrugged.

"Who knows? Or cares?" he said, impassioned into dialect. "I dinnae want to analyse it. All I know is this: I may have nae overcoat, but as recompense I've got a whole world instead!"

Heady stuff! Even as all feeling left the side of me nearest to him, I felt the glow of something so unfamiliar to me this last arid decade I didn't initially recognise it. Without first introducing itself, hope just felt … weird. Weird but warming …

Words failed me – but something seemed expected. So:

"So ...?"

Maclean again turned to me full-face, focussing the personal force that had made him a giant of his time.

"Gift horse, son," he counselled. "Leave its mouth alone: that's my advice. Here's a world as real as any other, but a bloody site better than most – excuse my language. And everyone gets their own tailor-made world! I can get you into yours ..."

Abruptly, Maclean's face fell. If forced to interpret, I'd read it as realising he'd gone too far ...

Equally abruptly, he was also gone. I sat alone again in ... *okay*, I suppose, but basically business-as-usual Tarbert. Which would no longer *do*.

That morning I'd thought my reality was all there was, and had been sort of resigned to it. Now, before midday the same day, it just left a sour taste in the mouth that was nothing to do with *bridies*.

*

My performance slipped, the Director turned (still more) sarky. I took to taking long lone walks in Kilmichael forest.

Which is a dead and commercial place. Just rows of pounds & pence pines, ringed with logging roads designed to carry really big rigs. You learned to give a wide berth to those – once going fully laden with slaughtered trees they weren't stopping for anyone.

Yet for all its faults, it would do for me, for now, for to brood in. It had been real once, you could see that much. There was a proper deserted village from the *'Clearance'* days, and a WWII POW camp where Glaswegian lumberjacks now slept off their work and play. I even found a 'secret' waterfall set in its own little canyon, which I bet no one bar me had stopped to admire since the forest was founded. Like with everything and everywhere else, there were *just* sufficient remnant scraps to keep me going.

Those evening strolls-more-like-marches were meant to steel me. Or heal me: the good old 'walking cure'. As with so many things, the Romans had it sussed: *solvitur ambulando*: *'It is solved by walking.'*

And it *almost* was. That particular slog, striding along in twilight silence with only my own personal midge cloud for company, I nearly sorted things. John Maclean? Deceased 1923? What a load of ... That Tarbert beer must have been stronger than I thought. And, before it, the air atop Dunadd rarefied and head-deluding. Lord alive, *New Labour* was easier to believe in than any of that supernatural stuff.

109

Then the forest beside me spoke. At that point the logging road narrowed to a darkening tunnel of trees. To either side, the pine shade was profound; I couldn't tell what was happening mere feet from me – but something was. The tree cover at my shoulder groaned and heaved as a more-than-human happening headed my way.

I had a long second to prepare, and in that time all my flimsy barricades fell. I knew it was *him* and that I'd been a bairn to deny my own five (maybe six) senses. Only children and cowards cling to delusion. I accepted and surrendered.

I *had* conversed with Scotland's greatest Communist, even though our lives did not coincide. And I *did* want Joy – joy with Joy. Of course I did. Every molecule of me did. Marriage and babies and all the trimmings. Forever, till I died in her arms. And, yes, I did hunger for Peace and Socialism: worldwide human solidarity and mutual assistance. *'From each according to their abilities, to each according to their needs'*. With a vanguard Party to guarantee it. Those things were my entire world, my real one, and I *did* want a world with them in it Why prolong the deadly drought of the last decade?

So, in that short space I decided. If a dead man offered me miracles I'd not inspect that aforementioned equine oral cavity. I'd damn well take my due – and sod the implications.

Whereupon a red deer: a huge *Monarch of the Glen*-style stag emerged from the forest edge. He was every bit as stunned to see me as I was him. It was 'just' him, no one else, not even the harem he probably had somewhere, but a big enough commotion-causing old-boy all the same.

'Struck comical' as I was, His Majesty could have trampled, maybe even speared, me with his probably (I didn't count) sixteen-point tines, for spoiling his evening promenade. In the event, he just graciously progressed by. Crossing the road (without looking), His Highness then barged through the opposite tree cover and out of my life.

But not without leaving his mark. Before the noise of that departure died away, even before I'd metaphorically crammed my heart back down where it belonged, this crossing of paths had settled things. In the Party Congress of my mind my earlier 'decision' was formally proposed, seconded, voted on, and then passed unanimously to tumultuous acclaim.

'Democratic Centralism' now dictated that all comrades should follow the new Party line.

*

I hit the hill at first light, knowing – *knowing* – he'd be there. En route I met the Director, an early riser who'd already been out and got his *Guardian*.

It was a blustery day, and my face must have matched it. Seeing me was shock enough to make him drop the plump *Public Appointments* supplement.

"Oh – I mean och," he said. "What's up? Where are you go –"

"I quit!" I told him.

"But your contract ... notice ..."

I didn't even pause on the path up.

"Tough. What you gonna *do* about it, Taffy?"

Nothing was what – you could bet the farm on it.

John Maclean was waiting at the summit. Always Mr. Dependable: as in life so in ... whatever.

Unfortunately, also present were a primary-coloured gaggle of *cagoul*ed hikers – early birds who saw and heard me – but not him, I think. Which explains their *looks* at me, and then swift leaving when conversation started.

"Why here?" I asked, without preamble. Incredibly, it was the one thing still puzzling me. "Why survey the scene from Dunadd?"

Maclean smiled at the scenery. Answer came easy.

"Because of you, I presume," he said. "We seem to be fated: linked like with handcuffs. But also for the *contrasts*. I often bide here for them."

I looked but couldn't see anything. The Crinnan peninsula was pretty monocultural till you got to Glasgow. Maclean took pity.

"Beginnings and ends," he explained. "Alphas and Omegas. There's so much to relish. *Progress*. Think about it, son: from here, home of kings – and barbarian warlord kings at that – to ..." he waved at the – his – *'Red Highlands'*, "to Human Liberation Day!"

It was a thought. Though I also had another one.

"But don't barbarian kings get their own – horrible – heavens too? What do *they* look like?"

Maclean shrugged his shirt. "Don't know. No idea. I've never so much as glimpsed one. They probably don't get to go there ..."

I could have baulked at that, this blush-making brush with theology. I could have brought out my fig-leaf 'Many Worlds Theorem' again, but, characteristically, Maclean wouldn't take the easy way out.

"Aye, I know," he said, as near to tetchy as I'd heard him, "it's getting close to *'God'* and all that Kirk cack. Well, I didnae believe in Him or it in Life and I'm damned if I will now. So what? Mebbe

111

the Big Man's love is infinite like the pastors said – but so are all His worlds. That'll do for me."

Why did I maintain my life-membership of the awkward squad, even on the threshold of Paradise? Joy was calling me and yet here I was quibbling. I realised now what a fool I was – and always had been.

"So you can even *ignore* Him," I said, "if that's your thing – to keep sort of honest … consistent …"

Maclean gave the curtest of nods. "He doesnae mind – He's no touchy."

And then John had had enough of 'that sort of talk'. He turned and put a cold hand on my shoulder.

"So, what *is* your problem, man? Tell me. Cough it up …"

And, amazingly, I did. It all came blurting out. Joy, the Party, the fall of the Wall; ten years of wandering the world wounded, I sobbed the lot up like a great big *Jessie*.

Maclean didn't judge (though I saw him shudder when I said about the USSR). He just rested a fatherly (and anaesthetising) palm on me, and endured the Olympic-gold whine.

Then, when I'd done:

"You too, eh?" he said, kindly avoiding my red eyes, back to looking out over *his* world again. "D'ye know, the only folks I seem to meet these days are in despair. One foot in the grave …"

That struck a cord – or maybe alarm bell. But I couldn't recall why.

"I won't show you," he said, "but I can see it, plain as anything: your future here. It's not much. Two years from now you'll be unemployable: even as a *'nomad digger'* – whatever *that* is. Alcoholism, unreliability, *delirium tremens*. A couple of criminal convictions even: *silly*, boozed-up crimes. And you'll never have another woman …"

"I don't want one!"

"Aye, I know. You only want *one*. Because you've a good heart. Your sort often suffer the worst. But now there's no need. I can give her to you."

Wow! The utterly impossible and irrecoverable – all lined up waiting for me!

I was *gagging* for it – but still a well brought-up boy. Highland homes of my vintage had 'manners' on the core curriculum. No *'please'* got ignored; no *'thank you'* got whatever you'd been given snatched back. And maybe a clipped ear too. Too late to change now.

"Thank you. Oh Christ, *thank you*, Mr. Mac – *John*. But how? No, *why?* Why do you do this?"

112

John Maclean turned his head to smile: a real thirty-two teeth dazzler.

"I just want to do good, son; to make things better. Like I did in life. Like with that coloured comrade ..." He tugged one shirtsleeve to remind me. "It's just a shame Life makes you use death to do it."

Screech of brakes. Emergency stop.

"What?"

Mr. Maclean held my shoulder all the firmer. A death-grip.

"Well, *obviously*, son," he said, "you can't get into your perfect world alive. There's a wee entry fee to be paid."

"But ..."

"Steady on now; you're one of us: a comrade. You know what the great Vladimir Ilyich said: you cannae make an omelette without breaking a few eggs ..."

For the first time in my adult life I no longer cared what Lenin said.

"No!"

"S'true. Omelettes and eggs; revolutions and heads ..."

I now saw John Maclean's world plain. Saw *exactly* what he did. The landscape I'd known was gone.

"No!"

The collectivised farms were famine factories. It wasn't just sheepdogs who worked seven days a week all their short lives. In the hamlets there were scaffolds: they sagged with *examples* bearing placards strung round stretched necks. From Lochgilphead I heard the crackle of a distant firing squad. Dunadd was now crowned with a statue of Stalin. We two stood in its titanic shadow.

And, somehow, I could see Joy. She scowled at me – and everything. Joy was in uniform, a dead-eyed commissar buttoned up to *here*. Completely contemptuous of bourgeois deviations like *'love'*.

John Mclean saw too. "It's for their – and your – own good," he said. "*'False consciousness'* must be crushed. Mercy is just milksop sentiment. The proletariat requires firm guidance by a vanguard! A steel vanguard. Hard as steel. Cold as steel. You must be cold! *You must be cold!*"

This last was delivered in a rising scream, touched by what only the kind would call madness. But screamed with a *smile*.

At last it occurred to me to wonder just who was the *'He'* we'd been talking about. Who precisely was it that had created this world for Mr. Maclean?

Or part of him. I now knew what portion of John Maclean had survived to meet me. The majority best bits were long gone elsewhere.

113

The dead are supernaturally strong. I was picked up like a toy (which to him I suppose I was) and aimed at rocks far below.

I expect the coroner blames a freak wind for hurling me off the hill. Or yet another Dunadd *'failed flying lesson'*.

GLAMIS CASTLE

Of all the ancient fortified structures in Britain, none have quite so terrifying a reputation as Glamis Castle in Angus. Glance through any gazetteer of Scottish ghosts, and this ominous stone edifice will figure prominently. In the writings of none other than William Shakespeare its name alone has the power to induce shivers, while another great literary icon, Walter Scott, said of his visit there, "I began to consider myself as too far from the living and somewhat too near the dead".

Superficially, Glamis is a handsome residence. Owned and maintained by the Earl and Countess of Strathmore and Kinghorne, and at one time the home of Queen Elizabeth the Queen Mother, in appearance it is an elegant 17th century mansion set in acres of rolling, manicured parkland.

But it wasn't always so.

The refurbishments we see today were made piecemeal between the 1680s and 1920s. Before then, Glamis was every inch a gloomy medieval stronghold, and it played a key role in the cutthroat politics of some of Scotland's darkest, deadliest days. Its legends have become infamous. Tales of witchcraft, diabolism, ghosts and even monsters abound through its history.

Some are transparently untrue. For example, the myth that in 1034, Macbeth, Thane of Glamis, murdered King Duncan at the castle is an entire fabrication. The real Macbeth, who was later king of Scotland himself, had nothing to do with Glamis Castle. However, Malcolm II of Scotland, who died as the result of a wound received in battle, did expire there that same year. His spirit is said to be one of many that roam its eerie corridors. In fact, on several occasions during the castle's lengthy history, spectral patches of blood – Malcolm's blood, it is believed – have been reported dabbling the walls and floors.

Other stories are equally colourful.

John Lyon, who was Thane of Glamis, and was also Chamberlain of Scotland in the 14th century, is often blamed for the castle's ills, as he is rumoured to have removed a family heirloom, a priceless chalice, from the Lyons' original seat at Forteviot, near Strathearn, where tradition insisted it had to remain. We can never know whether he did this for certain, or even whether such a chalice existed. But from Lyon's death in 1382 onwards (he was killed in a duel), Glamis was allegedly plagued by weird and fearsome events.

For example, one of his descendants, Alexander Lyon, the 2nd Lord of Glamis but better known as Earl Beardie, was an ill-tempered and inveterate gambler who came to a spectacularly mysterious end. One night in the 1450s, while playing cards with friends in a small side-chamber, the earl was so angry to be out of money that he staked his very soul. Chilled, his associates refused to continue, but now another party joined the game, arriving at the castle unannounced and garbed in black. He accepted the earl's stake, and it is said the twosome played long into the night until such an hour that even the castle servants had gone to bed. In the morning the curious stranger had vanished, but Earl Beardie was found dead in the side-chamber. The general opinion was that he'd bet his soul against the Devil himself, and had subsequently lost it. So disturbed were the earl's family that they walled up the small room and erased all reference to it from the castle records. To this date it lies undiscovered, and it is still said that in the depths of night, the muffled tones of Earl Beardie can be heard from behind the walls, groaning as he plays endlessly for the restoration of his soul and always loses.

It is certainly no myth that Glamis Castle has many secret places. One time in the 19th century, as part of an experiment, staff hung towels from the windows of every known room. Yet from the outside, numerous windows were seen from which no towels had appeared. What these rooms are, why they were walled off and how they can be located are in most cases still unknown, but one was supposed to be the lair of the Monster of Glamis Castle.

This Glamis tale, more than any other, sounds like popular horror story hokum, and yet it was one of the first of its kind. Sometime in the early 16th century, a child was supposedly born to the Lyon family so horribly deformed they could hardly bear to look at it. Rather than put the child to death, they sealed it into another secret chamber and were done with it. How the poor creature was supposed to survive was anyone's guess, but stories lingered around the castle for centuries afterwards that the thing had grown to adulthood in its miniature domain, and having found a way out, would wander the corridors at night, attacking lone servants or guests. If this sounds fanciful, visitors to Glamis in the 18th century were badly distressed when one of their party, a young woman, reportedly woke in her bed to find an indescribable something glaring down at her.

But it isn't only because of the monster that women have suffered at Glamis Castle.

In 1528, a terrible injustice was done to one Lady Janet Douglas, then owner of the estate, when James V of Scotland, at the *time feuding with the Douglas family, had her framed for witchcraft and murder. Despite her beauty and wit, Lady Janet's word was no match for the king's, and in 1537 she was taken to Edinburgh, where she was burned at the stake, with her young son forced to watch. Her unhappy ghost also manifests at Glamis. A smell of smoke is said to precede it, and when her apparition appears, it is wreathed in flames and twisting in agony.*

Glamis Castle's other ghosts are of a similarly lurid ilk. An escaped madman was once hunted and killed in the castle grounds; his spirit is said to dance maniacally across the rooftops. A tormented, tongueless woman has attempted to make contact with people, while the shape of a brutally beaten boy is often seen slumped by the Queen's Door.

As always, the truth about these things is difficult to discern. Many famous ancestral seats boast about their ghostly occupants to drum up interest from tourists. But long before central and northern Scotland proved the visitor attraction it is today, when it was still a dangerous place of courtly intrigue and warring clans, Glamis had a reputation for being somewhere one didn't spend the night if one could possibly avoid it.

Make of that what you will.

THE FELLOW TRAVELLERS
Sheila Hodgson

It is possible to suffer quite severely from the benevolence of others. Do not misunderstand me. I have nothing but admiration for the great and good, students long gone who have made their mark and their money in the rarified heights of Science – Art – Politics – giants of commerce, leaders of society, pillars of banking, or generals renowned in battle. However, from time to time these gentlemen die and remember us in their wills. It is kind of them, estimable, most praiseworthy. And I do wish they wouldn't do it. Mind you, some of the legacies are welcome. Some, to be frank, are not. The Anglo-Indian who bequeathed us eighty-four stuffed elephants' feet bound in brass and mounted on mahogany, for example … now, whatever happened to those feet? I seem to remember innumerable hours spent in committee, though what we finally decided escapes me. There was the eminent divine who left a fortune to found a scholarship for the sons of sailors lost at sea; we were hard put to it to *find* any lost sailors, and when we did they were bachelors to a man.

And then there was Lord Duncan Mellinger. That business began in 1907, when one hundred and twenty crates of books arrived at King's, the gift of the late lamented earl. My friend and publisher came upon me in my study, lamenting.

"This is quite impossible, Masterman! I have no time to study all these volumes, and if I did we have nowhere to put them."

They lay in piles on the floor, leather-backed, linen-backed, some tied together with frayed tape, others coming adrift from their bindings, and all of them smelling strongly of dust and mould. George Masterman picked up a book at random.

"*Little Thoughts of a Layman*. Printed in 1823. Privately, I suspect."

I was not, alas, very taken with the *Little Thoughts*, and my own choice – *The Memoirs of a Sussex Farmer* – promised not much more, dealing as it did with the price of wool in 1792 and the effects of the French Revolution on the breeding of sheep. The truth is that an object does not *ipso facto* become interesting merely because it is old. Why Lord Mellinger had seen fit to include so much trivia in his collection –

"Is there a catalogue?"

118

"There is. But there is very little attempt at classification, I'm afraid." I handed George the list, sighing. I had so far examined only the first seventeen crates.

"Who was Lord Mellinger?"

"A humanist. A follower of Darwin, I believe. I cannot pretend to know much about the gentleman."

"He seems to have had a taste for the obscure." Masterman frowned. Being an editor, he is more patient and more adroit than I at hunting out the best examples. His finger paused halfway down the list. "Have you seen this?"

"What is it?"

"*New Thynking on Mortalitie*. 1526. Printed at the Elston monastery, with engravings. I've heard of Elston, James, but I thought their library had been destroyed during the Reformation."

Masterman really is a man of surprises. Could it, he asked, could it be valuable, this book? I assured him that anything from the Elston library would, by reason of its extreme rarity, command a high price. His interest clearly lay in the volume's market value. Mine, I confess, was in the title. *New Thynking on Mortalitie*. A treatise by a monk which had somehow survived the Reformation. Yes; I felt a pleasant twinge of anticipation. I should like to examine this book.

We couldn't find it.

We spent five days meticulously searching through one hundred and twenty crates. The book was not there.

Strange how such things work on the mind. What started as idle curiosity became, as the hours went on, a burning desire to find the wretched volume. By the fifth day Masterman and I were of one persuasion: we had to have it.

On the sixth day we called on Mr. Arthur Sinclair, solicitor, and executor of the Mellinger estate. He proved to be a small man with ferrety eyes, and teeth which gave him the appearance of having a perpetual grin. He professed himself delighted to see us and bounded across the room.

"Dr. James, a pleasure to meet you, sir, such a long way, so good of you, so kind, will you not take a seat?" He dragged two chairs followed, urging us to sit, then skipped backwards and retreated behind a vast desk entirely covered with papers. The whole office seemed to me to be in a state of considerable disorder, and I could discern no sign of a secretary or clerk. Small wonder articles went missing.

I explained the reason for our visit. Mr. Sinclair looked startled and then dismayed. He clicked his tongue against those all-too-prominent teeth and glanced around the room, as if expecting the volume to materialise and put him out of his misery.

"*New Thynking –*?"

"I wrote the title out for him: *New Thynking on Mortalitie*.

"Ah. Yes. Oh, indeed. Quite. This would be philosophical, no doubt? An academical work?"

"It is a sixteenth century manuscript," I told him. "Written at the monastery of Elston, possibly containing illustrations in colour."

He nodded. "You have seen this book?"

"No. But it is listed in your catalogue."

"Ah! Which is not to say the article exists, Dr. James. How can I put it, sir? You are not under the impression I have *looked* at the Mellinger library?"

"You haven't?" The exclamation came from George Masterman.

"Good heavens, no! Oh dear me, I would be in a poor way of business if I wasted my time reading!" His mouth still grinned, yet his eyes looked anxious.

I rose. The conversation was clearly getting us nowhere. I thanked Mr. Sinclair for his time, and asked for the name and address of any member of the Mellinger family who might be in a position to help us.

"Oh, there we find ourselves in some difficulty. I myself would be only too happy to oblige you, rest assured, you may rely on my complete co-operation –"

"An address?" murmured George. He had crossed the room and appeared to be examining the bookshelves.

"Indeed – ordinarily with the greatest of pleasure – but unfortunately, no."

"I beg your pardon?"

"How can I say this? Regrettably – unhappily – the late Lord Mellinger died without issue."

"Aunts," said Masterman tartly. "Uncles? Nephews? Nieces? Second cousins twice removed?"

Something had irritated George. He was definitely losing his temper. I glanced sharply at him. There was no need to be cross.

"Are you saying there are no relatives left?" I asked.

"Not one. A melancholy state of affairs, my dear sir; I lament it as much as you do."

"That's odd," I commented. George continued to scowl.

"Not in the least, on no, no no. It is precisely that lack of kith and kin from which you benefit. Then entire estate goes to various charities, while the contents of the library are gifted to your good self; or, rather, to King's College, where I understand his Lordship spent many happy days."

I felt my patience beginning to slip. I had, I told Mr. Sinclair, one hundred and twenty crates of books back at Cambridge. Somebody had clearly compiled the list, checked the catalogue, packed the volumes, sent the crates –

"Oh, most certainly, oh indeed, dear me, that would have been Miss Drummond, poor soul."

Masterman swung round. Who, he asked, who and where was Miss Drummond?

Arthur Sinclair looked at him very reproachfully. He could not, he said, be responsible for the movements of others. No doubt the lady was in bonnie Scotland. Further questioning uncovered the fact that this was not some vague generality. Miss Drummond was the secretary who had once worked for Lord Mellinger, and who still lived on the island of St. Wulfran, where her employer had spent his final years.

We shook hands – at least we had winkled an address out of him – and prepared to leave. It was only as we were departing that I thought to ask Miss Drummond's Christian name – it is as well to be precise in these matters – and I turned back to ask the question.

Mr. Sinclair was standing behind his desk. I could have sworn he was laughing at me.

It must have been those teeth. Yes, yes; an unfortunate physical attribute gave him the appearance of having a secret grin. All the same, I mentioned my reaction to George.

"I do not care for Mr. Arthur Sinclair."

"I don't trust him." My friend spoke so vehemently that I felt compelled to ask his reason. You really cannot accuse a man of bad faith without evidence.

"My dear James!" He lifted an eyebrow. "Didn't you see the books lining his office?"

"Not in any detail."

"John Stuart Mill. Thomas Hobbes. Desidarius Erasmus. And this is the fellow who tells us he has not even *looked* at the Mellinger library!"

He had a point. While neither of us believed – *seriously* believed – that Mr. Sinclair had stolen the Elston manuscript, something unusual was most certainly going on. Collectors in the grip of an obsession have been known to act out of character; the most honest individuals may yield to temptation. The more elusive it became, the more determined I became to see that book.

That is why, some days later, we found ourselves staying at a gloomy little inn called the Tontine Arms, while long Atlantic waves rolled towards us from a leaden horizon and the island of St. Wulfran squatted like a toad on the horizon.

Our first encounter with the locals proved unfortunate. In the haste of our departure north I had entirely forgotten the date; when I asked for a boat, the landlord eyed me and replied that it was the Lord's day. His tone implied that only an unbeliever (and probably a Londoner) would be travelling at all. He himself was only persuaded by Christian charity to give us a bed for the night. There was, he said, a fire in the back room, and we would find a copy of the Bible by our bedside; oh aye, dinner could be provided at six-thirty, kindly oblige him by not being late. I had resigned myself to this state of affairs when – surprisingly, incredibly – he had turned in the doorway and said, "If it's the island you're wanting, you can walk across on the causeway."

I have no idea why he had not told us that in the first place.

Masterman showed some reluctance to leave the fire; but it was still afternoon, and I felt a great desire to get on with it, find Miss Drummond, and be off. On reaching the causeway I must confess that I began to share George's doubts. It was a long spit of broken stone, largely covered in green slime and dead mussels. On either side the water slapped and hissed, and through a drizzling mist we could just see the jagged shore of the isle of St. Wulfran. Slipping and stumbling, clutching on to each other for support (twice I almost fell, and once I feared George had twisted his ankle), we made our way to the beach, and were astonished to find a woman wrapped in a cloak standing on the cliff path, waving her arms.

"No, no! Not today! You canna come here today!"

Masterman pointed out that we had come here at considerable inconvenience, not to say personal danger, and that we were looking for a Miss Isobel Drummond.

"I'm sorry. There's nothing I can do for you. The island is never open on a Sunday, and neither is the house."

"Are you Miss Drummond?" I asked. She nodded. She was a tall, handsome creature with the high cheekbones sometimes found in Scotswomen. "I am Dr. Montague James. I sent you a letter." I had indeed written to the lady requesting an interview.

"Goodness, you should have said! I had no idea you were meaning to travel so soon." Her manner changed, and she led the way up the path, enquiring anxiously whether our shoes were damp. I think she found it odd that two gentlemen of our age had attempted the causeway; she kept giving us small astonished glances. The house itself proved to be a hideous mock-Gothic building set well back from the shore and mysteriously called The Manse.

122

"Oh, it had that name when Lord Mellinger bought it. To be honest, he couldnae be bothered to change the sign; besides, it would have annoyed the postie."

Miss Drummond ushered us into a hall crammed with dark furniture and dominated by a picture framed in gold. A study in oils, it showed a tall man in academic robes, clutching a scroll in one hand a patting a dog with the other. He had a great deal of fluffy red hair and the strangest mouth; a soft mouth, with the lips puckered up as if he was about to whistle. As with all good paintings, the eyes followed you whenever you moved.

"Lord Mellinger?" I asked; yet somehow I had no doubt.

"It's considered a very passable likeness."

"A fine piece of work," said I. Still the eyes mocked me.

"You'll have come to pay your respects?" Miss Drummond sounded positively reverent. She seemed to regard her late employer as some kind of god, and she herself the guardian of his work, his reputation and his fame. She gave us a catalogue of eminent scientists who had visited the island since his death; and led us from room to room like a professional guide – which I suspect she now was – pointing out his study, his favourite chair, his last known written words, and the window where he stood to admire a favourite view.

"It's no' raining much," she declared. "You'll have to watch the tide. Never mind, there's time to visit the tomb before you go."

Neither of us particularly wanted to see Lord Mellinger's tomb, but it was vital to keep on the good side of his secretary, so we followed her obediently to the cliff top where a mausoleum had been erected; a monstrous edifice of marble topped by an angel pointing out to sea. We made suitable notes of appreciation. I was quite interested in the prescription, which read:

ALISTAIR DUNCAN, LORD MELLINGER
1831–1906
EGO VENIAM AD TE

"You'll be aware of the meaning?" She seemed eager to tell me.

"Well, yes. 'I shall come to you'."

"That would be an angel, or happen St. Peter himself, come to guide his Lordship into heaven. I had it done by a stonemason in Inverness."

Masterson uttered a comment which, mercifully, I failed to hear.

"Was Lord Mellinger religious?"

"He had his convictions," said Miss Drummond primly.

123

I remained curious about the Latin. The lady explained that she had found a scrap of paper amongst the bedclothes after her employer died.

"I canna tell you how it got there. He lacked the strength to have written it himself; perhaps some visitor did it for him. He had so many visitors towards the end." And then, as if seized by a horrid doubt, she said anxiously, "I take it the words are quite proper?"

Oh yes, I assured her; entirely proper and appropriate. She smiled at that, and led us back into what she described as the Green Drawing-Room. It had really gone on long enough; I decided that we could fairly state our business now. I brought the conversation round to Lord Mellinger's bequest, the books she had so kindly had sent to me, and (carefully, anxious not to give offence) the one book which seemed to be missing.

"Oh, my goodness!" Her discomfiture was painful to see. One hand flew to her mouth. She was clearly appalled by the suggestion that she had failed in her duty, that she had not carried out Lord Mellinger's dying wish. It became even more obvious to both of us that she worshipped the man. She kept repeating, "*New Thynking*? *New Thynking*?" Then she darted from the room, and could be heard moving about upstairs.

It was all very unfortunate. To make it worse, the light began to fade; grey shadows appeared on the carpet, while Mellinger ancestors leered at us through the gloom. I had no desire to cross the causeway in the dark, and said as much to George Masterman.

"I canna find it!"

Poor Miss Drummond looked so flustered, so utterly cast down, that I had to reassure her.

"Come," I said, "I feel certain the book will turn up. Please don't upset yourself." An idea struck me. "Tell me, did Lord Mellinger remember you in his will?"

She drew herself up, lips pursed, eyes widening in reproach. "Oh no," she replied. "I never expected nor received any legacy myself. It would have been most unsuitable."

I had offended her. Never mind, I had discovered a useful fact: Miss Drummond was in need of money. On a slip of paper I wrote the title of the volume and printed my name and address. I would, I told her, be most grateful if she would post the book to me when he found it. Moreover, I would be happy to pay her a reasonable price for it. "Shall we say fifty pounds?"

"You'll not be serious! Fifty – oh no! I couldn't. You mustn't. His Lordship gifted it to you."

"Ah, but since you are going to a great deal of trouble, and may have to spend a lot of time searching for it, it's only fair that I should recompense you."

I smiled, and she blushed and thanked me. She seemed content, and so was I – confident that the moment we had gone Miss Drummond would tear the house to pieces to find *New Thynking on Mortalitie*. As we shook hands there came a kind of howl from George Masterman, who had been standing at the window.

"James!"

"All right, George, we can go now."

"You think so? Look!"

I joined him. Outside the grounds lay thick in mist. Beyond the beach waves heaved towards the shore, and the causeway –

There was no causeway.

The tide had come in.

Poor Isobel Drummond started apologising all over again; she should have kept her eye on the clock, she had entirely forgotten the time of day … Under questioning, she admitted that there was no boat. Lord Mellinger had valued his privacy, and travelled to Edinburgh no more than twice a year. Provisions were delivered to the island from the Tontine Arms, and since his Lordships died there was a ferry, which brought the visitors across to pay their respects plus four shillings to view the house.

"But not on Sundays."

There was no need for Masterman to sound so peevish. It was an accident, nobody's fault. It would not do to blame the lady, who in tones of mounting distress offered us a bed for the night.

"And you'd like some tea and a bit of Cumberland sausage? Oh dear me, what an awful thing to have happened." She bustled about making preparations, leaving us in the main hall where the great portrait of Lord Mellinger loomed above our heads.

And still the eyes mocked me.

Eventually we were shown into a bedroom with one curved window looking out across the Atlantic. By now night had fallen in a black swoop, brushing the coastline away and leaving nothing behind save a cluster of lights which betrayed the presence of the Tontine Arms. The Tontine Arms. Dinner. Oh dear. It must be at least half past seven; our landlord would not be pleased.

I do not sleep well in strange houses; I dislike impromptu arrangements. Planned visits can be most agreeable, but to be stranded on an island with some unknown Scottish lady … Either the surroundings or the meal (which consisted of a circular object full of mince, altogether too much hot tea, and a plate of what Miss Drummond called Baps and Butteries) had thoroughly disturbed my

125

digestion and I slept not at all. Around two in the morning I gave up any pretence of rest and wandered over to the window, wrapped in my overcoat. The worst of these misadventures is that your find yourself without the basic necessities, such as night wear, a toothbrush or a razor.

It had grown abominably cold, and a full moon lit up the cliff top in glacial light. I could see the Mellinger monument. I could see … Good heavens.

"Masterman! Wake up, wake up!"

He stirred, then sat up in bed, grumbling. "What is it? What's the time? What are you doing?"

"Look!" I cried. "No, I'm not mistaken. Look! Look at the tomb!"

Even as I spoke, two figures broke clear of the mausoleum and stood etched against the sky. They leapt in the air and clasped hands; one threw back his head in what seemed to be triumphant laughter. Then they wheeled, swung down the path, and were gone."

"Dear God!"

"Grave robbers!"

We both moved together, George pausing only to put on shoes and grab his coat. We hurled ourselves down the stairway and struggled with the massive front door bolts. The next moment we were out in the icy night air and running, running, running; along the path to the mausoleum, then down the cliff path and onto the beach.

The place was not big, and yet we could not find them. Two men had most certainly run from the tomb, and there had not been time for them to vanish. We stopped. Our breath formed little puffs of mist, and poor Masterman gasped in distress.

"James, James, how did they get here?"

"What's that?" I gazed around in bewilderment.

"The causeway is still covered! How did they get here? By boat?"

We listened, but could hear no betraying splash of oars, no sound of any engine. We walked across the whole island and could find nothing: no dinghy hidden in the curve of the cliff, no trace of any men. The island held very little in the way of vegetation; there was hardly a tree, only a few coarse bushes, and no buildings apart from The Manse. The villains must be hiding. But if hiding, then where?

Footsteps crunched on the stone. George swung round, crying "There they are!" But it was Isobel Drummond, wrapped in a cloak and carrying a lantern. She looked understandably frightened. We told her the reason for our search, and in my mind's eye I once more saw those two figures leaping in the moonlight, giving an impression of overwhelming joy. Together we made for the mausoleum, to see what damage had been done; and there we suffered the worst shock of all.

The monument had been broken open with an axe or some such tool. The doors gaped wide open, giving a clear view of the coffin. Wood lay in splintered pieces on the ground.

The coffin was empty.

On the whole, Miss Drummond behaved with admirable composure. I feared the lady might faint or succumb to hysterics. But she led us back into the house and suggested hot tea. Far into the night we sat debating the whole horrific incident. Ultimately, only two solutions presented themselves: either Lord Mellinger's body had been stolen for unspecified medical reasons, or Lord Mellinger had not been buried on the island at all.

With this last hypothesis in mind, we crossed back to the mainland the next day and called on Dr. Ian Rossiter. His reaction was not, perhaps, surprising.

"That is a very wild story, gentlemen."

Dr. Rossiter was a stocky fellow in tweeds. He pulled on his pipe and eyed us sardonically. Yes, he knew Miss Drummond well. Yes, he had attended Lord Mellinger in his last illness, and had signed the death certificate when his Lordship died of bronchial pneumonia on March the fourth.

"Forgive me," I said, "but there is no doubt the man was dead?"

Dr. Rossiter lifted one eyebrow.

"What kind of question is that? I am a doctor, sir."

I apologised. The fact remained, however, that we had found the grave empty and the body gone.

"If you query my professional competence, you'd best have a word with the Reverend Matthew Craigie," said Rossiter bleakly. "He buried the man."

We left in some confusion, and retreated to the Tontine Arms, there to be met by an angry landlord who declared that we had ordered dinner and not appeared to it so we would be charged for the wasted food; and where in the name of Godliness had we spent the night? He bolted the door at half past ten, all decent people being asleep by that hour. On hearing that we had been stranded on St. Wulfran's island, he gave a grim smile, apparently well pleased that the heathen had met their just deserts. I changed the subject and asked him for the address of Mr. Matthew Craigie. This pacified him, indicating – as it seemed – that we were not entirely lost souls.

The Reverend Mr. Craigie had a small beard. Notwithstanding this, he seemed young, and excitable. He spoke at length of the subject of Lord Mellinger.

"He published a large number of ... questionable books."

"Oh, come," I protested. "He was a famous person, a scientific humanist. Have you read any of his works?"

"I have not." His beard positively bristled. "I go to considerable lengths to avoid seditious literature, and I am happy to say that none of my congregation would touch it."

"You would forbid them?"

"I would."

"Did his Lordship ever visit this part of the mainland?" asked Masterman.

"Not sufficiently often to corrupt us."

"Ah." My friend pressed his point. Evidently a new theory had occurred to him. "But people went to the island? Visitors from London, Paris, Berlin."

"Only after he died, sir, by which time he was incapable of further harm."

I seized the cue. That, I told him, was the reason for our interest. Lord Mellinger had died ...?

"Even the wicked come to dust, sir."

"Indeed, yes, quite – but is he dead?"

Matthew Craigie looked astonished, as well he might. "I buried him myself, disregarding the fact that the man was a free thinker."

I hastened to explain – before he began to doubt my sanity – that we brought the melancholy news that the tomb had been broken and the body stolen.

"Oh, aye."

He knew. Beyond question, he already knew. Mr. Craigie shook his head sadly. "This is the devil's work, sir."

"It is also," said Masterman tartly, "a matter for the police."

It was not, it turned out, so very odd. It emerged that Isobel Drummond had sent Mr. Craigie a message. Well, why not? The poor lady must be distraught, and would naturally call for her spiritual adviser.

The Reverend Mr. Craigie?

But Craigie never set foot on the island.

Disaster makes strange companions. Her employer had certainly been a humanist, but Miss Drummond herself might be ...

What?

Oh, come, come, come! An unhappy woman had turned to the nearest person for comfort.

Why had she done it so quickly?

128

To get help?

Or to forestall us?

We argued the matter all the way back to the Tontine Arms. Miss Drummond had remained calm in circumstances which might have driven a lesser character to hysteria. Was there some undercurrent we had failed to detect, a hidden plot? As we came into the bar, the landlord stopped us, saying, "There's a visitor for you. I put him in the snug?"

A visitor? We exchanged glances. Very few people knew we were up in Scotland, and nobody had the address of the Tontine Arms.

A figure rose from the fireside. "Dr. James! We meet again. This is indeed a joyous occasion, how are you, my dear sir?"

It was Arthur Sinclair, complete with grin.

At this point my suspicions came bubbling to the surface once more. Very well; Isobel Drummond had sent for Matthew Craigie, but who had sent for Mr. Sinclair – and how, come to that, had he got himself there at all? The journey north took a minimum of three days and involved four changes on the railway. Only one explanation held any water. The wretched man had been following us.

Why?

One can read too much into coincidence. The fellow was, after all, executor of Lord Mellinger's estate. It would be normal for him to travel to St. Wulfran's island on business; his appearance might have nothing to do with ...

I was proved wrong again. He threw his arms wide, advanced on me, and cried, "I took the wings of the morning! Rejoice! Rejoice! I bring good news!"

And he handed me *New Thynking on Mortalitie*.

It was a small volume, bound in dark leather, the pages uneven and creased and stained with age. A first glance showed at least two beautifully illuminated texts. Wonderful! I turned the pages with reverence, while Sinclair babbled on about lost crates, incompetence, endless regret, and eternal shame. I could not wait for him to stop so that I could be alone with the book. George Masterman was saying something about the island.

"... you heard? Lord Mellinger's tomb has been robbed."

"Oh dear me, yes indeed, I had word of it only this morning when I arrived. What a terrible visitation; what heathen times do we live in! A sad world, Dr. James, when even the dead cannot rest in peace!" His eyes rolled in suitable dismay, and still his mouth grinned.

129

No matter. I had the book. Clutching *New Thynking on Mortalitie* to my chest, I thanked Sinclair and fled upstairs to my room. I lit a candle, for the light had almost gone, and settled down greedily to examine the text.

Masterman came up some time later, only to hear my cry of indignation.

"Oh, no no no! This is altogether too bad!"

"James? What's wrong?"

"Someone," I said grimly, "someone has torn three pages out of the book."

"Are you sure?"

"See for yourself!" I held it out to him. It was only too easy to see where a sharp instrument had been run along the binding; at one point a fragment of parchment still remained. I rose, slightly incoherent with anger.

"Upon my word, I shall have something to say to Mr. Arthur Sinclair! The impudence of the man! He can't do this ..."

"I'm afraid he's gone, James."

"What? Gone? Where?"

But Masterman, not unnaturally, had no idea. Neither had the landlord, who merely volunteered the information that the gentleman had drunk a glass of port wine and left. He had seemed, added the landlord, to be in high good spirits.

"Confound his impudence!" My first instinct was to rush across to St. Wulfran's island and protest in the strongest possible terms to Miss Drummond. It was George who pointed out to sea and indicated the difficulty here: the causeway had again vanished under water. It was late, and no boatman would agree to ferry us across. There was nothing for it but to contain my fury, wait for morning, struggle across those slimy stones ... It might be easier to hire a boat instead; in daylight there should be no problem.

There was not, and next morning saw Miss Drummond receiving us complacently and offering tea. The police had visited the island; the tomb appeared to be badly damaged; official investigations were under way. On hearing my news she smoothed her skirts and said, "So you've found your wee book? I'm awful happy for you. Now you can both go home."

Why did I begin to believe that all these people were in a conspiracy against me? There were, I told her, three pages missing from the book. Someone had deliberately cut out and removed ...

"Oh, aye. Will you take sugar?"

No apology! No surprise! I could have sworn the lady already knew. I said as much.

She nodded. "Lord Mellinger did that."

"He cut them out *himself*?" My astonishment showed in my voice.

"During his last sickness, it would be. He asked for the book, cut some bits from the binding, and told me to burn them."

Masterman put his head in his hands. I could not hide my own dismay. This marvellous volume had been deliberately ruined and by the owner … a flicker of hope came to me.

"I suppose – forgive me, Miss Drummond – I take it you did carry out his Lordship's orders?"

"I did indeed." The prim mouth tightened; she was understandably offended. "I took them from his very hand, carried them into the kitchen, and pitched the lot straight into the stove."

George groaned.

"Oh, there was no problem about that, they burnt awful easy."

"Thank you," I said, and rose. "There was no point in staying; the disaster had been complete. I made for the door and she stopped me, blocking the way out.

"You'll excuse me, sir, were you wanting to read those pages?"

"It can't be helped, madam. Never mind." It was, after all, not her fault.

"I can show them to you if you're minded to have a look."

I stared at her. So did Masterman.

"Naturally," said Miss Drummond sedately, "naturally I copied the words before ever I burnt the original. I thought to myself, maybe some day someone could want a wee peep. Is it worth money to you?"

Well, well, well. I continue to be astonished by the oblique reasoning of some women. I paid her without argument and we hurried back to the Tontine Arms in triumph.

She had given us a child's exercise book, filled with several pages of careful lettering. Many of the words were either misspelled or miscopied. No matter. We had the essential material, the complete text of *New Thynking on Mortalitie*. My friend lit the candles, locked the door, and together we sat down to study it.

I am not sure what we expected.

I don't know why we locked the door.

The contents seemed bizarre, macabre; a story of the two monks – Brother Simeon and Brother Elihu, both at the monastery of Elston – who grieved over the death of learning. It seemed to them monstrous that a man must die before he could acquire true wisdom. The one of them (it did not say which) by the grace of God discovered – Oh, no, no, no.

"James!"

George had left the translation to me; he has some Latin, but not enough to cope with a mediaeval text. "What does it say?"

"If we are to believe this," I told him, "they discovered how to raise the dead."

Someone knocked at the door. "You'll be careful with those candles?" shouted the landlord. Yes, I cried, yes, we would be careful.

"This is nonsense." Masterman took the copybook from me.

"Yet the grave was empty."

We gazed at each other, neither of us prepared to accept that these long-dead monks could perform miracles. I must have misunderstood or mis-translated. I reached for the book and continued.

After many days spent in fasting and diligent prayer, they determined that the knowledge was not for the generality of people, but for them alone as holy Christian scholars. Then did they petition Almighty God and swore a pact, by which whoever died first would be resurrected by the other, and so it was to be century after century until they heard the very shout of Judgement Day.

Masterman rose impatiently. "You've made a mistake."

Certainly it defied all reason; the image of these two men leap-frogging down the years, surviving, immortal. And yet Lord Mellinger wanted his library to be kept intact at King's College in perpetuity, the collection on no account to be split up.

"For pity's sake, James! What are you saying? Do you expect Lord Mellinger to materialise in some form and continue studying his work?"

Put that way, it did indeed sound preposterous. I had a sudden memory of that great portrait hanging in The Manse, the tall figure in an academic gown, the fluffy red hair, the too-small mouth pursed as if to whistle.

It would not do. I re-read the Latin and realised there were further complications. "If," said I, "if for the sake of argument Lord Mellinger was the reincarnation of Brother Simeon – or Brother Elihu – then who and where do you suppose is the reincarnation of Brother Elihu – or Brother Simeon?"

He stared at me.

"There were two of them," I reminded him.

George Masterman seized the candle, causing long shadows to rush across the wall. "In the name of sanity, let's go down to warmth and dinner!"

The landlord informed us that we were too late for dinner, and he could only offer cold lamb pastry and cheese. Both were singularly nasty.

In the morning we escaped from the Tontine Arms, driven by a powerful curiosity and à determination to resolve the matter. Heavy rain clouds masked the sky, and a thin drizzle hid St. Wulfran's island from our view. Alas, our enquiries came to nought. Mr. Sinclair had vanished; Mr. Rossiter was visiting the sick on some remote Western isle; Miss Drummond had left the night before, giving no address; and the Reverend Mr. Matthew Craigie had departed for his annual holiday, which he always spent at the Kirrieglen Health Spa.

When there is only one lead, you must of necessity follow it. I left a message at The Manse in the faint hope that either Sinclair or Miss Drummond would reappear. Then, through a Scottish mist which was turning rapidly into pelting rain, we set out for the Highlands and the Kirrieglen Health Spa.

It resembled nothing so much as a French chateau imperfectly remembered by a drunken architect. It had a great number of steep-angled roofs, rounded turrets, thin windows and a twin tower at either end, and stood in vast area of very beautiful grounds kept to perfection. A number of persons (patients, presumably) were wandering contentedly along the paths. We made ourselves known, and were greeted by a smiling gentleman of foreign extraction.

"Good morning! If I might present myself – I am Joel Liebeck, Director of the Kirrieglen Spa, and you are –" He beamed amiably at us, and we gave our names. "Excellent! Welcome! You have been recommended, perhaps? Your doctor advised you to come here? What is the complaint? *Ach*, no, you do not tell me, I shall tell you. You have rheumatism. A hardening of the arteries. A difficulty in breathing and a touch of gout in the great toe."

I assured him that either of us had any of these multiple disorders; we were simply looking for a friend, a clergyman. Was there a reverend gentleman staying with him?

"Of course. Large numbers." We must have looked surprised, for he continued, "When I opened the spa in 1886 it was with monies supplied from the Church, and on the understanding that members of the clergy should have the most inexpensive charges and sometimes even free treatment. There are always clergymen here, my dear sir. Which one do you want?"

"Craigie," I replied, "Mr. Matthew Craigie."

"Come! Come! We shall look!"

I think both of us believed we were going to search for the Reverend Mr. Craigie. It seemed that Mr. Liebek had other ideas; he clearly intended to give us a conducted tour of his Spa. He led us down innumerable passages, opening doors as we went.

"Here you see our Hydropathic chambers. In here we have the Vichy Douche; three jets of water are directed forcibly against the striped body."

George let out a chuckle, instantly suppressed. "Stripped," I whispered. "I think he means stripped."

"No zebras amongst his patients?"

"Do be quiet, George. Let us at least remember our manners."

"For rheumatic diseases we recommend the *Fango di Battaglia*, or Volcanic mud bath – *ach*, so sorry, I believe one person is in there at the moment."

A bubbling noise escaped into the corridor, followed by muffled curses. The whole place reeked of some peculiar herb. We had a duty to be courteous but this could not go on. I caught up with our host.

"Mr. Liebek, we are not ill. We merely wish to find Mr. Craigie. Would you be kind enough to see if he is on your register of guests?"

"With the greatest pleasure. Please wait for me, I shall return here."

He left us standing in an echoing hall. From time to time uniformed figures – presumably nurses – hurried by. One of them stopped and said to Masterman, "You should be in the Electric Impulse Chamber." Then taking a closer look, he added, "I beg your pardon, sir, I thought you were somebody else."

It was my turn to suppress a laugh. It was very difficult not to be amused by such outlandish apparatus. What earthly good were they supposed to do? However, health does, to a certain degree, lie in the mind. If the patients were satisfied with their treatment …

A man wrapped in a Turkish towel came down the passage towards us. I caught only a brief glimpse of his face as he went by, but that one glance gave me a considerable shock.

"Good heavens!" I exclaimed. "I've just seen a friend."

"What? Who? What are you talking about? Where are you going –"

There was no time to answer him. I made off in pursuit, and saw my quarry vanish through a door labelled 'Vibrator Room'. I reached for the knob as George caught up with me.

"Monty, you can't go in there!"

"Why not?"

"Because you've got your clothes on!"

I knocked. The next moment a scarlet face appeared, snarling. "Go away, sir! I am booked in Vibration for the next half an hour!"

"Good morning," said I. "My apologies, sir. Masterman, you do remember Dr. Rossiter of course?"

The doctor stood there, half-visible through clouds of steam, and manifestly rather startled. At this point the situation was complicated by the return of Mr. Liebek, who was clearly not pleased to find us wandering through his establishment on our own. Before he could give rein to the full extent of his displeasure, I told him that we were most impressed, and wished to sign on for a weekend cure. He smiled at that, a slow, fat grin, and led us away to register. Dr. Rossiter had vanished.

At least now I had the opportunity to examine the guest registry. I found Craigie's name with no difficulty, but there was no Rossiter listed; the man had obviously booked in under a false name. I tried to pacify George, who seethed beside me in Reception.

"Are you mad?" he hissed. "We shall have to take medicine, and we shall probably be subjected to those lunatic machines: the Vichy Douche, the *Fango di Battaglia*, the Schnee Four Cell Electric Bath …"

"I hadn't noticed that one."

"Monty!"

I tried to pacify him. We should now, I told him, be in a position to confront Dr. Rossiter and discover why he was at a health spa and not on one of the Western Islands comforting his patients. I anticipated a tricky and time-consuming search – always supposing the good doctor had not already fled – but in the event it proved quite simple: Dr. Rossiter came to look for us.

He appeared – fully clothed – in the Aquatic Gardens, sounding apologetic. He admitted freely to the false name of Smith, and begged us to respect his secrecy. It seemed that his friend, Matthew Craigie, invariably took his holidays at the spa, and came back speaking in the most extravagant terms of the various treatments, the wonder medicines, the miracle cures. Dr. Rossiter regarded these claims with deep suspicion, suspecting them to be bogus. He feared that his old friend was being swindled; in brief, he was there to conduct an investigation, and possibly to expose Mr. Liebek.

It sounded so confoundedly reasonable.

We located Matthew Craigie, who told us that he was enjoying a well-deserved rest. We discussed the robbing of the grave on St. Wulfran's island, and we were assured that the police had the matter under control. Neither of us could bring ourselves to mention *New Thynking on Mortalitie* or raise the question of the missing pages. Away from the island, and in the respectable atmosphere of this spa for the benefit of the clergy, our fears seemed altogether too unlikely.

Masterman wanted to leave at once; but we had paid for the weekend. There were also, I must confess, doubts lingering in my mind. Everything was so plausible.

Too plausible?

There had been something in Dr. Rossiter's eyes when he explained his presence at Kirrieglen; as if he were laughing at me.

Frankly, I mistrusted the whole pack of them. It would not have surprised me to see Miss Isobel Drummond walking through the gardens. No; there was an explanation, and I had to find it.

Thus it was that next morning, despite George's yelps of protest, we found ourselves undergoing treatment in the Nebulor Apparatus. This consisted of a box-like cell where we lay prone, strapped to a couch, while noxious gas hissed through pipes in the ceiling and Mr. Liebek himself could be observed nodding his head behind a glass partition. He urged us to relax, shouting above the hiss of the vapour to assure us that the Nebulor Apparatus had been used by foreign royalty, and was unsurpassed for purging the system whilst stimulating the liver.

I decided the man was a charlatan, and hoped Dr. Rossiter would succeed in unmasking him.

Dr. Rossiter?

Did we really believe his story? Come to that was the Reverend Mr. Craigie really here on holiday? The mist now filling the room smelled disgusting. Where was Miss Drummond? Where had Arthur Sinclair gone? Suppose we had accidentally stumbled on a gang of villains bent on some horrid crime? A very nasty thought struck me. It would be all too easy to dispose of Masterman and me as we lay there, helpless.

"George!"

My companion had gone to sleep.

I tried to rise, but broad straps prevented me. I rolled on one side, but choking fumes filled my lungs and sheer dizziness cause me to roll back. By now I was convinced we were about to be murdered …

A gust of air swept into the cell.

"You feel much better," declared Mr. Liebek. He shook me vigorously, peered down my throat, and undid the fastenings, explaining all the time how very well I had become. Then he said, "Be pleased to dress yourself. You have a visitor."

A few minutes later we were following him across the gardens into the main building. There in the entrance hall stood Arthur Sinclair.

"Dr. James! How very wise, a health cure, oh, capital, capital, worth the money I'm sure."

This was pushing coincidence altogether too far. I asked how in heaven's name he had managed to find us. He seemed rather hurt, though his grin remained in place.

"You sent for me, dear sir."

"What?"

George reminded me in a whisper that I had indeed left a message at St. Wulfran's island, giving our movements and probable address.

"There is a problem?" continued Sinclair. "You are in difficulties? How can I be of assistance?"

"The grave robbers," I stammered, somewhat incoherent in my confusion.

"Oh dear me, they have not yet been caught, though Mr. Craigie – you'll be acquainted with the Reverend Mr. Craigie? – has prayed for further information, which will no doubt be forthcoming before long, and will guide the police to the original sinners."

I had had enough of play-acting. I came to a decision.

"Matthew Craigie is here. So is Dr. Ian Rossiter. So are you."

"Well met, sir, well met." The grin broadened.

"Mr. Sinclair," I said, "I propose to be frank with you."

"Oh, excellent! Very good, very good. Openness is all. Let there be honesty between us!"

"Yes!" I stared him full in the face, while doors banged, machinery hummed, and the corridors filled with vapour from the Kirrieglen baths. I put my cards on the table, omitting nothing. I even produced the notebook, and read him the history of Brother Elihu and Brother Simeon. "What do you make of that, sir?"

His mouth dropped. I waited for fear; confusion; even a full confession. His eyes held mine.

"Did you offer Miss Drummond money?" murmured Arthur Sinclair; and his words held unmistakable irony.

Do you know, it had never occurred to us. Yet now that he said it, the thing became obvious. That wretched woman had faked the story.

"Oh dear me, what a shame to disillusion you both! I am not questioning her character – heaven forbid! – only the lady is in straitened circumstances, you see. Don't think too badly of her! You asked for a mediaeval text, and you got a mediaeval text – in her own handwriting, too!" He grinned. He really had far too many teeth.

My heart sank. He was right. I had put the offer to Miss Drummond; I had put the idea into her head myself. We made some excuse and retreated to our bedroom.

Masterman flung himself down and asked, "Well? Where do we go from here?"

"Home," I said bitterly. It was a complete anti-climax. Dr. Rossiter was simply a country doctor. The Reverend Mr. Craigie was just a parish priest. *New Thynking on Mortalitie* was merely a piece of sixteenth century hocus pocus.

The missing pages?

An accident. Only too probably after so many years.

The empty grave?

A rather nasty, but definitely modern, crime, best left in the hands of the police.

To complete my discomfort, they were all present at dinner. Dr. Rossiter saw me and dodged behind a pillar. Mr. Craigie raised one hand in blessing. Mr. Sinclair half-rose from his seat and bowed. I studied the room – old discoloured faces, young bland faces, mouths opening, mouths shutting, false teeth clamped tight on threads of dangling celery –

None of them looked in the least like Lord Mellinger.

How did Brother Elihu and Brother Simeon look once they had been resurrected? Did the monkish travellers retain their youth? Or acquire a new body? Had both of them been invented by Miss Drummond? My stomach heaved, partly from the absurdity of my thoughts and partly from undigested red lentils. I rose and suggested we retire to bed.

"You mean to leave tomorrow, James?"

"I do indeed," I replied. "Before Mr. Liebek has an opportunity to try any more of his monstrous cures on us."

Some time in the middle of the night I woke from a disjointed dream, in which I had been caught and imprisoned in the Schnee Four Cell Electric Bath while Mr. Liebek loomed over me crying, "You are much improved, Dr. James!" It was a strange remark for him to make, as my body seemed to be shrinking to half its normal size. I fought against his clutching hands.

"James, James, wake up!"

Somebody was shaking me violently. I struggled free of my dream, but still the nightmare persisted. A mist hung over my bed; an acrid smell of burning. Even as I rose to fumble for my shoes I heard a sound of running footsteps, distant shouts, and a piercing scream.

"Fire! Fire, fire, *fire!*"

"For God's sake, move! The hotel's on fire!"

The whole room seemed to be filling with smoke. Masterman seized a towel and plunged it in the water jug, then repeated the process with a face flannel, which he flung to me. Together we made for the door, keeping as low as possible and holding the damp cloths across our noses and mouths. In the corridor, several people were running for the stairs. We clung to the bannister rail, for it had become extremely difficult to see. We reached the great hall and emerged, gasping, into the night.

A hundred or so people were gathered on the lawn. Most were in their night clothes, though some had obviously had time to throw on overcoats, and a few carried belongings – a jewel case, a fur coat, even, ludicrously, an umbrella. A woman who appeared to have lost her child pushed hysterically through the crowd. Several men were draped in blankets. I saw Matthew Craigie, his hands clasped in futile prayer, and Mr. Liebek, his legs bare under a hunting jacket, staring blindly at the building while tears slid down his cheeks. Presently a young girl came and led him away. Rossiter went past me, shouting, "Check all the names! Has anyone got the register? Check the names!"

The babble sank to an appalled silence as we gazed up at the Kirrieglen Health Spa. Flames spurted from the top windows, light flared behind the turrets and vanished to reappear further down, and parts of the roof which were still untouched showed in black silhouette against a night sky which had turned crimson. There was a crash of falling masonry.

"Get off the lawn!" cried Rossiter. "Everybody move away! Move away! Get as far from the house as possible!"

Nobody moved. We seemed frozen in a horrified set piece; it was as if we were all turned to stone. As we stood there, a figure broke loose and ran towards the blazing entrance, screaming as he went, "I must have the body! I must have the body! *I must have the body!*"

It was Arthur Sinclair.

Before anybody could stop him – before any of us fully realised what was going on – he evaded Rossiter's restraining hand and vanished into the inferno. A single cry echoed above the splintering wood and exploding glass.

"*Simeon!*"

They never found his corpse.

Come to that, they never found the corpse of anybody else.

*

A year or so later I read an item in the paper to the effect that the Kirrieglen Health Spa had been rebuilt, and would reopen to the public with suitable pomp and ceremony.

I shall not visit it. I wish Kirrieglen well, if only for the sake of poor Mr. Liebek; long may he live to practise his outlandish cures. They may well benefit his patients, so long as they believe in them. Belief is all.

What do I believe? Ah. I find myself forced back into my usual position. I neither believe nor disbelieve. I await the evidence. *New Thynking on Mortalitie* was, alas, destroyed in the fire. Time has dulled my memory, and I think it entirely possible that I misheard that final, frantic scream from Arthur Sinclair.

"*Simeon!*"

He may have said something else. Only – did it never occur to Brother Elihu and Brother Simeon that they might die together?

The books still lie, undisturbed, on the shelves of King's College. Late at night, when the gas jets flicker and small shadows leap along the wall, I have a horrid fear. One day a young man may present himself in my study, demand to see the books – and display a wisdom quite out of keeping with his age.

DAEMONOLOGIE

Throughout the history of modern Britain, Scotland has been an intellectual powerhouse. From the Age of Enlightenment onwards, Scots have contributed enormously to the cultural development of the United Kingdom. Yet in the not-too-distant past, like so many other regions of the British Isles, Scotland was cursed by a period of extremely irrational thought. During the 16th and 17th centuries, mainly as an offshoot of the Wars of Religion following the Protestant Reformation, Scottish paranoia that the Devil and his minions were on their doorstep became all-consuming. In fact, in Scotland, witches and warlocks were more feared than almost anywhere else in Britain.

Partly this was due to the fact that James VI of Scotland (1566-1625), who became James I of England in 1603, was a firm believer in witchcraft. In 1597 he published his own book on the matter, 'Daemonologie', in which he proposed various means by which to detect and punish such felons. It was hugely influential – after all, if the king himself said witches were real, there was surely no argument. As such, the penalties in Scotland were excessively severe: conviction for merely practising sorcery carried the death sentence, whereas in England only the commission of murder by sorcery brought that final sanction. And in Scotland it was death by burning, whereas in England it was death by hanging.

Three particular stories from the Highlands of Scotland give deeper insights than most into the practise of and belief in witchcraft in that chaotic era.

The trial of Isobel Gowdie in 1662 is particularly informative. An Auldearn housewife, Gowdie was arrested that year for reasons unrecorded. But she freely admitted crimes of witchcraft without having been tortured, and produced an amazingly detailed confession in which she claimed to have been baptised by Satan himself (calling him "a meikle black man"), participated in demonic orgies, and had transformed herself on occasion into a hare, a cat and a jackdaw. She even claimed that she had feasted with the Faerie Queen underneath the Downy Hills. Perhaps more seriously, she also admitted that she and other Auldearn witches were responsible for the untimely deaths of the Laird of Park's children, having roasted their effigies in a magical fire. Given that so much of the confession has been preserved, it is difficult to understand why no record was kept concerning Gowdie's fate, but *though it is possible she was spared after turning evidence against her coven, most likely she too was burned.*

An even more sensational case is that of the Goodwife of Laggan, a well-regarded village woman who sometime in the mid-17ᵗʰ century suffered a brutal death at the hands of her neighbours. A local hunter and a noted hater of witches (!) was out one night in the Forest of Gaick, near Badenoch, when he was caught in foul weather. Taking shelter in a bothy, he lit himself a fire and lay down to sleep with his two hounds – when a voice suddenly called his name from the darkness outside. The hunter demanded to know who it was. The voice replied that she was a woman who had sold her soul to Satan but now repented of this and thought he was the person to help her. The hunter bade her enter, but she requested first that he tie up his dogs. Suspicious, the hunter only pretended to leash the two beasts. To his astonishment, a cat then entered the bothy. To his even greater astonishment, this cat transformed into a woman he knew and respected from his own village. She spat and hissed, telling him that only that morning she had drowned a famous witch-hunter in the Sound of Raasay, and that now she would kill him too. She leapt forward with cat claws extended, but the two hounds attacked her savagely, sending her shrieking into the night. The following day, when the hunter returned to Laggan, he found the woman ailing in her bed, under the care of neighbours who'd presumed she was ill. The hunter told his story, and when the bedclothes were torn away, the woman's wounds were visible for all to see. The villagers were so persuaded by this that no trial was deemed necessary. Despite her protestations, the Goodwife of Laggan was hauled from her cottage and hanged on a nearby tree. Later that night, another local man who had not been present at the lynching, arrived breathless in the village, claiming to have seen the Goodwife stumbling bloodied and wailing along the moorland road, under pursuit by a masked black rider and two hellish hounds.

While there may be some truth in that latter tale, namely that a village woman was suspected of witchcraft and died at the hands of a raging mob, belief in witches and their powers was widespread enough even among the educated classes of the Highlands to create some peculiar circumstances.

In the mid-16ᵗʰ century for example, George Gordon, 4ᵗʰ Earl of Huntly and Chief of the Gordon Clan, was an influential nobleman and proficient soldier. He won an impressive victory over the English at the battle of Haddon Rigg in 1542, and survived the Scottish defeat at Pinkie Cleugh in 1547. In 1560 he joined the Lords of the Congregation, a group of Protestant Scottish noblemen, but later gave his allegiance to Mary Stuart, the Catholic

Queen of Scots, only turning against her when she awarded the Earldom of Moray, a traditional Huntly property, to her own half-brother. Gordon went fully to war with Mary in 1562, when he marched against her forces at Aberdeen, meeting her at Corrichie. On the eve of the battle, he sought the advice of the notorious Strathbogie Witches, who prophesied that when the war was done he would lie in the Aberdeen Tolbooth without a wound on his body. During the course of the fighting, which the Queen of Scots herself watched from a chair-shaped stone high on the Hill of Fare, Gordon, encouraged by the prophecy, was fearless but ultimately unsuccessful. Once it was over and his army broken, he was taken prisoner but left physically unscathed. He toasted the knowledge of the Strathbogie Witches – then fell from his horse in an apoplectic fit, which subsequently claimed his life. As the witches had foretold, he did indeed lie in the Tolbooth without a wound.

But he was dead all the same.

SHELLEYCOAT
Graeme Hurry

He was in a white cell of billowing cloud a metre or so wide. Thick mist isolating reality, hiding destination and departure point. But worse was the *clink* and *rattle* noise. Continuously circling, just out of sight ...

Two hours before it had been so easy. Three o'clock in the afternoon, a lovely bright day and hours of daylight left for him to walk to his designated B&B. The train had dropped Colin off at the slightly touristy village and he had tramped in the direction his iPhone suggested. On his way out through the outskirts of the town he had found a pub. As he had stood outside it he looked over the grassy glen and, in the near distance, had seen the guesthouse where he was to spend the night.

Within easy reach. Surely less than an hour's walk? So what was the harm in spending an hour or two having a meal and a pint?

Homemade food and locally brewed cask ales enticed him from the pub signs. It would also be nice to rest his shoulders from carrying his heavy rucksack for a while.

He pushed open the inner glazed door and walked into the baking heat of an open fire, which was both stifling and welcoming, reminding him that though the sun shone brightly, the air temperature outside was in single figures. The bar contained four people. The barman, one solitary drinker at the bar, and two older men at a table with an unopened box of dominoes.

"Good day, sir." The landlord nodded without a smile. "What can I get you?"

While unbuckling and lowering his backpack to the floor, Colin assessed the beers on offer. "Are you doing food at the moment?"

"Only sandwiches and rolls at this time of day, sir."

"That's great, can I have a pint of ... Shelleycoat Pale? And what sandwiches have you?"

"Tuna and cucumber, cheese and tomato and ham," the barman recited as he pulled the hand pump, filling the glass with foam.

"You stoppin' in town?" asked the drinker sitting on a stool at the bar.

Colin looked at him and determined him to be a similar age to himself, about forty two, but while the drinker was thin, almost emaciated, Colin was slightly overweight. One reason for his decision to try a hiking holiday in the Highlands, to get fitter.

"No, I'm booked in at the Glenview B&B." He pointed in the vague direction where he had seen the cottage.

The drinker nodded solemnly. "Goin' over the glen then?"

"Yes." Colin laughed slightly nervously. "I can see it, so it shouldn't take too long."

The man grunted and lifted his half pint and drank the last mouthful. This left both the short glass and the beer glass empty. Colin was used to meeting many kinds of people working as an antiques valuer in Brighton. He knew he could easily offer the man a refill and get offered nothing in return. He was used to English scroungers and he doubted the Scottish equivalent were much different.

"'Nother one, Tam?" The barman asked topping up Colin's pint of golden ale before placing it in front of him.

Tam nodded, and Colin breathed in relief.

"That'll be £3.25, sir."

Colin paid and the barman went to replenish Tam's glasses. Colin realised he had lost his chance of ordering food. "Cheese and Tomato," he blurted, attracting the attention of the whole, underpopulated bar.

"Right you are, sir," the barman replied, "Have a seat and I'll bring it you when it's ready. It'll be £2.50."

"Thanks." Colin pulled a fiver out of his wallet and handed it over. He perched on a stool at the end of the bar and sipped the beer in front of him. Delicious. There was a slightly malty undercurrent but the sharp bitter hops offset by fruity citrus made his taste-buds sing with pleasure.

"This beer is great," he exclaimed, again attracting scowls from the bar's patrons.

"That it is, sir. Got a local brewer who comes in and brews in my cellar. Not paid for itself yet, like, but I have managed to sell some barrels to a hotel or two in Fort William."

"Did you come up with the name?"

"Ah, well it was me and that brewing chap. He said it needed to be local, but myths and folk legends make good names. So we picked the local ghoully."

After taking a heap of change from Tam, the barman hunted under the counter and came out with a beermat and handed it to Colin. On one side was a design of shells and water with the name, *The Highland Shelleycoat*, and on the reverse a short piece of text about the 'ghoully':

The Shelleycoat is a well-known folklore spirit in Perthshire, but less is known about its Highland relative, which doesn't content

145

itself with playing pranks and leading travellers astray, but finds ways of stranding them in desolate places and then attacks them for all their misdeeds in life. It can be heard from afar, as the Shelleycoat wears a garment covered in seashells which rattle and clank as it closes in on its victim.

"You don't want to get lost on the glen with a Shelley after you, son," Tam growled, apparently in all seriousness.

Colin laughed. "I must admit it makes a great story, but half an hour tramping over your glen out there and I'll get to the B&B. Though thanks for trying to frighten me." He laughed again and took another mouthful of the hoppy beer.

"Not trying to frighten you, son. Just trying to help. There are all sorts of traps out there, rabbit holes you can break an ankle in, streams and small ravines making you divert again and again. Paths which lead nowhere."

"Tam's right," the barman added, placing a plate with Colin's sandwich on the bar in front of him, complete with a paper napkin. "There's more in the wilds than can be dreamed of. Especially for someone brought up in civilisation and who has turned their back on nature."

He took Colin's payment and returned the appropriate change.

Colin eyed the Scotsmen and gave another nervous guffaw. "Okay, what alternative is there ... can I get to the B&B by road?"

The barman shook his head. "The only road comes from the other direction. You have to go back into the village and along the main road about seven miles, then up the mountain path. That's about ten miles. It'll take hours. I suggest you take a taxi."

Colin felt relief flood him. All this pushing of his buttons was to get him to pay a relative over the odds for a long taxi journey. "Good try, but I'm heading over the glen. There's still four or five hours of daylight and not a cloud in the sky."

"Well, you must be the most guiltless man I've met. or the most reckless." Tam shook his head. Again, no smile.

This trying to trick him out of his money was starting to slightly bug Colin.

If they had treated it as a bit of a joke he could perhaps join in with the laugh. But deadpan Scots humour was not for him. He ate his sandwich, which proved to be a bit dry, and ordered another pint of the Shelleycoat beer. The silence in the pub was broken only by the *clack* of dominoes and the *click* of a glass on wood.

Colin was determined to make the trek across the grass and low hills and through the sparse trees to his destination. Although he did not have a tent, he had lots of warm clothes, so even if he did get lost he could keep warm until help came. After all, he had his mobile phone.

What forced his decision more, though, were the circumstances of his holiday: his need to get away from his job and Brighton and all things that reminded him how he had failed. Backing out of his determination to be energetic and decisive would put him back into the piteous position he had been in before this break. No, he needed to prove himself to himself. His possible failures as a father and husband were behind him. He had a future and must not let past failings destroy his life again.

He shouldered his rucksack after finishing the sandwich and beer, feeling slightly light-headed as the weight of his load wobbled precariously when he tried to get his arms through the straps.

"You sure you don't want a taxi?" asked the barman, again looking worried.

"No, thanks. This is something I have to do."

"Beware the Shelleycoat," Tam added with vibrato in his overly dramatic voice.

"Shut up Tam," the barman scolded him. "He'll have enough trouble with the paths without worrying about fairy stories."

Colin waved 'goodbye' and jostled himself and his backpack out the door into the cool bright air. He breathed deeply.

"Ah! An hour's walk in the country is what I need." With one last shake of his head at the weird locals and their legends, he crossed the road and stepped onto coarse grass.

*

The ground alternated between springy tufts of grass, hard rock and peaty mud. The going was indeed slow but his destination was in his sights and even streams and gullies were not going to deter him.

Getting about a third of the way across had taken him three quarters of an hour, enough time to congratulate himself on a job being well done. He sat on a boulder and looked back at the pub by the road and the few houses of the village behind it. It looked a long way off. It seemed strange to sit and listen and not hear a car or any other man-made noise: just a few birds and the ripple of a nearby stream, and a quiet *rattle*, perhaps of the wind moving pebbles on the unseen stream bank.

But no, there was no wind; it must be the stream rattling through the pebbles. He shut his eyes for a second to breath in the cool peaty air, and a *clacking* noise forced him to open them again and look around. Impossibly, in the second or so he had closed his eyes, a light mist had descended. It was not too troubling for navigation, but its sudden appearance was perplexing.

Colin stood up again feeling his rucksack pulling him back, so he leant forwards slightly to compensate. The beer he had imbibed had been stronger than he'd usually drink at home. Five percent ABV or thereabouts, he guessed.

Maybe that had not been a good idea when carrying an unwieldy load. He could still see his B&B in the distance, though the mist did make it drift in and out of focus a little. *One step in front of the other and avoid those rabbit holes*, he joked internally.

As he trudged, his thoughts turned to his past. No matter how he tried to banish them, memories returned, inviting grief and pain.

When he felt a tear rolling down his cheek, he stopped to get a grip on himself.

I'm here to put that behind me, idiot ... not responsible for Jessica catching meningitis ... but away so much... no chance of spotting the signs ... my fault ... I missed her childhood ... she was only eight, for God's sake!

His eyes were blurred with tears as well as the thickening mist, and he tumbled over a tuft of grassy earth and fell heavily. The ground was slightly damp but soft and springy, so he sat up and roared the arguments into the mist.

I was not responsible for Beth slashing her wrists! I know I should have noticed her depression and got her help ... Why did she use the cut-throat razor from my wardrobe ... the one I found clearing my father's house after he died. Almost an antique, German-made. Deadly. What made her use that? Did she blame me or was it just convenience?

Colin no longer had an idea if he was keeping his thoughts internal or if he was raging to the wilderness. Then another noise intruded, dulling his long worn guilt. A *slither* and *rattle*. Light hollow stones. No ... like shells moving across each other!

He looked around wildly, the mist was thick now and he had lost his direction in the tumble. With a sob in his throat, he dug out his iPhone and stabbed the icons for a map. It showed him as a blue dot and the glen around him as bleak emptiness, but indicated no directions. He'd have to start moving, and see if the distance to the B&B decreased or not.

Twenty-three percent of his battery left. Jesus.

A *clanking* of shells and a *crunch* of heavy feet interrupted his thoughts. From somewhere to his right. He had to go left, away from it. Maybe there was a logical explanation for these sounds, but his emotional state was pulling phantoms from the very mist.

There was still no path under his feet so he had to be wary of the uneven ground. At any time a river bank might appear, or a gully deep enough in which to break his leg.

He tried the small bright torch he had felt so clever about remembering to bring along, but all it did was highlight the minuscule space the clawing mist allowed him to see.

The *clanking* noise which could be, but surely mustn't be, a coat of shells worn my some goblin beast, became regular. Like a walking man rattling sacks of pebbles at each step, and now slowly circling him, just out of sight.

Suddenly a path appeared and the mist elongated down it.

He stepped gratefully onto its worn earth and gravel surface, adding his own *crunching* footsteps to those of his unseen companion. Faster. Dangerously fast, he walked. Glancing uselessly at his phone map. He couldn't remember where he had been in order to work out the direction he was moving in. If only he had invested in the more expensive hiker's map app with tracking software.

Then a thought hit him.

Tam.

That bastard from the pub was playing a trick!

He probably did it to all Englishman. Hateful bastard!

Colin's fury was blinding and he stumbled off the path and tumbled down a short steep slope.

Freezing water lashed at his legs as he tried to keep from falling and soaking his rucksack. Arms outstretched, the mist whipped around him like a living thing. At times it thinned, exposing the stream and then the bank – and a moving shape coming down from the path.

Colin howled, no longer conscious of whether it was in rage against Tam or through insane fear of the unknown. But he balled his fists and moved towards the noisy figure as it *clanked* and *rustled* like a knight in delicate china chain-mail.

As the mist cleared again fractionally, Colin saw a tall, thin figure clothed from head to toe in long, brittle-looking shells, each one of which so resembled the blade of a cut-throat razor that Colin screamed.

Man or ghost, this thing was taunting him. Enflaming his guilt, fanning his anger.

Colin launched himself at the shell covered figure, and with the weight of his backpack became a formidable force. Colin smashed his fists into the Shelleycoat's chest, and felt the shells explode into glass-like shards, lacerating his hands and arms.

His back convulsed in pain as gravity threw his heavy load from side to side.

The Shelleycoat screamed back, its shell coat broken open and body exposed to Colin's unrelenting fists, which were now streaming with his own blood. Deep cuts in his hands and along his arms and face turned his skin red and glistening, blood splashing onto the broken shells. The apparition leaned forward and screamed again, directly into Colin's face – and he went rigid. Hands full of grit, sand and gravel, Colin fell back into the stream, life-blood pumping around him, turning the stream pink. His fury abated as his energy waned. The broken and tattered figure stood over him, a face of squirming mollusks gyrating in their cracked, broken shells.

The monster stopped screaming and Colin shut his eyes. Strangely, a sort of peace descended on him, and for the first time in years he felt at ease. The demands of his job, of his family, his guilt at being a failure … all faded away.

Colin had no control as he rolled over from on top of his rucksack. Just in time to see the Highland Shelleycoat dissolve into the pink waters of the stream.

The mist thinned as the shallow water splashed over his face and head, washing him, baptising. Cleansing his soul of sin, diluting his guilt. Colin bled his final energy into the stream and tranquilly breathed cold water into his lungs. Purifying.

EVIL MONSTERS

It is a common misconception that the Scottish Highlands are an ancient Celtic homeland, formerly the realm of one people with one society, one culture and one religion. The truth is much more complex. The Scottish nation is a conglomeration of many races and creeds: the Picts, who entered from the northeast; the Gaels, who entered from Ireland; the Cumbrian Britons, who entered from the south (what is now northern England); and the Vikings who entered from Scandinavia – and even that list does not account for the unknown Stone Age people who occupied northern Britain before the Celts even arrived and almost certainly mingled and intermarried with them.

The upshot of all this is that native Scottish mythology, particularly in the Highlands where old beliefs and traditions died hard, is rich, diverse and multi-layered. It is also peopled with demi-gods and deities from a range of lands and belief-systems, the fading memories of which, especially since the conversion to Christianity, have cast them as monsters and devils.

Hence the Highlands' vast array of terrifying creatures. Nowhere else in the British Isles can boast so many. Here is a relatively small sample:

The **Fachen** is a feathered, one-legged monstrosity so hideous to look upon that it kills its victims primarily through shock. It is mainly associated with the Glen Etive district, close to mysterious Rannoch Moor. To date, no viable explanation has been offered as to what this creature may really have been, or where it came from.

The **Bean-Nigh** is a classic Celtic entity and a clear derivation from the Irish banshee. Evidently based on long-ago recollections of a sub-goddess or 'fate', this enigmatic being appears on riversides as either an ugly hag or a beautiful girl, and engages in washing blood from the clothing of those due shortly to die. She will respond to politeness and may answer questions, but that won't necessarily save you.

The **Pech** may be familiar to readers of John Buchan's supernatural Highland adventures, and are described as a subterranean tribe of tough, hairy gnomes who are always hostile to man. It is possible they represent folk-memories of the region's previous inhabitants or maybe even Neanderthals.

The **Glaistig** is a notorious female vampire, superficially beautiful, though she will always wear a long gown to conceal her goat-like legs and hoofed feet. Having enticed a male victim with her singing and dancing, she will kill him viciously and then drain his blood.

The **Cù-Sìth**, or faerie dog, is reputedly a native of the Outer Hebrides, and appears as a gigantic hound with shaggy green fur. If it commences baying, anyone within earshot must block their ears immediately – if they fail, and hear more than three calls by the Cù-Sìth, their imminent death is certain.

The **Bodach** are among the most mysterious denizens of Highland legend. Some folklorists argue they are the souls of warriors killed in battle while outside God's love, and thus are doomed to wander the moorland mist, while others contend they are evil spirits who have never known God. Either way, they are invisible, predatory and rumoured to snatch misbehaving children – archetypical bogey figures, in fact.

Of course, no pantheon of Celtic cryptids would be complete without a dragon or two, and though these regal beasts are strangely rare in Highland myth – many no doubt having been subsumed into 'loch monster' culture – they are not completely absent. For example, the **Stoor Worm** was a sea-dragon who lived off the Orkneys, and who was so ferocious that the only way to placate it was by offering human sacrifices. The name 'Stoor Worm' is most likely descended from the Old Norse term 'Storoar-gandr', which also meant 'Jormungandr', the great sea-serpent of Viking legend. Another oceanic god-turned-monster is **Seonaidh**, a vast undersea presence just off the Isle of Lewis. He was deemed formless but no less terrible for that, and constantly in demand of sacrifice, though in this case, rather oddly, barrels of ale would suffice.

The most famous Highland water monster of all is surely the **Kelpie**, or water-horse. Irredeemably evil, the shape-shifting Kelpie features in numerous Highland fables, wherein he lures humans to a horrible death, usually by posing as a fine stallion and the moment he is mounted, galloping into the sea or the nearest river or loch, and there devouring his drowned rider – many stories tell about grisly fragments of human corpses washing up on shingle beaches or floating in loch-side backwaters. Even today there are degrees of belief in this most heinous of Highland fiends, mainly because in the Christian era he was confused with the Devil himself – this was because another of his abilities was to assume the guise of a desirable young woman or man, and thus draw victims to their doom by sinful seduction.

But the Kelpie has various cousins, which if anything have even worse reputations. The **Each-Uisige** was a hybrid man/horse mainly associated with deep-water lochs. One such beast was allegedly snared on the Isle of Raasay after supposedly accounting for several victims off the coast there, only to disintegrate into a heap of disgusting jelly (which possibly hints at the capture of a giant squid). Likewise, the **Nuckelavee**. He too is a water-horse, but he is skinless, one-eyed and sometimes two-headed, and he revels in galloping across farmland, withering both crops and animals with his foul breath, and spreading plague to humans. There are clear etymological similarities between the Scottish Nuckelavee and the Norse demon, Mukkelevi, who was first imported to the Shetland Isles by the Vikings.

A pantheon of monsters then, but as stated earlier, this is only scratching the surface. The Scottish Highlands are without doubt the land of beasties.

THE OTHER HOUSE, THE OTHER VOICE
Craig Herbertson

'...thou art born into Dis-Ease; where are many false and
perverted Wills, monstrous Growths, Parasites, Vermin are they,
adherent to thee by Vice of Heredity, or of Environment or
of evil Training'
Liber Aleph, "De Via Libertatis" Crowley

And suddenly, breaking through the sullen clouds, a spear of
blinding light, chromatic in its brilliance, reflected from the
glass of the high-flung window. In that moment, with the
utter certainty of discovery, Mulholland experienced a variety of
emotions unencountered since, as a teenager, he had gazed
transfixed in wonder through the lens of MacAteer's haunted
kaleidoscope.

At the foot of the short scree slope, the mist grew like the
billowing of some warped theatrical effect. Glancing behind,
Mulholland saw the hulking figure of Corporal Danforth rise up
from the dank tarn below, an archetypal Grendel in search of prey.
The call of a distant osprey, lonely and brittle, echoed from a granite
cliff wall – one of many impassive jagged slopes they had traversed.
Their leviathan forms, spewed out by prehistoric cataclysm, swept
over and over, upward and upward, until they merged into the
distant range of the Cairngorm massif. All around his chilling body,
Mulholland watched the mist billow, and all above, he felt the
oppressive weight of the dark sky that had remained a constant
backdrop to the journey. With the single exception of the piercing
ray that had so suddenly cut the underbelly of the malignant clouds,
they had struggled through a growing dark. But now above
Mulholland's head, the emblazoned bay window like the lamp of
some dread lighthouse cut into the very cliff – the unmistakable
window, whose counterpart he had seen many years before at
Boleskin house.

"Danny! We've found it, Crowley's other house. We've found
it!"

As the light died, Mulholland discerned the rough steps cut into
the living rock. They led to a short shelf carpeted in withered ferns.
This formed a portico, above which, rose the outlines of a vast door.
Beside the door he could vaguely discern the other windows,
decorated it seemed with some indefinable carvings.

This eerie tableau was the external visible world made insanely claustrophobic by the ghastly mist and the burdened dark. Internally, in that invisible world we loosely call the soul, there were other visions. They were carved like the rock into Mulholland's being and he was overwhelmed with a wave of emotions – fear, pride, joy, wonder and uneasy nausea – the deep and inexplicable thrill of the occult. It drew him forward, feet stumbling on the scree of the gully basin.

"Come on Danny. This is incredible!" Mulholland paused before the first of the series of stone steps, laboriously etched in flat slate-like treads that spiraled up the side of the low cliff face. His skin felt clammy. Moisture dripped down his cheek from his eye patch and a dank smell like corrupted marsh water assailed his nostrils. The mist increased in density and he could only see some five paces ahead. Beneath his feet the blasted heather seemed to grapple to hold him back. Above his head to the left, the window gave the sinister appearance of a half-closed eye – for some inexplicable reason Mulholland was caught with the singular impression that the window had suddenly closed and in doing so had brought down the preternatural night.

It was a jarring occult sensation. Exuberance gave way to misgivings as Corporal Danforth's vast bulk hovered over his shoulder. Steaming breath accompanied by slow grunting lent a new timbre to Mulholland's doubts. The treads of the steps were clammy and slimed with an unhealthy moisture. Mulholland hesitated and then, unwilling to allow the corporal any misgivings, he took the first: carefully. The climb was only the height of three large men, but there was little room and a fall on the scree could be ugly. He paused when he reached the shelf of the portico, a space wide enough for them both. Before him, two grotesques carved in black marble had been erected on either side of the wooden door. They supported an architrave emblazoned with cryptic symbols, and their abysmal faces gazed out to the east.

"Ugh," hissed Danforth.

"Masterworks by Harris," said Mulholland after a space. "Taken from the original drawings in the *Book of Thoth*. There are no other symbols here except the usual Thelemic cursigram and that inscription. I sense nothing but a vague malignance. I …"

Danforth, uninterested in art or the occult, took a pace forward and gave the door a shove. It was swollen with moisture but swung back easily. An insidious reek seemed to suck them both forward. Mulholland placed his hand on the Corporal's powerful shoulder. "Not yet, damn it. Look!"

On the wooden floor of the porch in pools of shadow, a pair of leather walking boots stood a good pace apart, the left boot pointing forward and the right actually in the room beyond.

"So?" said Darnforth.

"Professor Cameron's boots, I believe"

"It's just a pair of old boots. So what if they were Cameron's?"

"Look a little closer," said Mulholland bleakly. "His feet are still in them."

*

There comes a time in the life of some young men when they fully realise that they have loved and lost. For Mulholland the moment came some years after the crisis of his heart and it came in the capacious formal hall of the club. Here, before the frowning gaze of MacAteer, Mulholland sat on a small stool with his head in his hands. Moments before, MacAteer had switched off the ancient Dictaphone when it became apparent that Mulholland, wracked with emotion, was no longer capable of a logical response.

Mulholland had been invited to join the Order by his mentor at the tender age of sixteen, not long after he had lost his eye in a foolish schoolboy prank. It was a decision MacAteer had never regretted. The boy had grown to a determined young man. The Order fuelled by the elite occultists of the day, those who walked the selfless path to enlightenment, had never had a better student of the esoteric arts. But now Mulholland's past had caught up with him, as is inevitable, and the needs of the Order were never greater.

Behind the large walnut desk, MacAteer paused and pursed his lips. He tugged the sleeves of a tweed jacket that had been unfashionable in the 1960s and looked no less démodé twenty years on. For a number of minutes the head of the Order sat with his elbows placed on the desk and his hand thrust upwards in a pyramidal parody of the ancient Egyptian symbols emblazoned above the lintel of the great hall. In these moments, it seemed that the incredible acoustics of the domed ceiling still carried the whispered echo of the voice.

Finally, Mulholland raised his head and lit a cigarillo. The smoke curled up through the still air. The portraits of ancient dignitaries, gowned and wigged, glowered from the pale walls. The skylight sent shafts of bleak morning sunlight to cash shadows on the mosaic floor where Mulholland's patent leather shoes tapped an unconscious rhythm.

"Sorry about that," said Mulholland after a deep breath. "Took me completely by surprise. "That voice on the Dictaphone. It was Jeanie Brown. How?"

"No," said MacAteer. It was at moments like these that the head of the Order could only suppose that there was no such thing as coincidence. He looked at his student carefully. "It was not Jeanie Brown. It was in fact, her great aunt on the maternal side, Lady Jane Akhtar."

"I see," said Mulholland after a space. "Came as a shock. You know Jeanie has never been found? Of course you do."

MacAteer nodded. From the manila file he drew forth an old black and white photograph. Gingerly, he rose from the leather chair. He handed the photograph to Mulholland.

"Good God, how can this be possible?"

Mulholland was looking at the very image of Jeanie, the girl who had been lost in a snowstorm in the mountains near Criach two years before. The black and white photograph was old, the pilot's costume quaint. The young woman was holding a leather aviation helmet in one hand and with the other was making a mock salute. Behind her slim figure the fuselage of the old Sopwith Camel made a canvas backdrop, the pilot's cockpit, glittering in the sun, contrived a portraiture frame for her beautiful face. Her voice, metalised and muted by the hissing of the old belt, had sounded quaint and lonely in the echoing hall but now Mulholland could imagine it emerging from these sensuous lips. He could almost hear her laugh and he knew that laugh would send shivers of painful delight through his own body in reminder of a thousand sleepless nights. But it was not Jeanie. It was her long dead ancestor. Reluctantly, Mulholland stood up and handed the photograph back to MacAteer. The older man rang the service bell. "I think we need a couple of stiff whiskies," he said quietly.

Together they walked over to the bay window overlooking the Royal Mile and gazed at the panoramic view over the old Nor Loch to the Georgian new town and beyond to the rising Lomond hills. Further to the north, dark clouds gathered over the distant Highlands.

The steward, discrete in his white jacket, paced across the echoing hall. He placed the decanter of malt whisky on the small deal table with two crystal glasses. He whispered a few terse words. MacAteer frowned. "Just tell Corporal Danforth I might be quite some time. Perhaps better make an appointment."

MacAteer raised his glass. "Slainte Mha. Now, to Jeanie Brown's great aunt. I concealed these revelations from you because I knew you were still hurting from the loss of your ... friend. There

157

was no need for you to know. However, things have come to a head. Lady Jane Akhtar, as you know, was a founding member of the Order. She also disappeared in tragic circumstances some years after this photograph was taken." MacAteer placed the photograph back on the deal table with a sigh. "Until a month ago, her disappearance was still an utter mystery. Then, remarkably – an ancient portable Dictaphone turned up at the foot of a mountain with the recording that you have just heard."

"Crowley," said Mulholland under his breath. "She talks of Crowley." He made a quick mental calculation. "Given the exalted circles she moved in, it's just conceivable she may have met him as a child. And there was another voice – a young voice I think. They seemed –"

"– on the edge of a discovery of vast importance," interrupted MacAteer. "And you are correct. Crowley it is." He allowed Mulholland a space to collect his thoughts. They were mostly of Jeannie. He shuddered.

"When exactly did the good lady disappear?"

"Not long after the Second World War. I believe the Dictaphone, whose rusting remains were found in the mountains, was even invented by her. A prototype of the Lexan plastic belt, a cumbersome sort of device that rotated on a metal cylinder. Lady Akhtar was something of a technical genius – as well as a master of esoteric knowledge. Much of the plastic belt was damaged but surprisingly, enough remained intact – perhaps because it was frozen in the mountains – for us to get about ten minutes of the sound of her voice on the contraption. The laboratory up in Aberdeen has a copy and they're trying to get some more of the monologue but we won't know until next week whether or not we can understand any more than we have. They built this from scratch to play what we have just heard."

"Was she murdered?"

"All that we know, we know from this damaged recording. Her body has not been found. Nor that of her companion, her young lover, Adeline Walton."

"This happened near Criach?"

"The Dictaphone was found in the dry bed of the river Lough in the summer – under rather gruesome circumstances: it was still attached to a skeletal hand. The hand of a woman: Lady Akhtar no doubt or her young companion. We believe the body was washed down from some hidden cave on the west side of the mountain and frozen in for a few seasons before it was finally laid in the river bed. It is not uncommon to die climbing in the Highlands, but to die clutching a somewhat cumbersome recording device doesn't suggest climbing. Our people in Aberdeen had some difficulty detaching the hand from the device – it had rusted in. We really don't know enough and this is where you come in ... Mulholland, I would never normally ask you to investigate but the reality is that there is no one else capable. Your nemesis, Farantino is in Paris at the mathematical convention. Most of our men are keeping a little bit of an eye on him. The rest are still out in Egypt checking on that riddle in Kazakhstan. And you, more than anyone else, know how important that could be. However, this could also have immense consequences: Crowley, the Great Beast, the 'wickedest man in Christendom' by his own account! We always thought Crowley's entire opus had been covered but apparently not. It's like a Chinese warlock discovering a clue to the whereabouts of the Book of Bai Ze."

MacAteer paused as if contemplating this unlikely discovery. He recovered himself. "Now, Lady Akhtar was an expert on Crowley; she met him briefly in the early 1930s as a child, which prompted her interest in the occult and provoked a later obsession with the man. Her research turned up something rather interesting. This has been substantiated by papers which we have here." MacAteer produced various documents: manila folders, typewritten scripts, a letter yellowed with age and written in a crabby hand. "You know of Crowley's house on Loch Lomond of course?"

"The devil's paradise," said Mulholland. "Boleskine House."

"Quite," replied MacAteer. "The house is simply a seething pit of demons, jinns, astral monstrosities and everything bad. People die in the environs. Locals never call on the house at night; strange emanations and so on. Our people have long established that there are certain psychic forces in existence drawn up by Crowley in his first experimentations in the occult. The said forces are contained and relatively harmless – at least to the people of our order."

"Yes," said Mulholland. "After the mirror of Kazakhstan I feel I could quite happily breakfast at the Gog Magog. Boleskine House would be a tea party."

"Quite. I'm not asking you to visit Crowley's known residence though. Have a look at these papers." MacAteer spread them on the deal table. Mulholland fingered through the manuscripts for a few moments.

"Well, it says here that thirty-two Irish labourers were hired in 1922. There are wages here – gosh, labour was cheap then ... We have some official documents. Tickets for the Luciternia, an ocean liner bound for the Americas. And this is interesting," said Mulholland scratching his head. "The labourers are indicated here on the passenger list. But they do not arrive."

"They did not arrive. In fact, like the unfortunate Lady Akhtar they simply disappeared."

"Interesting," said Mulholland.

"Yes, and more intriguing, Professor Cameron made a very careful study of certain of the Equinox periodicals and other paraphernalia not generally available even to those very deep in occult circles. What he seems to have established is that Crowley had another house."

"Another house," said Mulholland slowly. "He had several."

"Yes, several houses in several lands, but there is one single unaccounted period in his life which occurred between these dates." MacAteer slapped the papers. "Here and here, where we have no records of his whereabouts. I'm afraid to say that during this period the labourers may well have been called in to build a house somewhere in the Highlands, offered a ticket to the New World and for reasons that we can guess, once that house was made, like the builders of an Egyptian tomb, the labourers were no longer required … at least on this earthly plane."

"Crowley. It's hard to imagine he could have an even bleaker side."

"Yes, our old friend, Crowley. Back in the Sixties he was all the rage – the great misunderstood guru of the spiritual world. Now, in the avant-garde Eighties, he's seen as an innovative but misguided cult figure. If what we have here is true, Boleskine House was merely a cover for a much darker and deeper secret. Unfortunately, for want of anyone else available, I am afraid that you must go and discover what that secret is. Certainly before someone like Farantino gets a sniff of it."

"What could be darker than Crowley's esoteric corpus?"

Mulholland paused as MacAteer said nothing and the full implications impacted. In desperation Mulholland continued: "But what about Professor Cameron? Did you not say that he was also in the Highlands?"

"Was in the Highlands, but like many of the people who seem to have become involved, he has simply disappeared. It's your job to find him, young man. When you do, follow his instructions. If you don't, do what you can."

Mulholland took a long dram of his whisky. He placed the glass carefully back on the deal table. "Professor Cameron is the acknowledged expert. I'm not the best man for this job. I'm only a student; papers to write for university … after Egypt?"

"Your experience with the mirror of Kazakhstan is something that you have to surmount. You seem to spend most of your time at university partying. In any case, you are the only man for the job."

"So be it," said Mulholland.

Leaving their whisky on the table they walked slowly back to the Dictaphone that lay like some funfair anachronism on MacAteer's large desk. MacAteer gave it a slow thoughtful glance. "Professor Cameron found some helpful geographical indications in Lady Akhtar's old papers and the gruesome discovery of the skeletal hand gave him enough to charge off alone and investigate. He was always a bit tempestuous. I suspect that he thought he was on the find of the century."

"It could well be. But sometimes one must be careful of what one finds"

"Quite. Perhaps we better listen to the rest of the recording".

"You said that you couldn't recover it all?"

"The first section is very partial. The laboratory worked on it for ages but there are whole sections missing. In the latter part of the original belt the voice is hopelessly distorted. The laboratory in Aberdeen is still fiddling around with it but it's old and there's a very slim hope that they can do anything. Unfortunately, time is of the essence."

The recording began, the sultry tones of the familiar voice again sent Mulholland back to times that he wished he could forget. He focused on the voice.

"… characteristic of Boleskine House located on the south-eastern shore of Loch Ness near Foyers. It looked designed by Fraser outside. Inside, it's not like the drawing room. The bay window simply looks on the opposite cliff although when – Adeline, don't go near that." The speech was interrupted. The tiny recording gave some indistinct reply, too difficult to discern. "Best not touch anything." Movement as though objects were being shifted. "There"s a silver lamp on the ceiling and an open fireplace. Decorations same as at Boleskine, as with the figures at the door. But the whole sweep of the room – it's different, circular, dome ceiling, the inscriptions as one would expect. Effectively, it's the inner temple. Those statues, Horus, Thoth – recognisable, but the others …" The recording distorted and buckled like a train leaving the tracks. The voice faded, indistinguishable from background hiss. There was a lucid moment through the static. "Adeline …" The single word repeated, a gap and then repeated again in a higher pitch. And then suddenly a dreadful screaming, distant but piercing and growing hysterical with each second. The voice cut. Desperate, scrabbling movements sounded. Then the belt gave only a harsh hiss. For a full fifteen seconds the two men stared transfixed. Mulholland was about to speak but MacAteer raised his hand.

Slowly, inexorably, the hiss transformed to a low pulsating threnody. Mulholland leaned forward. Was that a human voice, deeply masculine, penetrating the ether like a dull bell sounding through depths; or was it some massive, degenerate beast grunting in visceral agony? Either way, the diabolical sounds seemed to envelop the great hall.

Suddenly, cutting through the preternatural vacuum like the pure voice of an acolyte rising from a pit, the distinctive and beautiful tones of Lady Akhtar railed against the invisible horror. The voice faded. Again the belt played its monocratic hiss; and without warning the voice lapsed, buried in static until a few moments passed and it returned – but hopelessly distorted, twisting, increasing and slowing down, rising and falling in a grim parody of speech.

"Was that the lesser banishing ritual?" whispered Mulholland, "but why?"

"I assume in the moment of extremity, faced by whatever she was facing, she would employ her only defense ... regardless of its obvious futility."

"The circle. Of course Crowley's existed already, the pentagram. Everything in place and she within it. But the circle was not hers ..."

At this point, and for many years after, Mulholland could only remember that he had nearly died of a heart attack. There was a violent crashing as the great doors behind were thrown open. The yelp of the steward's feeble protests. Mulholland, whose eyes had been glued to those of MacAteer, read his expression immediately. It was a look he had seen as an adolescent pupil in the old man's class: steely but amused. Mulholland's every reflex was set to leap to assistance. A body, breathing heavily, drew up beside him. A voice, low and harsh shouted at MacAteer.

"They wouldn't let me in, sir! But it was important and ..."

"Danforth!"

Sensing no immediate threat to life and limb, Mulholland looked up. What he saw in that second was nearly as great a shock as the violent noise that followed the horrific last moments of the recording. A twisted raw mask in profile, an ogre like countenance with bared teeth and a gaping hole of an eye socket. The face turned, revealing that the burn damage had only affected one side. The other showed a brown cow-like eye, bleary with drink, a half potato nose, a heavy lower lip beneath.

"Snap," said Danforth when she saw his eye patch.

"Corporal Danforth!" shouted MacAteer.

"Yes sir!"

162

"For pity's sake stand at ease but shut up!"

"Yes, sir! Sorry, sir."

MacAteer drew his wallet from his breast pocket. "You're bored, Danforth. Here's twenty pounds. Book the train from Waverley. Be there at nine o'clock tomorrow morning. Do not, I repeat do not spend the rest on drink. This is young Mulholland. He's a student at Edinburgh University. Far cleverer than you. He'll give you instructions on the train and a bit of extra cash for expenses. Now, get out."

Without a murmur Corporal Danforth took the money and left.

Mulholland grinned feebly. "Expenses?"

"A few quid."

"Who the hell was that?"

"Corporal Danforth, ex British army."

"Her face?"

"Middle East, special operations; well before all hell broke loose. She was attached to the Mobility Unit and, from what I heard, a jeep she was escorting took a hit. Everyone died except Danforth. She got that trying to rescue her men."

"God."

"She's out now. Bored senseless. She gets bored easily and that's why she'll be accompanying you on your little trip." MacAteer looked pleasantly smug to have killed two birds with one stone.

"But how on earth could she help?"

"She passed the tests but was still rejected by the SAS. Caused quite a stir when she floored the captain."

"And?"

"Useful if you get in a scrape. If she sees one of Crowley's demons she'll probably knock it out too."

Mulholland threw up his hands in despair.

When Mulholland left, subdued and disconsolate, MacAteer picked up the phone. "Put me through to Nepal. Mulholland? I've told him. He knows something of the risks. He's young, inexperienced, but who else do we have? I want everyone available in the Order, all those above the seventh level, to search the astral plains; any disturbance, any sign that Cameron might be attempting contact, or God forbid, that he has … gone over. Anything.'

*

Mulholland entered the first class compartment of the Highland Main Line and settled into his window seat. It had been a night of broken dreams; images of Jeannie Brown as he had last seen her

163

walking out into the relentless snow. These images mirrored by the picture of Lady Jane Akhtar, her twin in beauty. Although he was trained in the disciplines of the Order, Mulholland was young enough to feel the full force of that emotional loss and fragile enough to still feel the shock of the manner in which it had been delivered. He sighed and then with an almost furtive air, scanned platform six, empty with the exception of a guard and a young couple. He stared absently at the couple locked in an embrace and, with a rueful nod of his head, spread out on the table various papers he had received from MacAteer. The guard blew his whistle. Mulholland pondered MacAteer's final words on leaving the club and took his much handled tarot set from his pocket, the Crowley set, which he had always favoured but which now seemed singularly appropriate. Professor Cameron's last known act was to telephone from the hotel and say he was setting out and to expect his next location in the post. MacAteer had received a hand drawn diagram of a tarot spread.

The train set off, westbound towards Haymarket. Mulholland glanced again at the empty platform. Five hours to Fort William and time to read up a little and also solve the problem set by MacAteer. He could breakfast after. He drew out the six cards – suit cards from the minor arcana – and, as he examined MacAteer's copy of the diagram, noted with interest that they were all Discs. He glanced again at the diagram and frowned. Professor Cameron was the acknowledged expert. Mulholland had expected to see the Celtic Cross or Mandala spread, both of which he knew Professor Cameron favoured. Instead he found a simple setting of six cards. It was the mirror spread missing the Querent and probable result. Or if he was more honest, it wasn't a real spread at all. Just six cards laid side by side like the number six on a die. "Most unusual," he muttered. "Still, can't be all that difficult. Two of Discs, three of Discs –"

For the second time in the last twelve hours, Mulholland was riveted to his seat. The first intimation of trouble was the repeated shout of 'shot'. After initial bewilderment Mulholland managed to pick out an unmistakable guitar riff.

Shot by Both Sides had plagued his evenings as a fresher. It had been Jeanie's favorite track by the Manchester band, *Magazine*. The door crashed open as a steward tried to obstruct a grotesquely large figure carrying a cassette player set at full volume. He was shuttled aside like a toy. Corporal Danforth, clad in dirty overalls over a shapeless grey woolen jumper, was shouting. In her left hand she held a six pack of pale ale and three bottles that, to Mulholland's horror, appeared to be the cheapest wine. "I've got a fecking ticket somewhere!" Giving the man as much attention as a tank rolling over a doll, Danforth pressed in beside Mulholland, crushing him against the window and dislodging a number of priceless documents.

After a brief but heated conversation, Mulholland managed to find the 'off' button of Danforth's cassette player. He paid a supplement for her ticket, which was finally discovered crumpled at the bottom of her canvas kitbag.

The steward left without offering coffee. Mulholland's stunned ears began recovery. Danforth set her stash of alcohol on the table, opened a bottle of ale with a bayonet and settled in with her good side a hand's breadth from his face. "Right chief," she said smiling cheerily. "Orders? Like a beer?"

"No thanks," said Mulholland bleakly. "Let's keep it … formal." He looked at the tarot cards, reflected on the two hours he had spent in meditation that morning specifically to approach the problem and looked out of the window as Haymarket station came into view. He calculated that there were approximately four hours and fifty three minutes before they reached their destination.

"Cards, good idea. It's a long trip. Fecking boring." Danforth reached for the cards. Mulholland's hand leapt out and gripped hers. This provoked a leering beery smile and, despite its apparent impossibility, she edged in closer.

"They're tarot cards …" Mulholland searched for an explanation. "Magic cards." Instantly, he regretted it.

"Tricks? I love tricks?"

"Not that kind. You can't touch the cards; only the owner can – that's me – and look, they're set in a pattern. It's a puzzle I have to work out …"

Danforth examined the cards in the manner of a child observing a ball cast into the grumpy neighbour's garden. Mulholland looked too. "This one, the seven – see here, it's called Failure – falling into Netzach, the fields of anarchy and destiny according to the Crowley writings." His voice sounded a shade pompous even to himself. "In astrology, that would be Saturn in the third decan of Taurus. The card expresses unfilled promises, loss of fortune, dealings that first sound good but later don't work – cheating, false successes. It's all part of a … puzzle we have to solve to find Professor Cameron."

For fifteen minutes Mulholland explained the nature of the cards dividing them into Earth, Air, Water and Fire elements. At one point he got quite excited as he drew Danforth's attention to fact that all the cards in Cameron's spread were from the Suit of Pentacles. "They are all Coins," he said.

"Coins?" said Danforth betraying a momentary interest.

165

"Coins, disks – no not money for goodness sake. Earth cards!"

Danforth stared at the cards, then at Mulholland, then her beer.

"This one's off," she said in a tone of incredulity. Draining it in one effort, she pulled out the bayonet and opened another bottle. Slowly, Mulholland lit a cigarillo and packed the cards carefully into the silk scarf he had brought back from Egypt.

Sheep on the line delayed the journey by two painful hours. Mulholland tried again with the tarot but Danforth's repertoire of songs was more than off putting. At Pitlochry, Mulholland gave up the ghost. The party of elderly gentleman who entered the carriage at Carstairs complained so bitterly about "bad language," "vulgarity" (belching) and "littering" (two empty wine bottles had fallen on the floor) that he had been forced to move into second class. Here they had lasted two stations before the hardened farmers going up north displayed a body language that often preceded the Glasgow kiss. In the unwritten rule of Highland etiquette, the woman herself could not be struck – the task of defense was by long custom left to her male partner. While Danforth's whole physique and attitude seemed to stretch this chivalrous point, it was, in any case, academic. Danforth would probably wreck the carriage in a paroxysm of violence and although Mulholland intuited that she might not lose the fight he had no wish to test the theory.

They disembarked in disgrace to meet a blanket of drizzle; the tiny station might as well have been the moon for all its human occupation. As the train departed, Mulholland looked north but the summit of Ben Vrackie was shrouded in mist. After the headache of the journey, even a long walk though bleak Drumochter Pass would be a welcome relief. It was a dreech, dark afternoon with the sky utterly clothed in voluminous skirts of grey. The unpredictability of Highland weather had armed Mulholland with the usual wax jacket and boots but he still felt the chill. From her kitbag, Danforth pulled out a crumpled duffle coat, which seemed a size too small. She stalked off, mouthing obscenities. Mulholland threw up his hands in despair and found a phone booth. He called the operator and, in a fit of spite, reversed charges to MacAteer's private number.

After a few moments, MacAteer answered.

"Glad you called," he said cheerily. "Everything going well?"

MacAteer listened patiently to Mulholland's steam of objections and ignored them completely from the benefit of his comfortable armchair. When the younger man finished, the cheeriness dropped from his tone.

"I phoned the hotel. Make your way there immediately. Cameron hasn't shown up. Worse, I've had reports from some our senior members. Cameron is almost certainly in a great deal of trouble. Any contact on the astral plane is obfuscated. There is some kind of barrier between his astral presence and those of Order members. Every report suggests something has upset the balance. Very unusual and somewhat disturbing. So, watch your step."

When Danforth returned she was smoking some brutal unfiltered cigarette. Mulholland was young enough to feel almost cheerful despite the grim forebodings. He had managed to get something from MacAteer – a lift to the Criach Hotel.

"We're being picked up by a local. Do not pick a fight with him or it's a two day hike."

Danforth slumped onto the bench and hunched over her cigarette. Mulholland looked mournfully at the unrelenting sky.

Through the drizzling rain the local arrived in the shape of a young Glaswegian, as tall as Danforth with blonde, shoulder-length hair and a canty glint in his pale blue eyes. He introduced himself as Bannerman, assistant chef, and eyed the sullen Danforth for a few seconds. "Naw sma' are ye. Is it muscle or tae mony pies?" Danforth seemed subdued or perhaps she was unable to understand the dialect. She took the backseat without a whimper. Mulholland was impressed. He climbed into the passenger seat of the battered Range Rover and Bannerman sped forward through pine-clad winding roads drowning in rain.

"Ye picked a bad time," said Bannerman. "Whisky tasting. Hotel's cram fu' o Dutch tourists."

"We won't be staying long."

"Your boss said you were efter a Professor Cameron. He left us last week. Didnae come back for his things. I'd put you up in his room but we had tae book it oot. You and your … wife will kip at mine above the kitchen. Naw ideal but any port in a storm."

Mulholland was unsure whether this reference to 'wife' was standup comedy but when they entered the hotel reception the Criach was packed with Dutchmen, every room was booked and it seemed that he would be stuck with Danforth. She had taken his glumness as a signal to share a drink with Bannerman. Mulholland heard her raucous laughter as he walked over to the bay window. He found a free seat at a small table. Next to a stuffed fox, an old ordnance survey map of Scotland was framed above the table. The map seemed to taunt Mulholland with his inability to find a solution to the mystery.

In typical Scottish fashion, the rain stopped and through the tattered clouds the sun shone on the dark surface of Loch Criach: a magnificent view. Far away, through a ragged line of Scotch pine, shone the mare's tails of the Criach Falls, which Mulholland had climbed once, nearly losing his life in the process. But beyond the

167

falls with their twin ribbon tails of shimmering water like tears on a cragged cheek, the mountains soared over the glens where Jeanie had walked out into the snow never to return. Her aunt, Lady Akhtar, had preceded her and now their voices seemed like one tantalizing call from the past. He could hear Lady Akhtar now, overshadowing Jeanie, a mournful hopeless wail from beyond. The voice grew stronger, disturbing his thoughts.

The trout rose, sending concentric ripples across the water as they leapt, reminding Mulholland of the Discs on the tarot cards. He laid them out on the small table.

Three of Discs, the Tree of Life: in Crowley's corpus – the understanding. Ironically, it represented the perfect precondition to go ahead with a plan. And here beside it, the four of Discs representing completion. What was Cameron trying to say? Mulholland sat until the darkness fell and the cards were emblazoned on his brain like the blood red orb of the sun. He started suddenly as Danforth hovered above him. "Still playing with these cards?"

"It's a puzzle, Danny. Cameron sent this diagram to tell us where he is."

Danforth looked at the cards through a haze of beer and spirits. "It's time for bed," she said. "Bannerman's shown me where we sleep."

Bannerman's attic-room was tiny. Books, video tapes, boxes of plates and glasses, paper napkins and ashtrays made it a Chinese pagoda in which the bed appeared like a bargain houri's four-poster. The floor, covered in empty whisky bottles and full ashtrays, left no room to pitch a sleeping bag.

"Looks like it's me and you," said Danforth. She dropped her overalls, revealed a musculature that would shame a shot-putter and pulled the grey woolen jumper over her head. With no ceremony she lay down on the creaking bed. Mulholland, reminded of a beached walrus, stared at her for a few seconds. "I'll find a chair downstairs," he said.

"Jesus," slurred Danforth. "I don't bite. We're on a job."

Mulholland sat on the bed. He undid the laces on his patent leather shoes, removed them and neatly hung his shirt on the back of a tottering bookcase. He put out the light, stared at the tiny skylight through which the vast panorama of the stars appeared framed like a mezzotint, and eased in beside Danforth's naked frame. They lay for some moments under a moon whose cratered surface bore an unkind resemblance to the profile of Danforth's face. Mulholland felt the warmth of her body next to his, heard her breath lightly on his cheek.

"Have you ever done it?" she slurred.

Mulholland tensed.

"You were in love with that Jeanie girl. Bannerman told me. You were on the mountain rescue team here when they searched for her. But did you ever do it?"

"No," said Mulholland finally. "She was fiancée to a friend. I just loved her from a distance."

"I never did it really. At the care home when I was a kid there was a man; he made us all do it. But it wasn't natural. He liked the boys and the girls but it wasn't natural what he did and he had a dog as well. He did terrible things. I hated him."

Mulholland felt a great gulf where his stomach should be. He said quietly, "I've hated evil all my life."

Danforth was drifting off to sleep. "But we could do it, if you wanted. You're not like the men I've known, the soldiers, that bastard at the care home. You're cute."

Danforth snored quietly. The moon glittered above, framed like Crowley's tarot card. Two virgins, thought Mulholland, seeing the tarot spread before his eyes, under the moon. The dark knowledge of the soul's depth, the subconscious, a look into the abyss; illusion madness and great, great danger.

It seemed that Crowley planned their journey from the grave.

*

Through a sleepless night the siren voice called to Mulholland. He left the snoring Danforth at dawn and spent two hours without breakfast at the little table under the bay window staring at tarot cards.

MacAteer called the hotel. Senior members of the Order had worked through the night on the problem and were none the wiser. They had noticed that the initials on the diagram were not Cameron's usual signature but no one had found it significant. The cards were all Discs. It must mean something. Danforth joined the table munching a sandwich. She had her kitbag over her shoulder.

"We'd better get off."

"We need to know where we're going," said Mulholland wearily. "To do that, these damn cards have to be interpreted."

"Wind, Fire, Air, Earth. You said they were Earth cards didn't you," said Danforth. "It's an Ordnance Survey grid reference. Usual six coordinates." She looked at the map above the table and pointed. "Just there."

Mulholland stared at Danforth, then the map.

"Army training," said Danforth. "Are you coming or not?"

169

Under a dreechit sky, Bannerman launched the fishing boat. They traversed the dark still waters of Loch Criach, debouched into the lesser Criach beyond the roar of the waterfalls and the thrumming air. Dark pines marched down the northern slopes of Ben Criach under the grey skirt of the scree slope before it spilled into the lochs; they passed the indomitable cliff face between the two waterfalls, glistening with emerald lichen; its ancient granite surface like tortured sculpture; shaped in cataclysmic events lost in antiquity, under the cragged overhangs where so many climbers had tried and failed.

Bannerman pitched the boat on a shale beach. He had no desire to go further and he watched in ominous silence as they took the virtually untrodden path through the smaller Glen Criach, where the Cairngorm massif spilled like a petrified ocean until the grey green summits blended into the storm clouds.

An osprey winged its silent way across the sky as the glen gave way to the forbidding Criach Moor, shunned by local people for reasons that were rapidly becoming apparent to Mulholland. The air itself was not simply oppressive with the shifts in pressure before the storm. There was an undoubted malignancy, occultic and pervasive, which made shapes of the forbidding crags on the lower reaches of slopes that rose like gaunt skulls and tortured, withered hands. Danforth appeared unaffected and marched stoically over the heather. When they reached the far end of the glen, the hills on either side began to rise. The path was unclear but with unerring instinct Danforth led the way through the gullies. By late afternoon they had begun to scramble over rocks, only to descend into unknown ravines where in the silence Mulholland, with his greater sensitivity, began to hear the voice of Lady Akhtar whisper in his ears – a sure indication that the barriers between living and dead were being dissolved and that Danforth was an expert guide. Finally, he spotted an old rusting sign standing by a bush.

Danger, Military firing range. Keep out

Danforth grunted. "It's a fake." She took a compass from her pocket. "The range is about six miles due west."

*

An hour later, they were gazing at the remains of Professor Cameron at the threshold of the door – a sludge of putrefying flesh, massed in a pair of walking boots.

Then Mulholland made the classic misjudgment of the young. He stared at the boots, watched flies rise in an aerial necklace of black, smelt the sickly odour of rotting flesh mixed with the dank hollow reek of empty unused rooms. But there was more – Even at the opened door, Mulholland sensed the deep reek of evil, of chaos, of things nameless and unknown, dread and delinquent. He knew it was time to run but he could not. He gripped Danforth by the shoulders. "When we go in Danny – keep your mouth shut, obey my every word. That's an order."

Danforth smiled her damaged half smile." You're the boss. But mind if carry this?" She drew out a regulation Browning from her kitbag and inserted the magazine.

"If it makes you feel better." Mulholland held up a bag of salt. "I've got this."

Mulholland stepped a pace into the hallway. To the left and right, open doors revealed dimly light rooms where the light from lichened windows shone greenly on a dust covered floor: rows of bookcases with mouldering tomes on one side, a vast kitchen with a large oak table, rusting pots on a far wall, row upon row of corroding meat cleavers and knifes. At their feet, a gutter, stained darkly, split a stone floor. The hall broadened, a large room to the left full of peculiar *objets d'art* buried in dust, a framed abstract hanging from a whitewashed wall above a grinning bust on a plinth. With every step the gloom thickened and the sense of doom crept like a thief; the ineluctable miasma of emptiness holding in its hollow breath the sense of something darker like the phlegm of a rotten lung. The air became a stifling madness. Mulholland paced forward infected – unsure whether by inner curiosity or the magnetism of a stronger will.

At the last they entered a large empty anteroom, stone-flagged and lit by a circular skylight which appeared above them like the mouth of a well as seen from the carved stone throat below it.

Here, Mulholland paused peering into the shadows to where a huge columned doorway splayed outwards into a greater emptiness. The sense of evil beyond normal sensation clutched at his throat. He gagged with the noxious reek of it. With trembling hand he took the salt. Muttering incantations he began to lay out a circle. "Danny, under no circumstances leave this circle."

Danforth hissed in reply. He caught the gleam of her drawn gun. "Eheieh. Eheieh. Malkuth Ve-Geburah …" He began to chant, placing himself to north, east, west, south; making gestures incomprehensible to Danforth who stood like a sentry staring into the gloom. In these moments, the clutch of despair wrung at his throat, his chest heaved with emotion, his breath hung dank on a moistening air. Far away, beyond the limits of sensible hearing a low thrumming chant appeared in his brain like the misting of a warm breath on a mirror. He heard again the voice of Lady Akhtar as though she were the contralto to his baritone. She seemed to be joining him from the ethereal plane. Every ounce of his being rebelled against the stupidity of his actions and yet with unwavering discipline he took a single pace forward to the edge of his circle.

From the skirt of the columned door frame Mulholland looked within to where a circular chamber the length and breadth of a marquee revealed a grey green floor on which rested an acacia altar within the square of Tpareth. Above it hung an old silver church lamp shining on the great pentagram with its Star of David surrounded by Hebraic inscriptions. The entire room, its makings and furnishings, the symbolic projection of the Great Beast Crowley's temporal shape. In effect his spiritual avatar. Mulholland felt an almost physical emanation.

Beside him, Danforth shouted in cracked guttural. "They're moving!"

Drawn to Crowley's circle, Mulholland had not seen the statues surrounding it. They stood in recesses in the wall: Horus, Kali, ibis headed Thoth, Buddha – others beyond even his deep occult knowledge. Whether they moved to the promptings of imagination or not, Mulholland spoke quickly: "Don't look at the eyes, Danny or it'll be the last thing you do."

Then he heard the voice of Lady Akhtar ringing as clearly as that of Danforth beside him. "Eheieh, Eheieh – Adeline don't touch that. Don't …"

It became a mosaic of words with no sensible pattern, as incomprehensible as the jeweled patterns of MacAteer's haunted kaleidoscope. The floor before him began to revolve, turning ponderously like the great wheel of a galleon. Mulholland stared open mouthed as the entire pentagramic floor sunk lower and lower, revealing as it did a vast architrave of obsidian darkness from which a glutinous mist began to spill forth. The voice rose in his head. He heard Danforth scream, in itself a terrible sound. He saw her gun arm point forward. A shot rang out. The head of the statue of Thoth splintered in a burst of stone. The floor ceased its dreadful movement, tilting at an angle. Around its circumference a circle of Doric pillars like the supports of a Tholic temple, could be seen through the swirling mist, beyond them impenetrable darkness. A great thrumming rose upwards, the sound of distant roaring water – an underground river heard but unseen, flowing in blinded cataracts through unseen depths. From the mist, vague tortured shapes rose in a hallucinogenic tapestry. The mist seemed to dance to the now

172

shrill and desperate voice. Danforth began to scream and fire indiscriminately. Mulholland drawing on his last reserves held his hands aloft and began the warding chant, then watched incredulous as the mists swept upwards like a huge grappling hand clutching towards him. Danforth threw herself forward and teetered on the brink of the circle. Mulholland reached out his hand but she was gone, twisting and falling into the blackness.

Mulholland's last vision of her, before he was blasted off his feet and thrown unconscious to the floor, was of a piteous face dissolving in a screaming hell.

*

A search party led by Bannerman found Mulholland three days later unconscious in a ravine seven miles from Loch Criach. He was suffering badly from exposure. It took a month for him to recover his health but it was summer before he actually made any rational sense. His sanity had retreated to some far corner of the mind where it lay dormant like an infant. His soul had been blasted to the outer reaches of the astral spectrum and although senior members of the Order were skilled in recovering damaged property even they had doubts. MacAteer had phoned the MOD and arranged that the false firing range be extended to certain geographical coordinates, and the area of the other house was officially written off as a dead end, never to be explored. MacAteer was there in the great hall of the Order as Mulholland delivered his stumbling report before lapsing into a profound silence.

"Shame about Danforth," he said quietly.

Mulholland nodded. "In her own way she was quite ... beautiful."

"Nothing you could do," said MacAteer. "You must have been drawn to it and whatever horror Crowley raised from the abyss needed a sacrifice."

Mulholland gathered himself. "Did the lab in Aberdeen get any more of Lady Akhtar's voice?"

MacAteer shook his head.

Best not to tell the young man that the lab results had arrived, revealing that the last words on the Dictaphone, the hopelessly distorted voice, were neither corrupted by time nor the denigration of the Lexican belt. Twisted, shattered beyond the realms of madness the recording was horrific in its parody of a human being.

But it was simply Lady Akhtar's voice.

173

THE MULL PLANE MYSTERY

L ate on the stormy Christmas Eve of 1975, former RAF flying ace Peter Gibbs left his hotel on the Isle of Mull with a bottle of claret in hand, boldly declaring that he intended to take a trip in his Cessna C150 G-AVTN. Given the weather, his fellow diners were astonished, but Gibbs was adamant he would fly, even though he declined to offer any explanation. Why the famous aviator decided to undertake such a bewildering and exceptionally dangerous mission is only one of several unanswered questions about the curious events that would occur on Mull that very wild and very cold December 24th.

For example, Gibbs's girlfriend, Felicity Granger, would later insist that only she was standing on the runway, holding a torch by which to aid his take-off, despite other witnesses claiming they saw the light of two torches moving independently of each other. Could someone else have been there? If so, who? Why? And why would Granger deny it? As Gibbs ascended, heavy sleet began to fall, so from the moment he was airborne conditions that were extremely poor beforehand became exponentially worse. In which case why, when it was blatantly obvious this was a deadly risk, did Gibbs not turn back? The concern felt by his fellow patrons in the hotel had clearly come with good cause. Even those with no flying experience had been worried. But when they'd expressed this, he'd merely been flippant with them. Again, why?

Whatever the reasons, Gibbs vanished that night.

No trace would be found, either of him or his Cessna, for the next four months – when a corpse was discovered on a Mull hillside, 400 feet up but less than two miles from the hotel where Gibbs had stayed that Christmas. It was identified as the man himself. There was no sign of his plane, so the initial assumption was that for some reason he had jumped from the Cessna while it was still in flight – until it was established by a pathologist that Gibbs had died from exposure, and that the only damage to his body was a slight wound on his leg. The proposition was put that he must have crash-landed in the sea and managed to swim ashore before expiring. But if that had happened, why would he then struggle so far uphill, crossing the road to his hotel in the process. In any case, this theory was put aside when examination of his remains showed that he'd had no contact with salt water. The conclusion must therefore be that Gibbs had landed on land somewhere, relatively safely, and had then died afterwards.

But if this was case, where was the plane?

This particular part of the mystery would remain unresolved for the next 11 years, until matching wreckage was discovered by a clam fisherman, over 100 feet under the Sound of Mull and smashed to such a degree that it seemed certain no-one on board could have survived the impact. In addition, its doors were locked, which itself defied explanation. Had no-one been flying the plane when it crashed? If not, how did the pilot exit? And did he seriously stop in the process so that he could lock the plane's door behind him?

Perhaps unsurprisingly, fanciful theories have emerged since, suggesting that Gibbs, thanks to his RAF background, was involved in some kind of espionage or intelligence work, possibly in Northern Ireland. Was it conceivable the IRA had captured Gibbs, killed him and then returned his body, leaving it out in the open as a lesson to the British? The answer had to be 'no'; Gibbs's body showed no marks of violence. In addition, it could never be easy killing someone by exposure, and why bother doing that if the aim of the exercise was to teach his paymasters a lesson? – death by exposure would normally equate to death by accident.

An adequate answer remains as elusive today as it did then. The great Mull Air Mystery remains one the eeriest and most baffling puzzles in the history of the Highlands and Islands.

MYSELF / THYSELF
D.P. Watt

'S muladach mi 's mi air m' aineoil, ...
'S èisleineach mi sa chuan rainich.
—from a Gaelic song

The bird broke the snow, plucking the young hare from the mouth of its burrow – a line of blood trailed across the white shroud of the hillside. Moments later a man approached, crunching through the thick, cold dunes. The bird circled twice about him, swooping in again, the sun behind it; its wings spread a moment, dappled grey, brown and black, and it settled on a thick leather gloved arm that the man held out, a chunk of mangled meat gripped in his forefingers. As the bird tore at this with its sharp beak he knelt to the dead hare, eviscerated it with a couple of slices of a stubby knife, and flopped it into a stained knapsack. The whole scene had taken a minute or so, and had been enacted a thousand times before, by other hands, with other birds, upon other hares.

After a moment or two he stood and surveyed the hill, looking around for any sign of the strange blueish light that had brought him here – for he had not intended to hunt this morning, and certainly not so high on the hills that were so deep in snow. As he searched for signs of what the unusual light might have been he looked back towards the sea and noticed a storm beginning to form. He started the climb down from the hillside, towards the magnificent castle, Dunrobin, which he had been lucky enough to call home for nearly a decade now. From up here it looked like a toy; some odd corruption of a French Chateau, with many turrets and spires, stone as white as the snow itself, and immaculate gardens that stretched out right to the edge of the cliff.

It reminded him of pictures he'd seen in travelling exhibitions of great majestic European castles, of kings and queens and stories of fairies and goblins.

There was something rather childish and silly about it, even with all its grandeur – or maybe because of it. It seemed out of place and rather alien, tucked away on the edge of the Sutherland coast, as though a giant child had cast it aside in favour of other playthings.

However unusual the place was, and however estranged his masters were from the life of the local Scots, he was grateful to have finally found work that he was passionate for. His years in Birmingham at a tannery had left him little time to devote to his real

176

love, the training and rearing of his birds. Here – at the patronage of the Duke, who was rarely present at the castle, and even when he was who would rarely call upon his services to walk out and hunt (the game here being less grand than the African variety the Duke had developed a lust for from his time fighting the Boers) – he had time to devote himself fully to his craft.

He had three birds now: Lucy, the peregrine, his most promising bird in years, and Toby – a juvenile dusky hawk that he hoped would replace Lucy as his main hunting bird when the time was right. The third was a barn owl – Florence – that he had found with a damaged wing following an attack by a pair of nesting sparrowhawks; he rarely hunted with her now, only the occasional nocturnal trip.

The castle grounds were perfect training for the birds; despite their ornateness they could easily be strung with training feeds and lures, and the surrounding woods allowed good cover and vantage for them as they swept across the structured hedges and pathways of the gardens. Indeed the woods were his favoured places to walk as he prepared the birds for the evening – there were few places more tranquil and contemplative than the open floors of a Scottish wood, he thought.

There was only one thing he did not like in the woods – 'the Museum', as it was called.

It was a small building just outside the walls of the castle grounds, dominating the pathway heading north. It had been built, originally, as a summer house, but without extensive clearance of nearby trees could never have offered much warmth, or even a view of the sea. The 3rd Duke had extended it and used it as a trophy house for the gruesome souvenirs of the sport that his son had recently come to adore.

He had only been inside once, at his master's invitation; accompanied by him as he proudly explained the trophies therein – stuffed animals from every continent; great glass cabinets filled with birds and animals posed for eternity in crude landscapes that gestured only faintly at their true habitat.

He found the place the most terrible building he had ever been in; a charnel house of macabre obsession. At least his world was a true encounter with the brutal fluidity of life, the endless exchange of blood and sinew in never ending pursuit of life – death, *out there*, was the only giver of life and to have swapped its relentless mutability for this exhibition of feather, fur and dust was, to him, an abomination.

About the only items in the Museum that interested him were some stones, carved with odd symbols that spoke to him about history, and the land, in ways he found difficult to articulate. The Duke had said they were etched by the ancient Picts and that they had yet to be deciphered, although a professor from Edinburgh University had expressed some interest and the Duke was hopeful that he might be able to sell the collection at some point – in the interests of science, naturally. That the stones might have been moved from their sacred ground was bad enough, but to have them begin a journey from institution to institution to be decoded and demystified seemed almost as terrible as the deathly frozen faces staring out from the cabinets.

He never returned to the Museum, but wandered the woods surrounding it almost every evening, keeping his distance from the unwholesome building as though it were some blight upon the ground. It was emerging from the northern edge of those woods that he had first seen the light – some two years before, one April evening at dusk. Since then he had seen it only twice again, on a bright November morning, when he initially thought it a reflection of binoculars, or the refracted light from a discarded bottle. Then again, in late December, high on the hill, where he had gone hunting for the hare as a premise for finding the wondrous light.

Something in its starlight twinkle had captivated him and he'd begun to yearn – even hunger – for it. He watched the hills every morning for a year. The light did not return. And yet, at the point that he was about to put it behind him as an hallucination or trick of the light, it appeared, just after dawn on a snowy day in early December.

It took him only ten minutes to reach it, going at an almost run, with Lucy circling and swooping about him.

The closer he got he began to hear words, becoming gradually more distinct against the harsh wind. The words were unclear, but it was certainly a voice. His ears – so tuned now to hear the slightest of sounds, especially when the birds had gone astray and could only be followed by the gentle tinkling of the bells on their jesses – strained to capture what it was saying as his eyes remained focused on the oddly shimmering blue light.

He felt his heart pounding with desperation as he willed the light not to vanish. His breath raged as it fought the cold air to carry him to his goal.

Then the voice called out, loudly, "mi-fhein", and a moment later responded with an enchanting melodic tone, "thu-fhein".

He was bewitched.

Lucy screeched and whirled around him, but he could not hear her now. Only the whisper of "mi-fhein", and the sing-song answer of "thu-fhein".

He began to mutter along with the voice, as the silvery-blue light sparkled and danced about him, and his final weary steps through the snow brought him to it, with arms outstretched as though to greet a returning lover. A shadowy shape within the light seemed to beckon with what might have been an arm, "mi-fhein, thu-fhein". And, enraptured, he stepped into the hill, and as the light blinked out of existence, his desperate falcon, Lucy, flew after him.

In an instant soil filled the shallow hole where the light had been, and the grasses knitted themselves together as though the ground itself was healing an ancient scar.

*

George Mills had seen the man three times now. The first time had been last Michaelmas term, the week before the holidays began. He had spotted a bright light – a sort of silvery-blue – out on the terrace overlooking the sea (the place where the headmaster, Dr. Crake, liked to talk over things when you had done something wrong). It had been the kind of light George imagined happened when stars were born, and from it there had walked a man – a strange man, wrapped up tight against the aching cold in leather trousers and a padded jacket, with a long black cape and tall black boots. He had a low-slung brown bag that knocked against his right leg as he strode along the pathway between the parterres. On his right arm there sat an eagle, or similar bird, it was difficult to tell with the brightness of the light. He was purposeful and George felt as though the figure had come to speak just with him. A moment later though the vision was gone and George considered it simply that – *a vision*.

But now, almost a year later, he had seen it again. In late November there had been a sudden snowstorm and that night, while all the boys struggled to sleep against the wailing winds, George had sat at the window by his bed and watched as the majestic garden was hidden beneath a layer of snow, the waves raging and soaring in the distance so that they too were as white as the land. Then the light erupted again, amplified by the blanket of whiteness that surrounded it, and the figure, with his bird, appeared, striding faster, almost running, down the path to the castle. It had almost reached the first set of stairs that began the long climb up the terraces from the gardens but vanished again as suddenly as before.

For two weeks since then George had held a vigil at the window to see if the man returned.

Sleep always took him, at some point in the early hours of the morning, when he could not fight his eyes closing anymore, however much he tried.

179

Then, on the last night of term, just as all the boys had been warned – by a very red-faced Mr. Slade (their year tutor) – for the "very last time!" that their pillow fighting and hijinks had to stop or they'd all be for a week's detention on their return in January, George saw the light again. The other boys were all busy telling ghost stories together, in whispered tones, so George pretended to be asleep to focus on the light. Either Tom Whittaker, who had the bunk above him, was also asleep or he hadn't noticed it – which would be strange because it was very bright.

The man stepped from the strange blueness and, as he had before, made hurriedly over to the steps up to the castle. This time he didn't disappear when he got to them, but neither did he make any attempt to go up them. Instead he raised his arm, pointing directly at George, as the bird flew about him in ever faster circles. The man said something. George could hear it as though spoken by someone beside him, and he spun around to check that there was nobody there. No, the dormitory was dark and the boys were all either asleep, or busy with their stories. The words whirled around him like a whispering breeze: "You are sad, in a lonely place."

And then, as before, the figure vanished, but the words continued to reverberate in his head and sleep refused to come.

The next day was one of the busiest in the school year, as cars came to collect pupils, sometimes driven by their parents who would greet them enthusiastically – much to the boys' embarrassment. Sometimes they were driven by a chauffeur who would load the trunk, and other belongings, as the boy sat in the back of the vehicle, enjoying the first moments of a luxurious few weeks away from the austerity of school.

Like many of the boys who lived quite far away, George had to catch the train home and so his belongings were loaded onto a coach that had been hired to take them down to the station in Golspie, and then on to Inverness and beyond. After the goodbyes in Inverness, he was finally alone and welcomed some peace and quiet to think about what had happened the night before. He sat in the carriage, idly tracing the passing scenery in the condensation on the window glass, as the heathery hills gave way to grassy lowlands, and the jagged interruption of villages, towns and cities began to accumulate.

A lady on the seat opposite him kept looking over, eyeing him with a strange mixture of curiosity and admonition – as though she wished both to care for, and scold, him.

"*You are sad, in a lonely place*," George muttered.

"Pardon?" said the woman, abruptly.

"Oh, nothing," he said. "I was just ... well, *just ... remembering* something."

"I see," she replied, followed by silence.

George started humming a carol.

"It's lovely countryside," she said, in a voice as soothing and quaintly southern as his mother's. "Are you going home from school?"

"Yes, Miss," he replied, "for Christmas."

"That's very nice," she said. "I'm sure your parents will be looking forward to seeing you very much."

"Yes, I *suppose* so," George said, rather doubtfully. His father always seemed to find him an interruption, even at the weekends, when he didn't have to go into London to sell people bits of paper that promised to pay them money when they died (a job that George found as morbid as he did perplexing – what need did you have for money when you were dead, after all!). And mother left most things to Mrs. Green, who cooked and cleaned the house, and looked after George while she went into Oxford to meet up with her friends. He knew his return would elicit the usual day or so of jubilant reunion followed by growing frustration until he was on the train back to Dunrobin in early January.

"Of course they *will*," the lady said. "Christmas is a magical time, for children especially, *with* children *particularly*!"

George wasn't sure if the lady had children of her own; there was something spinsterly about her that suggested she didn't.

"I suppose so ..." George repeated, his thoughts beginning to drift back to the scene in the castle gardens and the image of the man pointing and mouthing words at him.

"I'm sure you like to wonder what you will be getting for Christmas," the lady continued.

"No, not really," George said, distantly. "I think I know what it will be anyway."

"Well now," she said, excitedly. "What do you think your present might be?"

"It will be new cars for my Scalextric track that I got last Christmas," he said, flatly.

"That's wonderful," she said, her enthusiasm oddly excessive. "I bet they'll go very fast. You'll have an absolutely champion time with them."

There was a long silence. Then George turned to her and said, very seriously, "I see things that happened *before* ... *people* that once lived."

After a long silence, during which the lady seemed to be considering carefully how she might react; she just shook her head and frowned. "Oh, that's silly now ... that's *very silly* indeed."

"I don't mean *that* – I don't mean *ghosts*," he said quickly, hoping to be able to talk to someone, however briefly, to help understand what had happened. "I mean people that were meant to be dead but aren't. Or maybe they are and they want me to help them find out how to go away. I don't know ... I don't really know, but it's just that I see them anyway ... well, *him* – I see *him*, and his bird ..."

As he listened to himself he knew how *very silly* it all sounded, very silly *indeed*.

The lady held up her book and he turned back to the window. She got off the train at Birmingham without another word.

The Christmas holidays were always a lonely time for George. He wandered around the family's five-bedroomed house, on the outskirts of an Oxfordshire village, looking for things to amuse himself with. Books sufficed to while away some hours, and give him a sense of some other place and imagined company, but what he really longed for was the company of his friends and the fierce Highland countryside, and the odd symmetry of the school grounds; the wildness of the woods leading to the curious Museum and, of course, the oddities therein. But, most of all, he longed to lay at night and see the light, and the figure and to know what those words it had spoken really meant, and – what he wanted more than anything in the world – was to meet the man, and his bird.

On Christmas day he was as keen and over-excited as all the other children around the country must have been, but by late morning it was wearing off. He looked at his Scalextric and watched the bright new blue and red cars whizzing around the track. They were a Sunbeam Tiger and a Triumph TR4, from a catalogue that had come out a couple of years previously (George had been hoping for the Ford Mirage and a Ferrari P4 from *this year's* series), but he wasn't ungrateful. His father seemed more keen on them than he did anyway, or perhaps he was just feeling obliged to spend time with George. He shouldn't do, George thought, he was used to it now, and besides, all he wanted to do was think about the light, and the man, and the bird.

The beginning of Lent term came as a relief, for George and – no doubt – his parents. He was back at Dunrobin and had managed to get the bed by the window again (although, as ever, there had been no competition for the draughty bunk). Tom Whittaker wanted the bunk above him again and soon it felt as though his few weeks at home had been as much a myth as Father Christmas.

It was towards the end of the first week, during which lessons had been replaced by daydreaming, that the figure reappeared at dawn one Saturday morning. The light erupted towards the northern side of the parterre nearest the castle, and the figure strode from it, right up to the steps, the bird flying about the edges of wood.

The man pointed up at him and George heard the room echo with words again, but this time he could not understand them, "Mi-fhein ... thu-fhein ... mi-fhein ... thu-fhein ... mi-fhein ... thu-fhein ..."

Over and over again he heard them, to the point where, although he did not understand them, they still took on the horrible strangeness of language at the limits of disintegration.

He had to get outside and see the man.

He'd heard a rumour that there was a window in the larder that was always open, but nobody had ever checked because you could be expelled just for going in there, let alone going outside. But George, who was never normally disobedient, was impelled now by other demands – the last thing he wanted was to steal food from the school; he just wanted to get outside and find out what was happening.

The window wasn't open, but it wasn't locked either, so, after standing on a couple of boxes of tinned carrots, George managed to open it and crawl out onto the upper terrace. It opened onto some steps that led up outside the headmaster's office. At this time of night, there was nobody around and so, in the half-light offered by the waning moon, George was able to creep down to the gardens.

The man was gone, but the light was not. George headed across to the tall hedges of the northern parterre as stealthily as he could – always looking back up at the many windows in the castle, all of which were – thankfully! – dark. He could see the blue-grey light and prayed it would not vanish after he had risked so much to reach it – his father would kill him if he got expelled!

The hedges walled a trimmed lawn, with a patterned sequence of smaller box hedges within. To enter you had to go through an arched hedge that was the pride of the head-gardener. It was at the end of this twenty foot arch that the light appeared. It filled the opening at the other end and looked like one of those portals to another galaxy that George had seen in his *Eagle* comics. It had a shimmering blue colour that seemed at one moment like water and the next like some kind of mist. He felt as frightened as thrilled.

Before he had much chance to contemplate the light further though, the man appeared from inside it and the light was gone. Rather than the confident stride forwards he had adopted before. it

183

was as though the man were drunk, or injured. He lurched backwards, stumbling and flailing.

As he staggered back onto the lawn the moonlight caught him, and his bird leapt from his arm into the skies. George could hear the jingle of the bells on its talons and saw the stream of its leather jesses.

The man sounded as though he was choking as he gurgled out those strange words, "Mi-fhein… thu-fhein."

He held out his hand to George and, just as he fell backwards over one of the low hedges, he murmured, "Such a *sad*, and *lonely* place …"

George rushed over to him as he beckoned.

"Mi-fhein … thu-fhein."

George held out his hand and the man reached for him as though he were blind, his fingers, dirty with mud and blood, shaking violently as he did so.

"Oh, *Lord*," the man said, with a smile of exhausted delight, his eyes sunken and distant, "the things that *I* have seen – what *worlds* there *are*, and what *things* reside within them."

He clasped George's hand with a great exhalation of breath. The man's whole body seemed to go grey, as though lit by a gentle inner glow; and then he crumbled into an ashen heap upon the grass.

From behind the neatly trimmed hedges George heard a screech. A shadowy shape flew at him, the nascent glow of the morning sun behind it. His cheeks were furrowed by sharp talons, as fresh snow yields beneath the harrow. His eyes lay plucked on the glistening, frosty lawn, a dark ashen shape of a bird beside them, and – until the boys, and their masters, found him – he dreamt of other truths, and other histories; his imagination probing realities undreamt of by those who saw only the sad and lonely place about them. He was enthralled by visions of realms vibrant with other-worldly iridescences and astonishing alien colours, alive with peoples and creatures wild and noble, savage and serene; lands that would steal you away from this world whether you had eyes or not. And from that moment on George Mills was lost to us, a traveller in other places, as gently ominous and aberrant as they were violently wonderful and enchanting.

THE BAUCHAN

In traditional Highland mythology, the Bauchan is a kind of hobgoblin or bogle, an evil spirit capable of physically interacting with human beings. As so often with Highland lore, fables range across the spectrum from those in which the Bauchan can be bribed or befriended to the point where it will carry out chores, to those in which it delights in molesting, tormenting and even murdering any persons unfortunate enough to encounter it.

The latter of these myths is best embodied by Coluinn gun Cheann, a hideous Bauchan who at some unspecified date in the Middle Ages was regarded as a loyal defender of the MacDonalds clan of Morar. In appearance it was described as a lumbering headless corpse, massive of stature and wearing only a kilt. Though bloodied and pale as death, it wielded a broadsword and was adept enough in its use to slaughter and mutilate all those men who crossed its path. Its main weakness – in fact its only weakness – was that it could only manifest at night.

According to the most ancient tales, Coluinn gun Cheann first appeared in Trotternish, the northernmost region of the Isle of Skye. Allegedly still in possession of his head in those early days, the ghastly brute would leap out and ambush any man he saw, and put him to the sword, though women and children he spared. He later travelled to the mainland and continued these ruthless attacks in the Arisaig district. By now apparently, his head had been severed, but all this meant was that he carried it around with him and sometimes used it as a weapon – until it was finally stolen from him by an unknown hero. From this point on, the headless Bauchan became the guardian of the MacDonalds residing at Morar House, just across the water from the Point of Sleat on the Skye coast. He haunted a coastal path called the Mile Reath, and once again slew every man he met during the hours of darkness – a number of butchered corpses were left in his wake, some of whom were supposedly friends and neighbours of the MacDonalds.

Posterity does not actually mention how the MacDonalds felt about this, or even how or why this uncontrollable monster had ever come into their service, assuming it actually was – its many murders suggest it was only nominally defending their ancestral seat and in actual fact was terrorising the whole district for its own ends. This reign of fear finally ceased when a certain warrior, Ian Garbh, the son of McLeod of Raasay, sought to avenge his friend, the Bauchan's latest victim, and engaged it in an all-night battle, at the end of which, though his weapons were broken, he managed to catch his foe in a grip it could not shake off. As the sun arose, Garbh exacted a promise from the Bauchan that it would leave and never return, which it duly did, lamenting eerily as it dissipated into the morning mist.

The story of Coluinn gun Cheann is a curious one, a classic fairy tale in tone and yet exceedingly macabre. The brutal murders imply that a protracted series of violent incidents, murders or robberies, lies at the root of it. Almost certainly, their origin can be found in yet more clan feuding, with the local branch of the MacDonalds at the centre of it, though it may also be that the real Coluinn was simply a brigand who eluded capture for a significant period of time, and maybe was beheaded once taken.

All this said, the idea of a living creature that is nothing more than a trunk with limbs is not as unique as it may sound. Pliny the Elder, the Roman historian, described a race of headless men called the Blemyah, who he said lived in Numibia, southern Egypt. A generally reliable annalist, Pliny treated their existence quite seriously, giving much detail about their appearance and habits. Early medieval writings also discuss these bizarre beings as if their society in the Middle East was common knowledge, though their gruesome aspect became most familiar when it was adopted into medieval church architecture, to sit among the gargoyles, green men and other grotesques warning of the tortured forms men could take if they strayed from the path of righteousness. But how one such monstrosity found its way into West Highland folklore is still a baffling mystery.

BROKEN SPECTRES
Carl Barker

Any mountaineer worth his salt will tell you that climbing is all about trust. Putting your life in another man's hands on the end of a rope is a serious business, and Martin was a firm believer in the theory that a close relationship with your fellow climber enhanced the safety of both. That was before he'd started sleeping with Jenny though, and as Steve's Range Rover tore up the narrow track towards the north face of Ben Nevis, he began to wonder whether this ascent was a good idea after all.

For months now, he'd known that he would have to come clean to Steve about the affair, but despite several weekends spent together throughout the autumn on various endeavours, it had never seemed like quite the right time. In part, Martin had hoped that Steve would simply get bored of his new spouse and move on to something else, much as he did with everything in life once he'd taken full possession of it, but as the year drew to a close and winter's bite grew fresh teeth, Martin had finally made his mind up to confess this newest of sins to his oldest of friends.

The car lurched violently to one side as Steve stubbornly drove over another pothole, inadvertently throwing Martin against the passenger door and causing the contents of his stomach to voice their disapproval. Martin opened his mouth to grumble but then thought better of it.

"That ought to wake us up before climbing." Steve grinned maliciously as the road opened up into the meagre Torlundy car park.

Loose gravel splayed across frosted tarmac as Steve slung the Rover into the nearest bay and shut off the engine. Smoothing back thinning grey hair, Martin stared vacantly out at the tree line, listening to the random clicks of the engine cooling whilst Steve climbed cheerily out. Half-heartedly puffing out both cheeks in an attempt to convince himself he was ready to do this, Martin eyed his reflection in the overhead mirror. The pin-pricks that gazed back seemed somehow resigned to their fate: a slightly podgy middle-aged man sick of being a coward. He still wondered what a woman like Jenny saw in a man like him, but when Steve strutted past the window like he owned the whole forest, Martin was reminded that love and attention were sometimes more important than looks. He exhaled decisively and threw open the passenger door.

The close confines of the car park seemed eerily still. Trudging round to the rear of the vehicle, he found Steve industriously unloading their gear with his usual gusto. Allowing his companion to fill his boots in the role of porter, Martin eyed their surroundings, stuffing benumbed hands into pockets and watching his breath billow out. A thick frost covered much of the ground, hanging ponderously from the surrounding trees like anaemic tinsel. He stamped his feet and was slightly perturbed by the lack of an echo. Over in the far corner, a dilapidated hatchback poked from beneath the low-hanging branches of a deceased conifer, its filthy moss-covered windows and old-style number plate demonstrating amply that the vehicle had stood abandoned for years. Martin eyed it thoughtfully, wondering who the driver had been.

He watched Steve proudly withdraw a set of brand new carbon twin axes from the base of his bag and hold them up in the early morning sunlight, as though making an offering to the god of the mountain. Dull black in colour, except for the aluminium fittings, each bore a hooked top-shaft and saw-toothed steel pick, giving the appearance of nightmarish, petrified seahorses. Steve extended them proudly by the tails and took a couple of practice swings through the damp air. Taking note of the curved one-piece design and adjustable pick-angles, Martin let out a low whistle of appreciation.

"Very nice, mate but what happened to the Ushba?"

Steve shrugged, unable to tear his gaze from the blades.

"Chipped the tip off of it last week, didn't I," he replied.

Martin frowned.

"How in the hell did you manage to chip a £200 titanium ice axe, Steve? You only bought it last winter, for God's sake."

Steve looked at him sheepishly then and an odd smile played over tightly pursed lips.

"Guess I don't know my own strength," he shrugged.

*

The path through the trees extended a hundred metres or so before joining up with the 'Old Puggy' railway line – closed down in the Seventies when heavy rainfall had washed away part of the tracks. Though the narrow gauge rails had been taken up shortly afterwards, the occasional sleeper could still be glimpsed, half-buried beneath the undergrowth; defeated remnants of progress. They walked in silence for twenty minutes or so, the only sounds their boots and warring birds in the trees. Rounding a bend in the trail, they found a solitary piece of discarded rail-track disinterred from the earth, its rusted blade stabbed down through the back of a long fallen tree. To Martin, it resembled a knife and the weight of guilt on his shoulders shifted uncomfortably at the thought of his imminent confession.

Bearing left onto a more recent path, they hiked southwards into Leanachan Forest, the snow-laden conifers looming down on them like densely packed sentries. The track steepened in places, making the hike more difficult, but both men ignored the occasional bench, enlivened by the prospect of a challenging climb. Within the wet darkness of the trees, Martin's thoughts also shrank from the light, repeatedly playing over that last frantic encounter with Jenny till he felt himself stiffen. He'd never had anything remotely like this with a woman before and though he knew Steve's temper became almost feral when frayed, he knew he couldn't go back to the way things were before.

Emerging from the shadow of the forest, they were greeted with their first real sight of the Ben: the mountain's scree-laden ridges emerging from the low-hanging cloud like a behemoth in the fog, its towering bulk still half shrouded in mist. The plateau rose gradually towards the base of the mountain, where a complex system of andesite buttresses and exigent crags comprised the north face of the Ben. Despite their familiarity with the route, both men stopped for a moment to catch their breath, drinking in the view of the imposing cathedral of granite.

"Makes you feel almost sorry for the tourists, doesn't it?" Steve commented, referring to the pony track from Glen Nevis, which non-climbers used to reach the summit.

"She looks a little moody this morning," Martin muttered, eyeing the early morning cloud dubiously.

"Nothing we can't handle though, mate." Steve chuckled and marched on through the snow. Martin trailed forlornly along in his wake, still contemplating how to own up to his crime.

At the intersection with the Allt a'Mhuillin path, they crossed over a small stile and began the steady trudge up the east side of the burn. Despite a snow-hardened layer of topsoil, the ground remained boggy in places and it was an hour before they reached the CIC hut at the base of the scree pile.

*

Steve spotted them first, his keen eyes picking out the two climbers as the mist receded briefly from the face of the mountain like breath on a window. The men were about fifty feet above them, making their way steadily out of Zero Gully, along the shelf towards the base of Observatory Ridge. From their limited equipment and lack

189

of waterproof clothing, Martin took them to be either amateur enthusiasts or determined thrill seekers, and his spirits sank further. There was a well-known adage about there being old climbers and bold climbers, but no old and bold climbers, and the last thing that he and Steve needed was to be sharing the Ridge with a pair of adrenaline junkies in search of a fix. As they ascended onto the shelf though and gained ground on the pair, he saw that something was clearly amiss.

Both men looked under thirty, clad in rough tweed trousers and jackets, with only a single coil of old-fashioned rope each in place of kernmantle lines. Instead of gaiters, they wore tightly wound bands of coarse cloth, spiraling from ankle to calf, so as to protect the lower parts of their legs. The nearer of the two wore a brown derby hat and he turned at their approach, letting out a short yelp of surprise and brandishing a long-handled ice-axe, backing up against his companion.

Well aware of how quickly things could go wrong on a mountain, Martin took a placating step back.

"Alright now," he soothed. "Let's not get excited."

Reaching over his companion's shoulder, the older of the two men plucked the axe from the youth's trembling hands and bestowed a reproachful glare.

"It's alright, Angus," he chided through a hoar-frosted beard. "It's not him. It's not Wilson."

"Rag week again is it, fellas?" Steve muttered, visibly unhappy about the presence of two rank amateurs in such difficult conditions. "Got nothing better to do than get dolled up in fancy dress and come try get ourselves killed, have we?"

Toweling moisture from his face with his sleeve, Steve surveyed the pair's heavy clothing with a distinctly unimpressed expression.

"Do I take it, sir," the bearded man queried, squaring broad shoulders and drawing himself up to his full height, "that you take this to be some sort of jape? With those strange trappings and gay colours you gentlemen come bedecked in, I'd wager that it is you who are wearing the costumes."

Steve laughed brazenly, his short argumentative bark making clear the absurdity of the stranger's question. Behind him, Martin took stock of the pair.

The two men were like something out of a history book, clad in the primitive attire and simplistic equipment that one might have expected of Victorian climbers. Their rucksacks were made of simple cloth fabrics, fastened with leather buckles, each one containing barely enough room for a second rope, let alone the numerous screws and crampons required on a climb of this sort. The long-handled axe which the older man held, though, was a thing of exquisite beauty and Martin found it hard not to stare. The axe's three-foot shaft was fashioned from what looked to be a single piece of seasoned hickory or some similar wood, and the immaculate spike and metal collar which protruded from its tip gleamed hazily against the surrounding backdrop of snow like fine jewels upon mink. Martin figured it was probably an antique of some kind and as such maybe worth a small fortune. He found himself wondering why they'd brought it along when he noticed Steve also eying the axe. In his companion's case though, the expression was one of possession, not envy.

"Are those puttees?" Martin enquired, staring pointedly at the cloth wrappings which each man wore round his shins.

The bearded man ignored the question and removed wire-rimmed spectacles, agitatedly clearing his throat.

"Good sirs," he announced, somewhat formally. "I must regretfully inform you that our climb here today on the ridge is one born not out of recreation but of necessity, for there is an urgent situation unfolding at the observatory above. At this very moment, a man's life may well hang in the balance and any assistance which you can offer to our ascent will be most gratefully received, for neither my companion nor I are seasoned climbers of any particular worth."

Confused, Martin stared at the pair. The stranger's language was eccentric at best but the observatory to which he referred to was presumably the one built up on the summit at the end of the nineteenth century. But that had been abandoned for well over a hundred years, hadn't it? Martin seemed to remember reading somewhere about the building having fallen into disrepair during the First World War, before being gutted by fire. Steve and he had climbed to the summit many times over the years and could attest to the fact that the building was now little more than a ruin.

"You want to run that past me again, chief?" Steve muttered, arching his eyebrows.

"It's true!" cried the younger man, adding his voice in support. "We already tried to get up to the observatory via the pony track yesterday, but poor Mr. Wilson's taken leave of his senses. Screaming something about figures in the mist he was, and firing his rifle off in all directions, before he turned it on us."

"Wait," Martin asked. "Are you saying there's a man up there on the summit …with a gun?"

He and Steve exchanged a brief glance of concern.

"Of course," snapped the older man, testily. "Why else do you think we would be attempting such a hazardous climb if it weren't for the seriousness of the situation? With Wilson wandering around armed as he is, this is the only way to approach the buildings unseen."

The man's face softened with a mixture of fatigue and beseechment.

"Won't you please help us, gentlemen?" he pleaded. "My younger brother Charles is up there somewhere and we're growing understandably concerned for his safety."

Steve scratched the back of his head lazily and glanced over at Martin.

"Sounds like bullshit to me," he opined.

Martin was less convinced though.

"I don't know," he replied. "If there's even a hint of truth to their story, then maybe we ought to call for help or something?"

The two of them turned away, conferring in hushed tones whilst Steve pulled out his mobile and thumbed the hotkey for mountain rescue. The man with the beard continued to watch them intently, whilst his companion collapsed shakily onto the loose shale, clearly on the verge of hysterics. The scowl which Steve adopted when he held the phone to his ear told Martin they were on their own for the moment.

"No signal" he grunted in disgust.

Noting the strangers' open-mouthed expressions, he waved the mobile sarcastically at them.

"What? You fellers never seen an iPhone before?" he smirked.

The bearded man peered suspiciously at him.

"Am I to take it, sir," he enquired haughtily, "that you expect me to believe that object is some form of telephonic device?"

Now it was Steve's turn to stare.

"Look just what is it with you two?" he growled, having already decided they were being played for fools. "You just escape from somewhere or something?"

Martin laid a hand on Steve's shoulder, ignoring the brief pang of guilt which traversed his arm.

"Cool it," he urged. "Let's just get to the bottom of this and make sure no-one's hurt, okay?"

Steve rounded on him.

"You saying you agree with this whacko?" he blurted, nostrils flaring with indignation.

Martin let out the breath he'd been holding and watched it ebb round Steve's fiercely set jaw. "I'm just saying that if there's been an accident of some kind then we have a duty as fellow climbers to help in any way that we can."

"Well said," observed the man with the beard, grasping each of them by the shoulder. "And spoken like a true humanitarian. Tell me, friend, are you a medical man?"

Martin shook his head, allowing his hand to be taken.

"Doctor George McRae," the stranger announced, giving Martin's arm a friendly shake before turning to Steve, "and my young companion over there is Mr. Angus Rankin, assistant Superintendent of the Ben Nevis Observatory."

The young man feebly raised one hand in salute and Martin returned the gesture, concerned by the boy's dwindling colour.

"Between you and me," he muttered to McRae, "I'm not sure that your friend is in any condition to climb."

The doctor shook his head vehemently.

"Nonsense," came his matter-of-fact voice. "Young Rankin there is fit as a fiddle and besides, he knows a damn sight more about these rocks than I do, so he'll be coming along."

"Wouldn't it be simpler to just go round to the south face and walk up to the top?" Steve asked, keen to take charge once again. "Oh yeah, that's right, I forgot – the man with the gun."

His sarcasm betrayed his opinion and Martin heard Steve grinding his teeth. Being the alpha male that he was, Steve clearly wanted to remain leader of the pack and gathering up his rucksack and axes, he strode to the head of their column, eager to be at the forefront of any further ascent on the mountain.

"Well, if we're going up top, we'd better get started hadn't we?" he urged, making his way sure-footedly across the scree pile, never once looking back.

The other three exchanged a hapless nod of consensus before trailing after him. As they began to move forward, somewhere up above the stones shifted uneasily. Loose shale scratched its way down through the rocks, and the mountain seemed to rouse at the prospect of violence.

*

As the morning unfolded, their progress up Observatory Ridge was almost intolerably slow, the clear lack of anything resembling modern equipment on the part of McRae and Rankin quickly becoming a limiting factor. For the most part, the two strangers were fairly competent climbers, but the old-fashioned hobnail boots they wore were not best suited to the icy conditions and more than once, Martin was forced to come to the doctor's assistance when he lost his footing.

193

They belayed after just fifteen metres or so, Steve keen to set-up an anchor for the less experienced pair and so prevent all four of them being pulled back down the mountain. He added another line a further twenty metres up, to take some of the strain, and by the time the four men had conquered the first slab within reach, they had all broken into a sweat.

Taking a quick breather, Martin perched himself beside the doctor and watched the loose strands of mist swirl round the jagged edges below, coalescing into ominous cloud. A wandering breeze tugged mischievously at the powdered snow, coaxing it from every nook and cranny till the mountain resembled a giant snow globe of sorts. Above them, Steve donned a pair of expensive climbing goggles, their tinted circular lenses transforming his face into a dark mask of concentration as he ascended the next stage of the Ben. At the base of the slab, Rankin held fearfully onto his trailing line, his expression one of terrified admiration for the superior climber.

"He's been through a lot recently of course," Doctor McRae observed with a nod to the boy, "but young Rankin's a staunch sort of chap. I'm sure he'll be alright to the top."

Martin bit down on his lip, keeping his concerns to himself.

"You mentioned something about your brother earlier?" he asked, still unsure as to whether to trust McRae's outlandish tale.

"Yes, yes that's right," the doctor replied eagerly. "He's a physicist of some considerable note, a terribly clever chap. Perhaps you've heard of him?"

Martin smiled at McRae's obvious pride for his sibling.

"Charles has been staying at my home in Glencorse for a couple of months, but for the last fortnight or so he agreed to take up a temporary relief position here at the observatory so that Mr. Ormond – that's the Superintendent – and one of his assistants could enjoy a short holiday. Charles simply couldn't pass up the chance to continue his experiments at such a remarkable elevation."

Snippets of half-remembered facts slithered from Martin's memory as he began to piece this mystery together.

"So there's just your brother, Charles, and this guy, Wilson, stationed up at the top?"

The doctor frowned darkly.

"Young Rankin there is the only other officially sanctioned assistant to the Superintendent. No sir, Mr. Clement Lionel Wilson is what one might refer to as an unwanted interloper."

"What exactly do you mean by that?" Martin asked, but it was Rankin who answered.

"He means old Inclement's gone stark raving mad," the boy whispered. "I swear as the Lord is my witness, he pointed that hunting rifle at the two of us like a man half-possessed. If it hadn't been for the good doctor's quick thinking in flinging us down behind that outcrop, we'd be dead men for sure."

"That's enough, Angus," McRae admonished, not wishing to over-dramatise his part in the tale. "You be a good chap now and keep charge of that rope for Mr. Martin's companion."

The wind churned round the ridge, buffeting the three of them against the rock-face like marionettes. Martin shivered and found himself hoping there wasn't something nasty waiting for Steve when he climbed over the top.

"But what's it all about?" he probed. "What's Wilson after, I mean?"

The doctor cocked his head to one side, as though considering how best to phrase his reply. "I can't rightly say. There are rumors of course, but a gentleman never puts stall in such talk."

Martin nodded in bemused agreement.

"I'm led to believe that poor Mr. Wilson did not take kindly to being overlooked for the position of Superintendent when the Observatory opened last November. Especially not after he and his wife had invested so much of themselves into the acquirement of readings during the previous year."

McRae leant forward conspiratorially.

"There has of course been talk of a marital rift in the gossip columns of late, but I don't believe it myself."

The doctor clearly knew more than he was saying, but that bit about the readings struck a chord with Martin and he at last recalled some vague history from a guidebook he'd read –

Clement Wilson had been the man tasked with first setting up the observatory on Ben Nevis, back in the late 1800s. During his first year on the mountain, Wilson had reportedly taken a daily walk to the summit, to take various meteorological readings, whilst his wife, Annabelle, had recorded an identical set of readings at sea level, for comparative purposes. The data had formed the basis of a convincing argument for the building of a permanent station and within another year, construction of the observatory had been completed with funding from the Scottish Meteorological Society. The fact that the responsibility of running the observatory had then been handed to someone else had not sat well with Wilson in the following months and occasional snippets of rumour from the papers of the day had pointed towards his resultant alcoholism driving a wedge between him and his wife; a rift which had ultimately resulted in her leaving him and his descent into violence.

But that had all taken place over a century ago, hadn't it? Martin's head swam with the implications of what he was hearing.

If Wilson were still alive today, he'd be over a hundred and certainly not able to make his way up to the top. And then there were McRae and Rankin's clothes, and the antiquated equipment they carried. Somewhere deep in Martin's brain, the answers were screaming aloud, but the rational part of him refused to accept them. Clearing his throat nervously, he voiced the unspoken question birthed in his mind.

"I need to ask you something that may seem like an obvious question, but please humour me?"

McRae smiled pleasantly, having clearly taken a liking to Martin. "But of course, my dear fellow."

"What … year … do you think this is?" Martin asked, his voice emerging hesitantly in one long drawn out breath.

The question hung in the air between them – a moist punctuation mark – and as Martin waited for a reply, he felt the rope tethering him to his sanity fray. When McRae answered, it was if a great precipice had opened up between reality and him.

"Why it is the year of our Lord eighteen hundred and ninety four, as any fool rightly knows. Why my dear chap, are you quite well?"

Martin's face had gone as pale as fresh snowfall and he gripped the granite shelf till his knuckles went white. Taking firm hold of his shoulder, the doctor peered at Martin with a look of mild concern.

"Come now," he smiled reassuringly. "You look like you've just seen a ghost."

Martin stared down at the doctor's hand, reasoning with himself that nothing so corporeal could be a phantom or spirit. Despite their attire and old-fashioned speech, McRae and Rankin couldn't possibly be what they at first appeared to be. Yet, here they were on the mountain, like perfect excerpts from history, as real as anything else within reach. Time travel Martin mused, but by whom? Had they somehow trespassed into the past? Or were McRae and Rankin merely echoes into the future, projected forward through time's impenetrable mists? Either way, Martin still felt he had a duty to help them, but before he could consider things further, Steve's voice called down from above.

"Right lads, you can come up now, but take it steady, 'cos the powder's real fine."

*

Once they reached the halfway point, the going became easier. As the temperature continued to drop away, the loose snow which had so hampered their earlier progress gave way to more compacted drifts and a thickened layer of névé. Forced into relying on his new ice-axes for traction, Steve's expression became one of almost childish excitement as he carved out a usable channel for the four of them through the narrow gullies and outcrops, pausing every once in a while to affix a new ice screw, or to readjust his crampons.

The light mist that had roamed the lower parts of the ridge now became a soup-like fog and as Martin cleared a particularly difficult pitch, he saw that he could no longer make out the shapes of the others above. The bright red line clipped to his belt vanished up into a ceiling of mist. He coughed nervously, the sound unpleasantly wet in his throat, and for a moment the mist seemed to force its way down his esophagus; a watery snake.

A cry of warning sounded from above and he glanced up to see a cloud of loose shale come raining down out of the murk, throwing himself to one side just in time. As Steve's apologetic call filtered down, Martin glumly reminded himself that once this particular crisis was over, the two of them still had to bury the hatchet.

*

They reached the summit shortly after twelve; Martin crawling wearily over the top like a shipwrecked mariner washed up on a shoreline. He found his three companions stretched out on the ground, already well rested, and was permitted only a brief respite before Steve urged them on.

The mist in the crater was thicker than that encompassing the ridge, hanging malignantly on the ground like distended smoke, wrapping eagerly round anything within reach. Peering into the fog, they failed to locate any distinguishable structure and so elected to move forward in single file, taking a direction that young Rankin assured them would eventually lead to the buildings.

In the firmament above, a white haloed sun struggled valiantly to pierce the thick hide of the fog-bank, splintering instead into partial strands of light which stabbed down through the brume and were reflected back off the snow. Lagging a little behind, Rankin caught sight of movement and his breath snagged in his throat. Turning, Martin found him pointing fearfully away into the mist.

"Over there, Mr. Martin," the boy motioned, hand noticeably trembling. "There's someone watching us."

Following the boy's gaze, Martin eyes picked out a shadowy figure hovering at the edge of the mountain and he tensed instinctively, thinking it might be Wilson. The shape was humanoid, in outline at least, but that was where the similarities ended, for its

197

thin limbs were distorted to an almost impossible length, hanging from shoulders like rags. Noticing the rainbowed halo surrounding its head, Martin quickly came to his senses.

"It's just a glory," he laughed, "nothing to be afraid of."

The boy stared at him in wild-eyed incomprehension, the use of such an ethereal term having done little to dispel the fear of being hunted by some malignant entity.

"You know? A Brocken spectre?" Martin reassured him. "It's just a trick of the light – nothing more sinister than your outline being magnified onto mist by the sun."

Rankin peered over his shoulder and then back at the elongated figure. The look of terror on his face suggested that he wasn't convinced.

Holding his arm out, Martin moved forward till a second distorted shape appeared beside the first, copying his gesture.

"See?" he urged. "It's just your shadow, that's all."

He smiled at Rankin and ruffled the boy's hair.

"Come on," he smiled. "Let's catch up to the others."

Rankin stood rooted to the spot though, peering back at the spectre.

"For goodness sake, Angus," Martin cringed. "Don't tell me you're afraid of your own shadow as well?"

"That's just it, Mr. Martin," the boy mumbled. "I don't think it is me own shadow."

"Of course it is" Martin argued wearily, turning back to the glory. "Whatever makes you think that it isn't?"

"Well, because you're still standing next to me," the boy whispered, "and now there's only one shadow."

Martin hadn't noticed it before, but Rankin was right. The narrow distance between them was such that he should still have been able to discern two distinct figures in the mist. But as he stared back the way they had come, he saw that only one shape now trailed in their wake.

The figure moved, raising its wispy, incorporeal arms and beckoning them in a slow and deliberate manner. Martin felt the hair on the back of his neck stand on end and he took an involuntary step away, dragging Rankin with him. The spectre bobbed its head up and down, like a bird responding to movement, and then glided forward, its sickly gray outline detaching from the surface of the fog with a wet puckered sound.

They turned and ran, darting away into the mist before the shadow could reach them. Martin felt his heart in his mouth as he charged blindly forward, Rankin a mere second behind. The clang of his steel crampons on the rocks was like the cold chatter of teeth.

Staring wide-eyed into the blanket grey, Martin picked out Steve's hulking form up ahead. Quickening his pace, he drew up alongside and was near decapitated when Steve swung his axe instinctively round.

"Jesus, Steve!" Martin exclaimed, ducking away. "Be careful with those bloody things, will you?"

Steve eyed him grimly before returning his attention to the mist.

"That's bastard's out here somewhere," he whispered. "No way I'm letting some nut with a screw loose get the drop on me. No way in hell."

He noticed the distraught look on Martin's face and then the panting shape of Rankin beside him.

"What the hell happened to you two?" he asked.

Before Martin could reply, a shot rang out and Doctor McRae's clipped tones were heard calling for help. Charging through the mist, with Steve a clear yard out in front, the three men scuttled over a nearby rise to find the doctor cowering behind a low dry stone wall. Ahead, they could make out the squat circular buildings of the observatory and a thin tower above. Thick frost crystals had built up on the outer surface of the buildings till they resembled layers of dirty white fur and the complex resembled a family of woolly mammoths clustered together in the dip of the rocks. It took Martin a moment or two of stupefied gawking to realise the impossibility of what he was seeing in place of the ruins, before Rankin yanked his legs out from under him and they fell to the floor.

McRae was propped into a seated position behind the wall, one hand clutching his shoulder, where a dark patch was slowly spreading across the thick tweed of his jacket.

"It's Wilson," he wheezed, doing his best to ignore the pain.

A second shot rang out and the four of them ducked lower, Steve peering out through a hole in the wall as he tried to spot their would-be assailant.

"Of course it's fucking Wilson!" he hissed, eyes hungrily searching the fog for something to charge down and kill.

"Maybe we should get inside, out of range of that rifle?" Martin suggested, trying to gauge how long it would take to reach the observatory door.

A third shot went wide, pinging off the anemometer up on the tower and sending it spiraling madly. Within the miasma, they heard the low grate of a rifle being chambered.

"Are you sure that he's shooting at us?" Rankin asked, peering fearfully back the way they'd just come.

"Of course he's shooting at us!" Steve grunted. "Who else would he be bloody shooting at up here?"

As if in answer, Wilson's voice emerged from the fog, scraping through the gaps in the mist like dry sandpaper across skin.

"Why won't you leave me be, woman?" the voice yelled. "You know I can't take it back. I'm sorry, I didn't mean it to happen!"

Martin flashed Steve a warning look and began manhandling the doctor towards the observatory.

"Angus, give me a hand will you" he whispered, struggling to keep the now semi-conscious McRae upright.

They managed to haul him to his feet and prepared to make for the doorway.

"Steve," Martin hissed, hoping his companion would provide a distraction to aid their retreat. But only a space remained where Steve had crouched, and Martin silently cursed his friend's competitive edge.

Looks like we're on own," he informed Rankin, and together they managed to half carry, half drag the doctor to the observatory door.

The heavy oak swung open at his first kick and they ducked quickly inside, laying the doctor out on a nearby work bench before setting about barricading themselves in. The laboratory's worktops lay cluttered with broken glass and smashed instrumentation, someone clearly having taken out their rage on the room. Of Charles McRae there was no sign, save a pair of black Wellington boots which stood upright beside the workbench, as though the missing physicist had been plucked from them mid-experiment and dragged out into the fog. A threadbare carpet of mist skulked round their boots and Martin found a small locket on the floor at his feet. The glass within was badly cracked and, peering closely at the faded image, Rankin informed him that it was a picture of Clement's wife, Annabelle – the find confirming their worst fears, that the madman had been here before them.

Having at least a rudimentary understanding of first aid, Martin set about trying to staunch the doctor's bleeding, removing the lining of his jacket with a pocketknife and tearing it into strips to use as a tourniquet, whilst McRae continued to mumble deliriously. Outside, everything had gone quiet and Rankin peered fearfully out through the solitary window.

"Do you think he's coming back?" he asked. It took Martin a moment to realise he was referring to Steve.

Having seen the crazed look in his friend's eyes, Martin wasn't entirely sure that there weren't two madmen out there.

"Steve doesn't like to lose," he muttered.

200

Having made the doctor as comfortable as possible, he joined Rankin at the window and for the next twenty minutes they kept watch, jumping at every creak from the door. The afternoon sun which had previously hung overhead had now vanished and as the light faded, the fog's morose grey tones darkened to more sinister hues.

Casting off his usual mantle of caution, Martin stiffly walked to the table and picked up the doctor's antiquated ice axe, hefting it in one hand before pulling the barricade aside.

"Come on," he motioned. "We'd better go look for Steve before he freezes to death, or worse still goes and gets himself shot."

*

Frost crystals littered the ground outside but Martin's boots made only a slight crunching sound now he'd removed his crampons. As he stole cautiously over the rocks, watching for movement, he reflected on how strangely reassuring it felt to take charge of the situation.

He'd never considered himself a hero. Even when the two of them had been young, it was always Steve who gave the orders, his slightly combative manner making him a natural leader. But now that Steve wasn't here and the terrified Rankin and wounded McRae badly needed his help, Martin found that being in charge wasn't quite as frightening as he'd always assumed it would be. If dealing with the deranged Wilson and getting these people to safety was what he needed to do then he'd rise to the challenge, and once they were safely back down the mountain, he was going to tell Steve that he was in love with his wife.

The click of a trigger roused him for his thoughts as Rankin and he were thrown roughly to the ground, the shape of Clement Wilson coming barreling out of the mist. The axe slid from Martin's hands and he fell onto his back, staring up at a snow-laden giant.

Wilson's face was a mess of disheveled hair, his matted beard streaked with frost and dark blood. Having run out of bullets, he raised the rifle as a club, snarling down at Martin like a man half-possessed.

"It was you, wasn't it?" he screamed. "You brought her up here, didn't you? You showed her the way!"

Martin kicked out at Wilson's shins but the blow only served only to enrage him further. He glimpsed Rankin's crumpled form nearby, blood oozing from a blow to the boy's temple, his part in this over. Back-pedaling away, Martin quickly ran out of room and, as Wilson bore down, he found himself wondering whether Jenny

201

would have said yes if he'd asked her. He half-closed his eyes, not wanting to see the final blow coming but still unable to look away, and it was then that Steve appeared like a wraith through the fog.

The blade of the first seahorse made a slushy ripping sound as it tore into Wilson's back, opening him up from behind. The madman's mouth dropped open in a silent scream as Steve dragged the second blade across his throat, the axe's jagged teeth sawing open his gullet with a minimal fuss. Clement sank to his knees, gurgling thick blood as he toppled forward, spilled innards quickly melting the snow and staining the rocks beneath red. Steve wiped his hands on his jacket and launched a gob of spit at the eviscerated body, marking his territory like some victorious buck.

Shell-shocked, Martin crawled to the motionless Rankin and felt unsuccessfully for a pulse. He watched Steve drive his one remaining seahorse down through the top of Wilson's skull and leave it embedded there whilst he retrieved the hickory axe.

"We have to get back to the main building," Martin called weakly. "McRae needs medical attention and we have to get him down to the hut before he loses too much blood."

"No." Steve stood rigid, half-wreathed by the mist, the axe clutched possessively against his chest. When he spoke, his voice was strange and faraway. "We can't go yet."

A cruel smile snaked across his lips as he grasped the hickory shaft in blood-stained hands, plodding methodically forward.

"Did you think I didn't know?" Steve spat, slapping the flat head of the axe into his palm. "Did the pair of you think that you could make a fool of me and get away with it, Martin? Surely you know me better than that?"

Martin stared, first at the axe and then at Steve, all thoughts of rescue now fading. Looking into that cold smile, he suddenly realised how Steve had come to chip the tip off his Ushba, and he felt tears sting his eyes. Jenny wouldn't have been able to put up much of a fight against a man of Steve's considerable size and having just seen him crack Wilson's head open like an egg, Martin knew with agonising certainty that Steve's perverse need to possess all that he saw had led him to butcher his wife. Rather than suffer the indignity of losing one of his most prized possessions to another man, he had caved in Jenny's diminutive skull and now stood ready to do the same to the friend who he knew had betrayed him. Steve's manic grin widened when he saw that Martin finally understood and he stamped down with one boot, driving the steel teeth of his crampons into Martin's calf. Martin roared with pain and tried to drag his leg out from under Steve's boot, but the movement only ripped the wound further. Black spots danced across his vision and everything began to go fuzzy.

Then something else emerged from the mist.

Steve stood with his back to the observatory and so never saw the spectre approach. It dissociated itself from the fog like water ebbing from a much larger pool and sailed forward so quickly that Martin barely got a look at its face. The shape caught Steve in the middle of his back, wrapping its elongated body round his torso, long shadowy limbs snaking round arms and legs. Martin got a sense of something vaguely feminine as Steve was dragged towards the edge of the mountain, and he rolled over onto his belly, attempting to follow. Steve fought wildly, hacking repeatedly at the indistinct shape with his axe, but the honed blade merely passed through the mist, unable to make contact with this ethereal thing. As the spectre lifted him up and over the lip of the crater, Steve swung the head of the axe down into a groove in the rock, desperately anchoring himself there in an attempt to prevent being pulled over the edge. With blood spilling from his mouth, Martin crawled forward, watching Steve steadily weaken till his fingertips finally relinquished their hold on the axe and he was dragged out into the darkness.

No sooner was he gone than the vast curtain of fog receded from the mountain, as if tugged away by oversized hands. A cold wintry sun bore down onto the summit and to his surprise, Martin saw that no trace of the observatory or his companions remained. He lay back exhausted on the ice, eyelids falling closed as he replayed those last few moments again. When the spectre passed by, with Steve clutched in its deathly embrace, Martin had caught a glimpse of a familiar face in the dark heart of the shadow.

It was Annabelle Wilson.

*

Despite the occasional flash of warm sunlight from the overcast sky, almost two weeks of rainfall had left the plateau waterlogged, and as Helen made her way gingerly up the burn, she was forced to stop more than once, to dislodge her boots from the quagmire. Mountain climbing was not the kind of thing she usually went in for at the age of fifty-three and she was beginning to feel more than a little delicate as the years drifted by.

This trip had been the brainchild of her eldest son, Jack, and as she watched him stride purposefully onward, head raised towards the Ben with unbridled defiance, she reasoned that he was perhaps a little too much like his late father. Justin on the other hand had always been the more agreeable child and as he hung back to assist his dear mother, she smiled, letting his hands guide her over the rocks.

An angry shout from Jack summoned his younger brother, and as Helen watched them argue over the best place to begin their ascent, she wondered whether she had spoiled them both too much with her money.

"We'll go up via Observatory Ridge I think, mother" announced Jack, preparing their equipment.

Justin hovered obediently behind his older brother, nervously chewing on his lower lip.

"Are you sure this is a good idea, Jack?" Helen asked. "I mean, shouldn't I at least have had some rudimentary training before a climb of this sort?"

Jack gave a sly smile that did nothing to quiet her nerves.

"Nonsense" he said. "Both Justin and I are experienced climbers, and with both of us to guide you, I'm sure you'll have no trouble at all."

Not entirely convinced, Helen peered up at the Ben, her unease growing further with the sight of dark clouds overhead.

"But are you sure this is entirely safe?" she queried.

Justin opened his mouth to say something, but a fierce glare from Jack silenced him. The two youths exchanged a look of cold understanding and then took their mother gently under each arm, guiding her brittle bones towards the unforgiving wall of the ridge.

As the three of them began the slow scramble up the scree, Helen spotted two climbers on the rock face above. She glimpsed a tweed jacket, reminiscent of something her father once owned.

"Looks like we'll have company at least," she observed, pointing up at the pair.

Both boys glanced up and Jack's features darkened, the taut mask of concentration slipping momentarily to reveal a monster beneath. Stroking the knife at his hip, he recalculated for a moment before breaking into a wide grin.

"They don't look too experienced do they, Justin? Shall we go up and give them a hand?"

Justin's smirk mirrored his brother's.

"I'm still not sure about all this you know, boys" Helen panted, already struggling for breath.

"Oh come along, mother" Jack chided. "What's the worst that could happen?"

Atop the Ben's darkling summit, a morose bank of fog bore down from the clouds to enshroud the top of the mountain. At its edge, two elongated feminine shadows patiently watched the climbers below. A slow wind played over the rock face, tugging loose shale from its many hollows, and once again the mountain stirred at the prospect of violence.

THE BIG GREY MAN

"I was returning to the cairn on the summit in the mist when I began to think I heard something else than merely the sound of my own footsteps. I heard a 'crunch', and then another 'crunch' as if someone was walking after me but taking steps three or four times the length of my own. I listened and heard it again but could see nothing in the mist. I was seized with terror and took to my heels."*

So spoke Professor Norman Collie in 1925, describing an experience he had near the summit of Scotland's second highest mountain, Ben Macdui, in 1891. It is an account many climbers today will be familiar with, because the unknown beast of Ben Macdui is still one of the most mysterious and terrifying beings in British mountaineering mythology.

Ben Macdui itself contributes in no small way to the aura of very genuine fear this oft-told tale creates. Standing 4,295 feet above sea-level on the southern edge of the Cairngorms, it is a remote and lonely fixture; it also suffers from extremely severe weather – heavy snow in winter and much mist and fog for the rest of the year. Stories that its high slopes and passes are home to an enormous, aggressive biped have been told for generations.

The creature was certainly known about in ancient times, when its old Gaelic name was 'Am Fear Liath Mor' (literally 'Big Grey Man'). In the late 18th century, the great Scottish author, James Hogg, described a blood-chilling encounter with what he estimated was a 30 foot-tall giant, whose close details were hidden in frozen vapour, though Hogg said it was dark of aspect, "like a blackamoor". In 1903, renowned mountaineer Henry Kellas reported something very similar. In 1943, climber Alex Twenion claimed that he shot three times at a colossal shape in the fog as it lurched menacingly towards him. Shortly afterwards, in 1945, a former mountain rescuer, Peter Densham – a man very experienced in the high peaks of the Cairngorms – told friends how he'd fled the mountain in terror when a massive, two-legged form chased after him.

There always seems to be an overwhelming sense of terror and panic in the presence of this unknown thing, though one or two witnesses have hung around just long enough to get a better look at it. They describe a burly, "crudely-made" humanoid form, somewhere between 12 and 20 feet tall, which is either grey in colour, or covered in short grey fur. Its face has variously been described as "malign", "inhuman", "apelike", or weirder still, "non-existent".

Owing to the harshness of the terrain, no major searches have ever been launched on Ben Macdui, but the majority of the sightings centre around the Lairg Ghru Pass, and perhaps not surprisingly, more than a few climbers no longer use that route.

Theories abound as to what the Big Grey Man could actually be. An optical illusion is one possibility – mountain mist, refracting sunlight, rapidly altering perspectives and so on, with the accompanying panic caused by exhaustion in the presence of this awesome landscape. However, other theorists dismiss this explanation as too pat, pointing to the very solid, very real nature of the phenomenon so many reliable witnesses claim to have experienced. One question raised is could the Big Grey Man be a relict woodwose – a mysterious hominid rumoured to have lived in the very wild parts of Britain during the Middle Ages, and supposedly glimpsed much more recently in the Highlands – in effect, a Scottish Bigfoot?

The reasons why this must be nonsense are almost as many as those given for why the North American Bigfoot must be nonsense, and yet – as in North America – the reported sightings continue. As usual in these kinds of cases, no real answer will be possible until some carcass or other type of physical evidence is discovered. For as long as it isn't, scary rumours will persist that an unknown something prowls the desolate slopes and icy ridges of Ben Macdui.

JACK KNIFE
Gary Fry

"Is your boot still broken, Baz?"

Loading their luggage back into the car, Barry turned to his brother and nodded. "I haven't got round to having the latch fixed yet," he explained, realising that their holiday in Scotland had accounted for most his disposable income this month. But then he touched the coolbox in which he'd stashed what little remained of the beer he'd taken along for the break. "Not that we've anything worth nicking, Sam."

"There's all my books!" the young man protested, referring to the collections of myths and legends he'd insisted upon taking on the trip. "There's a lot of ..." – he fought for the word, the way he'd once been taught in his special school – "... of *classified* information in them."

Yes, thought Barry, recalling the many unlikely stories he'd heard during the last few days, *I'm sure the Scottish authorities are quite unaware of all the werewolves, kelpies and selkies that occupy the area ...*

But he shouldn't be dismissive; his younger brother, seventeen years old, had been born with a severe learning disability and needed all the encouragement he could get.

This was why Barry had taken Sam away for a weekend, up to Loch Ness where they might hunt for monsters. They'd had a fine time in a budget hotel near Inverness, the only thing Barry could afford given his economically impoverished status as a medical student. He was between academic terms – training to be a GP – and had relished the chance of a few days out in the wilds, drinking beer, revisiting childhood memories involving himself and Sam.

Certainly his parents – with whom Sam lived permanently, after leaving school last year – had been glad of the break. Barry had also just split up from a girlfriend and had thought putting some distance between himself and her back in Leeds would help. It had kind of worked.

After slamming the car boot on its faulty latch, he accessed the driver's seat, starting up the engine and assuming his brother would join him at his side. Sam soon did so, clutching another of his scaremongering books, which hardly made Barry feel excited about the long journey back to England. But looking around as the car began moving, he figured there were worse places to be.

The Scottish Highlands were magnificent, so many barren hills set alongside beautiful glistening lochs. During the last few days they'd gone in search of the famous monster, eaten haggis in a traditional inn, listened to bagpipes, drank whiskey, and laughed at men in kilts – the whole Scottish deal. The people they'd chanced upon had been charming, not once demonstrating that infamous but clearly mythical hostility to visitors from over the border.

Barry was glad he'd come – he'd always found travel good for mental well-being – but would also be pleased to get back on campus, to his studies which were now reaching a critical period. Heading for such an empirical world as the modern health service, he was unlikely to learn much useful from his brother.

As the car chugged towards an A-road south, Sam started quoting from another of his collections of myths and legends.

"There are lots of names for the Devil in Scotland, Baz. One is *Black Donald*, a figure who can disguise himself as many different things, but who is always given away by his cloven feet." He paused, looking at his brother. "What does *cloven* mean, Baz?"

Barry had never much liked Sam calling him 'Baz' – it made him feel young again, when he'd been frightened and confused. They'd both grown up in a modest suburban house, and Barry had attended a comprehensive school, where, despite finding it hard to mix with his fellow pupils, he'd done well in his exams and ended up getting a place at university. He felt he'd come a long way since being so shy and uncertain, but as ever, his insecurities lay beneath the surface, especially when out in places like this, miles from civilisation.

"Cloven means split in two, Sam." Barry demonstrated with his gear-changing hand, coupling index and forefinger alongside third and pinkie.

"But I don't get it. Aren't *all* feet cloven, then?"

"How do you mean?"

"Well, if cloven means split into two and we all have *two* feet, why is Black Donald different from the rest of us?" He hesitated, thought for a moment, and then added, "Shouldn't the book say the Devil has a cloven *foot* – or rather, two of them?"

This was part of Sam's problem. Despite a keen analytic nature, he often interpreted linguistic shorthand – the kind used with common sense – quite literally, worrying concepts to death, so that other people could also lose their grasp on what was factual or otherwise. It could be draining, and Barry pitied his parents putting up with this all the time. After finally qualifying as a GP, he was determined to do as much as possible for families facing similar difficulties.

209

"Tell me something else about him," Barry said, keen to escape the tortuous logic of Sam's earlier question.

His brother rose to the challenge, quickly readdressing the book as the car hit the A-road and then passed a national speed limit sign.

"Another name for the Devil in Scotland is – ah, *here* we have it – is *Clootie*, meaning 'one division of a cleft foot'." If Sam had sounded like he'd just quoted the text verbatim, his next comment was back to his usual fussy self. "But if a Clootie is only part of a foot, why is a Devil with two feet named after just half of one?"

Barry sighed, accelerating the car in protest against such verbal convolutions. Observing miles ahead of open road, flanked by patches of woodland, he said, "I meant tell me more about that other Devil's disguises – *Black Donald*, did you say he was called?"

But Sam had grown tired of his research, mercifully tossing the book into the backseat and looking through the windscreen at all the glorious landscape sweeping by, a blur of greens and browns.

"Go faster, Baz," he said, a familiar request during their drive north a few days earlier, as the younger man had tried to derive fun from the otherwise long journey.

"I can't," Barry replied, knowing he must handle this moment sensitively. His brother could sometimes be violent when he didn't get his own way; he'd commonly hit fellow pupils at his special school, as well as a number of teachers. But then Barry appealed to an obvious fact. "Don't you see the speed cameras up ahead?"

In truth, Barry had yet to see even a single camera, but plenty of signs in the roadside had announced them. He suspected that most were there to bluff, but it was impossible to know which weren't. And so he must obey the law.

"I don't get it," Sam exclaimed, not the first time today. "How come we have to go *this* slowly when there are no people or even houses around?"

Barry didn't consider sixty miles-an-hour particularly slow; he'd seen footage during his studies of damage transport could do to pedestrians at even lesser speeds. But on this occasion he had a sound explanation; Barry had got talking last night to a local in Inverness, who'd provided a sensible reason for the prevalence of cameras in this area.

"A lot of trucks come off boats back in the port we visited yesterday. In continental Europe, especially Germany, the speed limits on roads like these are far higher than in Britain, and drivers from such countries sometimes forget that. It's common for trucks to jack-knife out here, blocking the route for other motorists – maybe even folk like us."

"Jack Knife," said Sam, focusing on the most inappropriate part of Barry's response. "That sounds like a killer, doesn't it? Like *Jack* the Ripper who used a *Knife* to murder women!"

These unsavoury interests – first the Devil and now serial killers – unsettled Barry, to such a degree that he tried to keep the discussion in safer territory.

"As I say, Sam, that's why the authorities keep the transport here moving at a sensible speed."

A long silence followed, during which Barry observed the day declining, long shadows appearing under the clusters of trees they passed. It was late autumn, a time for spooks and ghouls, but in this landscape there was little movement, only unmistakeable birds of prey wheeling high above, prowling the grim sky with imperious silence. Barry was still looking there, away from the road, when his brother spoke again.

"Well, *that's* a coincidence."

Barry initially worried about what Sam had meant – a serial killer, perhaps? A goblin? The *Devil* himself? – when he glanced up and simply saw it: the truck laying in one side of the road, its cab and trailer toppled over and sitting at ninety degrees to each other.

"Oh *Christ*," said Barry, a barked exclamation, which Sam found amusing, sniggering until his brother quickly turned his way. "Don't laugh, man. This looks serious."

It certainly did. Drawing the car to a halt, about fifty yards from the wreckage, Barry rolled down his window to observe more of the accident, which had failed to seal off the road but made a chopstick mess of woodland to the right. One tree had almost been uprooted, while others were snapped at sharp angles. Steam rose from the felled behemoth, and although its engine had died, there was an uptight hissing sound, like a punctured radiator swiftly losing liquid. The driver's compartment was laid on its side, the windscreen smashed into multiple fragments scattered across the pine-strewn ground. Barry was unable to see the trailer's flanks and couldn't work out what its load might be, whether harmless stuff like machine parts or maybe something more dangerous – gas, perhaps, or chemicals. At any rate, this was why he'd parked so far from all the mess.

Sam reached for his door handle, as if about to exit and go investigate. But Barry stopped him, one hand gripping his arm. "No, mate, stay here. Let *me* go."

"That's not fair," his brother replied, which wasn't the response Barry had hoped for. "*I* want to see something exciting, too."

This certainly wasn't why Barry had decided to approach the accident site. With his incomplete medical training, he had a responsibility to provide support. What if the truck driver was still alive, crumpled in the cab and losing blood by the moment? Barry might be able to help, or at least call someone who could.

Plucking his phone from one jacket pocket, he climbed outside and started edging forwards. By the time he'd moved half the distance, he heard no sound from behind and assumed that, for once, his brother had obeyed him. Then he was right up close to the wreckage, smelling its sulphurous scents, observing burnt rubber smeared onto the tarmac, and becoming aware of coils of smoke fading into the sky.

It was getting dark, but sufficient daylight remained to assist Barry's approach. He went first to the front of the truck, squatting to see what travesties awaited, blood and gore likely possibilities. That was when he spotted the driver, a pale-faced man pressed into the crippled contours of his seat, head burst open like a fruit against the vehicle's collapsed metal roof. He wasn't merely dead; he was *hideously* dead, impossibly mangled, like a doll whose limbs defied conventional anatomy.

"Jesus Christ," muttered Barry, not knowing why he kept invoking his race's alleged saviour, since he had no religious sense at all. "What the hell am I supposed to do about th–"

Still crouched in front of the ruined vehicle, he thought he heard a noise from nearby, something sharper than the failing engine sounds, and coming from one or the other side of him. But after flicking his gaze in both directions, he spotted nothing other than a dark bird to the left, pecking at the ground with disdain. Perhaps the hungry creature awaited an opportunity to stray closer to this fresh source of sustenance, the impromptu meat-shop to which Barry now redirected his attention.

Something wasn't right about the corpse. He'd felt this while first inspecting it, but now, once the shock of seeing so much red had diminished, he was much surer. It was clear that the man had died of a head trauma and maybe even a broken spine, but a further injury seemed inconsistent with many suffered by victims of similar accidents. There was more blood than there should be in the chest area, where the ribcage looked crushed, with a ragged, gaping wound at the centre. Barry observed that the man still wore his seatbelt, the tight strip ensnaring his lower gut like a noose around a neck. But if his injury hadn't resulted from a collision with his steering wheel, what *had* caused it?

"Is it *really* bad, Baz? Can I come and look?"

His brother's sudden use of his truncated name made Barry want to yell with anger. But, turning to view the younger man standing only yards behind him (but mercifully out of sight of the driver), he wondered what good that would do. Barry had other matters to attend to, the most crucial of which was calling authorities and reporting this incident. Despite so many signs along the road announcing camera monitoring, it was possible that nobody knew about the crash, that he and Sam were the first people to chance upon it.

Which suggests that the accident occurred recently, thought Barry, only now reflecting on how deserted the A-road was this Sunday afternoon. *In which case, what – or who – had caused that damage to the driver's chest?*

But he refused to think about that, merely stood to cross to his brother while hoisting his phone. So far away from a town, he'd be lucky to get a reception, but he noticed one scant bar above the photo of his ex-girlfriend he'd yet to replace as his homepage wallpaper. He dialled 999.

"What's happening, Baz? Why won't you let *me* look?"

"Not now, man," Barry replied, the line connecting slowly. "Come with me back to the car."

His purpose on this occasion was to protect his brother from distress. For all his adult interest in dark human issues, Sam was easily disturbed and could become uncontrollable. When Barry steered the younger man back to the vehicle, someone answered his call, a faint voice but definitely there, like the whistle of a master to some wayward dog.

Barry asked for police and an ambulance, despite suspecting there was little that paramedics could do for the truck driver. But in such circumstances, he guessed that procedures must be followed and that medical staff were best placed to deal with them.

After offering his location and hanging up, he joined Sam back in the car and struggled to suppress a mental image of a gaping chest wound, as if … as if someone had fished inside there and plucked something out.

But that was ridiculous. Stupid. Foolish.

He turned to face his brother. "I *told* you not to leave the car. Why *did* you?"

Sam looked forlorn, all his usual insecurities writ large across his man-child face. "Don't shout at me, Baz. I just wanted to see the crash."

"Oh, for God's sake, man. Real life isn't a book or a film. Blood doesn't look like ketchup." Barry reached into the backseat and snatched up the book his brother had been reading earlier. "Things can get messy and … and the Devil … the Devil *doesn't* exist."

Barry had hesitated because, while delivering this preachy monologue, he'd spotted something moving outside, off to the left where he'd spotted that bird near the truck. Indeed, *this* looked like such a creature, despite being blurred, as if he was focusing somewhere short of its actual location. But how could that be true when it appeared to cling to a tree close by, watching silently like some reticent funeral attendant? Barry couldn't be looking at something – or some*one* – much farther away ... could he?

But no, that was impossible, even though moments later, with a burst of black wings resembling folds of a cape, this shape launched into the air, either from that tree nearby or ground way beyond that.

Black Donald, a figure who can disguise himself as many different things ...

Barry, still holding the collection of Scottish myths as if it was all nonsense, suddenly felt as if he was getting drawn into his brother's unsettling mind-set. But then he passed Sam the book, started up the car engine, and found his gear.

"If you've called the police, you'll have to wait till they get here," said Sam, with surprising good sense. But he also looked at the volume Barry had just handed him, as if it was a snake he'd wanted rid of. "What's wrong, Baz? Why do you look so ... *scared*?"

Was that true? Was competent, intelligent, *normal* Barry being supported by the usually helpless younger man?

He was unable to figure it out. All he knew with certainty was that he was frightened and must get away as quickly as possible. In his mind's eye, he saw again that savage chest wound and then a figure nearby becoming airborne on wings too blurred to belong to what he'd first taken the thing for. *But what the hell was the alternative*, he wondered?

The car started rolling towards the capsized truck. By this stage, Barry wasn't looking at the crash's steaming hulk – there could be nothing dangerous in the cargo; that would surely have manifested by now – but at the road ahead, at predictable white markings down its centre. Just beyond the sprawling accident, these appeared to develop a *reddish* strand. But there was more: moving away from the site, the entire width of the lane was covered with the same bright marks.

Upon closer inspection as the car rolled on, Barry realised that these could even be footprints, but such unusual examples that they mightn't be that at all. They were shorter than any adult's foot, but broader than a child's. Each imprint seemed to have *two* segments, one on the left, the other the right.

Black Donald ... who is always given away by his cloven feet.

214

Now shaking, Barry depressed the accelerator, sending his vehicle beyond the truck and its single occupant, a man who appeared to have had his heart torn clean from his body.

Yes, Barry had to admit that this was a real possibility; he'd seen similar images during his studies, autopsy shots taken mid-operation. Despite all the damage it had done to his body, there was no way a transport incident could cause such an invasive injury; someone must have done that to him *after* the event.

He'd driven at least a mile before Sam spoke again, his voice sounding needy. "What's happening, Baz? Why did we leave so fast?"

"Can you stop calling me *Baz*!" Barry snapped back, but immediately regretted the outburst, sensing his panic ease as he spoke. He turned to face his brother. "Hey, look, I'm sorry, man. Pay no attention to me. I ... I just saw something horrible back there."

"That's what *I* wanted to look at," Sam replied, but then Barry, tired of such naïve nonsense, slammed on his brakes.

It was then that they both heard the bump from the car's rear.

There was nothing in the backseat but a jack, foot-pump and car tool, in case Barry ever got a puncture. And so the noise couldn't have come from there. But as Barry parked the car against one kerb of the still deserted road, his mind raced back to when he'd started out on this journey, loading the boot with their luggage.

The boot with a faulty latch, he was immediately reminded.

Turning slowly to look at Sam, who now sat as upright as his brother, Barry said in a whisper, "Before you spoke to me back at the accident scene ..."

Sam nodded, attention sharpened by the situation. He probably wondered why his brother had talked quietly and might be scared, rattled, liable to act unpredictably. But then he quickly added, "What about it?"

Barry held the younger man's stare while finishing: "...how long did you leave the car unattended?"

"What do you mean?"

"Long enough for someone to sneak up behind us and ..." He hesitated a moment, as if weighing up the implications of revealing more; but then he asked, "... long enough for someone to climb into the boot?"

"Who? Who'd want to do that? And ... *why*?"

Barry failed to reply, thinking hard.

"What did you see back there, Baz ... I mean, Barry? What *was* it?"

Barry recalled the red marks on the road, close to the violated truck driver. It was as if someone – or at least some*thing* – had caused his body further damage, before departing with booty, leaving behind wicked footprints – *specific* footprints, their form was split into two, like the cloven hooves of an animal, but one that could ascend to become bipedal.

Now Barry rebuked himself for not checking other parts of the road for similar markings, perhaps even including the area behind his parked car at the time. But he and his brother were now long gone, maybe a mile away. Police would arrive there soon, anyway. But what use was the law to them *here*, where perhaps the true threat existed, secreted in the boot with its faulty catch?

Barry turned to address Sam again. To tackle the next step, the younger man must be fully informed about the case. "Listen," Barry said, and told him all he knew – especially about the dead truck driver bearing such an unlikely chest wound – in a voice too low to be heard by what might lie in waiting nearby.

Barry grabbed the car tool – a big metal wrench – from one of the rear footwells and then climbed outside. He'd instructed his brother to do the same, walking to the vehicle's rear.

The plan was for Sam to lift the boot while Barry stood alongside with the car tool raised high. If anyone pounced from inside, Barry would do what he had to do; if not, they could both relax and even drive on. The authorities had his name and would be in touch; he could tell them that he'd had his brother to consider, someone with special needs. No law would ever question that.

"I'm scared, Barry," Sam announced, now only a stride from the boot. Barry recognised his expression as one that usually marked his difficult episodes, sometimes even violent ones. He tended to lash out because he was afraid, and it was only now that Barry realised that maybe Sam's obsession with the world's darkness was an attempt to understand dangers he might face.

But there was no time to dwell on such insight; he now had a task to complete. "Don't be frightened," he whispered to his brother, even though his arm – the one holding up the wrench – also shook. "Just remember what I told you: lift the boot and then run away several yards. Can you do that for me, Sam?"

"I … I think so."

"Good. Okay, then. After three."

Something made a sound nearby, like a bird chuckling through its vicious beak. But Barry wouldn't be distracted. He observed the motionless surface of the boot, listening for any violation of the silence within. Then he spoke again.

"One …"

Sam's hand reached forwards.

"… two …"

Sam's hand gripped the latch.

"… three!"

Sam hoisted the car boot, sending it flipping up in a rapid arc, which caused the ageing springs to groan … and exposed its creepy, uninvited tenant.

Their cases. That was all that was in the luggage compartment. Those and the coolbox in which Barry had placed the few unopened cans of beer he'd brought back from their short holiday.

Relief sweeping through him, he felt as if he could use a shot of alcohol now. Yes, he was driving and had a future responsible career to consider, but surely this situation justified excess? And so he reached into the boot to access his treasure chest.

Sam – who'd just obeyed his brother's instruction, pacing back several yards from the car after opening the boot – came racing forwards, halting at Barry's side. "Did we get him, Baz?" he asked, his former enthusiasm resurfacing, involving serial killers and devils, ghouls and monsters. "Did we get *Jack Knife*?"

Something about this comment – the way it made Barry feel as if, since they'd reached that damaged truck, he'd been sharing one of the younger man's hallucinations – forced him to acknowledge that a problem remained, that the driver he'd observed back at the crash site had still been violated in a sickening way. But then he plunged one hand into the harmless coolbox.

And screamed.

When his hand came back, he held an object familiar during his studies: a human heart, plucked from a space reserved for beer cans.

He flung the thing aside and it landed like a fish on the ground between his brother's feet.

That was when Sam also started screaming, all his brave talk this weekend withered away like old fruit on a vine. There was genuine horror here: a human heart, dripping and pulsating.

"*Jesus Christ*," said Barry, flinging out his arms. His body felt limp and he didn't immediately acknowledge the way his brother took the car tool from his hand, as if now eager to defend them both.

But then Sam also found his voice. "No, not Jesus. The other one. The Devil. *Black Donald*. With cloven feet. Two of them. A master of disguises."

Just then, another bird – or maybe even the same one as earlier – issued a loud squawk, which again sounded like impish laughter, the kind usually accompanying pernicious tricks.

But Barry refused to pursue this line of reasoning; that way lay madness and perhaps even his brother's twisted logic. *Jack Knife*, had the younger man suggested? A killer at large in the area? And now that had to be true, hadn't it? Evil needed no supernatural excuse. Barry understood this from his studies, all the victims of suffering he'd had to assess.

"It's him! It's the Devil! It's Black Donald!" cried Sam, terror making his voice shake as he hoisted the heavy wrench. "He plays tricks on people! It says so in my book! And he can change into different creatures!"

"No, *no*," Barry replied, feeling no more assured by the only other interpretation he could think of. Indeed, how could he start to help his brother understand that? Barry looked at the heart on the ground, its chambers bloated, raw and red. If the person – yes, *person* – who'd extracted the organ was playing a sick game, after sneaking up unseen on the car and depositing this evidence, it surely wouldn't end here. Barry knew better than to believe that the police would suspect he'd committed this act, let alone his brother. They conducted sophisticated forensic tests, and although Barry's hands were now covered in blood, none of the rest of him was, which would surely have been the case if he was guilty.

And now all he needed to do was reach the police.

But as Sam continued babbling nonsense – more about Scottish folklore and now something about mythological birds that could become bulls or horses – the police found them.

The car arrived at speed, roaring around a sharp bend in the road just behind. Barry heard it first, above his brother's increasingly frantic comments, and when the vehicle finally approached, he experienced a renewed surge of relief. They were safe now, him and Sam; they'd be driven away from whatever evil certainly waited out in this threatening landscape, watching with demonic amusement.

When the police car halted only yards from his, Barry struggled to see who was inside. The light was poor, clouds conspiring with the early evening sky, making everything look murky. The driver's seat door swung open and a young officer exited, dressed in full uniform and surprisingly female. Pacing forwards, she slotted on a peaked cap with hands which looked too delicate for her profession.

"Hello, gentlemen," she said with a light Scottish accent, but while drawing nearer, one arm dropped to her side, where a brutal truncheon dangled against one leg. "I'm assuming it was you who made the emergency call about the accident a few miles back. I've left colleagues back there, but you should have stuck around, you know. We'll need statements."

Barry, his diffuse mental state forcing him to view himself and his brother through the policewoman's eyes, realised how this scene must appear: him standing with blood on his hands; Sam alongside him, muttering nonsense and carrying a hefty car tool. *Just wait till she spots the heart on the ground*, thought Barry, and almost laughed out loud with delirium.

But then he took control.

"Be quiet, mate," he said to his brother, placing one red finger over his own trembling lips.

"*Jack Knife*," said Sam, lapsing into one of his ungovernable fugues. "*Killer, killer…*"

"We'll talk all about that soon." Barry turned back to the police officer, who'd now reached them and could surely see all the blood on his hands. "I'm sorry we drove off, but I can explain. I can even give you character references, if you like, and numbers to call. I mean, I'm … well, *we're* not responsible for any of this."

Now close up, the woman looked taller than she'd appeared after exiting her vehicle, but once her eyes had followed the direction of Barry's downwards pointing finger, she appeared bigger still, one hand reaching for something inside her uniform.

"Maybe *she* did it," Sam said in a whisper, putting into words what Barry – feeling as crazily paranoid now as his brother was – had begun to suspect. "Maybe the *real* policeman came after your call and *she's* the killer. She might have killed the policeman and then dressed in his clothes. And perhaps now she's going to … to …"

Before Barry could prevent it, his brother brought down the heavy wrench on the officer's head.

She fell in a heap, gore weeping from the wound Sam had inflicted. Hearing something nearby cackle and gloat – an animal, surely; just impartial wildlife awaiting its feed – Barry stooped to the body's side, feeling for a pulse in the neck, the way he'd been taught during university workshops.

The woman was dead, her central nervous system shattered by the blow.

Barry glanced up at his brother.

"*She* was Jack Knife." Sam dropped the car tool, as if beginning to understand the horror of his act, but then pointed at the officer's side. "Look at her fingers. There's *blood* on the nails."

In a daze, Barry could indeed observe traces of red against the woman's cuticles. This might be residue of recently removed varnish; a police officer wouldn't wear cosmetics on duty.

Or it might be blood.

"She was reaching in her jacket for the knife, Baz," Sam went on, his voice now nearing hysteria. "She was going to cut out our hearts, like she did to that man in the truck. I … I saved us, Baz. I saved us both."

"I know you did, mate," Barry replied, but then saw something stir at a distance, at the top of a nearby field. If this was someone standing farther away – human in shape but with dark wings and an unusual stance, as if its feet were less than normal – would its sudden burst of laughter be so loud?

He didn't know and refused to think about it. As the black figure now in his peripheral vision seemed to stumble away with a bestial gait, Barry returned his attention to the body on the ground. He hoped his brother's reasoning was correct, even if this meant sharing his troubled mind-set. He hoped the woman had a knife in her jacket, a big one capable of ripping open a man's chest.

And as Sam talked again about the Devil in disguise, Barry reached forwards to conduct a thorough investigation.

TRISTICLOKE THE WOLF

Like every other country on Earth, Scotland has had more than its fair share of serial killers. Perhaps understandably, the vast majority of these human monsters hunt for their victims in those heavy areas of conurbation in the Scottish Lowlands. Even Sawney Bean, the infamous Galloway Cannibal of the 16th century, if he existed at all, was located in the far southwest. However, Bean, assuming he was real, wasn't the first to play this grisly game. He had a forerunner further north in the Highlands, whose gruesome activities might well have inspired the Galloway Cannibal and his hideous inbred family to their multiple vicious acts.

This forerunner was the much mythologised Christie Cleek, a brigand and murderer who lurked in the wilderness with a band of like-minded degenerates and preyed on lone travellers, butchering them alive and feasting on their flesh.

The big difference in the case of Cleek is that a plausible explanation is often given for his activities. Unlike Bean, Cleek lived in the Middle Ages, the mid-14th century to be precise, a time of incessant hostility between England and Scotland, and constant strife among the greater Scottish barons, the net result of which was desolation and famine on a widespread scale. Cleek, whose real name was Andrew Christie, was a butcher in the town of Perth, who finally had to abandon his failed business – there was no meat and therefore no customers – and head north into the Grampian hills. Here, he and a few compatriots eked out a miserable half-life on roots and berries, but in the way of many desperate groups lost in a brutal wilderness, they finally turned to cannibalism when members of their own party expired.

From feeding on the dead, it apparently was no great leap to feeding on the living, and it was at this point in his career when Andrew Christie gained his notorious moniker – because a 'cleke' was the Scottish word for a hooked pole, and it was one of these that he allegedly used to snare unwary travellers. According to the stories, Cleek and his men would crouch in the wayside undergrowth, drag their victims from the saddle as they passed, and fall on them with clubs, stones and knives. Whatever was left afterwards was divided up and cooked over open fires.

No details are given as to how the villains were finally exposed, but we are told by various sources that an armed and mounted force was eventually dispatched from Perth. It prowled the hills and glens for several days, finally uncovering the cannibals' camp and attacking without mercy. Most of the band were killed resisting arrest, though others were taken back to Perth, where they were presumably tried and hanged, though again very few details are given about this. One thing we do know is that enough human bones were recovered from pits and shallow graves surrounding the camp to reconstruct the remains of at least thirty victims.

The most important detail of all, however, is absent – the outcome for Christie Cleek himself. We don't even know if he was captured. There is certainly no record of his execution. Perhaps it's no surprise, then, that from this moment on Cleek's name became a byword for evil throughout the whole of Scotland, not just in the Highlands. Even decades later, the belief was rife that Cleek was still roaming free, creeping up on lone villages during the hours of darkness and stealing away livestock and even young children. Centuries afterwards, additional stories emerged that various elderly men in different parts of the country had confessed to being Cleek as they lay on their deathbeds, in each case the fellow having admitted to his stunned family that he had changed his name and managed to merge back into normal society, and in some cases – though not all – that he repented of his sins.

As with any story originating from such a distant period, it is difficult ascertaining the actual facts. Unlike Sawney Bean, for whom there were possible genuine reasons why the chroniclers might have wanted to fabricate such a tale (demonisation of the Jacobite movement), there are virtually no politics in the Christie Cleek story. Moreover, while Bean was first written about over 200 years after the events are said to have occurred, Cleek's tale was committed to paper in less than 50, when in 1420 Andrew of Wyntoun's 'Orygynale Cronykil of Scotland' told us that a killer called 'Chwsten Cleek' murdered and fed on diverse women and children. Further evidence can be found in a later document, from 1577, which reports that an 'uplands man' called 'Tristicloke' behaved 'like a wolf' as he attacked, murdered and devoured countless women and their babes.

In a modern court of law, two witnesses to a story would be regarded as excellent corroboration of its truthfulness.

THE FOUL MASS AT TONGUE HOUSE
Johnny Mains

he Week of Christmas, 1927

He wasn't to be disturbed when he got into 'one of his states', as the staff liked to call it. The house was locked down and the Master would be left uninterrupted for a week or so. There was fresh meat and vegetables in the cold store and plenty of cured pork and beef available, so his hunger would always be sated. But as Mary McDougal busied herself in her cottage kitchen a mile and a half away in Tongue, she remembered that she hadn't brought up the champagne before she left, as the coalman had arrived expecting his monthly bill to be paid.

The Master always demanded that he had fifteen bottles to see him through the week and would become apoplectic with rage if his needs weren't met. It was always better to have him happy, as that made him easier to deal with.

Putting on her thick woollen shawl, Mary slipped out into the crisp winter night, her oil lamp burning brightly. She quickly left the town behind, walking down the Stone Road, the loch to her left and the forest to her right.

The lane sloped up into a gentle hill and edged away from Loch Duibh. Ten minutes later she was walking past the cemetery where several of her ancestors lay and then up one of the many dirt paths that led through the estates grounds to Tongue House.

The front of the house was in darkness. The Master performed all of the rituals either in his studio or in the Library at the back of the house where he had many books to hand, filled with strange and exotic script the like of which Mary had never seen before. Her visits to the Library were always taken when the Master was walking in the hills behind the house or during his trips to London when the house needed airing. Even though he had never told her to stay away from the Library, Mary thought it best to be discreet.

She let herself in at the servants' entrance next to the kitchen and when she opened the door a gust of icy air froze her to the bone. The house always seemed to be colder than it was outdoors, which was a blessing on long, hot summer days, but in the chill of midwinter only roaring fires in the kitchen, reception room and the Library gave the house any chance of warming up.

The wooden soles of her shoes *click-clacked* on the granite floor as she walked the length of the kitchen to the heavy-looking cellar door. She put the lantern down on the solid oak table and took the

223

door key that was hanging from a small rusty hook hammered into the side of the dresser. The lock was stiff and took a considerable amount of effort on Mary's part to turn, but she gritted her teeth and the ancient lock gave way with a resounding and satisfying *clunk*.

Mary lifted the lantern by its thin metal handle and walked down the stone steps into the dank staleness of the cellar; the soft yellow light glinting off the rows and rows of wine and champagne bottles. She walked to the row at the far end of the cellar and removed bottle after bottle originating from the champagne house Möet of Rheims. In daylight, the bottles gave off a ruby glow and the Master once told her that this was created by throwing gold coins into the molten glass. Mary had been permitted to have a sip of the Rheims; she had nodded her head in approval, but in reality had thought it rather bitter.

She loaded seven of the bottles into a wicker basket and carefully carried it up the stone stairs. A slight tinge of light from the lamp below permeated the inky blackness of the kitchen as she took the bottles out and carefully placed them onto the heavily scarred preparation table. She was about to go back downstairs to gather up the second load when suddenly the house began to shake; the bottles clashed together then fell from the table, smashing as they hit the granite floor. Mary used the heavy door to steady herself and after a few seconds the tremors subsided; only to be followed by a deafening crash that suffused every part of Mary's being, taking the wind from her and bringing her to her knees. She blacked out momentarily and when she came to, there was no light coming from the bottom of the stairs, the lamp was extinguished.

An excited chatter seemed to drift down the hall from the direction of the Library. Mary gathered herself together and got up, knowing that her aged body would pay the price in the morning. The notion of an earthquake wasn't in the housekeeper's reality; she thought that the Master must have been experimenting with his potions and had probably taken half the house away with the explosion.

Mary had come with the house when the Master had first moved there fourteen years previously. Before that she had catered to two generations of the Fraser family for most of her life. Mary could find her way around the house blindfolded; she left the kitchen and turned right, going down the open corridor on which hung painted fabrics embellished with the signs and figures that were unfamiliar to her, which she had never seen before. The closer she got to the Library, the louder the chattering became, but there was another noise, extremely low and droning.

By the time she got to the main Library door, the droning sounded like a swarm of angry bees. She had to put her hands over her ears, rooted where she stood, unable to move. She tried to scream, but she couldn't open her mouth. Her breathing whistled through her nostrils.

The heavy oak door in front of her was flung back. Mary saw her Master, dressed in the finest robes she had ever seen, resplendent in purple with gold braided letters and symbols decorating them. She spied Jock Holdstock, the local bobby and the Very Reverend Edward Lee. All had their eyes concentrated on the foul mass of creation in their magic circle.

It was seven feet tall, and from the light of the candles Mary could see that it was made out of hundreds of thousands of whispers of black smoke. She stared at it, amazed. Mary felt compelled to walk towards it, to be close to it, and as she stepped into the circle the black mass was …

Only now did the dark art practitioners really see her. The Master frantically tried to dismiss the demon back to the void from where it came.

The demon started to feast on poor aged Mary.

*

In a short time of frantic incantation they had banished the demon and now stood staring at the mess in from of them. One bite had taken her face. Through the ruin you could see the odd tooth, a splinter of nose cartilage, lots of frothy blood.

Poor Mary. A hard life had she. Washerwoman. Cook. Loyal. Forever silenced by her Master's folly, his dark arts.

The Master, known to the village as Dr. Sharman Summers, but not the town's doctor, knelt by her side and felt for a pulse. It was there, a silly little rhythm.

When he looked up, his eyes were only mildly panicked.

"Stupid *mulier*. She knows the rules. Though she is not dead yet. I cannot lose her. Who would fetch my champagne?"

Jock Holdstock nodded sagely, his normally perfect hair savage and windswept, such was the static in the air around them.

"Aye, she would be missed, and it would be out of character for her to be found at the bottom of rocks with her neck broke. However, being exposed in the outdoors like that, the marks on her face could be explained away as a fox. That would ring true."

"Would have to be a bloody big fox," muttered Edward

"Bring me the Greek translation," Summers said softly, and knelt back on his haunches.

225

"Sharman, no!" Edward gasped. "Do not use it, the power contained is too dangerous. It won't just consume you. It will consume us *all*!"

Summers sneered incredulously. "Don't be simple, man. Do you think I would *dare* to use the Mad Arab's book if I didn't know how to bend it to my will? Holdstock, fetch the book. You are familiar with the one."

Jock nodded again, the obedient servant.

Summers grabbed the book from him, opened it and furiously rifled through the pages. He shouted in Greek those arcane words written by Alhazred many centuries before.

With a final gargle, Mary passed away. It wasn't until Edward grasped his shoulder and shook him out of his reverie that Summers realised she was dead.

"Ah, cursed be this *damnation*!" Summers shouted, throwing the book away from him. It landed on the floor, the room seemed to tremble, the minute shockwaves disappearing into Mary's corpse; though no-one noticed it; they were too preoccupied with the inconvenience of the matter.

"Can we conjure a bear to let loose into the countryside?" Holdstock asked meekly; the normal stature and poise that the community saw and respected was nowhere to be seen.

"I'll have to perform a final spell to make her face look *better*," Summers said, defeated. "She'll need to be identifiable."

*

The news that Mary had died on her way back home from Tongue House, and that it appeared that she had been attacked by a bear, sent desperate shockwaves throughout the community, as Summers, Holdstock and Lee had known it would. All three men fitted their roles as respected pillars of the community in which capacity they reassured, comforted, advised.

Groups of men went out into the deep countryside to find the bear, which people surmised had escaped from a laird's estate in some other part of the country. Summers had been right in saying that it didn't need to be created, the very mention of it being out there would suffice, and indeed, all that the groups of men would bring back were foxes, and on one occasion, a boar, an animal that was believed to be extinct in Scotland.

Mary's body was identified by her husband, Tavish; she was loosely wrapped in fine linen and placed on her bed at home, and would remain there for the next seven days, after which she would be buried. Mary's family moved out and into the home of Tavish's brother, Fergus. It would be a sombre Christmas for them all.

The tragedy aside, the village of Tongue was called to the Christmas show, as it had been every year ever since Dr. Sharman Summers' arrival in the area all of those years before. In the beginning there were only a handful of people who would attend, as newcomers should never be trusted, but the delights that were to be had by those first few visitors spread, and by the third year everyone packed into the banquet hall of Tongue House, trying to glimpse Summers perform a new magic trick and listen as he read a tale of ghostly imaginings from one of the less blasphemous books in his Library.

The hall was noisy, the rabble digesting the free food that had been laid out for them. There was no drink as it was a Sunday.

Dr. Summers strode on stage, wearing a purple velvet jacket, his finely clipped beard looking particularly pointed; as some of the gas lighting was extinguished and only his stage bedecked with candles, some thought he looked like the devil himself. A delicious thrill went through the audience as a softly played recording of classical music drifted over them.

Summers sat in his chair, and closed his eyes, his hands grasping the rests on either side of him, his breathing gradually becoming hoarse, more ragged with each effort, before his breathing stopped altogether. At this moment, the classical music also stopped.

His eyes widened He opened his mouth to speak, but what came from him was the voice of an old woman:

"Oh, dear, what can the matter be?
I'm scared to go to the cemetery,
There are ghosties in there who commit all kinds of blasphemies
I don't like who's hiding in there!"

The crowd laughed and clapped its approval as Summers stood up and began to jiggle about, as if his body had been taken over by a drunken spirit.

"But now, what's this? What is this coming towards me?" he said suddenly, his voice returning to normal, maybe a little fear had crept into it. "Ah!"

Towards him, a bottle, from his precious champagne collection, a bottle that looked like it was floating in mid-air. He reached out for it, and then, between his hand and the bottle, was something about the size of a small coin, which hovered and glowed a dull red.

227

He stood there, appearing to be petrified, his hand held out to the bottle. All of a sudden the candles snuffed out. There was now no light in the large room and yet the object shone with a light of its own, as though from within. It hovered terrifyingly between him and the bottle. The crowd began to gasp, unable to comprehend what they were seeing.

"Weird sprite, begone!" The red light exploded. Summers grabbed the levitating bottle and one of the servants dragged open one of the main curtains, flooding the hall with dappled sunlight.

The audience gasped, and then there was the sound of rapturous applause as Summers grabbed a knife from the table next to him, and with one fluid motion whipped the top off the champagne bottle and drank from it. Nobody seemed to remember it was a Sunday.

"And now, for a story," Summers said. "A ghostly tale this will be, of things returned from the dead!"

The curtains were slowly drawn again and the candles were relit.

*

Cold.

So incredibly cold.

Mary tried to move, but found she could not. She opened her mouth to make a noise, any noise, but none were forthcoming. She tried to breath, let those complex organs whose workings she would never have any knowledge of fill up with air, then she could slowly get up and go and see her husband.

She wasn't breathing.

Mary panicked, her arms and legs finally starting to thrash, brushing aside the linen that loosely bound her, but it was as if she was only able to move seconds after she first thought about it. She placed her hand over her chest, searching for a heartbeat. There was no familiar thudding, just a mocking emptiness, a deadness that was all for her.

Och, no, I cannae be deid, she thought to herself, she was too cold for that. If she was dead there would be nothing, no sensations, no awareness.

She knew it to be blasphemous, but she had never believed in God, and nothing that awful Reverend Lee of the Church of the Holy could do about it. Using as much will as she could muster, she jerked her body outwards, and promptly fell out of her bed and onto the stone floor. The linen drifted down on top of her, lazily, eternally hers.

The impact was all that was needed to bring her back to her dulled senses, get her scrabbling to her feet, albeit clumsily. Then slowly, oh, so slowly, the memories of what happened that night came to her – that awful thing in the Library and … Mary made her way towards the table at the far corner of her bedroom and grasped at the long handled mirror that was there. She tried to scream when she saw her awful reflection, the face cloven in half – but she could not. What had her Master done to her? What was he?

These thoughts were slow and ponderous, but they came to Mary, half-formed. She knew that she must go and see him. But there was something else, something in her that was driving her to the Master. Something that was swirling there in her deadness, striving to be born outside her.

*

"'No one had any knowledge, fortunately of any William Ager living in the district. The evidence of the man at the Martello tower freed us from all suspicion. All that could be done was to return a verdict of willful murder by some person or persons unknown. Paxton was so totally without connections that all the inquiries that were subsequently made ended in a No Thoroughfare. And I have never been at Seaburgh, or even near it, since.'"

Summers closed the book with relish and stared out at the faces in front of him. It was the first time he had read *A Warning to The Curious* by M.R. James, who was indeed a friend, and Summers had actually been in Aldeburgh with him on holiday when the inspiration for the story had taken place. There actually *had* been a chap found dead. As suspected, the story had gone way above the heads of the village folk. A creeping contempt started to settle on him, and he wished for a moment that they would all die. He could do that if he wanted to of course. He had the means. He certainly had the power.

Only a few people were clapping at his prowess, at his domination of the text. He nodded and smiled and told the audience that there would be one last trick, one last fancy to see them on their way and at the door on the way out would be a present, as every year, for the children to take back home.

"Can I have someone from this fine gathering? You there, you." Summers pointed at a young girl, who looked unsure. Her mother smiled and nodded, giving her approval, pushing her out of the crowd and towards him.

The girl was just about to reach Summers's outstretched hand when someone began to scream. He looked up sharply. He hadn't even commenced his soporific spiel to put the girl into a trance. He saw Holdstock look at him with dumb horror. Holdstock managed to hold his arm up, pointing one trembling finger at the travesty of a living being that had managed to infiltrate Tongue House.

Mary. Dead, destroyed Mary.

Summers fled, leaving the girl in the path of Mary, who simply ignored her and lurched after him.

Mary's dress, the finest she owned, wafted over one of the lit candles on the stage and caught alight instantly, engulfing the poor, dead woman. Those already sundered features bubbled and burst. Her whole body turned black within moments, such was the intensity of the heat. But still she continued, one torturous footstep after the other, and slowly started to disintegrate. Once the shell was totally ruined, the thing that was inside Mary, the thing that was born the day Summers had no more use for *Al Azif*, the mad Arab's book, and threw it contemptuously to the floor, broke free and *truly* revealed itself to the scrambling rabble.

Summers fled deep into the Highland night as Tongue House burned to the ground. And the thing with all form and no form gave chase, more powerful than anything that had stalked every known universe before it. There was no hope that yet another who'd dared to try and master the book's arcane knowledge would evade a terrible, terrible end.

THE DRUMMER OF CORTACHY

Cortachy Castle is another of those dramatic fortified manor houses that dot the Scottish Highlands, in this case occupying a gorgeous position in the heart of Angus, not far north of Kirriemuir. A former stronghold of the Stewart Earls of Strathearn, the current handsome building was erected in the 15th century on the ruins of a more warlike structure, and has been renovated many times since. During the course of the castle's existence, in both its early and later more stylish incarnations, it was much damaged by conflict, as a result of which Cortachy is now the site of what is possibly Scotland's eeriest ghost story.

The castle first came of age when in 1473 it was granted by King James II to the hugely powerful and influential Ogilvy clan. Though up until then it had seen skirmishing action thanks to incidents of local baronial strife, from this point on it would be embroiled in the larger, more violent politics of Britain as a whole: Cromwell attacked it in 1651 in retaliation for the sanctuary it offered Charles II, while in 1745 the entire estate was seized by the Crown as punishment for its support of the Jacobite cause. But it was back in 1641 when something truly terrible happened at Cortachy Castle.

That year, Archibald Campbell, 1st Marquis of Argyll and to all intents and purposes the head of government in Scotland during the English Civil War, enacted a policy of 'fire and sword' against all royalists in Atholl and Angus, and marched his army on Cortachy, still the ancestral seat of the Ogilvies, who were ardent followers of the king. The battle that followed was no contest. Argyll's forces were vastly superior, but he also drew advantage from the neglect shown by one of the Ogilvy sentries – a young drummer boy, who for reasons never completely established failed to warn anyone that the enemy was approaching. There are various theories as to why this happened, though most owe more to suspicion than historical certainty. One holds that the drummer was having an affair with the wife of Earl Airlie, and that he was busy with her in her bedroom rather than standing at his post on the high parapet. Another, which maybe has more weight to it because subterfuge was often employed in the Highland wars, insists that the drummer was an Argyll insider and that not only did he ignore the approaching army but that he was the one who opened the gates when they arrived.

Whatever the truth, Argyll's men managed to force entry to Cortachy Castle and set alight to it. Though the Ogilvy garrison resisted fiercely, they could not prevent their ancient seat going up in flames, but Earl Airlie took a savage revenge on the young drummer before he fled. Legend holds that the lad was stuffed into his drum while still alive, and then either thrown from the parapet where he'd been supposed to be standing guard, or hanged from it until he was consumed by the fire (and in fact, the relics of an ancient drum still kept at the castle clearly display extensive scorching).

Of course, this was only half the story. From this point on, it was said, a ghostly drumming would sound throughout Cortachy Castle whenever disaster was approaching the Ogilvy family, and tales to this effect have persisted until relatively recent times. In December 1844, a visitor, a certain Miss Dalrymple, departed the castle in distress after hearing the incessant beating of a drum she could never locate. Sometime in the next few months, the lady of the house committed suicide. Another visitor to the castle reported the same weird sound in August 1849, and the 6th Earl of Airlie died the very next day in London. In later decades, a mysterious drumming at the castle preceded the death of an Ogilvy family member over in America, and recurred again in 1900, on the eve of a Boer War battle that would claim the life of David Ogilvy, the 9th Earl.

Since then, there have been no further reports of such death omens. In truth, there are question-marks against any of them ever having happened at all – many of the stories concerning Cortachy Castle appear to contradict each other, while in others the dates are different. Some even place the incident involving the faithless drummer centuries earlier in the depths of the Middle Ages. But Cortachy casts an uncanny spell even today. It figures prominently on the Highlands paranormal tourist trail, and many visitors still listen out for that mournful drumming, sincerely hoping that they'll hear absolutely nothing.

THERE YOU'LL BE
Carole Johnstone

Black.

No lights or life, no strata of shadows, no discerning anything at all either ahead of or behind me, though I spin around all the same, arms flailing, feet nearly tangling. I can't afford to fall down, I realise – the assertion is sudden and acute – I *cannot* fall down. Though I want to. I want to let go of the shriek inside my head and inside my mouth, open and washed dry by the wind. I want to run. But most of all, I want to fall down. To make myself small. And then I want to crawl away from this place as fast and as far as I can.

But I'm not entirely blind. I can feel the soft give of sand under my heels, cool between my toes. I can smell and taste briny ocean, and I can hear its crashing approach over even the howl of the wind. There is a narrow run of stars overhead, solid and nearly linear like the lintel of a door.

And I have a torch. Its rubber weight lies heavy inside my hand. I don't switch it on. I don't want to see any more than the little that I can. I don't want to see what is between me and the rhythmic surf. What I can already feel, smell, taste, *and* hear is coming for me across the sand: whispering, choking, crawling. Drawing sharp rings from the rock and muted creaks from the sand.

Until the stars vanish overhead. Until the empty black curtain of horizon, and its downstage of chattering, choking noise become too much. Until I have to look.

The torch's narrow beam shakes across dark waves spitting grey foam. My mouth opens and shuts in dumb imitation of the sounds that close in from the sea and rocks, moors and hills. I sink deeper and deeper as my yellow light shudders over dozens, hundreds, *thousands* of dark jostling shapes, each one as large as a man, their shining carapaces knocking together in echoless combat as their tide clamours and scuttles towards me.

*

The room is bright with sunshine, its pine panelled walls and trite portraits of cats and cherub-like children reflecting the light and washing it back, making me wince, squint, change position. My legs are caught up in the sheets, and I fight my way free in slow panic before an arm presses down across my torso, pulling me back against solid warmth.

A tickle of breath at my hair, my temple. "*There's* my beautiful wife."

I close my eyes, lean into the reassurance of what I expect always to be there, and am rewarded by a low chuckle, a fiercer, harder pressing back.

"You're bloody hot."

"Nice of you to say so."

"Another nightmare?"

I close my eyes and smile as your fingers stroke my thigh, my stomach. They're cold and I shiver.

"Alright," you say, flipping me onto my back before straddling me, holding my hands high above my head. Your grin is sharp, eyes sleepy. "I'm going to have to insist on no more afternoon flirting with Mad Graham, okay?"

"Mean. He's a nice guy," I say, but my protests are too distracted to carry any weight.

"What was it this time then? The quicksands at Seilebost? Clan massacres on the machair?" You press a hot, open-mouthed kiss against my neck. "Or marauding Norsemen come to rape and pillage in their big bad galleys?"

*

I shoulder open the living room door, hunched and freezing. The sound of the shower camouflages my cry when I see the dark figure bent over the kitchenette sink, its head hidden between grotesquely hunched shoulders black with wet and dusted with shell-sand. Long straggles of hair whip towards me, and I stagger back into the tiny porch, yanking the door shut again. When you come out of the bathroom, a towel wrapped around your waist, you arch an eyebrow before opening the living room door and disappearing inside. I follow, and she's gone, of course. Nothing bad ever happens when you're with me.

*

I end the day on Luskentyre beach, just as the rolling clouds settle lower over the Teampall and the sheer cliff face of Liuiridh to the south. I walk along less than half of its vast length before stopping to watch the big distant waves crest and break in glorious roars, feeling their echoes foam around my feet as the soft sand yields to us both. I crouch, watching the horizon through my viewfinder, waiting until the dark shadow becomes discernible enough to set focus points flashing, and then I take the picture, hear the long snap of the shutter. I'm still crouching when Graham clears his throat in his usual hello. The mini horizon is beautiful: the sky clouded puffy white above, the waves frilled white below. Nothing at all between.

"Another spectre ship?"

"Maybe," I smile, standing up, fitting the lens cap.

"And where were ye the day then, hen?"

From that first day when I'd seen him limping along the single track into Borve, and he'd answered my eager "are you a local?" with a sardonic "no, hen. My lot only came o'er fae Skye five generations ago", he has filled my head with tales of tribes and clans, Christians and Vikings, fortresses and watch towers. He has fired my imagination with Neolithic pyres set above underground caves and chambered cairns; dun beacons warning of danger from the sea in relays of light along headland and cliff; blackhouses set to burn while their crofters farmed the land, because there were no trees with which to rebuild on the island – every last roof beam and timber joist had been rescued from the sea.

Today, I walked from the base of Beinn Dhubh, and then along the grassy, sandy bluffs above Seilebost and Luskentyre, my macro lens capturing the wondrous turns and twists of ten dozen or more warren entrances, a city crouched and waiting to come alive once I'd gone. I followed the machair back towards the sea, trampling my way through its blanket of tiny-flowered, riotous colour before reaching the wild headland of Aird Nisabost.

The twelve foot MacLeod's Stone would have represented little more than good composition – stark relief against the endless blue Atlantic swell – had Graham not told me of all the events that it had seen, all the things that it had *been* for more than five thousand years. Everywhere is ancient, of course, but here is on the edge of nothing and everything. Here there are no streetlights, no crowds, no pubs or office blocks, no shouting or screaming or music or sirens or wi-fi. Here there was once conflict and hardship and suffering to spare, but not anymore. Now there is only peace and the witness of silent stone. Here is everywhere and nowhere to hide.

"Ach, nearly everyone sees them, ken," Graham says. "S'nothin' tae worry aboot. The Outer Hebrides are famous for the spectre ships."

"I didn't see anything," I say, feeling vaguely ashamed, even more vaguely persecuted.

"This is a sad place, a bad place," he says, as we both look out at the vast bowl of blue sky, as the sea froths around our intrusion and the white sand gives way underneath it, as the warm breeze blows inland against our skin, and those low rolling clouds over the

Teampall begin glowing rose pink.

It's this kind of morose proclamation that has earned him your sarcastic epithet of Mad Graham. You think that he fits the dour Islander stereotype entirely. You think – we think – that this place is an unexpected paradise. Warm and wild and nearly uncannily beautiful, full of a light and colour so at odds with the bronze overcast desolation of the mainland bens and glens less than forty miles east. But, through him, I can see what neither of us wants to: that what seems perfect rarely ever is.

*

When I get back to our blackhouse, it's nearly dark. Its tiny windows glow bright against the stormy clouds sweeping inland. The dangling weights of quarried rock that hold down its thatched roof dance and sway. Though Graham told me weeks ago that it was only a replica of what had once stood in its stead, I still like to think of it as our outpost, our temporarily borrowed protest against all those fancy weekend holiday homes with gunmetal frames and sea-facing walls of glass. Though our blackhouse is west of the coastal road and less than a hundred yards from the sea, we have to stand on our tiptoes to glimpse it, leaning across recessed stone sills more than half a foot thick.

I try not to think of quicksand pockets, or scuttling black creatures, or of Graham's sad, bad place as I hurry across the gloomy last few hundred yards, dodging cattle-holes and boggy puddles, the wind wild enough to knock me off course, only our little square lights keeping me true. As I push up the latch on the door and step inside orange warmth, I try even harder not to think about a figure with dark, hunched shoulders and wild straggled hair bent over the kitchenette sink.

When you smile at me, a stupid lump fills my throat. The living room is warm and bright. The stove crackles and smokes behind glass as you pull me into your chest, squeezing the right side of too hard. I anticipate your long exhale; press my cold cheek against your warm ear.

"Monkfish," you say, pulling me towards our tiny table. "Chablis. Weird, indistinguishable vegetables from the Co-op in Stornoway." You wink, pull out my chair. "Don't say I don't treat you nice."

"I'm sorry I took so long."

You shrug, smile, pull the cork before pouring. "Did you get many good shots?"

I sit down without answering, abruptly aware of all that you do for me, and what little I do in return. What little I even think of doing in return. It makes me feel both ashamed and resentful, like being caught photographing something that isn't there.

After dinner, we loll on the couch under a blanket of Harris Tweed, playing a lethargic game of whist.

"How was Mad Graham?"

I look at the black, red-cracked lumps of coal inside the stove. "He told me more about the Clearances."

You roll your eyes and pretend to yawn. "It's hardly wrecked fortresses, Viking longboats, and wiped out villages is it?"

I don't argue because I'll never be able to do Graham's bleak tales justice. I won't be able to pass along to you the shivers that cricked my neck and tightened my scalp as we stood on that empty and beautiful sand-shell beach – behind us nothing but grass bluff and the wink of those occasional gunmetal holiday homes; ahead of us nothing but the big breaking waves and nearly four thousand miles of empty ocean until Canada – while Graham described a whole other place of noise and people and industry and life. A world wiped out more effectively, more cruelly, than centuries of foreign invasion or local warfare, and for no other reason than the recognition that there was more profit to be made in sheep than in people.

I looked southwest towards the beaches and machair of Borve and Scarista, and I could see the burning blackhouses that were people's entire lives; I could hear the screams of the crofters as they tried to rescue what little they could; the cries of the dispossessed as they fled along the Coffin Road, driven like cattle over the Harris hills and onto the peat moors and desolate rocky lochs of the Bays in the east.

"Just the way o' things," Graham said in his stoically grim way, and I felt a burst of fury that it was and always would be, not because of the greed or ownership or spite of a few, but because for so many others nothing was more certain, nothing more inevitable than the bloody *way of things*.

"He's an okay bloke, you know," I say, feeling guilty. "I'd rather be interesting than cheerful any day of the week. Why don't you come out with me tomorrow and actually meet him?"

You pretend to consider it, but you know that I work better alone. "Need to go into town. They've forecast a big storm tomorrow – got to prepare for the worst: stock up on booze and slice and fire lighters." You fake a big shudder. "Remember when we went camping in Helmsdeep and you ran out of vodka?"

I smile, run my knuckles against your bristly cheek, burrow my toes under your legs. "Remember when you always gave me foot

237

rubs?"

You cock an eyebrow. "Remember what else we always used to do?"

I smile. "We still do plenty of that." Though it's not entirely true.

"We don't spend all day in bed."

"No one spends all day in bed."

"We did." But you're smiling a little too, your fingers already rubbing slow circles against the cold soles of my feet.

Sometimes I find your reticence difficult, unsettling. I watch other couples and imagine that we somehow come up short. I complain that you never buy me flowers, never post loved-up pictures of us online, never tell an entire roomful of strangers how much you love me.

One night, you looked at me and sighed. You've always been slow to anger; I used to see that as a lack of passion too. "D'you really want to know what I think of those people? The ones who run through smug profile pics like water? Who can't ever stop shoving every other poor bugger's face in it – the exes, the single friends, the lonely strangers? All those fuck-awful declarations and personal conversations they put on show for everyone to see when they're probably sitting right fucking next to each other?"

"Maybe they're just happy," I said.

"And maybe they're just trying too hard. Maybe they're shit scared that everyone else – and more likely the person that they're sitting right fucking next to – will find them out, see them for the insecure pricks that they really are."

When I didn't answer, you became fiercer still, and I secretly basked in it: the angry flash of your eyes and press of your hands, so like the moments when you grabbed me and kissed me as if you had to, as if nothing else mattered at all.

"I don't care what a bunch of virtual strangers do or don't think. I only care about what *you* think. I love you more than I've ever loved anyone else. And I don't need anyone else to fucking know it as long as you do."

I look at you now as you start to drop off, my feet still in your lap, and I feel such fear and tenderness and doubt and discontent. I don't know why. Despite all my complaints and demands, I'm forever uncertain, forever unfulfilled, where you're always so sure, so calmly complacent.

*

When I wake up, I'm still on the couch, and the blanket has been

238

pulled up to my chin where it scratches. The wind has grown much louder: I can hear it under the eaves and in the thatch. Rain batters against the dark windows, and I can hear the sea too, bellowing and angry.

I shiver as I push back the blanket. The coal in the stove has stopped burning. Only one lamp is still lit; it throws low shadows against the couch and faded hearth rug.

I feel rather than see her. She never makes any kind of sound, and the kitchenette is behind me; I don't turn around. But I can see her all the same. Shoulders hunched high and shaking sand into the puddles at her feet, long ropes of hair heavy with rain or seawater. I can feel her grief and fear and fury as if the storm is inside our blackhouse.

I get up fast, the blanket slipping onto the floor as I run around the couch and towards the door. The living room is tiny – I almost collide with our dining table before grabbing hold of the couch's end and pushing myself away. I bring my other hand up to shield my face, my eyes, as I stumble nearer to the door. My gaze keeps slipping in her direction, even though all it can see is the shadowed cup of my fingers. When I struggle with the metal latch, I feel breath at my neck; I hear the soft, low chokes of her.

I run through the wooden porch and into our bedroom. All is terrible black, and for a more terrible moment I imagine that you're gone – that I'm alone – until I hear your slow, steady breathing, and realise that you've only closed the shutters against the storm.

I creep into bed, still shaking, still shuddering. I nearly cry out when you snake your arm around me, pulling me into your fierce heat. Even though you're sleeping deeply, you murmur soft comfort into my ear, and I slowly relax, slowly remember to stop being afraid.

Before, I used to wonder if she was one of the Christian missionaries murdered in the Norse raids of the 800s, or a sixteenth century islander caught between famine and clan battles for land and power. I wondered if her terrible grief was for herself or for those she had lost. Now, I wonder if she's one of Graham's evicted crofters. I wonder if her husband was burned or imprisoned or taken away to fight against Napoleon, while she was left with nothing and no one.

I am more terrified of her than I am of spectre ships or dreamed scuttling monsters from the sea.

She hates me. That's all I've ever been certain of.

239

The next morning I rise late – you've already gone to Leverburgh for supplies – and after a fast breakfast of porridge and black coffee, I head inland away from the beaches. I follow the Coffin Road to the centre of Harris, where I photograph the purple and brown moorland between rocky hills and glassy still lochs. Ordinarily, I find this landscape as bleak and uninspiring as the stony grey Bays on the east coast looking back towards Skye and the mainland, but today I want barren and eerie quiet instead of the wild wind and waves; I want the claustrophobic press of bens and high hills instead of the flat expanse of those four thousand miles of open ocean; I want the ugliness of peat bogs and the steel-shuttered eyes of abandoned shielings, instead of dizzying colour and white-gold sand.

Until I don't. Until staying there begins to feel like looking at the shadowed cup of my fingers.

The sun comes out as I leave behind the hills and clouds and head back into the west. I pick up speed along the causeway that has been built over the head of the bay at Seilebost, suddenly eager to return to what I wanted to escape. In the morning, as I walked the same route, I looked out towards the head of the river and thought only of Graham's warnings of quicksand and all those who had fallen foul of it. Now, I think of the salt-flats of thrift that greeted our arrival in early summer: the haze of sea-pink above the water that looked like a field of candyfloss.

When I find the blackhouse empty, I immediately make my way to our beach along the trampled pathway through the machair, across the little wooden bridge built over a stream. I climb the stile onto the grassy sand bluff, and when the sight of the flat sea and surf, the low clouds over the Teampall, and the slopes and sandbanks of Taransay catch hold of my breath as they always do, I let myself stop and stand and look. I let myself forget both my worries and my viewfinder just long enough to stop and stand and look. Nowhere is like here. Though I've been to admittedly few places, I know it's true. Irrefutable. I can feel it even in my bones. There is nowhere on Earth as wonderful or as alive as *here*.

When I see your shadow like a spectre ship on the horizon – sitting on our high plateau of sand sheltered by the bluff, but boasting the best views of the ocean – I nearly begin running, my camera battering against my thigh as I stumble down the steep bank, grabbing for flailing waves of grass, my feet sinking into the sand to my ankles, a smile stretching my mouth wide. While you stand and wave and wait.

Of all the places that we've known, that we've shared, this is the only one that is truly ours. For nearly eight weeks, we've shared this hundred yard space with barely another soul. We've walked and picnicked and got riotously drunk; we've paddled and even swum in the warm, wild surf; we've sunbathed and been caught unawares by storms rolling down from the hills; we've watched sunsets more colourful than the machair in midsummer, and shivered under the stars in the hopes of glimpsing early Northern Lights; we've talked and laughed and even cried. Here is away from the world and all its distractions. Here is where we're both the people that we want to be, that we've always tried – and mostly failed – to be.

*

When I wake up, the breeze has grown cooler and the sky a darker blue. The clouds have thinned into long cirrus streamers high above the sun. In all the time that we've been here, neither of us has seen a single contrail. You rub your beard against my temple as I sit up.

"Sorry," I say. "I keep falling asleep."

"This'll help."

You hand me one of two plastic bottles, and we raise them high, grinning at each other before turning towards the sandbar and low hills of Taransay across the Sound.

"To the rock! To the rock, ye lads of Lewis!" Our bellows echo unheard and unchallenged.

"I still think that's probably very bad karma," I say as I swallow two mouthfuls of horrible rum before shuddering, belching, laughing. It was the anniversary of the Battle of Taransay a few weeks ago, and although Graham has never come down to our beach, he described the invasion of the clansmen from Lewis in such detail that I was able to sit beside you on our plateau and point out the destroyed villages and townships on the northern headland, and the low sheltered cove on Taransay where the Lewismen's boats had beached before they massacred every soul on the tiny island. I was even able to single out the rock that the MacLeods of Harris had driven the clansmen onto before exacting their revenge, leaving only one man alive to tell a cautionary tale. Graham said that large numbers of men's bones could still be seen around the rock when the big storms came in and disturbed the sea floor.

"Nah, we'll be alright. They're all done with the massacring," you say, knocking your bottle against mine. "Sláinte."

I haven't told you about the spectre ships, or my nightmares of scuttling, chitinous monsters. I haven't told you about the woman in our blackhouse. You only believe in what you can see and touch and hold. You try to fix things; I try to understand them as they are. You live and I dream.

241

"You might get your perfect sunset tonight," you say, nodding towards my camera, and then the nearly midnight blue of the sky over Ceapabhal to the southwest. The storm, I realise, has cut a deep curving swathe through the sand of our beach, from sea to grass. The channel froths and fills with the rising tide, like a monsoon river. I don't like it. It reminds me of a carefully incised wound.

"Graham said this is a sad, bad place," I say. If we were to row over to the *smitten-rock* tonight, I wonder whether we'd see thigh bones and skulls rolling beneath the surf.

"Well, that's Mad Graham for you," you say, looking out at the horizon. "Always looking on the bright side."

You mean it's me too, but you won't say so. Any more than you'll ask me how I am, how I'm feeling, because you know I'll tell you. It makes me suddenly angry, resentful again. It makes me want to poke at barely healed wounds, even though I know it's perverse and pointless.

You and Graham are not as different as you'd like to think. Both of you would, I don't doubt, stand in the way of any savage invader – you once said that you would die for me, and I believed it without question – but neither of you would stand against what you accept as inevitable. *Just the way of things.* All I do is fight for what I can never have, and against what I can never accept, even if their sum is only impotent complaint. You never say that either, of course. Because then I might actually do something more.

"Sometimes I don't like it here either," I say, looking at that deep, angry wound of water. "When I think about all the terrible things that have happened on these islands, the fact that this place is so fucking beautiful it makes your eyes hurt makes it so much worse somehow."

"Horrible things happen everywhere. *You* wanted to come here. You loved it five minutes ago." I can't read your eyes in the fading light, but I can see the familiar set of your shoulders. "The grass isn't always greener, you know."

For once, I can hear the uncertainty in your voice, the question in it. But I *do* feel angry, I *do* feel restless, and I can't pretend that I don't. I want more out of life than I have, and can hardly understand why you don't – why anyone wouldn't. And you're my husband. Of everyone, you're the one who is supposed to be on my side no matter what, always trying to fight my corner.

"And sometimes it fucking is! For Christ's sake, d'you think anyone ever got to be anything if–"

"Maybe I'm just happy, you ever think of that?" You hardly ever raise your voice in a fight; I've always found it infuriating. "And maybe I go along with everything you want to do because you

242

never are."

"We wouldn't do *anything* if it wasn't for me. We wouldn't even have come *here* if it wasn't for fucking me."

"I know," you say, reaching out to touch my hand before I can flinch away. "I'm not saying that I don't need a kick up the arse every now and then. But you never ever stand still. You never enjoy anything. You're always taking pictures or making plans or getting ready to move onto the next thing." You stroke my jaw, run cool fingers across my lips, even though I know that you're angry too; I can feel it humming under your skin. "You'll never find what you think you want that way."

But I disagree. I find your small life stifling, claustrophobic. I loathe your lack of dreams or ambition, and the martyred acquiescence that always leaves me feeling like an overbearing witch. More than once you've said "I know I love you more than you love me", and it's never a question, we both believe it. But that doesn't mean you should live your life in quiet endurance; it doesn't mean I should have to let go of all that I want.

I look at the Teampall, and realise that the clouds have moved out to sea and the sun has become a low orange ball, its reflections sparking gold and silver across the calmed waves like spindrift. The sea-pools are calmer still, and the virgin banks of sand are alive with rippled shadow. I itch to pick up my camera, but I can never let you have the last word. I can never let you win.

"I don't want to fight."

"Me neither," you say, reaching for me, pulling me against your body. Your lips are cold, but your mouth is warm. It tastes of rum.

But I'm not finished, and I need to be clear. I need you to know that we can't keep living our lives this way: in pointless, repetitive arguments that are always about the same things, and never, ever resolved.

"Because the summer's nearly over," I say. "And then we'll have to leave."

You sigh, but I don't care that I'm doing what you say I always do. Not saying a thing, not acknowledging it, doesn't make it any less true. It just makes its whisper louder.

I love you, but the grass *is* greener, I'm certain of that too. And sometimes dreams really do become reality. Sometimes, colonies of shellfish deep inside ocean forests of seaweed are washed ashore in winter storms, and blown inland on wild, whipping winds. Creating grass that is not just green, but every colour of the fucking rainbow.

*

243

When I wake up in our bed, the storm is all around us, battering our blackhouse, sending great howling gusts up into its thatch. When something big bangs hard against the front door, I sit up and reach for you. You're not there.

I throw back the covers, ignoring the sudden chill as I feel my way around the bed, banging my shins against the electric fire close to the door. When I turn on the light, the room is still empty, and I barge through the door and the porch, into the dark living room.

I know immediately that she is there and you are not. Hairs crawl awake along my neck and scalp; my skin prickles into awareness. I blink towards the kitchenette, and imagine her hunched over the butler sink. I don't turn on the light. I think rather than say fuck off. *Leave me alone.* My nakedness and your absence make me feel too vulnerable, too afraid. Instead, I run back into the bedroom, and pull on a hoodie and jeans. In the porch, I grab a torch and the spare key fob from the hook next to the door, and then I bang through it, yanking and locking it shut.

The darkness is nearly absolute. It catches me by dismayed surprise, though it shouldn't, I've lived with its alien company for weeks. But tonight there is no moon, and even the stars are hidden behind invisible clouds, whose rain soaks me cold to the bone before I've stumbled further than a few feet. I shout for you, but the wind shouts louder. When I turn on the torch, its beam is thin and thready, picking out little more than the gravel path and the latched gate behind it.

I stop running and hunch instead, whirling my thin light around me in an unsteady circle. I don't know what to do. I don't know where to go. I can't go back to the blackhouse, even though I know that it's the only sensible thing to do – I can't, because she's there and you're not. I'm gripped with a terror that has both none and too many reasons to be, and so I keep moving because moving is the only thing I've ever been good at; moving is the only thing that ever makes sense.

I only realise that I'm heading towards our beach when I hear the roar of the ocean growing louder. My light glances off the defeated mats of machair as I trample my remembered way towards the grass banks. The sound of my boots against the little wooden bridge startles me, and I stop again as though yanked out of a dream. I squint against the rain, flailing my torch over the distant shadows of the gravestones at Na-Buirgh. The ocean howls and screams, and I know that this is a bad idea – a terrible idea – but still I keep on moving.

When I finally reach the stile, I clamber over it, and only narrowly avoid pitching straight over the bluff and onto the sand

244

many feet below by dropping the torch and grabbing hold of a fence post instead. The strength of the wind is incredible. Although I'm blind, I imagine its cold fury barrelling over all those flat thousands of miles towards this little defenceless coast, sweeping inland between the Teampall and Taransay, sending waves that sound like swollen and pitiless fists into the Sound, and against its rocks and sea pools, stirring up wrecks and bones, carving ugly fissures into the soft, yielding sand.

I've always thought that I knew fear, that I understood it. I've seen it, heard it, read about it; imagined that I've felt it myself many times – even here on our island paradise. But I haven't. I've felt the shivers and shudders, trembles and sweats; a heart that beats too fast and too hard, lungs that can't find air, screams that can't find a voice. But real fear is more than just the sum of its symptoms. Real fear is the constant dread that we pretend we don't feel, until we run out of ways to fool ourselves. It's the reason we build our little fortresses and watch towers and blackhouses. And in times of trouble, it's what drives us to light bonfires in the darkness; it's what makes us want to believe that we're never alone – that there will always be others ready and waiting to answer with fires of their own.

And fear is also lunging for a torch and training its light on all the things that we don't want to see. A foul and insurmountable tide, a beautiful paradise gouged deep with wounds, and overrun with jostling, chittering, scuttling horrors. Horrors that hunch and shift and suddenly stop, turning their heavy, hungry gaze up towards my light on the stormy black edge of the world. Horrors that *see*. And begin to rise, to reach, to run.

I scream when something lands heavy on my shoulder, and jump too quickly away. Graham lunges for me, yanking me back from that fathomless edge with surprising strength.

"Whit the hell're ye doin'?" he bellows.

My ears pop as if I've been underwater. He snatches the torch out of my hand.

"I went tae the blackhoose tae tell ye ye have tae move inland, and I find the door wide open and naeb'dy inside."

I grab hold of his coat. *I locked it*, I want to say but don't. She might be listening.

"Where's your husband, hen? Ye cannae stay here. We need tae get goin'."

Dread washes over me in fresh wet wind that tastes and stings of salt. "He's gone!" I cry. I scream. "He's gone!"

A look of weary and unsurprised comprehension settles over his face. That look pulls me free of fear's quicksand; it remembers

245

embarrassed outrage, resentment.

Graham yanks on my hoodie, ignoring my protests as he drags me away from the bluff. He manhandles me back over the stile, and then starts walking us back through the boggy machair. He doesn't use the torch.

"Didn't you see them?" I screech over the wind and the waves, even as their bellows grow more distant. *"Didn't you see them?"*

*

I wake up in a bedroom that is the same but different. Instead of cats and children, there are framed scriptures hanging on the wood-panelled walls. I'm warm, nearly hot. Bright sunlight streams through grey net curtains. When I sit up and then stand up, sore muscles and tendons complain. I'm still wearing my hoodie and jeans; they're stiff with salt, and sprinkle fine grains of sand onto the threadbare carpet under my feet.

I open the bedroom door and follow the smell of food down a narrow corridor into a living room even tinier than the one in our blackhouse. Graham straightens up from a spitting grill with a wince.

"Ye're up, that's grand. How are ye feelin' the day then?"

I feel bizarrely dislocated. My mouth moves into a polite smile. "I'm fine, thank you."

"You'll be wanting a decent breakfast, no doubt."

If it's a question, I don't know how to answer it. Instead I drop down onto a hard and uncomfortable couch, and it's only when I have to shove aside a pillow and blanket that I realise Graham has slept there; that I've been in his bed.

"I'm sorry," I say, and something starts to thaw inside me, cricking my neck and swelling my throat.

"Quite alright, lassie," he smiles. "Your need was the greater."

I sit on his couch, while he sits on a tiny stool, and we eat our porridge and bacon in silence. It's nearly as unnerving as the silence and sunny glare from outside. My ears roar with static noise.

"There's a ferry goin' back tae Uig at ten," he says, swiping clubbed fingers across his mouth. "I'll take ye o'er tae the blackhoose, so's ye can pick up your stuff."

"What?" I stand up. The thing that's thawing inside me knows more than what I've let myself believe for nearly two months, but even this is still too much – and far too soon.

"Now," he says, giving me the same careful look that he did on that black, stormy sand bluff – and there's a part of me that can hardly blame him – "I ken that your lease isnae up for another week, but the storms have come early, hen. There's a good chance that in a week there'll be nae ferries at all goin' back tae Skye, and then where'll ye be?"

I close my eyes. Even if he's lying, I know that his reasons for doing so are no less well intentioned. None of this is his fault. Even so, my chest squeezes tight at the thought of leaving. A fear older than the spectres of ships and monsters and ghosts grabs hold of my throat and my voice.

He looks at me and his eyes are kind. "Ye need tae go, hen."

*

The blackhouse is empty. Graham waits outside while I pack my clothes and bag up what I'll leave behind: the remains of our food and all the unbroken shells and pieces of slate that I collected from our beach. I fill the sink and clean the dishes, and I'm still numb, I still feel nearly nothing at all. I wonder if she stood shaking and choking in this very place because she was trying to feel nothing too; because she was trying just as hard not to think of those four thousand miles of empty ocean and the men waiting outside to take her to exile on the other side of it. My own will be much closer.

I don't look back at the blackhouse as I leave. I don't look up from the wet, boggy ground. I don't listen to either the wind or the waves.

*

The terminal at Tarbert is crammed with cars and roving men in hi-vis jackets. Graham is twitchily uncomfortable – it's probably more people than he's seen in weeks, maybe even months – and I'd feel sorry for him were it not for the fact that he's the reason we're both here at all.

When the ferry finally arrives and drops its creaking, heavy ramp, I turn to him with an urgency that I wish I'd felt long before now.

"You really didn't see them, did you? The creatures on the beach?"

He looks alarmed and nearly appalled before he hides both behind his stoic, wrinkled mask. "I've never seen a spectre ship either, hen," he says.

When the last of the foot passengers have embarked, and the men in hi-vis begin heading our way, Graham coughs, pulls me into a tight and fierce embrace.

"I'm sorry for your loss, hen."

247

It's only when I hear the low rumble of the ferry's engines that I leave the numb, noisy press of the passenger lounge. I stumble around with a growing sense of panic, until I find a steep stairway leading up onto the deck. The door at its summit is heavy, and the wind makes it heavier, as if both are conspiring to keep me inside.

The deck is nearly empty. I march around its red plastic seats and white-painted railings, my trainers slipping on wet metal as I try to find my way back to the harbour. When I do, the distance that has slipped between us is greater than I was expecting. Beyond the stacked lights and roofs of its houses, the low, tarmaced slope of its mouth is nearly indistinguishable, save for a few waving figures close to its beginning. I imagine that one of those figures is Graham, and wave frantically back; my fear – my dread and my sorrow – a horrible fluttering thing inside my chest.

My heart keeps on beating too hard and too heavy as the rocky edges of East Harris leave me behind. Tears sting my eyes when I lose sight of the low, grey clouds over the inland bens and lochs. I close them against the passing stony shores of Urgha and Scalpay, like the tips of reaching fingers whose hands I've waited too long to grasp. When I look back towards the harbour, both it and the waving figures have gone, replaced by grey-blue sea and a low rolling fog.

I think of Graham's sad, bad place. I think of Macleod's Stone high on the headland, standing sentinel over so much suffering. I think of agreeing that the island's stark beauty made all that suffering only uglier. Ugly like a hate-filled woman hunched over and choking with sorrow. Ugly like an invasion of monsters from the sea, scuttling and clambering their way across the beach in a malignant black tide.

But Graham was wrong about a lot of things. He was wrong about you.

The horror – the fear – was never on Harris. It was never in suffering warfare or invasion, hardship or poverty. The horror was in ever having to leave it behind: in being forced onto a rock to die, into the eastern Bays to starve, onto those spectre ships bound for an alien world so distant that there would never be any hope of one day coming back home.

You always knew that you were good for me. What I'd mistaken for so many other things – arrogance, disinterest, complacency – had only ever been that one quiet certainty. I remember your long exhales and fierce warmth and silent comfort. I never said thank you. I never thought that I had anything to be grateful for. It wasn't in me to wonder whether I was good for you. And every time that I complained about you not being on my side, it had never once occurred to me that I should have been on yours.

Why do we save the best of us for everyone but those who love us the most? Why are so many of us fools who already have everything, but always imagine that we want or need more? Until we choose to chase the lights of our dreams, like a headland of contagious fire. Until we give all that everything up for a man, a place, a life that we believed would be all things, but wasn't even one. Until what we always took for granted becomes only what we miss, what we long for.

As the engines rumble under my feet, the wind whips wet around me, and the fog closes in, I'm suddenly terrified of where *this* ship will take me. And what it's taking me further and further from. I dump my holdall, dropping to my knees on the cold, hard steel of the deck. When I find my phone, I watch its signal slowly return in white uncertain circles.

I stay crouched as it rings and rings. I squeeze my eyes shut against the freezing sting of the Little Minch, and I remember all those scuttling black horrors looking up at my torchlight high on the bluff as they tried to stand.

The rings stop, and I freeze, my heart beating too hard and too fast; those shivers and shudders, trembles and sweats nearly achieving their aim before I manage to find my voice.

"Hello?" The ferry is too loud, the wind too wild. When one of the deck doors slams shut, I flinch, my ear straining to hear anything that isn't here: a voice, a whisper, a breath. "Hello?"

And then I'm rewarded by the latter: a sigh that is nearly yours, but too sharp, too cold.

"I told you not to call me."

"I know you did, but I wanted to tell you where –"

"Leave me alone."

And I think of standing naked in our blackhouse just one night ago. I think of her hunched over the sink, choking and scattering wet sand. I think of me saying fuck off. *Leave me alone.* And while I don't hear the beep or click of disconnection, I know immediately when you do.

I don't stand up. I remain crouched and hunched and shaking. I close my eyes and remember that first day, weeks ago, when I came back to the island. Not the lonely, half mad widow that Graham now imagines me to be, but grief-stricken all the same. I remember standing on our beach, the sand sucking at my ankles as the tide came in and the rain soaked me to the bone. I remember returning to

249

our blackhouse, wringing my hair out over the sink, shaking sand and seawater onto the wooden floor. Sobbing and choking and mourning all that I'd lost; all that I'd given so blindly away.

A group of cagouled American tourists stampede noisily past, casting some curious looks my way. Though I still make no move to stand, I reach closer to the ferry's white-painted railings, and stare down into the grey-frothy water. When I look up again, the sun has broken through the southern clouds out towards Barra and the Uists. There is a double-arced rainbow between their low shadow and the dark clouds overhead, and the sight of it unbalances me, reminds me that beauty is as easy to find as fear.

I am no more that ugly, desperate woman than Harris is a sad, bad place. Or than you are a cold and cruel voice on the crackling end of a phone.

Co Leis Thu is a traditional clan greeting on the islands. It means *who do you belong to?* I belong to no one now. No one belongs to me. But there is where we once belonged to each other. There is where we once were happy; where we were the people that we wanted to be, that we'd always tried to be.

I remember that day on our beach all those months ago. When you stroked my jaw and kissed me with lips that tasted of rum, even though you were angry. When you said "the grass isn't always greener, you know", and I'd insisted that it was, without ever acknowledging it as a question.

If I could go back, I'd tell you that all those times I was so certain I was right, I was wrong. I'd tell you that I was always grateful. I'd tell you that I was sorry. And I love you. I love you more than I've ever loved anyone else. I'd die for you.

When the double-rainbow fades into grey and the sea-fog begins to lift, I stand up. A smile hurts my chapped lips as I look west beyond the ferry's white-trailed wake. My shoulders forget their hunch.

Next summer, I'll come back again. I'll cross this narrow strait into the narrower isthmus of Tarbert. I'll take the high road west above the harbour, winding between all those purple stony bens and glens and glassy lochs, through heavy clouds and peat farms and slate quarries, across flat lonely grazing plains and moorland.

I'll walk along the causeway above a blanket of bright pink sea thrift, and crest the last hill at Seilebost, just as the sun rises up over the Teampall. I'll run down through the machair beyond the coastal road at Borve. I'll cross the little wooden bridge, climb over the stile, clamber down the grassy sand bluff towards the beach, grabbing for flailing waves of grass, my feet sinking into the sand to my ankles. I'll look across to Taransay and the northern headland,

and out at the rolling white-frilled waves and the flat miles of Atlantic beneath a vast blue bowl of sky.

And there is where I'll finally stop moving. There is where I'll stop and stand and look. I'll take off my coat, my bag, my camera; I'll stretch my shoulders free of their hunch. And I'll watch all those others crawling their way out of the sea and onto the sand. I'll watch them trying to shed their own armour; trying to stop, to stand, to look. To believe that they're home again.

And last, I'll look west towards that high plateau of sand sheltered by the bluff, but boasting the best views of the ocean, a smile stretching my mouth wide.

And there you'll be. Standing and waving and waiting.

No matter where we go. No matter what either of us become.

There you'll always be.

SOURCES

All stories appearing in *Terror Tales of the Scottish Highlands* are original to this collection, with the exception of *The Fellow Travellers* by Sheila Hodgson, which was first published in *The Fellow Travellers* (Ash-Tree Press, 1998).

FUTURE TITLES

If you enjoyed *Terror Tales of The Scottish Highlands*, why not seek out the first seven volumes in this series: *Terror Tales of the Lake District, Terror Tales of the Cotswolds, Terror Tales of East Anglia, Terror Tales of London, Terror Tales of the Seaside, Terror Tales of Wales* and *Terror Tales of Yorkshire*. All available from most good online retailers, including Amazon, or you can order from http://www.grayfriarpress.com/index.html.

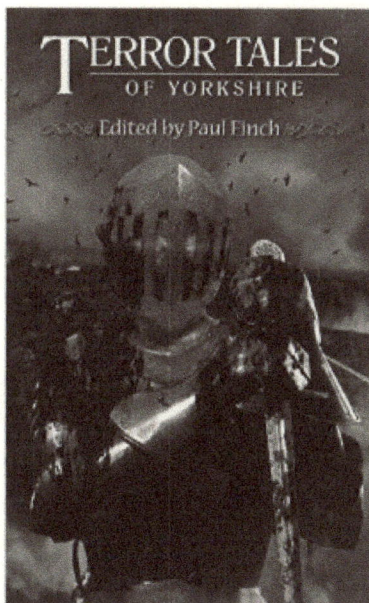

In addition, watch out for the next title in this series, *Terror Tales of the Ocean*. Check regularly for updates on this series with Gray Friar Press and on the editor's own webpage: http://paulfinch-writer.blogspot.co.uk/. Alternatively, you can follow him on Twitter: @paulfinchauthor.

Printed in December 2021
by Rotomail Italia S.p.A., Vignate (MI) - Italy